Cathy Williams can remember reading Mills & Boon books as a teenager, and now that she is writing them she remains an avid fan. For her, there is nothing like creating romantic stories and engaging plots, and each and every book is a new adventure. Cathy lives in London. Her three daughters—Charlotte, Olivia and Emma—have always been, and continue to be, the biggest inspirations in her life.

Melanie Milburne read her first Mills & Boon novel at the age of seventeen, in between studying for her final exams. After completing a master's degree in education, she decided to write a novel, and thus her career as a romance author was born. Melanie is an ambassador for the Australian Childhood Foundation and a keen dog-lover and trainer. She enjoys long walks in the Tasmanian bush. In 2015 Melanie won the Holt Medallion, a prestigious award honouring outstanding literary talent

Also by Cathy Williams

Shock Marriage for the Powerful Spaniard
The Italian's Christmas Proposition
His Secretary's Nine-Month Notice
Expecting His Billion-Dollar Scandal

Also by Melanie Milburne

Cinderella's Scandalous Secret
Billionaire's Wife on Paper
The Return of Her Billionaire Husband
His Innocent's Passionate Awakening

Discover more at millsandboon.co.uk.

THE FORBIDDEN CABRERA BROTHER

CATHY WILLIAMS

ONE NIGHT ON THE VIRGIN'S TERMS

MELANIE MILBURNE

MILLS & BOON

First Published in Great Britain 2020
by Mills & Boon, an imprint of HarperCollins*Publishers*
1 London Bridge Street, London, SE1 9GF

The Forbidden Cabrera Brother © 2020 Cathy Williams

One Night on the Virgin's Terms © 2020 Melanie Milburne

ISBN: 978-0-263-27831-6

MIX
Paper from
responsible sources
FSC® C007454

Printed and bound in Spain
by CPI, Barcelona

THE FORBIDDEN
CABRERA BROTHER

CATHY WILLIAMS

CHAPTER ONE

SOMETHING, DANTE THOUGHT as he nursed his whisky and stared out at the floodlit manicured gardens that comprised the grounds of his Spanish estate, wasn't making sense.

Behind him he could hear the muffled sound of voices and laughter—all those people, from dignitaries to old family friends, who had gathered to welcome Alejandro, his older brother by four years, and his fiancée.

It was a star-studded event, even though it had been arranged at fairly short notice. Such was the long arm of the Cabrera family's influence that an invitation from them—especially, Dante recognised, one that would be hosted at his own sprawling mansion—pretty much guaranteed attendance.

Intricate lanterns twinkled up the long winding private avenue that led to his house. Behind him, on a warm summer night, the bank of French doors at the back of his house had been flung open wide to a vision of exactly what extreme wealth could get. The serving staff on high alert for empty glasses, the blaze of yet more lanterns adorning the strategically placed trees and illuminating the still splendour of his infinity pool, the massive ice sculpture of a couple, which his mother had insisted on having. And, of course, the very elegant, barely noticeable and extremely expensive trio of violinists providing subtle background music. Here, in this setting, the women in their high-designer elegance and the men, formally dressed, were birds of paradise at home in a setting with which they were largely familiar.

His parents, naturally, were bristling with excitement at meeting a woman who, as far as they were concerned, was roughly five years overdue. Tradition was tradition and, as the eldest in the family and now in his mid-thirties, Alejandro should have been duly wed and well on the way to producing an heir or two to the throne.

The vast fortunes tied up with the Cabrera name needed to be kept in the family and Roberto and Isabella Cabrera had been making noises about grandchildren for some time now. How else could the family lineage remain intact if both their sons decided that playing the field was a far better option than settling down to the rigours of domestic life?

Dante was as keen as his parents were for Alejandro to get married and have kids because if he didn't, then it wouldn't be long before their parents began looking to Dante to do his duty in that area and he most certainly wasn't up for that.

So when Alejandro had phoned three weeks ago with the happy tidings that he was engaged, it had been champagne all round, a suitably lavish engagement party hastily arranged and expectations running high.

One small snag, though, was the fiancée.

Where the hell was she?

Shouldn't the loving couple have arrived together? Holding hands and staring into each other's eyes with undisguised adoration? It wasn't as though they had been dating for years and had had time to settle into the comfortable routine of taking one another for granted. Oh, no, the fiancée had been produced like a white rabbit from a magician's hat, so young love should still be fresh enough for the woman to have accompanied Alejandro to the opulent engagement party happening inside.

Except, she hadn't and—Dante glanced at his watch before swallowing the remainder of the whisky—it was a mere two hours before the elaborate buffet was set out and the speeches began. Half an acre of lawn had been meticulously roped off so that tables could be laid out with no small detail spared, from the linen cloths to the magnificent arrangements of red roses, as befitting a couple in love. The seating was casual because it was a party, and yet it still managed to feel incredibly formal in its opulence.

He wondered whether the mysterious bride-to-be would deign to make an appearance in time or whether his brother would have to mumble his apologies while the guests tucked into finest prepared rib of roast suckling pig in the absence of his fiancée. Certainly, Alejandro was strangely phlegmatic about the woman's appalling lack of manners. Maybe he had become a little too accustomed to the behaviour of a high-maintenance woman who felt that drama was some kind of selling point. Dante wryly thought that he had encountered a few of those himself.

He was about to turn away and head back into the sitting room, where champagne and canapés would be in full flow, when something caught his eye. In the twilight gloom, he glimpsed movement up the wind-

ing tree-lined private avenue that led to the courtyard
in front of the house.

Standing still, he squinted and there it was again, a
movement barely glimpsed between the trees.

He dumped his glass on the broad concrete ledge,
straightened up and headed down the sweeping arc of
stone steps that descended gracefully towards the open
courtyard and then out towards the drive.

Caitlin could barely see. Up ahead, the lawns and a
mansion of unseemly proportions were illuminated by
the sort of floodlit extravaganza that could be seen from
space. Here, as she half ran up the tree-lined avenue
leading to the house, the path dipped in and out of the
shadows. Any minute now and her already nightmar-
ish trip would be compounded by an even more night-
marish ending, which would involve her tripping over
something, breaking her ankle and having to be carried
ignominiously into the house on a makeshift stretcher.

Everything had gone wrong, starting with her mother
sobbing down the end of the phone just as she was supposed to be leaving for the airport, and ending with the
taxi, booked by Alejandro to fetch her from the airport
and deliver her to her own engagement party, for heav-
en's sake, getting a flat tyre just when she didn't need it.

Now, three hours late, she'd decided that creeping
into the house and at least having the option of getting ready somewhere private was far the more sensible choice, rather than the screech of a taxi alerting
everyone to her lateness.

She shuddered at the thought of all those assembled
guests piling out of the front door to witness her di-
shevelled appearance. In his understated way, Alejan-

dro had warned her that it was going to be *something of a bash*—which, in Alejandro-speak, meant that there would be ten thousand people there, all waiting for her arrival.

As luck would have it, Alejandro was, as always, nowhere near his mobile phone and her quiet entry through a side door somewhere was disappearing with each reluctant step forward. She'd tried calling him a dozen times and every single time it had gone to voicemail and she was fed up of leaving increasingly despairing messages.

They were supposed to be in love! In the real world, he would be hanging on the end of the line, worried sick about where she was!

Caitlin thought of him and couldn't help but smile because that was just Alejandro. He would have dumped his phone on a random table somewhere and would have to be reminded that she still hadn't arrived, which was something of a big deal because the engagement party his parents had arranged had been for both of them.

Not for the first time, she felt a twinge of intense discomfort at this story they had concocted. Back in London, it had seemed almost inevitable because it had satisfied so many disparate concerns, but here…

She stopped in her tracks to catch her breath and gazed at the mansion towering ahead of her, ablaze with lights. The courtyard was massive, as big as a football field, and it was crammed with high-end cars of every description. They were parked at haphazard angles but, when she squinted, she could make out two men in uniform and she guessed that they would be in charge of parking so that any of the luxury cars could be moved at the snap of a finger. She shivered with apprehension.

This was reality now. They weren't in London any longer. They weren't sharing their sob stories over a bottle of wine. A plan had been made and she had temporarily turned a blind eye to the fact that plans made in one country appeared completely different when viewed in another.

Posing as Alejandro's fiancée had been the answer to both their problems and, in London, that solution had seemed a logical conclusion.

But here...

With the sounds of summer insects around her and the grandeur of a sprawling house reminding her that this was where a simple game was always going to lead...

Her heart raced and she half looked over her shoulder with an instinctive urge to run away.

About to speed-dial Alejandro for the umpteenth time, she was only aware of a man stepping out of the shadows when he was practically on top of her and she didn't stop to think before taking action. It had been drummed into her by her parents the minute she decided to leave Ireland for the streets of London that it didn't pay to trust anyone. London, they had intoned worriedly, was a dangerous place. Accordingly, Caitlin had learned the basics of self-defence and now those ten lessons at the local town hall once a week coalesced into a blood-curdling shriek as she swung her holdall at the looming figure, striking a direct hit against his shoulder.

She had been aiming for his head, but the man was tall, way taller than her five foot three. She snapped her hands into action and eyed him narrowly for a few seconds as she debated which manoeuvre to take.

If only she were taller! Leaner! Stronger! Instead,

she was short, round and it was dawning on her at speed that she probably wasn't going to land any significant punches because this stranger was built like a house.

She grasped her holdall tightly and took the next most sensible option, which was flight.

She didn't get far. One minute, she was half running and panting with her eyes pinned to the mansion in the distance. The next minute, a vice-like grip was holding her back, at which point she spun round and kicked.

'What the...?' Dante demanded, holding her at arm's length as she struggled and tried to sling punches at him.

'Get *off* me!'

'Stop trying to kick me!'

'Stop trying to attack *me*! You have no idea who you're dealing with! I... I'm an expert in martial arts!'

Dante released her. He was temporarily stunned into silence. He couldn't quite make her out because it was dark, but he could see enough to realise that the pint-sized spitfire rubbing her arm was about as expert in martial arts as he was in ballet dancing.

'I don't know who you are,' Caitlin gritted, backing away just in case he decided to lunge at her, 'but if you don't clear off, I'm going to make sure that the police are contacted as soon as I get to...' she nodded brusquely at the house, which should have been a lot closer considering how far she'd walked but still seemed a hundred dred miles away '...that house you can see up there.'

'You're going up there? Why?'

'That's none of your business.' She spun round and began walking as fast as she could towards her destination. If the guy lurking in the grounds was up to no good, then he had obviously realised that she didn't

make a good candidate to be robbed. One glance at
her dress code would have given the game away. Long
flowered skirt, sensible shoes, her favourite flowing
blouse over which, because it was cool even though it
was summer, she was prudently wearing a cardigan…
not a diamond in sight.

She clasped her holdall ever tighter, because you
never knew… She didn't want to look at him, even
though her skin tingled because he had fallen into step
alongside her. She had no intention of making eye contact.

'It might be.' Dante had always had the knack of
making people stop dead in their tracks without raising his voice and, on cue, she stopped.

'What are you talking about?'

'Engagement party? Alejandro? Name ring bells?'
He folded his arms and stood perfectly, watchfully still.

Caitlin turned to the stranger. They had progressed
out of the shadowy overhang of trees, into more light,
and she could make him out far more clearly and suddenly her mouth went dry and her nervous system
seemed to temporarily forget what it was meant to do.

He had stepped back and she saw he was dressed
for—yes, an engagement party. Black trousers, white
shirt with the top couple of buttons undone as though
he couldn't be bothered with a formal dress code, no tie.
He'd shoved his hands in his pockets, dragging down
the trousers ever so slightly, and that seemed to empha-
sise the perfection of his muscular frame.

Her breathing went from fast to slow and back to
fast in record time. She blinked, confused at a reaction
that was so out of keeping with the person she knew
herself to be.

When she met his eyes, she had to try to ignore the impact of a perfectly chiselled face. The man oozed sex appeal. He was also ever so slightly familiar, but she knew that she would remember him if she'd ever met him, or even laid eyes on him. He was not a man anyone could meet and forget.

'You're here for the engagement party, as well.' She finally found her voice and then, because she was irritated with herself for being thrown by him, she belatedly added, 'In which case why are you lurking in the grounds and jumping out at perfect strangers?'

She began walking, once more, in the direction of the house. Time was of the essence at this point and she couldn't waste any more of it chatting to someone who made the hairs on the back of her neck stand on end.

But this time her awareness of him, once again falling into step alongside her, was acute. She could feel the rasp of her breathing, and the shadow he cast as the winding tree-lined avenue became ever more brightly lit sent shivers racing up and down her spine.

Only when she was standing to the side, with the massive edifice of the house in front of her, did she stop to take stock, at which point she tried Alejandro's number once again. She felt sick and out of her depth. She'd always known that Alejandro came from a wealthy background, but to be thrust into the very vortex of it, as she was now, made her stomach clench.

The cars that filled the vast courtyard gleamed with the patina of priceless machinery. Up close, the house, brightly lit, was beyond impressive and the distant thrum of noise was a sick reminder that the part she had undertaken to play was not going to be an easy one.

Predictably, Alejandro failed to respond.

'Problems?'

'Why are you still here?' Her voice was laced with agitation.

'I thought I'd personally escort you to the premises,' Dante said.

'Don't you believe that I'm a legitimate guest?'

At that, Dante inspected her with leisurely thoroughness, his dark eyes roving from the tips of her toes, along her body and finally coming to rest on her scarlet face.

She had gone into attack mode from the second he had surprised her and she was still in it. If she was a guest, then she was a highly unlikely guest.

'Are you? Because you don't seem to be dressed for the part.'

At that, Caitlin reddened even more. Her parents had always made a point of telling her that she was beautiful, inside and out, but parents were notoriously partisan and she had always been sensitive about her looks. She'd stopped longing to be five inches taller and fifteen pounds lighter, a leggy brunette free from the curse of freckles and hair the most skilled hairdresser would have found impossible to tame, but right now...

With this impossibly sexy and perfect guy lounging in front of her and staring with just the hint of a condescending smile on his face...

'I have clothes in here,' she said coldly, indicating her holdall with a curt nod. 'And in case you're in any doubt that I actually *have* been invited to this engagement party, I should tell you that I happen to be the... er... Alejandro's fiancée.' It wasn't a declaration that rolled easily off the tongue. Downright lies seldom did.

Dante said nothing. He was too stunned to speak.

'I'm running a bit late…ah…anyway…'

'Alejandro's fiancée?' He found his voice. He was seldom thrown, but this time he was.

'There's no need to sound so incredulous.' There was, actually, every need. Not even she, with her imagination going full pelt, found it easy to believe that she could possibly be Alejandro's fiancée. They came from such different worlds. Whatever his back story and however close they had become over time, he was Spanish nobility and it was there in the way he held himself and his casual disregard for money. He could do as he pleased, even if he was funny and caring and considerate, which always left you with the illusion that he couldn't buy the world, which he could. Somehow, you always expected the super rich to run roughshod over people and Alejandro completely disproved that theory. That, of course, was one of the reasons why she absolutely adored him.

They were also so different to look at. She was pale, with freckles and green eyes and copper-coloured hair. He was swarthy and dark-haired. They were both short, though, and plump and she felt wonderfully comfortable with him.

'Miss Walsh?'

'Caitlin. Look, I can't hang around here chatting to you. I have to…' She squinted at the imposing edifice of the house and tried to work out a possible side entrance through which she could sneak, although heaven only knew what she would do if and when she did enter the house if Alejandro was still missing in action. Fumble her way to the downstairs loo so that she could change into her finery? Hope that she didn't trip over anyone in the process?

So poorly conceived all of this, a plan born on the spur of the moment without much thought being given to the technical detail. It was just as well that once this engagement party was over and done with, they would both return to London where life would carry on as normal.

She pulled her long, tumbling hair over her shoulder and fiddled with it while she tried to work out various house-entry options.

'You were saying...' Dante prompted.

Caitlin looked at Dante and shivered again. The guy had the strangest effect on her. Since when had she ever gone for the brooding Alpha-male type? She'd learned long ago to steer clear of those sorts.

Besides, men this good-looking were always far too fond of themselves for her liking. And as a postscript, she belatedly thought, she was engaged. Or at least, for all intents and purposes she was engaged. Which amounted to the same thing.

'As you mentioned,' she conceded, 'I'm not exactly dressed the part and I can't get hold of Alejandro. He's terrible when it comes to his mobile phone. It never seems to be on him.'

'I'm surprised he isn't scouring the four corners in search of his errant bride-to-be,' Dante murmured.

'What do you mean?'

'Shouldn't he be out looking for you? If you haven't been able to get hold of him to warn him of your late arrival?'

'Oh, right. Yes. I see where you're going with that,' Caitlin mumbled. 'He... We are quite relaxed with one another when it comes to stuff like that.'

'What a novel approach to a serious relationship.'

'I need to change into my glad rags.' Something about the man's tone of voice triggered a wave of unfocused apprehension in her. 'And you never introduced yourself. You are…?'

She paused and stilled him with her hand. Her eyes met his questioningly.

For a couple of seconds, Dante's cool, rational mind seemed to shut down, then he drew back and returned her wide-eyed gaze narrowly.

'Do you know the layout of the house?' He smoothly changed the conversation, while at the same time politely removing her hand and hustling her between the cars and past the uniformed valets standing to attention outside.

Was this his brother's fiancée? Dante couldn't quite believe it, but then how was he to know what sort of woman his brother liked? He had never met any of Alejandro's girlfriends. Different countries, awkward schedules, fleeting meetings over snatched drinks in random bars. He and his brother had long mastered the art of saying absolutely nothing of any genuine importance to one another.

That said, Dante had always assumed that his brother would go for the same kind of women he did, refined thoroughbreds who moved in the same social circles as they did. When Dante thought about those women, he felt a certain amount of boredom, but the one thing he knew about them, and it was very important, was the fact that they were all independently wealthy. Largely they came from families who, if not in the same category as his, were in a similar ballpark. No gold-diggers and, from bitter experience, he knew that gold-diggers were a breed best avoided.

A memory pushed its way to the surface. He'd lost his heart once, at the tender age of nineteen, to a woman ten years older who had played him so well that he had ended up handing over wads of cash to her. A small fortune. He'd fallen for a tale of a broken marriage and a violent ex and a vulnerable toddler. She had been poor but still touchingly hopeful in the face of personal tragedies, desperate for a new start yet tentative about accepting anything from him, which had made him insist on giving her even more, and of course so breathtakingly beautiful that common sense had been quickly abandoned to a raging libido hooked on the thrill of the unknown. It had been wildly exciting after his tame diet of beautiful, predictable young socialites and privately educated heiresses. When he reflected on what might have been had he not caught her in bed with the father of her child, no less, he was filled with shame at his own stupidity, but every mistake taught a valuable lesson and he had never again strayed from what he knew. Rich, beautiful, well bred. Known territory. If they were self-absorbed and sometimes shallow, then that was a price he was willing to pay.

Caitlin Walsh was not known territory…and while *he* might have the nous to know how to handle any woman who wasn't known territory, did his brother?

A broken heart, Dante figured, was no bad thing. It made you stronger. But his brother was engaged, and once rings had been exchanged a broken heart wouldn't be the only thing to deal with. The family fortune had to be protected and Dante had no intention of letting that out of his sight.

If Alejandro was taken in by Caitlin Walsh, then

Dante saw no reason why he couldn't do a bit of probing of his own, for no other reason than to make sure Alejandro wasn't about to make the biggest mistake of his life.

Wasn't that what brotherly love was all about?

'I've never been to the house before,' Caitlin responded tartly, 'so it would be impossible for me to know the layout. I had hoped that Alejandro...'

'It's his engagement party. He's probably busy entertaining the troops. You're in luck, though. I happen to know the place very well. You might say that I know it like the back of my hand.'

Caitlin stopped and stared at him with undisguised relief. 'Would you mind...? I need to change and I would rather not...' She made a vague gesture to encompass her state of dress. 'I should have got here ages ago...but with one thing and another... If you know the house, I would really appreciate it if you could maybe...'

'Sneak you in so that you can change into your finery?' Dante stood back and looked at her from the towering height of his six feet two inches. The holdall was quite small for finery. 'Why would I do that when I've been accused of attacking you?'

'You surprised me. Naturally I reacted accordingly.' Caitlin's voice was stiff.

'You could have caused me permanent damage,' Dante inserted smoothly, 'what with you being an expert in martial arts.' Silence greeted this remark. He could see that she was itching to launch a few verbal missiles. His antennae were still on red alert, but the woman was in a league of her own, and what had promised to be something of a tedious social occasion was looking up. When you were someone who could always call the shots, a little bit of *different* went a long way. He was beginning to enjoy this little bit of different...

'Fortunately,' he carried on magnanimously, 'I am not a man to bear a grudge and I would be delighted to secrete you away somewhere private where you can freshen up.'

'I don't know how to thank you,' Caitlin said, in a voice that was far from oozing gratitude.

Dante said nothing but, just for a second, something weird and strong raced through him, heating his blood and tightening his groin. He spun round on his heels and began heading towards the side of the house, away from the brightly lit entrance.

'You'll have to be quick,' he said, slowing briefly so that she could catch up with him. 'The party's in full swing. The longer you take, the more dramatic the reception is going to be.' He glanced at her. The braid was not quite enough to keep her fiery hair in order and wisps floated around her cheeks. She was flushed and breathing fast. His eyes dropped to breasts that were more than a handful. Small-statured and large-breasted.

Infuriated by the sudden lapse of self-control, he stiffened. If the woman was up to no good then he intended to find out before the situation became financially messy, but she was engaged to his brother and he wasn't going to forget that. Forbidden thoughts would be culled before they could start interfering with what had to be done, and in very little time because if she had angled for a profitable engagement then she wasn't going to hang around waiting for the wedding ring to seal the deal.

He took her to one of the many spare bedrooms. Each and every one was permanently prepared to a high state of readiness although it was rare for guests to stay overnight. Dante loathed that sort of thing and, indeed, the only time the vast mansion saw an influx of people was when he happened to be away and it was lent out to friends or family members. He valued his privacy far too much.

'Make yourself at home,' he drawled as she stood still and looked all around her. 'I'll wait outside for you. You won't know how to find your way down to where the action is.'

As she was busy appreciating a level of luxury she had never seen in her life before, it was a few seconds before Caitlin responded, then she eyed her holdall.

'I'm sure I'll manage,' she said dubiously.

'I'll wait.'

'Why?'

Dante felt a twinge of guilt. He needed to get a feel for her, work out if his suspicions were well founded, and time wasn't going to be on his side. His intentions could not exactly be called noble and something fleeting in her eyes, an expression of helpless, vulnerable apprehension, made him flush darkly.

'Call it good manners,' he said brusquely.

'Okay.' She hesitated, then smiled tentatively. 'I might need a bit of moral support. I'm not accustomed to…events like this… When Alejandro and I…' She reddened.

'When you and Alejandro…?'

'I knew there was going to be a party,' she said hurriedly, 'but I had no idea that it would be on this scale.'

'Alejandro comes from an extremely high-ranking family,' Dante murmured, his keen eyes taking in everything, missing nothing. 'With more notice, it would have been even bigger. As it stands, two hundred is reasonably well contained.'

'I... The cars parked outside...' She sighed. 'I'm not sure I've brought the right clothes...'

Dante thought of the women milling around downstairs, dressed to kill and dripping in diamonds. He noted her anxious expression and reminded himself that the most efficient gold-digger would always be the one the least obvious. His lips thinned because he knew that better than most.

'I'm sure you'll...fit in just fine...'

'You haven't seen my outfit.' Caitlin grinned and met his veiled gaze with a roll of her eyes. 'Once you have, feel free to change your mind. I just didn't think...'

'You just didn't think...?'

'That it would be quite like this, like I said,' she told him honestly. 'I never thought that the place would be so...lavish.'

'Yet you knew that your fiancé came from a wealthy family...'

'Yes, of course, but... It doesn't matter. I'm here now so there's not much I can do about... What you can't change you might as well accept, and I definitely can't change the outfit I brought over with me. Anyway... I'm going to get ready so if you don't mind? I won't be long.'

He gave it forty minutes at the very least. Longer if something had to be done about her hair. She was so unexpected and novel an entity that he literally couldn't imagine what the transformation would be like and it annoyed him that he couldn't resist letting his imagination break its leash and run away. He responded to that by lounging against the wall, flipping open his phone and scrolling through work emails.

He was settling in for the long haul when the bedroom door was pulled open and out she breezed, all of a fluster.

He pushed himself from the wall and slowly moved to stand directly in front of her.

'That was quick.'

She looked...amazing. Gone was the fashion-disaster outfit she had been wearing. In its place was a figure-hugging jade-green dress that lovingly emphasised each and every delectable curve of her small but insanely feminine body.

The sight of it made Dante stiffen as he acknowledged, once again, just how inappropriate his reaction was.

'I forgot the diamonds at home.' There was a nervous edge to her voice and she fiddled with the thin gold chain around her neck, a sixteenth birthday present from her parents.

'I doubt anyone will notice the oversight,' Dante murmured. She was playing with a thin necklace round her neck and his dark eyes zeroed in on her slender fingers and then on the shadowy cleft between her breasts. He gritted his teeth and quickly looked away.

'It's kind of you to say so.' She fell into step with him, taking it slowly because the heels were stupidly high and falling was a distinct possibility.

'I doubt anyone has ever called me *kind*. How did you and Alejandro meet?' Dante realised that he had asked very few basic questions about the relationship that had materialised out of thin air. 'We were all...a little surprised by the speed of the relationship...'

Dante barely noticed the endless miles of corridor along which they were walking, although he was keenly aware of her wide-eyed awe. Telling but hardly surprising if there was an agenda to the fifteen-second relationship, he thought wryly. To one side, ornate wrought-iron railings offered a view of acres of marble on the ground floor and white walls on which were hung huge statement pieces of abstract art. An enormous crystal chandelier, as delicate as a waterfall, dominated the vaulted ceiling, dropping five metres down to the central hallway, which was manned by several uniformed men and which they had successfully avoided.

'We go back a way,' Caitlin said vaguely.

'He's never mentioned having a serious girlfriend in the past.'

'We were…er…friends…before…' Slanted green eyes collided with dark, coolly thoughtful ones. 'You still haven't told me who you are. I guess you must know Alejandro and his brother really well considering you're so familiar with this house. It's pretty amazing, isn't it?'

'Admittedly,' Dante murmured, completely ignoring her question, 'he hasn't let on much about anyone there in London.'

The noise was increasing in volume and then they exited into the massive hall manned by the uniformed guards, who half bowed but were clearly trained to remain in the background. The paintings here were more traditional, less abstract and more impressionistic.

Caitlin was drawn like a magnet towards one of them and inspected it minutely, lost for a few moments in the exquisite mix of colours and recognising the somewhat obscure artist behind it. It was the artwork of a connoisseur.

'It's a lovely piece.' She turned to Dante, her eyes gleaming with appreciation.

'You know about art?' Dante raised both eyebrows questioningly.

'Why shouldn't I?' Caitlin stood back. 'I'm a photographer but I studied art at college. I probably know a lot more than Alejandro's brother, even though he owns this house. I'll bet he hasn't got a clue who this artist is.'

'Why would you say that?' Dante asked silkily.

'He's a businessman,' she said with a shrug. 'I gather making money is his number one priority. I'd say that if that's the case, then he's probably commissioned someone to bulk-buy a fortune's worth of valuable artwork that will do its job and appreciate over the years and make him yet more money.'

'That's quite a statement,' Dante murmured. 'You must have gleaned that impression from somewhere... Is that what his brother has told you?'

'Of course not!' She cleared her throat. 'Alejandro never has a judgemental word to say about anyone. Not that I'm being judgemental...just expressing an opinion...'

'But surely you would be partisan, considering you're his besotted better half?' Dante was outraged that a woman who had catapulted herself into the centre of their family, for reasons that were open to a lot of question, should dare insult him in his own house. Actually, should dare insult him, full stop.

'Sorry?' Caitlin blinked then blushed. 'Yes. No. I mean, *yes*, of *course* that's what I am, but no, I'm not at all partisan. I don't know why I'm telling you all this. I still don't even know who you are!'

'Oh, haven't I introduced myself?' He gave a mocking half-bow and then fixed her with his amazing eyes. 'My oversight. I am Dante Cabrera, Alejandro's brother.'

CHAPTER TWO

'WHY DIDN'T YOU pick up your phone?' was the first thing Caitlin demanded when she had finally managed to corner Alejandro, who had already been tipsy by the time she'd located him.

When she and Alejandro had discussed this charade, and it had been a discussion that had not happened on the spur of the moment or even overnight, she had not foreseen the very real stumbling blocks she might encounter.

She knew that she only had herself to blame. An optimist by nature, someone who had been brought up to see the silver lining behind every cloud, she had spent months lost in the unfamiliar world of uncertainty and hopelessness. Misfortune had rained down on her from the very moment she'd found out about her parents' horrendous financial problems, and from that point on things had only seemed to get worse. Her parents had always been her biggest fans and the very backbone of her life, there for her through thick and thin, always in her corner. They had instilled positivity in her and a belief that things could only get better whenever she'd been a little low. She'd relied on them, and to see her father tearful and broken…to have faced the repercussions as they had unravelled over the past few months…

She had had to step up to the plate in a way she had never had to before. She had had to go into caretaker mode. It had been debilitating, especially as she had been working in London and commuting as often as she could back to Ireland, spending money she could ill afford because every penny she earned now had to be earmarked for the gaping hole the financial catastrophe had left in her parents' lives.

Alejandro's suggestion had, at first, fallen on barren ground. The thought of any deliberate deception had been anathema to Caitlin. Every moral code instilled from birth had risen up against the thought of lying, but he had persisted. He had his very pressing reasons, in many ways as urgent as hers, and he had persuaded her that she would be doing him a favour, that in return he, with his limitless millions, would be honoured to return that favour. As a friend, he had insisted, it would be an insult to him for her to turn him away in her moment of desperate need. If friends couldn't help one another when help was most needed, then what was the point?

He had said all the right things at the very time when she had been absolutely dazed at the speed with which disaster after disaster had been battering her naturally upbeat nature.

From the minute she had accepted Alejandro's offer, a weight had been lifted and the sun had tentatively begun to peek out from behind the bank of raging dark clouds.

She had been able to see a way forward. The silver lining had been slowly restored and that, she realised now, had been her undoing, because she had contrived to overlook the fact that what had started as a straightforward solution might throw up unexpected obstacles.

She hadn't banked on the brother.

She'd been apprehensive about meeting his parents but nowhere in that scenario had she given a second thought to Dante, even though there had been sufficient mention of him over the time she had known Alejandro to have joined the dots and worked out that he was ruthless. With a light at the end of the tunnel, she had allowed her optimism to take over and that had been a mistake.

When Dante had disclosed his identity, her brain had done a rapid overview of the conversation they had had from the moment she had attacked him on the walk up to the house and she had realised that she would have to be careful around him.

He had laid bait for her to take and if she didn't watch out, he would…do *what*? Caitlin didn't know, because what on earth could the man do in the space of twenty-four hours, after which she would be gone? But that didn't prevent a shiver of apprehension from feathering along her spine at the nebulous thought that she should be on her guard.

She determined to avoid him for the remainder of the party, which, as she glanced now at her watch, still had a long way to go. And where on earth was her wandering fiancé? He had become close friends with the champagne and, between trying to keep an eye on him and also on Dante, she had had a hellish hour and a half.

His charming parents had almost been welcome relief. They were over the moon that their eldest was finally settling down. She had been so distracted by the tug of war inside her at having to avoid Dante, while watching out for an increasingly inebriated Alejandro, that she had only paid scant attention to their polite but searching questions about what she did and whether she would continue doing what she did once she was married. She had tried to appear focused as she had listened to their gentle but insistent hints about the grandchildren they hoped would be forthcoming sooner rather than later while her brain had conjured up alarming scenarios of what a suspicious Dante might do should he decide to make mischief. Or worse.

She had barely had the chance to feel awkward even though she knew, on some level, that she really didn't belong with this glamorous, pampered crowd. So many of them, swarming in confident groups. So many beautiful women and expensive men, barely glancing at the waiting staff as they did the rounds with champagne and canapés. To the right, there was the glorious sight of tables laid out for outdoor dining. It should have looked casual and homely but it looked, instead, madly opulent. There was something strangely intimidating about tables formally dressed under the stars, manned by formally attired waiting staff, like a Michelin-starred restaurant in a five-star hotel, suddenly exposed to the elements.

She would have been a lot less nervous had she not been agonisingly conscious of Dante, a tall, brooding presence, glimpsed just enough for her to know that he was keeping an eye on her.

And it wasn't just the fact that he was an unknown threat that made her jumpy...

She also remembered the way her body had reacted to him, nerves all over the place and pulses racing a mile a minute. She hadn't known who he was and her response had been instinctive and physical and shocking.

Things felt as though they were getting beyond her control. She'd barely managed to exchange two words with Alejandro, just sufficient to scramble through what had happened en route to the big event.

Now, as everyone made their way through a huge archway of flowers and lanterns into the magical outdoor eating area, Caitlin felt that she had to vent some of her panic and frustration on her so-called erstwhile fiancé, before he tipped over the edge from too much champagne.

Thanks to his absent-mindedness when it came to his phone, and his preoccupation with hurrying along the occasion by drinking as much and as fast as he could, she had ended up in a place she had not banked on and she just wasn't equipped to deal with it. Subterfuge wasn't in her genetic code and she was terrified of blurting something out to Dante, who struck her as the sort who wouldn't release the bone once he had got it between his pearly white teeth. Which he had.

His watchful, speculative dark eyes brought to mind a shark in search of prey.

When she looked at Alejandro she realised that he was miserable, and she prayed that she was the only one to spot his unhappiness underneath the broad smiles and perspiring bonhomie.

Alejandro was not being Alejandro and he was clearly a lot more uncomfortable with the situation than she was. She cornered him.

'This is a nightmare.' Alejandro was busy relieving the waiter of another flute of champagne as he leant into her. 'And I'm sorry about the phone, Linny. No idea where I left it. Still haven't found it. It's probably buried under a cushion somewhere. There was a lot of sitting around earlier today. Talking. God, this is a nightmare. And I can't believe your bad luck running into Dante on your way to the house.'

'Slow down on the drinking!' was Caitlin's anxious response to that.

'I can't. It's the only thing that's propping me up.'

'Oh, Alex.' She sighed and rubbed his arm sympathetically. 'You need to be honest with your family.'

'I will. Just not yet. Once Dante finds a woman and settles down, then the pressure will be off me and then...' His voice drifted off. It was a conversation they had had before. 'Are you going to be all right?'

'What do you mean?'

'People can sit where they please but close friends and family members are at the top table. Wedding style. Look at where you're sitting.' He'd been propelling her along on unsteady legs and now he nodded to the one and only table with a seating plan. It occupied an exalted position on a makeshift podium that was adorned with striking flowers in urns of various sizes.

'Why have they stuck me next to your brother?' Caitlin was appalled and panic bloomed inside her. She had optimistically thought that she might have seen off Dante for the remainder of the evening. She had planned on vanishing with Alejandro at a respectable hour, when the guests started drifting off. A flight had been booked. He had assured her that his parents wouldn't bat an eye because they were used to work commitment cutting short all kinds of family gatherings, usually courtesy of Dante.

Still reeling from the prospect of sitting next to Dante, she raised her eyes to spot him heading in her direction. His gait was leisurely, his body language was relaxed but he was a man on a mission. She shivered.

The shark looked in the mood for a meal and she quailed at the thought of being the tasty morsel. She was barely aware of Alejandro. She was too busy telling herself that the evening would be over soon enough.

'I suppose,' she surfaced to hear Alejandro muttering gloomily, 'the intention is for you to get to know the nearest and dearest. Don't worry, Uncle Alfredo to your right is okay and Dante has Luisa next to him on the other side.'

'Luisa?' She was riveted at the sight of Dante weaving his way through the crowd, so graceful, so dangerously, darkly beautiful. He was compelling. She felt a little sick and wished all over again that she had stuck to her guns but, when she thought about her parents and the mess they were in, she could see why she had done what she had.

'Not here yet. She enjoys making an entrance. My hopes are high for Dante and Luisa to do what everyone expects they'll eventually do.'

'What's that?' she asked vaguely.

'Tie the knot. They dated a year or so ago and broke up but everyone thinks it's just a matter of time before it all kicks off again. Anyway, I have to go, Caitlin. You'll have my moral support from across the table. Feel for me. As the guest of honour, I will have both parents on either side so it's going to be an evening of the Spanish Inquisition. I just can't cope.'

'You'll have to,' Caitlin said sternly.

There was a bewildering array of wine glasses in front of them and she only hoped that his nerves wouldn't propel him to have them all filled so that he could duly empty them. He wasn't a drinker. Frankly, she was surprised that he was still standing.

When she shifted her attention away from him, it was to find that Dante was settling into the chair next to her and she shivered and began a hurried conversation in broken Spanish with Uncle Alfredo, as he wanted to be called, who was very happy to carry the conversation.

The night air was balmy and the sky was velvet black, dotted with stars. It was a perfect setting and were this a real engagement party, it would have been heavenly. She thought back to that distant time when it had looked as though marriage might have been hers for the taking and felt a rush of sadness. It had ended and it had been for the best, but sitting here, in this wonderful, magical setting, she could almost airbrush away the expensively dressed people and imagine what it might be like to be celebrating a true engagement to a guy she loved, under the stars, with the gentle sound of violins harmonising with the chirping of invisible summer insects.

'We meet again…'

Caitlin blinked and landed back on Planet Earth with a resentful bump. 'You should have told me who you were,' she said stiffly, bypassing small talk, which seemed irrelevant now, considering they were already acquainted.

'Is that why you've spent the evening avoiding me? Because you were embarrassed?'

'I wasn't avoiding you.' While there was a buffet service for the guests, this select table benefited from an array of assiduous waiters whose duty was to make sure they were fed and watered without having to exert themselves at all.

It was over-the-top luxury that Caitlin could have done without. No opportunity to take her time hovering in front of tables groaning with food. No opportunity to duck Dante's dark, fascinating, menacing presence.

There wasn't even Luisa there to distract. Whoever she was. Caitlin had paid scant attention at the time, but there was an empty chair next to him so the woman was obviously going to be a no-show.

'I, naturally, would have told you who I was but you gifted me a unique opportunity to get to know the real you. The real Caitlin Walsh, mystery fiancée.'

'There's nothing mysterious about me.' Her heart was racing and her mouth was dry.

'Which, in itself, is something of an enigma. I've watched your interaction with Alejandro and, yes, I can see that you two are close. He seeks you out with his eyes when you're not around.'

'Like I said,' Caitlin said, sotto voce, picking at an arrangement of appetisers on a plate that had found its way in front of her and pointedly making sure not to look at Dante, 'we've been friends for ages.'

'Yes, the friend bit,' Dante intoned smoothly, his low murmur matching hers, 'is evident. It's the other bit I'm not seeing.'

'I have no idea what you're talking about.'

'Where's the touchy-feely, loved-up, starry-eyed, can't-stand-a-metre-apart-from-one-another couple?' His voice oozed concerned curiosity and Caitlin gritted her teeth together and wished he would just disappear.

'We're not those people.' She shifted back as a waiter bowed to remove her plate. There seemed to be an army of them, moving as one, making sure that everything went to plan. 'We don't believe in public displays of affection. Not everyone does.' Refusing to be threatened, Caitlin peered past him to the empty seat on his left.

'And speaking of which, where's the guest who's supposed to be sitting next to you? Luisa, I believe? That's what Alejandro told me. He said that you two are practically engaged?'

Dante's lips thinned and he turned so that he was looking directly at her. 'Is that so?' he said in a sibilant murmur that would have served as a warning shot to anyone else.

'Yes...' Caitlin tilted her head to one side, considering his rhetorical question as though it were deserving of an answer '...but, of course, he may have got it all wrong. He said something about you two being an item in the past and everyone assuming that it's going to end in marriage even though you're on a break?' She couldn't help herself. She'd never thought that she could take pleasure in watching someone squirm, but for the first time since their paths had crossed Dante wasn't calling the shots and she liked it.

'This conversation is going nowhere,' he growled, under his breath.

'Lots of people go on breaks,' Caitlin murmured wickedly. 'Sometimes, taking a step back from someone can make you realise how important they are in your life. We don't know one another at all, so I hope you'll forgive me for saying what's on my mind.' She didn't give him time to do any such thing. The last thing she intended to do was stop saying what was on her mind. 'Marriage and tying the knot can be scary. Are you scared, Dante? I would say that you should let go of all those apprehensions and show Luisa how much you really care about her.' She wondered what this mystery woman was like. Beautiful, captivating...

she would have to be if she'd managed to get to a guy like Dante Cabrera.

'I don't believe I'm hearing this. No one—*no one*— has ever dared address me in this way!'

'In that case, please accept my apologies,' Caitlin said without a hint of apology in her voice. 'But you feel free to ask me whatever you want to so why shouldn't I return the favour?' Their eyes collided and she felt such a rush of weird *sensation* race through her body, like the surge of an electric charge, that she blinked in utter confusion and for a few seconds couldn't say anything at all.

Then the moment was lost because there was a sudden lull in the din of people talking and all heads, as one, swung round to the arch where a leggy brunette was poised theatrically, her beautiful face a picture of exaggerated remorse. The glow of the lanterns and the backdrop of light from the house did her a lot of favours. She was aiming for drama and she was delivering it in bucketloads. Her lips twitched with amusement, inviting everyone at the honoured top table to get in on the joke with her. Caitlin could only admire the spectacle.

Then Luisa was stalking towards them, tossing her hair as a waiter scurried to hold out a chair, then it was all about Dante.

Caitlin thought she might be gaping. Up close, the woman was even more stunning than she had appeared at a distance. Perfect features in a perfectly oval face. Her hair was waist length, curling down a narrow back and, although she was olive toned—just a shade lighter than the guy sitting next to her—she had the most incredible bright blue eyes.

Caitlin politely turned away as more food continued

to arrive, but she could hear breathless murmurs coming from the woman in question and not much from Dante.

Caitlin's head was whirling. She suddenly felt self-conscious. A little ridiculous in her newly acquired fancy dress and her silly high heels, pretending to be someone she wasn't.

She was back to feeling like that girl who had been ditched by the boy everyone in the village had assumed she'd end up with. Ditched for a five-foot-ten beauty from Latvia. All the insecurities Caitlin had felt then assaulted her now in a full-frontal attack, a reminder that this silly party wasn't real, that there was no engagement, that love and marriage were not things on the cards for her, and no amount of optimism and silver linings could camouflage that fact. This charade was a pragmatic solution to a problem that had been tearing her apart.

She wasn't a beauty queen like Luisa. She was the girl next door and she was ashamed of those taboo stirrings she had felt with Dante, that slow uncurling of something sexual that had blindsided her. Had she completely lost her mind? Had two glasses of champagne gone to her head?

She surfaced to find that the business of eating was beginning in earnest. The alcohol was flowing. The courses were coming thick and fast, each one a testament to what a talented chef could produce.

'I never remembered Alejandro drinking quite so much,' a deep, velvety voice to her left murmured.

Caitlin had glazed over at Alfredo's long-winded monologue about a game of golf he had played three weeks previously. She snapped to attention in a hurry at the sound of Dante's deep, dulcet tone.

She looked narrowly at Alejandro, who was flushed, before turning sideways to Dante.

'He…he…'

Dante's dark eyebrows winged upwards in a question.

'He's thoroughly enjoying his own engagement party?' Dante queried helpfully before she could think of something to say. 'If I didn't know better, I'd almost think that he was a man trying to drown his sorrows.'

'Thankfully—' Caitlin stabbed a piece of succulent chicken breast '—you don't know better.' Her skin tingled. Something about his voice, his accent, barely there and stupidly sexy.

'Mind you,' Dante mused thoughtfully, 'he's stuck between our parents. They will be asking him all sorts of probing questions he probably doesn't know how to answer.'

'Such as what?'

'Oh, the usual. Timelines…venues…food preferences for the wedding meal…'

Caitlin remained silent. Yes, she'd been plied with a couple of those questions herself but poor Alejandro would be squirming like a fish on a hook, trying to fend off *probing questions*.

'Poor Alejandro,' Caitlin murmured softly, without thought. Too late, she realised that that was the last thing she should have said because those questioning eyebrows now conveyed less mild curiosity and more scorching interest.

'That's an odd response. Why do you say that?'

'Because…'

'Because…?' Dante prompted silkily. 'I'm all ears.'

He had moved closer to her so that his shoulder was almost but not quite brushing hers and she could smell the warmth of his breath and whatever woody cologne he was wearing. Out of the corner of her eye, she could see that Luisa had turned the full, glowing wattage of her undivided attention to the elderly man sitting next to her. There was lots of noise, people talking, laughing, getting merrier by the second as the alcohol continued to flow, served by the army of solicitous waiters. The lanterns swayed in the breeze, picking up the glitter of expensive jewellery, adding a layer of mystery to the wildly glamorous gathering.

Amidst all this, the low murmur of his voice in her ear somehow seemed to wrap them in a bubble of their own.

'We haven't talked about…er…concrete plans for anything.' She tentatively tested the waters to see whether this evasive response would have the desired effect of shutting him up. The dress was beginning to feel uncomfortable, or maybe it only felt uncomfortable because she was beginning to perspire with a sense of rising panic.

Across the table, Alejandro was not helping matters. He was tugging at his collar and guzzling champagne as though his life depended on it. She would have to corner him, somehow, and steer him back on the straight and narrow, but she had no idea how she was going to do that because there was still a long way to go with the wonderful never-ending meal and then, presumably, speeches.

'I confess I'm surprised.'

'Why?'

'I always thought that once rings were on fingers, the first thing a woman wanted to do was pin her man down to a time and a place.'

'Has that been your experience?'

'I've never been engaged. I'm surmising.'

'I guess you and Luisa…must have discussed things of that nature?'

'It won't work.'

'What won't work?'

'Trying to get me off-piste with this conversation. Don't you want to set up house as soon as you can? Alejandro is no longer a boy in his twenties. I'm sure he's keen to set the date so that he can start producing heirs to the throne.'

Caitlin contained a shudder of horror.

'It may not have occurred to you,' Caitlin said stiffly, 'that in this day and age a woman might actually want to further her career before she starts having a family. I'm only twenty-five.'

'No, if I'm being honest.'

'No *what*?'

'No, it hasn't occurred to me.'

'I love what I do.' She slanted her eyes sideways and instantly looked away because the lazy intensity in his gaze unsettled her. 'I left Ireland to make my way in London and I managed to land a very enjoyable job freelancing at a magazine. Every day is different and I have a lot of opportunities to go somewhere with my career. I may not want to sacrifice all of that to have kids when I'm still young.'

'Photographer for a magazine…' He let that musing statement hang tantalisingly in the air between them for a few seconds. 'Very interesting. Tell me, how did you and my brother meet? There's quite a chasm between the world of business and the world of entertainment and I'm racking my brains but I'm pretty sure publication isn't part of the family holdings.'

Caitlin had a moment of sheer panic. What, exactly,

had Alejandro told everyone? She had been vague when questioned but the man sitting next to her wasn't going to let her get away with vague.

'No one spends all their time working,' she said faintly. 'Everyone has hobbies and Alejandro discovered that he enjoyed photography. It's…relaxing…'

'A straight answer, Caitlin. Is that asking too much? How did you meet?'

'He dropped by.' She took a deep breath. 'I happened to be renting space in a workshop. I still do, as it happens. He dropped by and we got chatting.'

'Why would he drop by a workshop?'

'You should ask him.'

'But you're sitting next to me,' he responded smoothly, 'and so I'm asking *you*.'

'He dropped by—' Caitlin glanced across to Alejandro, who was now looking the worse for wear '—and we just happened to click.'

'But you didn't start going out with one another. That happened later…'

'That's right.'

'Why is that? Was it not love at first sight? Maybe he was involved with someone else at the time? Or maybe you were?'

His low voice was a persistent murmur in her ear.

'Why are you asking all these questions?' she breathed. 'I get it that you're curious about our relationship, but, honestly, isn't it enough that I'm here? Your parents haven't pried into our…our relationship…'

'My parents are already in love with the idea that their eldest son is going to be tying the knot. They have grandchildren on their mind. They see what they want to see, but my vision is slightly less rose-tinted. Alejandro might be older than me but he's gullible in places I'm not. Gullible enough to fall hook, line and sinker in love with a woman who might not be…let's just say, right for him. So my curiosity? Natural. Your reticence on the subject of love and marriage, not to mention your reluctance to go into detail? Less natural.'

She was thinking hard. Thinking about how to address those suspicions. Loathing the man for putting her on the back foot, for not accepting what she had to say, for not being satisfied with polite small talk.

She was still thinking, still sweating with discomfort when it happened.

The crash was deafening. For a few seconds, she just couldn't seem to focus on what exactly had happened because everything seemed to have slowed down. Then she realised, in a flash, that Alejandro had fallen. He had begun standing up, but he'd had so much to drink that his legs had refused to co-operate. He'd fallen, dropped backwards like a stone, catapulting the chair behind him and crashing to the ground.

She sprang to her feet. Everyone had sprung to their feet. Then it was all a blur. She raced over to where Alejandro lay sprawled in an unnatural position on the ground, with one arm flung behind his head and his leg twisted underneath him. He was perfectly still and as she shoved her way to his side Caitlin desperately wondered whether he was breathing at all. Tears had sprung to her eyes and she was whimpering when someone pulled her back.

She felt the hardness of muscle against her back and then Dante was whispering urgently into her ear.

'Don't panic. He's alive and there's a doctor here. Take it easy.'

The voice that had filled her with discomfort and hostility only moments earlier now soothed her, but she barely had time to question the phenomenon because amidst the chaos someone was pushing forward and taking charge, ordering people to stand back while simultaneously reaching for his phone and jabbing at it as he bent towards Alejandro.

Caitlin couldn't bear to watch. She spun round and buried her head against Dante. He could have been anyone. She just couldn't look at her friend lying there on the ground. There was a roaring in her ears, which she wanted desperately to block out.

She wasn't quite sure what happened next. She knew that people were being ushered inside. So was she. Her feet were moving, propelling her towards a sitting room where she was settled on a sofa, a quiet place which was good, left on her own, time to gather herself. What had just happened replayed in her head in slow motion.

It was dark in the sitting room, with only one of the lamps on a side table on, but that suited her. Her thoughts were going crazy in her head and just when she was about to go out because she couldn't sit on her own any longer, the door was pushed open and she saw Dante outlined, a shadowy silhouette filling the frame.

'You need to sit down, Caitlin.' His voice was low and serious as he moved towards her.

She fell back against the sofa, too scared to say a word. He'd moved from the shadows into the pool of light from the lamp and his expression was as serious as his voice.

'What's happened, Dante?' she whispered.

'Sit and I'll tell you. Good news and bad...'

CHAPTER THREE

SHE WAS SHAKING like a leaf and she barely noticed the glass of brandy Dante had brought in with him. He'd been thinking ahead, she dimly registered, predicting her reaction and knowing that she would need a stiff swig of something to deal with whatever he had to say.

If the gravity of his expression wasn't enough, the very fact that he had come equipped with brandy said it all.

He'd sat her down on the sofa and he sat next to her and waited until she had fortified herself by duly sipping some of the fiery alcohol, even though she didn't feel she needed it.

'Just tell me,' she whispered.

'There was a doctor there. An eminent surgeon, as it happens. A relative on my father's side. Of course, he couldn't do a complete test but it would seem that Alejandro fell at an awkward angle. If I could draw a parallel, it's a bit like someone collapsing to the ground because the chair they'd planned on sitting on has been yanked out from under them.'

'An awkward angle…'

'He didn't fall far, but what's certain is that he's broken several small but significant bones in his ankle.'

Caitlin looked at him and blinked. Her thoughts were lagging behind but a few broken bones didn't seem like the end of the world and she said as much, breathing a sigh of relief and closing her eyes.

'Not so fast,' Dante said, and he held her gaze when she opened her eyes to stare at him.

A person could drown in those eyes, she thought distractedly. She hadn't noticed how deep and dark they were before, because she'd been arguing with him, resentful and defensive at his suspicions, which had made her question all over again the wisdom of embarking on the charade. They weren't arguing now, and something shifted and filtered through her defences. Now, as their eyes locked, she could see that his were the deepest shade of bitter chocolate and fringed with thick, sooty lashes that any woman would give her right arm for.

He was a good-looking guy and she was up close and in a state of shock. It was understandable that those first impressions, that whisper of sexual attraction, felt stronger now. 'You said he just broke a few bones…'

'Preliminary findings show that he struck his head on the marble flooring at an awkward angle. He's concussed at the moment and we won't know more until more detailed examinations are made at the hospital, but Roberto seems to think that Alejandro could slide into a temporary coma.'

'A *coma*?' Tears gathered. 'But he just had a little fall…'

'It's not a certainty so there's no need to start getting upset.'

'Of course I'm going to be upset! I should be there with him.' She stood up while Dante remained seated, his long legs stretched out and lightly crossed at the ankles.

Why wasn't he responding? How could he look so cool and collected at a time like this?

'I need to get to that hospital,' she repeated, with mounting urgency. 'You need to take me *right now*.'

'You're in shock and you're better off here. Rushing to the hospital isn't going to achieve anything. Right now, and for the next few hours, if not days, Alejandro will be out of it, undergoing a battery of tests. Trust me, I will be the first to know of any developments.'

Caitlin hesitated, soothed by his assertiveness. She realised that it had been a long time since someone else had taken charge and it felt good. 'I feel so helpless. He must be terrified.'

'Caitlin, he's in the equivalent of a deep sleep. He'll be as peaceful as a newborn.'

All that stress, she thought, riven with guilt. Yes, he'd fallen, but was a part of him retreating from the awkward situation he had obviously found difficult to cope with? Had his brain decided to conveniently shut down just for the moment?

There were so many cases of people forgetting traumatic events, relegating them behind closed doors in their head because they just couldn't cope with the memories.

Had Alejandro done the equivalent?

And yet, she thought feverishly, they had both been so cavalier about this arrangement.

Alejandro was gay. This was a revelation that had seeped out over a period of months and Caitlin had been more surprised at his shame at the admission than the admission itself. After all, in this day and age, who thought twice about someone being gay?

But she didn't understand, he'd said matter-of-factly. His background, generation upon generation of accumulated wealth, was mired in tradition, his elevated birthright an albatross around his neck.

He was the older and expected to marry and produce. It would kill his parents if they found out about his sexual persuasion. Nothing Caitlin had said over the months could assuage his anxiety but it was only when he told her that his parents were becoming increasingly vocal on the subject of his love life that she began to see just how much it was affecting his state of mind.

He'd begun playing truant from work. He'd stopped caring about whether his increasing absences were noted or not. If only his brother would get married, he'd told her. That would let him off the hook. He'd be able to remain free for longer, at least until he sorted out what he would do in the future. But Dante, he had said, just wasn't playing ball.

And his parents wanted to know what was going on. Why had they not been introduced to any girlfriends? They had someone in mind for him, a lovely girl, daughter of one of their friends. They were insistent on a meeting.

And from there, Alejandro and Caitlin's plan had been born.

He'd been desperate and so...had she.

She wasn't going to think of her own circumstances. This was about Alejandro and the fact that he was in hospital and she couldn't help but blame herself because she hadn't seen just how stressed he'd been at the whole mess and at lying to all his friends and family.

'Where are—what's happened to everyone?'

'Gone.'

'Gone?'

'Shuffled out in an orderly line. My parents went to the hospital but they've heeded the consultant's advice and returned to their place.'

'What is the prognosis?'

She'd been borderline hysterical but now her brain had re-engaged and she was a lot calmer. Dante's sense of calm was mesmerising and infectious.

'Excellent.'

'Would you lie to me?'

'Of course I would.' He smiled, and just for a second she understood how power, charm and incredible physical perfection could be an intoxicating mix.

Her heart picked up a beat and she suddenly felt hot and bothered.

'But,' he continued, still smiling, 'in this instance I'm not. Yes, there are broken bones, and it'll be a while before those completely heal, and, yes, he's been concussed, but all his vital signs are good and if he's out of it just at the moment, Roberto, the consultant who was here, has assured us that a full recovery is to be expected.'

'But you said that he's in a coma.'

'He's out of it at the moment, yes. Perhaps *coma* might be something of a dramatic term.'

'So how long do you think…does the consultant think…?'

'Can't put a timeline on it. Could be a day, could be a week. Doubtful that it'll be longer. All the signs are good.'

'That's such a relief.'

'It's a disappointing end to what should have been one of the best nights of your life,' Dante murmured, briefly lowering his eyes.

'Yes, it's a shame,' she returned politely as her mind hived off in other directions.

'You don't sound too distraught.'

'Of course I'm distraught.'

'You were certainly upset when he toppled over.' Dante was getting that feeling again, that vague, shadowy feeling that something didn't quite add up but he couldn't put his finger on *what exactly*. It was frustrating. In Dante's world, everything added up. There were no loose ends because he always made sure that there weren't any. He never asked himself whether he was missing out on the adventures that spontaneity could bring.

When he glanced back over his shoulder to the kid who had allowed himself to be carried away on the spontaneous adventure of straying out of his comfort zone with an older woman from a different background, it was like looking at a stranger. The stupid thing was that he knew that what he had felt at the time, and what had propelled him into throwing himself into his ill-advised affair, had had nothing to do with love. Infatuation, yes, and lust, most definitely, but that had been it. Everything else had stemmed from a defiant act of rebellion against a life that had been preordained from birth. Someone had to take the reins of the family empire and he had known, even then, that it probably wasn't going to be Alejandro.

How had he known that? Dante could only assume it was because his parents had begun, automatically, to turn to *him* for his opinions on the stock markets, on trends, on modernisation, *on the way forward*. Bound within the confines of this life, he had broken free in an act of rebellion that had cost him dearly and not just in terms of the money he had recklessly flung at the woman. His pride had been injured and he had glimpsed a vision of weakness inside him that had required eradication. He had shut down his emotions and ruthlessly taken control of every aspect of his life.

Vague, shadowy feelings didn't sit well with him. Neither did the way his body refused to obey his head when he looked at the pocket-sized redhead, who had no business getting under his skin the way she did. Her intentions were open to question and getting to the bottom of what she was up to with his brother was a straightforward matter. He would then respond accordingly.

So the jostle of unwelcome responses inside him that had nothing to do with the business of finding out what she was up to was an unwelcome reminder of a weakness he'd thought he had put to bed. It got on his nerves.

She wasn't lying when she said that she had, indeed, been distraught when his brother had hit the ground. She just didn't seem overly upset at the fact that he had hit the ground at their engagement party, thereby ensuring a premature and unwelcome conclusion.

Now that he thought about it, he couldn't remember her flashing the diamond ring at all. What excited bride-to-be didn't flash her engagement ring at her own engagement party?

He glanced at her finger. She was absently fiddling with the ring, slipping it off and on her finger, twisting it round and round. It was startlingly modest in its proportions.

Unwittingly, he looked at her, felt that tightening in his groin again.

'I knew he'd been overdoing it with the drink.' Caitlin spoke her thoughts aloud, eyes sliding away from Dante's over-the-top masculine presence. Her conscience still plagued her. This had been a terrible idea, an awful plan and she should have argued more against it, but she'd allowed necessity to override common sense, and now thinking about poor Alejandro, lying unconscious on some sanitised hospital bed in an impersonal, clinical hospital room, filled her with remorse.

'I should have done something about that. He's not used to drinking a lot. He's quite abstemious normally.'

'Yes, that's a curious one, isn't it?'

Caitlin looked at him. 'What are you talking about?'

'I did recall that my brother doesn't tend to hit the bottle hard. I just wondered why, of all nights, he should decide to sample every drink that went past him on a tray...'

He wasn't going to let up. That was the thought that ran through her head. There had been a lull in the attack amidst the chaos of Alejandro being rushed to hospital, and during that lull she had glimpsed another Dante Cabrera, but normal proceedings had resumed and he *just wasn't going to let up.*

The man was like a dog with a bone, and not just *any dog.* Nothing she could turn her back on and ignore. This dog with a bone wasn't a loveable poodle. He was a pit bull and he wanted to sink teeth into her until he prised every little secret out.

She had no intention of letting him do any such thing but her blood ran cold as she felt him circling her.

'Who doesn't feel nervous on an occasion like that?'

she responded smoothly. '*I* was a bag of nerves. As you know.'

'You *were* concerned about your outfit,' Dante agreed. 'But, moving on from the troublesome subject of my brother's alcohol intake and his hospitalisation, the question is what happens from here?' He vaulted upright and paced towards the window, his movements as elegant and as stealthy as a jungle cat. He stared out for a few moments, then turned to look at her. 'Like I said, Alejandro probably won't come round for a day or two, but even when he does there's the business of those broken bones. He's going to be off his feet for some weeks, I would imagine...'

'He's going to go stir-crazy.'

'We can agree on that,' Dante said ruefully. 'Not that anything can be done to change that situation. On the upside, he'll be able to keep on top of work. Much of what needs to be done can be done via email and conference call. Thank God we live in a connected world.'

'He'll be thrilled to hear that,' Caitlin said sarcastically, without thinking, and then she flushed as Dante looked at her through narrowed eyes.

'You think he should refrain from working while he recuperates?'

'I think...' She shot Dante an accusatory look from under her lashes because she was now in the awkward position of having to explain what she had meant.

Didn't he know *anything* about his own brother? How was it possible for there to be such vast gaps between them? She'd never had siblings. When she was young, she'd *yearned* for one. It was heartbreaking, really, to witness a relationship that was so fractured.

'Yes?'

'I think...' she toed the middle ground '...he might appreciate a bit of peace from...er...the world of business...'

'What are you trying to tell me?'

He sounded genuinely perplexed and Caitlin sighed and decided to take a risk. A *tiny* risk. Wasn't it a starting point for these brothers to know a bit about one another? Alejandro, one day, would find the courage to explain who he was to his family and, when that day came, it would be so much smoother if Dante at least knew how his brother felt about working for the company.

'I'm not sure Alejandro is as...*besotted* with working for the company as you are...'

'Besotted?' Dante stared at her with rampant incredulity at yet another intrusion into areas of his life no one dared to explore.

'I know Alejandro tries to be as diligent as possible...' For Alejandro that actually meant working the minimum number of hours as efficiently as possible so that he could spend the remainder of his time exploring all those creative interests that he was more intrigued by.

Dante scowled and raked his fingers through his dark hair. 'I realise,' he conceded grittily, 'that he, perhaps, doesn't have the same drive as I have when it comes to running the company. Why do you think I've succeeded in diverging from the family business to build my own computer-software research companies? Because I've had nothing better to do? No, Alejandro doesn't have the same drive, but I've had no complaints from any of the directors...'

Personally, Caitlin was sure that that was because Alejandro was loved by everyone he met. He could put in an hour a day and she knew that everyone would be loath to report him. The fact was that he did his job perfectly well, if he was to be believed. He just didn't enjoy it and he spent as little time as possible there.

'No…well…it's just…' She breathed in deeply and decided, like a diver staring down at a very tiny pool of water miles below, to take the plunge. 'It's not that he doesn't have the same drive as you do. It's just that his heart has never really been in finance and business.'

Fulminating silence greeted this remark.

'He's really a creative soul,' she ploughed on while Dante watched her without saying a word, his face wiped of expression. 'That's why we get along so well. He's very interested in all aspects of photography. He loves exhibitions. He's even thinking about dabbling in a bit of sculpture or maybe even going for a course in woodwork…'

'Sculpture? *Woodwork?*'

'So you see he won't mind not being connected to the outside world while he recuperates.'

'Why would Alejandro not enjoy the work he does?' Dante demanded. 'He's never had the responsibility for any decision-making. I run everything. The buck stops with me. He has always had the easy ride of keeping the customers happy. What's not to like?' He flushed darkly. There was an admission there somewhere and he refused to shine a light on it. For once, the forbidding wall of privacy he had constructed around him revealed foundations that weren't as solid as he had thought.

He wanted to lock the discomforting thought away, but a series of connections were happening in his head that made him wonder whether the distance between him and Alejandro didn't hark back to that gradual alignment of responsibilities. Had there been something inside him that had resented the fact that he, although younger, had been the one to assume the reins of leadership without asking for it? Had that resentment spilled over, gradually, into the relationship he had with Alejandro?

The clear green eyes searching his lean, rigid face made his jaw harden in proud rejection of any sign of weakness.

'Maybe you judge him the way you would judge yourself,' Caitlin suggested quietly. 'Maybe because *you* enjoy being a workaholic, he must also enjoy being a workaholic because you share the same genetic code. But that's not how it works.'

'No one *enjoys* being a workaholic,' Dante responded coolly.

'I've offended you. I'm really sorry.'

'Offended me?' Dante scowled. 'Don't flatter yourself, *querida*.'

Caitlin flushed as she recognised a kick in the teeth when it was delivered.

'You asked for my opinion,' she returned shortly. 'And I gave it to you. Forget I ever said anything. You said something about Alejandro being in hospital for some time to come. Is there any chance that he could be transferred to a hospital in London?'

'If my brother was miserable in his job, he should have said something to me. As for being besotted with work… This vast family estate won't run itself because I'd rather have fun lazing around and going on holiday.' Dante was annoyed that he couldn't give it up.

'That's not what Alejandro is about!'

'Duty demands that the business falls to the sons. As

it stands, I have my own concerns that occupy much of my time. The family business is now just part of something bigger for me, even though our father no longer busies himself directly in its running. However, it is up to the pair of us to take up where he has left off. Would Alejandro rather abandon his obligations so that he can pursue a life of fun and enjoyment?'

'Your own concerns?' Caitlin had latched onto his phrase...*duty demands*. It gave her a very clear idea of why Alejandro was so loath to be open about his sexuality.

'My parents built their company on import and export. I have single-handedly brought it into the twenty-first century and it has become a gold mine, but it is overshadowed by my own computer-software empire.'

'So you work hard. But you volunteered for that, didn't you? You weren't content to just run the family business. You wanted your own, I guess because you enjoy that kind of ruthless, cut-throat lifestyle. Alejandro just isn't built along the same lines. And the reason he hasn't said anything...' she sighed but it was too late to start wondering whether she'd got in over her head with this conversation '...is because of this whole duty and tradition thing. He knows he has to join the family business whether he likes it or not but...'

'He's never uttered a word of complaint to me,' Dante said roughly. 'I could...work this out differently... I have been thinking of taking my computer business into a different area—the leisure industry always has room for improvement.' He frowned, padded across to a chair and sat down, stretching his legs out to the side. 'The wheels are in motion for me to take over a couple of boutique hotels in South America. There would certainly be scope for some creative advertising.'

'He would absolutely *adore* that.'

'This is something my brother should have brought to my attention. It's ridiculous that I have only found this out via a third party.'

'Maybe he was scared of disappointing,' she murmured. 'Haven't *you* ever been scared of disappointing?'

'Disappointing who?'

'I don't know. Your parents...your girlfriend...'

'To answer your question, no.'

Such self-assurance, Caitlin thought with a fascinated shiver. Little wonder Alejandro, so full of insecurities and doubts, had never thought to confide in his much more confident younger brother.

What must it be like to go out with a guy like Dante Cabrera? Personally, she had never been drawn to tough Alpha-male types but something feminine quivered inside her just for a moment at the thought of being with someone so absolutely in command. He was born to take charge and she remembered how that had made her feel when she had been frantic with worry earlier on. *Safe*.

Yet, he was willing to make concessions because, whatever his relationship with his brother, however distant they were from one another and however wildly different their personalities, he cared enough to try to see things from Alejandro's point of view.

He wasn't just a man of action. He was a listener. The problem was that Alejandro had never tried talking and Dante did not invite confidences.

'We were talking about the fact that Alejandro will be in hospital for a while,' Dante picked up the conversation from where they had left off before they'd gone down various byroads, 'and I couldn't help but notice that you travelled over here light.'

Caitlin looked at him with puzzlement because she wasn't sure where he was going with this.

'You're going to need clothes, so we have to decide how we're going to play this.'

'What are you talking about?'

'Well, you won't be returning to London for a while. Presumably your company will allow you suitable time off?'

'Time off?' Caitlin parroted.

'Alejandro is here and he won't be going anywhere any time soon.' He paused, giving her ample opportunity to see where he was heading with this.

How could she abandon her fiancé after the first night when he was lying in hospital, unconscious?

She blanched.

'I… I hadn't actually banked on spending much time over here…' *Or any at all, for that matter.* 'I don't know what the company policy is on…on time off for…for…'

'Compassionate leave? That does exist in your company, doesn't it?'

'Of course, but you know… I'm a freelance photographer… Yes, I'm employed by them, but I get called on to do various shoots and I'm paid accordingly…'

'That hardly sounds a satisfactory situation.'

'I'm working my way up. It's not something that happens overnight…'

'So…what…? They're going to quibble over giving you time off because the guy you plan on marrying is lying unconscious on a hospital bed in Spain? What kind of crackpot organisation are we talking about here?'

'It's a very reputable company!'

'Good, then that's all sorted. You'll have to call them first thing in the morning.'

'Yes, but...' She'd been standing on fairly solid ground but now a roller coaster had whipped past, scooped her up and she was in mid-air and travelling at speed.

'I'm not getting what the problem is here, Caitlin. Either you want to be with Alejandro or you don't. Which is it?'

'Of course, I would love to be around to make sure that he's going to be okay!'

Dante frowned. 'Good. Then let's not put unnecessary obstacles in the way. Back, though, to what I was saying earlier. You seem to have travelled over here with next to nothing. You'll need clothes. Do you want me to arrange to have some of yours brought over for you?'

'That won't be necessary,' Caitlin muttered. The walls had well and truly closed in and there was no point trying to reconfigure the space. 'I expect if you point me in the direction of the nearest town, I'll be able to buy one or two things.'

Dante shrugged. 'I'd look at a fortnight here.'

'A fortnight...?' She tried not to sound appalled.

'And naturally, you will have to stay here.'

'Here?'

'Where else?' He raised his eyebrows and held her dismayed gaze. 'Unless you'd rather stay with my parents? They're not very handy for the hospital, but I'm sure they would not object to putting you up for however long you think you'll need to stay...'

'What? No!'

'Didn't think so. Not many brides-to-be would leap

at the chance of staying with their in-laws, especially when they've only known their in-laws for a matter of a few hours.'

'I wouldn't want to impose,' Caitlin objected faintly, and Dante took his time looking round the huge sitting room with its high ceilings and sprawling bay windows. His dark eyes were cool and amused when they finally rested on her face.

'I wouldn't worry about it. I don't think we'll be bumping into one another because I live in a shoebox. Fact is, I doubt my brother would appreciate me turning you away at the door, given the circumstances.'

Caitlin, in her head, begged to differ. Alejandro would understand completely if she headed for the airport, clutching her bag. They were friends, after all, and certainly not the couple Dante assumed they were.

That said, if she ended up staying in Spain, he would also have sympathised with her perfectly reasonable desire to hit the nearest B & B because sharing space with Dante would be like sharing space with a hungry tiger on the prowl.

Realistically, though, was there any way that she could turn down the man's offer? He was already casting his net of suspicion far and wide.

'If it makes you feel any better, I'm rarely around. Naturally the staff will be here so you won't have to worry about anything at all. I know you'll be worried sick about Alejandro…but, rest assured, he is in the best hands, which I'm sure you know because you're certainly handling the shock better than I would have expected.'

He had vaulted to his feet and was heading for the door. She followed.

'What did you expect?' They were back in the body
of the house and it was quiet. The army of staff who
had scurried with their trays of champagne and caviar
had had another role to fill and had removed all evidence of the party, so that now it was as though it had
never been. A dream. Except...*not*.

'Well...' He spun round so suddenly that she almost
crashed into him. She hastily stepped back and their
eyes collided, startled green meeting cool, speculating
midnight black. 'Call me stupid, but I thought there
might be some hysteria involved.'

'Hysteria?'

'Naturally, you were clearly upset and shaken, but...
let's just say I admire your self-control...'

'I'm not that type.' Caitlin licked her lips nervously.

'So it would appear,' Dante murmured lazily. 'I like
that. And yet that seems to contradict the firecracker
who attacked me outside the house.'

Caitlin flushed. How on earth was she going to manage spending a few *hours* here, never mind a few days?

He was so different from Alejandro. She wished her
so-called erstwhile fiancé had told her a bit more about
his forbidding younger brother. She might have, at least,
come prepared. As things stood...

'No matter,' Dante said smoothly, spinning back on
his heels and striding towards the curving staircase,
one of two that dissected the mansion, 'we all have our
different ways of dealing with distressing situations.'

'Where are we going?'

'Your rooms. Your bag will follow.'

He paused, pushed open a door and stood back so
that she could precede him into a self-contained apartment that was the last word in luxury, from the thick

velvet drapes to the rich Persian rug that partially covered the highly polished wooden floor. Through interlinking doors, she could see a sitting room.

'Thank you.' Gratitude didn't seem quite the emotion she was feeling. 'Please don't feel that you have to look out for me *at all*. I'll be more than capable of making my way to the hospital and into the town while I'm here. I'll call work in the morning and find out what sort of leave I'll be allowed…' His silence was oppressive.

'No need to thank me.' He lowered his lashes, shielding his expression, then looked at her. 'And banish all thoughts of making your way anywhere. I'll have a car waiting to take you to the hospital tomorrow and also to the town so that you can stock up on clothes.'

'Of course.' How on earth was she going to afford a new wardrobe? How was any of this making any sense at all? Why, why, why had they jumped head first into water without first finding out how deep it was?

'In the meantime…' he strolled towards the door and lounged against the door frame for a few seconds, looking at her with a veiled expression '…try and relax. Have a soak. By the time you're out of the bath, your clothes will be here. And when it comes to shopping? Buy a swimsuit. There's a superb infinity pool. I think you'll like it.' He straightened. 'When you're not agonising about Alejandro, kick back a little. You'll be waited on hand and foot. You may find that you won't be able to resist thinking of it as an unexpected little holiday…'

CHAPTER FOUR

HOLIDAY? *HOLIDAY? WAS the man mad?*

Caitlin peered out of the sitting-room window and wondered which of the cars parked outside might be the one designated to take her into the city. Would she be summoned by someone? One of the members of staff? There was no helpful chap in a uniform poised by an open car door to offer her any clues and she wasn't quite sure what she should do.

She'd had a restless night as the consequences of what had transpired began to take shape in her head.

A week here. At the very least. Work, at any rate, had been sympathetic but she was new to the job and freelance so she didn't know just how long the sympathy would last.

Her parents had been puzzled.

'Spain? Why are you in Spain, darling? You never mentioned going on holiday...'

No, of course she hadn't! This fleeting visit was supposed to last a handful of hours, after which she would have been able to see a clear way forward with all the problems that had disastrously landed on her lap without warning.

Instead, here she was, peering out of a window and wondering what more disasters lay in wait.

Lost in her thoughts, she was unaware of footsteps behind her until she heard Dante's voice.

'Have you been waiting long? After last night's adventures, I thought you might want a lie-in.'

Caitlin spun round to see him lounging in the doorway. She'd expected an empty house. Dante had more or less reassured her that if she stayed under his roof, there would be almost no chance of them bumping into one another. The house was as vast as a castle and she had assumed that he would be out of it anyway, back working, but now she wondered how she could have been so naïve. Whatever brief periods of respite there had been since Alejandro's accident, Dante was still determined to piece her together and dig deep to find out what was going on.

She had to be on guard, but as she looked at him she knew that she would have to fight her own physical responses to him, which threatened to undermine her resolve at every turn. She couldn't work out how someone who made her hackles rise and threatened her peace of mind could have the sort of effect on her that he did. Was it because she just hadn't been interested in any guy since Jimmy? Or was it because she had always assumed that if she ever looked twice at another man, he would be in her league, someone reliable and grounded, someone *who made sense*.

There was no chance that she had caught him on his way out because he wasn't dressed for work. He was in a pair of black jeans and a black polo-necked shirt with a distinctive red logo on the pocket. He looked darkly, sexily *dangerous* and her nervous system went into immediate overdrive.

'I thought you would be at work,' she said, already

on edge. 'I…er…wasn't sure what to do about transport into town.'

'You're looking at your transport.' Dante straightened and glanced at his watch.

'What are you talking about?'

'I've decided that it would be inappropriate to abandon you in your time of need. You don't know this part of the world, I'm guessing, and you're going to need someone to show you around while you're here.'

'Show me around?' Caitlin couldn't think of anything she needed less than Dante playing tour guide for the next few days. 'Why? Don't you have more important things to do?'

'What could be more important than making sure that my brother's beloved fiancée isn't left alone and floundering in a strange city? Come on. We can hit the hospital first, and then I will take you to the shopping district where you can buy sufficient clothes to tide you over.'

Caitlin quailed at the prospect of spending money she didn't have on things she didn't need.

Dante wasn't hanging around, waiting for any further protestations from her. He was already heading out of the sitting room and towards the imposing front door, barely leaving time for Caitlin to trip along behind him, clutching her knapsack.

The clean-up job on the house had been spectacular. As she was progressed along at fast speed, she could only guess that an army of helpers had been hard at it, wiping away all evidence of the elaborate party that had come to such a premature end.

It was not yet nine thirty and already it was hot outside.

Dante ignored all four cars parked in the massive courtyard and instead headed to the side of the house, beeping open a low-slung, steel-grey sports car that hadn't been visible from the sitting-room window.

He held open the passenger door for her.

Caitlin dropped into a plush leather bucket seat that made her feel as though she was inches away from making uncomfortable physical contact with the ground. Peering over the sleek walnut dashboard was a challenge because of her lack of height.

Dante, on the other hand, as he slid into the driver's seat and donned a pair of dark sunglasses, looked like a racing driver about to do a few winning laps around a circuit.

'Good news from the hospital,' he said as soon as the car revved to life. 'Alejandro is progressing well. He still hasn't regained consciousness, but all his vitals are good and those broken bones are the only damage he appears to have suffered. They can't work out how he lost consciousness and can only think that he must have dropped to the ground in a peculiarly awkward manner.'

'That's great,' Caitlin said with genuine warmth. 'Do we…er…have any idea how long he will be…out of it?'

'Absolutely none, but the signs are good for a speedy recovery on that front. I'm assuming you've contacted your people at work and been granted whatever time off you need?'

'I've phoned and told them that I will probably be here for about a week.' She braced herself for criticism.

Instead, Dante said smoothly, 'We'll head to the hospital first. You must be keen to see Alejandro.'

'Of course.' She noted the quick sideways glance Dante shot her but there was no way she could sound like a besotted lover, desperate to see her wounded fiancé.

Naturally, she was deeply concerned about what had happened and relieved that he had not had a more serious accident, given the wild abandon with which he had been drinking, but, much as she cared about Alejandro, he was, in the end, simply a very good friend and her pretence could only stretch so far. Not only would she have found it impossible to pretend to be loved up, but Alejandro would have had an even harder time of it.

It was just terrible luck that he happened to have a brother with eagle-sharp eyes and the prowling, suspicious nature of a trained sniffer dog.

'I guess your parents must be so relieved...'

'Naturally. They'll be visiting later today and, of course, they will want to see you, make sure you're okay, even though I've already told them that you couldn't be better. Given the circumstances.'

Caitlin gritted her teeth together at the implied judgement call in that throwaway remark but she remained silent, taking in the change of scenery as the grand and leafy outskirts of the city were left behind and the car began to nose its way into the main area of the very beautiful city.

She had never been to Madrid before, never been to Spain, if truth be told, and her artistic eye fully appreciated the beguiling mix of old and new, high tech and historic, sleek glass and pastel coloured.

'And you are okay, aren't you?'

Reluctantly she dragged her attention away from the passing scenery and focused on the aristocratic profile of the guy sitting next to her, one hand on the steering wheel, the other resting lightly on the intimidating gearbox.

So different from his brother, she thought a little helplessly. Chalk and cheese had more in common. She just had no idea how to deal with him or how to handle herself when she was around him.

Everything about him made her nervous, from his aggressive good looks to his cool, watchful self-assurance.

'Of course.' She cleared her throat. 'How far is the... hospital from here? Once I know the route, I would be happy to make my own way in to visit.'

'How would you propose to do that?'

'There must be some form of public transport close to your house?'

'Sadly not.' He shot her a sideways look that carried a hint of amusement. 'Of course, I could always arrange for my driver to take you but, like I said, I feel personally responsible for your well-being while you are here. We're twenty minutes away from the hospital, by the way.'

Caitlin was so tempted to protest, yet again, that he had no need to feel responsible for her in any way, shape or form, but why bother? The man was determined to take her under his wing and she hadn't been born yesterday. She knew that if she was under his wing, he would be able to keep a sharp eye on her and would be in a prime position to keep prodding away, poking into nooks and crannies, airing his suspicions and waiting for her to slip up.

How long would it take for that to happen? she wondered. How long before she slipped up?

Not long. She wasn't used to lying. Manoeuvring through the labyrinth she and Alejandro had innocently created was going to take the dexterity of a magician.

As they approached the hospital she finally allowed herself to think about the convoluted road she was now travelling down.

It had all seemed so straightforward not that long ago. She would pretend to be Alejandro's fiancée, thereby buying him time from his parents, who were pushing for a solid relationship from their eldest son and the inevitable production line of much-wanted grandchildren.

He would pay her, he'd said.

Caitlin had adamantly refused. Not only could she not see the reason for such drama, but the thought of being paid for it was ridiculous.

But then circumstances had changed in a heartbeat for her, and Alejandro, who had not abandoned his plan despite her initial refusal to co-operate, had found a way past her defences.

She had no interest in his money for herself because she didn't have a materialistic bone in her body, but when her parents had become involved, her love and loyalty to them had very quickly become the quicksand that had begun to drag her under.

'I don't believe it,' she had poured her heart out to Alejandro one evening, several months earlier. 'How could Dad have lost everything? There are news bulletins all the time about scammers, but he's gone and lost everything, Alejandro! His savings, his pension. Gone. *Pouf!* They have the house, of course, but how on earth are they going to afford to support themselves as they get older?'

'What about your mum?'

She'd known that Alejandro would be grappling with the concept of having nothing. The backdrop to his life was paved with gold and priceless gems. He, literally, would have no concept of just how agonising it would be for two pensioners to realise that their life savings had gone. But he had sympathised as she had talked to him about the situation, told him that, as the only child, it fell upon her shoulders to build up some kind of nest egg for them so that they wouldn't be terrified of growing old in poverty.

And even then, it had been awful but within the realms of possibility until her lovely, kind and gentle mother had had a heart attack and they had all been told by the consultant that stress could prove to be a fatal enemy.

The conversation that had been left behind, Alejandro's offer to pay her generously for helping him out, had begun to beckon.

When he'd raised the subject again, Caitlin's defences had been in a different place.

She had listened.

It still went against the grain. She still didn't get why he couldn't just come right out and tell the world that he was gay.

But she had listened.

Just a couple of days, he had told her with bright and breezy confidence. A small bit of acting, a make-believe relationship, enough to convince his parents that they were involved.

No dates would be set for anything and they would return to London, where they would resume their lives and he would be granted a reprieve.

Once his brother had married, he had assured her, everything would change and the pressure would be off. And of course, he had told her earnestly, he would tell them all the truth. It would be easier then.

And the money…

He had named a sum that had made her eyes water. All her parents' problems would go away. It would be like waving a wand. Caitlin had thought of her mother and the possible horrendous consequences of another heart attack brought on by ongoing stress... She'd thought of her father, who would never forgive himself for getting them into the mess that he had... She'd thought of two lives that would end in tatters...

And Alejandro's proposal had suddenly seemed like manna from heaven. She had swept past her hesitation and doubt and she had agreed.

Except, she was here now, and nothing was straightforward any more...

Not when Dante was in the driving seat, which he was. 'We're here.'

Caitlin surfaced and stared at the sprawling glass building facing her, abuzz with activity, its harsh, clinical contours softened by thoughtful planting of trees and shrubbery in strategic places.

Like royalty, Dante dumped the car right outside the building and it was efficiently collected by someone she could only assume was his driver, who had been forewarned to meet them there.

He strode into the white brightly lit corridors of the hospital and crowds parted. He glanced neither left nor right. He led the way with certainty and she tripped along in his wake, profoundly relieved that he knew just where he was going and what he was doing.

She spoke absolutely no Spanish and she couldn't think how difficult everything would have been had she come here on her own.

He spoke in rapid Spanish to a consultant who had been summoned, and then finally turned to her.

'I appreciate that you must find all of this very confusing.'

'I'm glad you're here,' Caitlin admitted with a smile. 'I have no idea how I would have coped. I would probably still be in a taxi trying to get the driver to understand where I needed to go.'

Dante shot her a sideways glance. 'I'm surprised you don't know any Spanish at all, given the fact that you're engaged to a Spaniard.'

For once, there wasn't that jagged edge of suspicion underlying his remark. He sounded genuinely curious as they began to walk along the corridor to the room previously indicated by the consultant.

'Alejandro did try,' she admitted. 'It only took him five seconds to realise that he wasn't going to get anywhere when it came to me picking up a second language.'

'Not interested?'

'Very interested but my brain just doesn't seem equipped to handle it.' She laughed.

Dante's dark eyes slid over to her. That laugh...as infectious as her smile. Unconsciously he glanced down at her sexy, round curves, the softness of her fair skin, the vibrant colours of her copper hair, which she had tied back into something resembling an untidy bun. She smelled faintly of flowers and sunshine. There was something intensely appealing about her lack of artifice and that appealing *something* dragged on his senses, made him hyperaware of her in ways he knew he shouldn't be. He knew the dangers of *different*. He knew what shame and wounded pride tasted like and he knew that the road that led there started with irrational temptation. It had that one and only time. It was a road he was never going to walk down again. On so many levels, the woman standing here was wrong and yet...

When he thought of the sort of woman he was destined for, a woman like Luisa, other thoughts pushed their way through, discomforting, uncontrollable thoughts that had no place in his life. Of course, he would never go there. He was supremely confident when it came to his ironclad willpower, but the mere fact that he couldn't stop his mind from wandering rankled.

'Somewhere along the line, I think my parents gave up on me being academic and so, in my head, I just ended up assuming that I couldn't do anything that wasn't creative. Hence my love of art and photography.'

'You should learn.'

'Why?'

'It might come in useful,' Dante interposed drily. 'Considering the circumstances.'

Caitlin laughed again. 'Oh, Alejandro and I won't be...' She went scarlet and came to a grinding stop.

'Won't be *what*?' Dante encouraged softly, his ears pricking up.

'Nothing,' Caitlin muttered. How could she have let all her defences drop with him? How had she managed to let that charm get under her skin and very nearly pull the rug from under her feet?

He was staring at her. She could feel the insistence of his eyes boring into her skin and she purposefully kept her head averted and, thankfully, they had landed up outside Alejandro's room so she had a very good excuse to ignore the guy towering next to her so that she could focus on her supposed fiancé, who was lying on the bed, for all the world looking as if he just happened to be in a deep sleep.

As peaceful as a baby, she thought, leaving her to deal with the fallout on her own.

'If it's okay, I'll go see him…on my own, if you don't mind.'

Dante didn't mind. He was still trying to work out what she had just said. It had slipped out and she had immediately regretted the oversight. He knew that and it wasn't just because she had gone a beetroot-red shade of intense discomfort, the intense discomfort of an adult who had very nearly broken the tidings to a gullible four-year-old that Santa wasn't real. He had *sensed* it, had sensed her horror at something that had very nearly been said.

What was it, though?

He was excellent when it came to reading people and reading, more importantly, what was between the lines. It was a talent he had ruthlessly exploited over the years, because it had always given him the upper hand when it came to the cut and thrust of dealmaking.

You never made it far by believing anything anybody said to you. He certainly never trusted anyone unless they had gone the distance to earn it. Few ever had.

Dante believed every word Caitlin had told him about her relationship with his brother, namely that they went back a way and had started out as great friends. He could see the *friend* bit clearly enough. It was what she *omitted* to say he found so intriguing, and that near slip-up she had narrowly escaped had compounded his suspicions.

She'd hurried into the room, closing the door behind her, and he watched through the pane of glass in the door as she pulled a chair closer to the bed and sat down, taking one of Alejandro's hands in hers for a quick pat and then leaning forward to talk.

There was no gentle caressing of the brow or tender kiss on the mouth, and after that perfunctory pat she had dropped his hand with shameless speed.

He would have given his right arm to have been a fly on the wall because, whatever she was saying, it didn't appear, reading her body language from behind, that she was soothing him with sweet nothings.

Dante spun round and was helping himself to some drinking water from a plastic cup when she approached to briskly thank him for delivering her.

'I can make my way to the shops from here,' she said firmly. 'We're in the centre of things. I won't need you to traipse behind me. If you want to visit with Alejandro, I can either meet you back here or else I'll grab a taxi to the house.'

'How did you find him?'

'He seems comfortable enough.' She sincerely hoped he'd heard every word she'd said when she'd told him in no uncertain terms that he'd been an idiot to have consumed his body weight in champagne and that she was really out of her depth having to cope with Dante, who watched her so closely that she felt uncomfortable every time she drew breath.

'Honestly, Alejandro,' she'd all but wailed, 'what on earth possessed us?' She wondered whether she had imagined the flicker of his eyes when she had said that. If he could hear her, then he was probably trying hard to blink in agreement.

'Wait here. I will come to the shops with you. You're about to tell me that there's no need but I wouldn't bother to waste my breath if I were you. You're new to Madrid and it's the very least I can do.' Under any other circumstances, Dante would have spent fifteen minutes with his brother and then continued on to his high-rise office in the city centre to pick up where he had left off on the work front, but the green-eyed, butter-wouldn't-melt-in-her-mouth redhead, trying not to look appalled, suddenly made all things work-related fade into the background.

'Fine.' Caitlin shrugged and took a seat outside the room and waited. For the first time, something loomed even more stomach-churning than the prospect of Dante lurking like a hangman's noose, and that was the thought of a shopping expedition she couldn't afford.

He wasn't long. Ten minutes at the most. Well, she thought, they barely had anything to say to one another when Alejandro was on top form, so lying unconscious on a hospital bed wasn't exactly going to be conducive to a lengthy visit.

'That was quick.' She'd aimed for sarcasm. She ended up with compassion because it was sad. Dante looked at her, his handsome face darkly rejecting the soft empathy in her voice and yet…as he raked his fingers through his hair and continued to stare, the atmosphere suddenly shifted. He wasn't retaliating, calling her to account, slamming the door in her face. He looked lost for words and, in that moment, intensely human and vulnerable.

'I'm sorry,' she said softly, reaching to rest her small hand on his arm.

'I don't do pity.'

'I'm still sorry. I always longed for a sibling but it wasn't to be. I'm sorry for both of you that, as brothers, you've drifted so far apart.'

'These things happen.'

'They do,' Caitlin agreed. Their eyes were locked and she had unconsciously stepped a bit closer towards him. 'But there's usually a reason behind it. I'm sad for you both because you seem to have just drifted into silence. It's crazy.'

'Not crazy,' Dante said roughly. 'In a busy life, things can sometimes drift. My fault. My brother's fault. Who knows? I agree…it's…not ideal.'

Caitlin smiled. 'Not how I would have described it…'

Dante smiled back. 'That's because you're emotional and I'm not.'

The silence that fell was brief, thrumming with something he couldn't put his finger on and broken when a woman said, from behind, 'Sorry, but am I breaking something up here?'

Dante spun round and Caitlin expelled a long breath and blinked at the leggy brunette staring at them with narrowed, assessing eyes.

'Luisa.' Dante pushed himself off the wall, his brain failing to instantly engage. It was sufficiently engaged, however, to bring home to him that Luisa was the last person he had any interest in seeing. She had been hard work at the aborted party the evening before, trying desperately to revive a relationship that was well and truly in the throes of rigor mortis. 'What are you doing here?'

Luisa pouted. 'I've come to see your brother, Dante. What else?' Her eyes were chips of diamond-hard ice as they briefly settled on Caitlin, who was fervently wishing that she could be anywhere but here. Deliberately eliminated from the conversation, she could only hover, acutely uncomfortable at being third wheel in whatever drama was unfolding between Dante and the other woman.

'I popped in to have a chat with your parents…' Luisa half turned, drawing Dante into a private huddle with her. 'They're so worried but I reassured them that Alejandro will be just fine.' She smiled broadly and lightly rested her hand on Dante's shoulder, making small stroking movements against the sleeve of his polo shirt. 'Maybe...' the smile was coquettish now and she had lowered her voice to a husky murmur '...you and I could go somewhere and grab a coffee? Maybe some lunch? That lovely little place we went to a few months ago would be perfect...'

'Did my mother happen to mention that I would be here?'

Luisa laughed nervously.

'No coffee, Luisa,' he said on an impatient sigh. 'No lunch. I'm heading into town. Caitlin needs clothes because she will be staying on. I am taking her shopping.' He glanced down at Caitlin and Caitlin saw a flash of venom cross Luisa's perfect face, gone in a heartbeat, replaced with a gentle smile of understanding.

'You're such a gentleman, Dante.' Luisa forced the smile in Caitlin's direction and flicked some non-existent fluff from her figure-hugging dress before shaking her hair and throwing back her shoulders. 'Of course, you must look out for your brother's fiancée, seeing that she has no one here at the moment and must be grief-stricken at what's happened. I'm sure I'll see you when things settle down.'

During this interchange, Caitlin hadn't said a word and she didn't as she and Dante both left the hospital and made their way into the bustling city.

CHAPTER FIVE

THERE WAS NO WAY to be polite and beat about the bush so Caitlin took the bull by the horns and said, bluntly, 'Is there some kind of market I could go to?'

She was discovering that going anywhere on foot was unacceptable to Dante. He had driven his sports car directly to the hospital, where it had been collected by his driver. She guessed it had been returned to the house, because no sooner were they out of the hospital and standing outside in baking heat than another car showed up, this time a black four-wheel drive with darkly tinted windows.

She was bundled into blissful cold and immediately turned to him to repeat her question.

'Why would you want to go to a market?' He frowned. 'Special dietary requirements? Tell me and I'll instruct a member of staff.'

'Not a food market, Dante. A flea market where I can buy clothes.'

'It's false economy buying cheap tat,' Dante returned smoothly. He spoke to his driver in rapid Spanish and she lapsed into fretful silence as they were driven to and deposited on a tree-lined avenue where elegant buildings with discreet pale awnings advertised a range of exclusive designer stores. Gucci rubbed shoulders with Louis Vuitton and Jimmy Choo, and some names she didn't recognise looked even more upmarket.

'Dante!' She turned to him with desperation as she was hustled out of the car to find herself on the pavement. 'I can't afford to shop in a place like this!'

'You're engaged to my brother.'

'What does that have to do with anything?' She literally had a vision of fifty-pound notes blowing away from her savings account.

'This is a ridiculous conversation. I can't believe my brother would not spend money on you.'

'I prefer to spend my own money buying my own clothes,' she retorted angrily. 'What sort of world do you live in, Dante? No, forget I said that! You enjoy throwing money at the women you go out with because it's easier than the other option!'

'You're crossing lines.' His jaw hardened. 'Be careful.'

'Or else what?' Caitlin rolled her eyes and placed her hand belligerently on her hips. 'Dante, it's easier to spend money than it is to spend quality time, isn't it?'

Dante flushed with outrage. 'More tête-à-têtes with my brother about me?'

'No! I'm just observant. I can see that Luisa is besotted with you but it's not returned—and, yes, Alejandro did say that you weren't keen on the notion of settling down.'

'Nor, presumably, is he, or he would have done it sooner.'

'It doesn't matter.' She sighed. 'I don't like accepting stuff from guys. It doesn't feel right. And I can't afford to buy anything in any of the shops on this fancy street.'

This was a first for Dante. The idea that a woman might resent having presents lavished on her puzzled him. What she viewed as some kind of insult to her feminism, he saw as an expression of appreciation.

'Caitlin, you're going to be here for at least a week. Who knows? Maybe longer. If you can't afford to spend money on yourself, then allow me. I do so on behalf of my brother. He can pay me back in due course, if it makes you feel easier. I hear what you're saying about not wanting to accept anything from anyone, but I feel that Alejandro would not want to think of you traipsing down to the local flea market. You're going to be entering a whole new dynamic when you marry my brother. Why not start adapting now? Besides, the flea market only opens on a Sunday.'

'Because people get engaged doesn't automatically mean they're going to get married,' Caitlin said vaguely. She realised that the deeper she dug her heels in, the odder it would seem to a guy like Dante, who lived in a completely different world from her. Alejandro shared that world. He would lavish gifts on whatever partner he ended up with.

She wasn't going to win this one.

'I suppose Alejandro—'

'Good.' He spun round on his heels and swept her along to a shopping experience she hadn't banked on.

This was how the other half lived. She'd seen it on a grand scale in his mansion. The priceless artwork, the acres of polished marble, the invisibility of his staff paid to make his life as fuss-free as possible.

For the next three hours, she experienced it first-hand when it was exclusively directed at her.

He had chairs brought for him so that he could sit,

his veiled expression revealing very little as clothes were fetched and carried. When money was no object, the attentiveness of the various boutique owners was ingratiating. They fawned and scurried and couldn't do enough.

And something deep inside Caitlin responded with a feminine enjoyment that was shameful because it just wasn't her.

Even before everything with her parents had fallen apart, plunging her into a financial nightmare, spending money on expensive clothes had never been her thing. Maybe it was her shape. In her head, expensive clothes were designed for a certain type of figure, one she didn't possess. Maybe it was the way she had been brought up. Her parents had always been sensible with money because they'd never had a great deal of it and it was an attitude that had been passed down to her.

Shopping with Dante Cabrera was not a sensible experience. The opposite. He snapped his fingers and people hastened to please. She was the beneficiary of his largesse and it was *thrilling*. She didn't want it to be, but it was.

Silk and soft cottons were laid for her inspection. The finest leather was brought out on show. She had had to resist the temptation to lovingly stroke some of the items of clothing.

'If you want an objective opinion,' Dante had drawled, standing next to her in that very first exclusive boutique, when the glamorous woman in charge had hurried off to find the right size for a dress Caitlin had guiltily admitted to really liking, 'then feel free.'

'No, thank you,' she had responded politely. But she had still *felt* his presence as he'd accompanied her on the shopping trip, had found her mind wandering back time and again to those dark, hooded eyes, his lean beauty, to the insane appeal of his lazy self-assurance.

His driver took bags of shopping to the car, patiently waiting wherever they happened to be.

It was exhausting and exhilarating at the same time and then, when it was over, when they were being ferried back to the house with half a store in the boot of the car, Dante murmured, softly, 'You should wear something you bought today to visit my parents. I accepted an invitation on your behalf. They're concerned about you…'

On a high from shopping, from breaking out of her comfort zone, temporarily freed from the unending stress of the past few months when every penny had had to be counted and allocated to a fund for her parents, Caitlin nodded. Yes. Why not? What was wrong with feeling like a living, breathing woman again? Just for an evening?

Dante's low-slung Ferrari glided through the iron gates, which opened silently at the press of a button.

It was mid-afternoon. He should still be at his glass high-rise in the Silicon Valley just outside the city centre.

Why was he here, driving up the tree-lined avenue towards his house?

Of course, he knew why. He hadn't been able to focus. He hadn't been able to focus for the past three days.

That shopping expedition…

Dante had been shopping with women before. He had always taken his laptop because, in between watching the inevitable parade of outfits, he had always been able to catch up on his emails as he'd positioned himself on a chair, in for the long haul.

He enjoyed lavishing presents on the women he went out with. Why not? He had more money than he knew what to do with. And women enjoyed being treated like queens.

Caitlin had not been one of them. Her remark about him throwing money at women because money was an easier sweetener to dish out than time and commitment had rankled. As far as he was concerned, it wasn't a case of one or the other. It was a case of him not being interested in commitment but enjoying being lavish. How were the two connected? He had refused to rise to the bait and had been outraged at yet another foray from the woman into his private life, which was and always would be out of bounds. She had accepted, finally, his offer to cover the cost of a new wardrobe, seeing that she was stuck in Spain, but he had then to persuade her that the purchase of cheap plastic shoes and disposable tat was out of the question.

What sort of man was Alejandro? he had privately questioned. Stingy? Surely not. He might not be on familiar terms with his brother, but stinginess didn't run in their family. So how was it that the woman he planned on marrying had to dip into her own pocket for essentials?

Dante knew that some might call him a dinosaur for thinking like that but he really didn't care. It was how he was, and he was shocked that his brother was not cut from the same cloth.

Accustomed as he was to the twirling of women as they tried on clothes, their insistence that he stay put so that he could give his opinion, Dante had been perversely fascinated by Caitlin's lack of interest in what he thought of her choices. Made sense, he knew, because it wasn't as though they were involved on any level, but he had still found himself dumping the laptop and watching what she went for even though there were no trying-on performances.

The three exclusive shops he took her to didn't offer anything he figured she would automatically make a beeline for. Nothing baggy. Nothing made from fabric better employed for curtains. Nothing designed for women who didn't want their bodies on show.

He'd found himself curiously keen to see the transformation and he had that very evening when he had stood there at the bottom of the stairs, glancing at his watch and waiting for her to emerge.

The dress she had worn to the ill-fated engagement party had revealed a figure she was at pains to hide. She had looked good but had clearly been ill at ease in it. The silk culottes and little matching silk vest she had worn to his parents' were much more her thing. She felt confident in them and that confidence spilled over into the way she moved, the way she carried herself, the way she walked. Did she imagine that, because they didn't cling to every inch of her, her figure was, somehow, less on display? If so, she was very mistaken. Knockout.

That was three days ago. The fierce pull of temptation had set alarm bells jangling in his head and he had dealt with the situation immediately. In between taking her daily to see Alejandro, he had cocooned himself away in his office at home and worked. He had told her that without the distractions that cropped up when he was accessible in his high-tech glass office, which was located some distance away from Madrid, in the equivalent of Silicon Valley, he could power-work and be at hand for any emergencies that might crop up at the hospital. They had met over dinner, prepared and left ready for reheating by one of his staff. They had made pleasant conversation about Alejandro, her job, the weather and various other bland topics. He had done his utmost to keep his eyes off her but, having told himself that she was out of bounds, he had been even more tempted to look.

He had noted the swing of her hips when she had carried her plate to the sink. He had been drawn to the fullness of her mouth every time she smiled. She had a tiny waist and that was apparent in the outfits she had bought—soft khaki shorts…a small denim skirt… a strappy dress with buttons down the front.

How could a man concentrate on work-related issues when the temptation of the forbidden had taken up residence in his head?

He had gone into his offices first thing that morning and had packed it in as soon as his meeting was over.

It was Friday. It was hot. He couldn't think straight. The constant interruptions had been getting on his nerves.

Made sense to return to his house and bury himself in his office as he had done previously. At least he wouldn't have to deal with his office door opening and shutting every three seconds.

So here he was. The simmering, dark excitement that seeped into his veins at the thought of seeing her was easy to dismiss as just the irrational pull of what was banned. The dangerous desire to hear her voice and indulge in those invigorating verbal sparring matches was a little more difficult to dismiss but Dante had every confidence in his capacity for self-control.

It was what made him the man he was today. No one ever rose to the top by allowing emotion to get the better of them and Dante, who had started with the sort of privileges most could only dream of, had risen to the very top, expanding his empire beyond belief, because of his ability to detach, his ability to suppress emotion in favour of cool-headed logic.

Cool-headed logic dictated that whatever temptations Caitlin posed, they were little more than titillating distraction in his high-powered but otherwise predictable life.

And anyway, he still wanted to find out what was going on with the woman, what the deal was between her and his brother, whether anything had to be severed before problems could arise.

So all in all…yes, it made complete sense to be returning home on a hot, sunny Friday afternoon…

From her bedroom window, Caitlin could appreciate the stretch of stunning manicured lawns, the clever array of trees that cast just the right amount of shade in just the right places. Facing towards the back of the house, she could almost delude herself into thinking that she was on holiday in some vastly expensive enclave for the super rich.

Dante was out of the house. She knew that because he had been leaving for work when she had descended that morning and had politely quizzed her about her plans for the day. His driver would be available, he had informed her, should she wish to go anywhere. He had already given her the guy's mobile number and she knew that, should she text Juan, a car would be ready and waiting to deliver her to any destination within seconds. When the wealthy snapped their fingers, people jumped to attention.

Were she on holiday, she now thought, stifling a sigh, then her head wouldn't be constantly buzzing with anxiety.

For the past few days, in between hospital visits and, on that one occasion, seeing Alejandro's parents for dinner, and generally trying to deal with Dante's unsettling presence, Caitlin had busied herself trying to sort out various stays of execution on loans she had discovered her parents had taken out, which they could no longer service. The deeper she dug into her parents' finances, and dig she did, the more rot she was discovering.

She communicated with her office but had already lost one job because she wasn't around to take it on. She felt their sympathy was not going to be limitless and her frustration was growing by the hour.

Dante had told her, on that very first evening, when Alejandro's fall had put paid to their carefully made plans, that when she wasn't worrying, she should see her stint out in Spain as a little holiday.

Caitlin had never heard anything quite so ludicrous but now, with the sun burning down on a vision of impeccable greenery outside the bedroom, in which she was trying vainly to concentrate on collating various archive photos for a project she had been working on for the past six weeks, she felt suddenly restless.

She had had eight months of unimaginable stress. She had functioned in her job, had tackled the problems thrown at her, had dealt with the horror of her mother's poor health in the wake of their financial woes, and she'd thought she was doing fine, all things considered.

But sitting here now, she felt that perhaps she wasn't. She felt weary, as weary as a hundred-year-old woman. Not only was she now anxious about Alejandro, but she feared she might lose her job if she stayed out here much longer and then where would that leave her? And her parents? She had worked out a repayment schedule for the loans with the intention of saving as much as she could to stockpile a little cash for them. What on earth would she do if she didn't have a pay cheque coming in? She certainly couldn't accept a penny from Alejandro, considering the outcome to what they had planned had crashed and burned.

Amongst the various items she had bought, there was also a swimsuit because, yes, she had seen the pool, and it had looked inviting and, besides, the swimsuit was the least wildly luxurious of all the items of clothing she had purchased. Two bits of stretchy black cloth.

Temptation beckoned. Dante wasn't around.

The house was vast and yet it still felt as though she saw too much of him when they were both in it. She tried to keep their conversation basic and polite whenever they crossed paths, but it seemed he had the knack of dragging confidences out of her because she always had to fight to stay true to the role she had taken on board, and not let her guard down.

When he fastened those dark, speculative eyes on her it was almost as though she were being slowly dragged into a vortex and she had to physically keep her distance from him just to hang on to some self-control.

Did he notice? She hoped not.

What mattered was that there would be no dark,

speculative eyes on her now. She had her window. Why not take advantage of it?

What else was she going to do? Think about all her problems and marvel that there was no way forward? Get depressed? Caitlin snapped shut her computer and headed for the chest of drawers to rifle through her meagre belongings for the bikini, which still had the tags on.

She changed quickly. She made her way down to an empty house. Everything that required doing had been done, and, in fairness to Dante, he was generous about letting his staff head home once their work was finished. It was Friday and the house was silent. Staff gone.

The unspoken rider to his generosity was that, should he discover any job half-done, then there would be all hell to pay. Caitlin assumed that that would be what he brought to the table in the work environment, as well. Total fairness. Big rewards for those who worked hard and deserved it but ruthless dispatch for those who failed to meet his standards.

She accessed the back garden through the kitchen door, which was spotless. There were always fresh flowers in a vase on the kitchen table and a balmy breeze lifted the muslin panels at the windows.

The scent of the flowers in the vase mingled with the smell of sunshine from outside and for a few moments the constant weight resting on her shoulders lifted, leaving her, for once, feeling like the young woman she was. Twenty-five, just, without a care in the world. The way it should be. Fresh in a job, going out with friends, with maybe a boyfriend in tow, and a future stretching out in front of her that promised everything even if, in the end, it fell short on delivery. Carefree. Happy.

Dante had told her that she should accept her enforced stay in Spain and enjoy it as a holiday rather than an inconvenience. He had said that with barely contained sarcasm as he had circled her like a shark in a small tank, letting her know that he suspected her motivations and would find her out in his own sweet time. At the time, Caitlin could think of nothing more unlikely than enjoying a second of her stay in Spain under his roof, but it was so glorious outside and she was so tired of being worn down and anxious.

The pool was wonderful, by far her favourite bit of the estate. It was crystal clear, a flat blue infinity pool flanked by decking that was slip proof but cleverly fashioned to look like glass. Around it, there was a veritable plethora of shrubbery. Flowers in the brightest hues of orange and yellow mingled with the deepest greens of leaves and ferns, and strategically positioned trees provided shelter from the sun, rather than umbrellas. It was like a lake within a park.

Out here was tranquil in a way the inside of the house never seemed to be. Even when there was no one to be seen, she was always conscious of the fact that there were housekeepers in the vicinity, cleaning and polishing and preparing food and making sure that life was as easy as possible for the master of the house.

Out here though…

Troublesome cares drained away as she basked in the sun, slowly relaxing and letting the accumulation of problems seep away. The water was wonderfully cool and she swam lazily, up and down, up and down, getting into a rhythm.

Her eyes were half closed, her breathing even when she surfaced at the deep end of the pool, blinked water out of her eyes and realised that someone was standing directly above her, casting a long shadow over the crystal-clear water.

Dante.

His towering figure took shape as she blinked into the dazzling sun, shielding her eyes.

She clung to the side of the pool, heart suddenly hammering.

He was in swimming trunks and a tee shirt and barefoot and he looked spectacular.

Her mouth went dry and she couldn't think of anything to say, although, roaring through her head, was the single thought... *Shouldn't you be somewhere else?*

And if he was here...why wasn't he dressed in a suit and tie, on his way to a meeting somewhere? Why was he in swimming trunks?

'Thought I'd join you,' Dante answered the question she'd been asking herself. He looked at the pool, the calm perfect blue. He hadn't been in it for months. Longer. No time. But today, heading down the corridor to his bedroom to have a shower, he'd happened to glance through the long window on the landing and seen her. She'd been swimming, taking her time, her long hair streaming out behind her. He'd abandoned work early. The woman had put a spell on him and he knew that he had returned to the house because he'd wanted to see her.

He told himself that she was an enigma and that could only be a bad thing when it came to the situation between her and his brother. With Alejandro laid up in a hospital bed, Dante would have time to solve the riddle of what, exactly, was going on between the pair of them and take whatever steps were necessary. He could be decisive.

She was hiding *something*. Whatever happened to be going on between her and his brother, it wasn't a passionate and loving relationship between two people desperate to tie the knot.

So what was it? If Dante could excuse his preoccupation with her as the natural outcome of wanting to protect the Cabrera dynasty from a potential intruder, he would have. However, she failed to conform to the one-dimensional cardboard-cut-out image he would have liked.

She was witty, sharp and disrespectful. She should have been desperate to curry favour with him, to get him onside if her plan was to marry his brother and then set herself up in the enviable position of being able to lay claim to the family fortune. Her mission seemed to be the opposite. She was either ostensibly avoiding him or else openly arguing with him.

She fascinated him because she was so different from all the women he went out with and because he just couldn't work out what was going on with her.

So when he had glanced through that window and spotted her, he hadn't stopped to think. He'd headed straight to his bedroom, rummaged and found his swimming trunks, stuck on an old tee shirt, grabbed a towel and headed for the pool.

And here he was.

And there she was. Looking up at him, her face still wet, her hair dark from the water and fanning out around her like something from a pre-Raphaelite painting.

He hardened, felt that ache in his groin. He wondered whether coming down here had been the best of ideas. Maybe not.

'It's a hot day,' he muttered roughly, turning away to

strip off the tee shirt and then diving with fluid grace into the pool, only to surface and shake his head before raking his fingers through his wet hair.

Caitlin edged back in the water. 'I wouldn't normally have come in...but...'

'Don't apologise, Caitlin. I'm glad it's being used. It's maintained twice weekly and yet so seldom used that I can't imagine why I had it put in in the first place.'

She could feel her cheeks burning. She was very much aware of him barely clothed, his body so close to hers that she could reach out and touch him with no effort at all.

He was so beautiful.

Seeing him here, bare-chested, she realised that, somewhere deep in her subconscious, she had wondered what he might look like underneath his expensive gear.

He lived up to expectation. Broad-shouldered, narrow-hipped, his torso the right side of muscular. There was a strength to his physique that made her think that he could pick her up one-handed and not feel the strain.

Plus, he wasn't asking those questions, those vaguely pointed questions that always made her so uncomfortable and guarded and on the defensive.

He was being *nice*.

'Why did you, in that case?' she asked, looking at him briefly, eyes locking, before spinning away and swimming towards the shallow end of the pool because all of a sudden she had to escape the stranglehold of his presence.

He followed her. He covered the length of the pool in slow, lazy strokes and somehow ended up by her side without looking as though he'd expended any energy at all.

'I had the entire place renovated when I bought it years ago.' He picked up the conversation where he had left off, as though there had been no interruption. 'The architect and designer at the time both agreed that a swimming pool would be an asset.' He shrugged. 'It's very ornamental.'

'But as you say, if it's not used...'

'Maybe somewhere, at the back of my mind, I had high hopes of using it now and again.' He smiled ruefully and a tingle of heated awareness shot through her body, making her fidgety and uncomfortable.

'But then what happened?'

'Really want to know?'

Caitlin nodded. She was uncomfortable with the conversation because it felt strangely intimate, and yet she wasn't sure why she should feel uncomfortable because they weren't sharing secrets and he wasn't telling her anything he probably hadn't told lots of people who might have asked the same question she had. And yet...

'I never seemed to find the time. Alejandro went to London but here, in Madrid—this is the heartbeat of the company, and not just the family business, but all the other networks I have subsequently developed on my own. The heart never stops beating and I am in the centre of it. Finding time to use this pool became an empty wish.'

'You sound trapped,' Caitlin mused, looking at him with empathy before turning away to sit on the step. 'I always got the impression that there was nothing you enjoyed more than working.'

Dante lowered his eyes, his lush, sooty lashes brushing his high cheekbones. He seldom, if ever, had conversations like this with any woman but he was enjoying talking to her, enjoying her calm intelligence, her refusal to kowtow to him and, most of all, the fact that she wasn't flirting with him, doing her utmost to grab his attention by flaunting her assets.

She wouldn't be, though, would she? She was engaged to his brother. It was a reminder that was grudgingly acknowledged. She didn't act like someone who was engaged, but why did he constantly catch himself overlooking it? Was it a Freudian slip? Since when was he the sort of man who suffered from such weaknesses? After that one and only youthful error of judgement, from which lessons had been learnt, he had led a gilded life, where success after success had made him untouchable and given him an unshakeable confidence in his ability to control his destiny, so he was ill at ease with the fact that there were gaps in his armour he had never suspected.

'I'm far from trapped.' Was he, though? For one piercing second he envied the freedoms his brother enjoyed. He had an easy show to run, working in an office that was so well oiled he was barely needed at all, free to pursue just the sort of interests that had brought him into contact with the woman sitting next to Dante. He wondered whether there was a low-level, unconscious resentment that had fuelled the distance between himself and Alejandro.

Had he taken time to explore that possibility, was there a chance the chasm between them might have been bridged? And how was it that a stranger had been the one to propel him towards realisations he had barely acknowledged?

Caitlin shrugged and looked away. She was so intensely aware of him and the potency of his masculine appeal that she could scarcely keep her thoughts straight. She didn't trust herself to have the normal, in-offensive conversation the situation required.

Dante was finding her lack of interest in pursuing that tiny morsel of information thrown to her oddly annoying.

'And you?' he asked gruffly, shifting uncomfortably because he couldn't seem to look at the woman without his body misbehaving.

'What about me?' Caitlin raised her eyebrows with a slight frown.

'Do you feel trapped in the road you're going down? What's life like for you and my brother? What do you do together?'

Caitlin blushed. *What do good pals do,* she wanted to put to him, *except hang out together, listen to each other's woes, meet up as part of a group...?*

The charade stuck in her throat and for a few seconds she didn't say anything, but he was watching her, waiting for a response, and so she said, eventually, 'The usual.'

'The usual? What's that? Tell me?'

'What do *you* usually do with someone you're going out with?' Caitlin threw the question back at him, flustered.

'I wine them, I dine them, I shower them with whatever they want...'

'And then you dump them?' Caitlin was thinking of Luisa, the desperate yearning in her eyes when she had looked at him at the engagement party and the vicious jealousy when she had seen them together at the hospital, chatting. Was that how he handled all the women he dated?

Caitlin took a deep breath. The hot sun made her feel reckless and daring. The intimacy that was sending shivers up and down her spine was unfurling something dangerous inside her and suddenly she was fed up of tiptoeing around the danger. If the shark was going to attack, then why not weather the attack now?

'You're suspicious of me, aren't you? You think I'm after his money.'

'And if I am?'

'I don't know why you would be. What have I done to deserve your mistrust?'

If she cleared the air, then maybe he would back off. She didn't have to lie. She just had to be tactful. He couldn't very well call her a downright liar, could he? And if he was forced to tell her why he was suspicious, then she might be able to fudge her way through a few answers that might just satisfy him. She wouldn't be here for ever. A few days of peace was all she was after.

'I just can't picture the two of you together, as an item,' Dante murmured softly.

Caitlin thought of the leggy Luisa and she stiffened at the implied insult.

'I suppose you think I should be more like that ex-girlfriend of yours?' she said coldly. 'I suppose that, because that's the sort of woman you like dating, it's only to be expected that Alejandro should follow the same pattern? The last sort of woman he would ever go for would be someone like Luisa, even if, in *your* opinion, that would be the sort of woman you might be able to *picture* with him. As an item.'

Dante raised both eyebrows and there was a moment's silence.

'Are you insecure about the way you look?' he asked

lazily, and if Caitlin could have gone any redder, she would have.

'Of course not!' She whipped her head away and stared out at the marvellous vista, not really seeing any of it but instead conjuring up an unflattering picture of herself alongside Luisa. She thought of the woman her ex-boyfriend had fallen for and hated herself for returning to that unfortunate place, which she'd thought she had left behind. She thought of all those leggy beauties next to whom she knew she often came up short in the eyes of the opposite sex. Tears gathered in the corners of her eyes and she took a deep breath, refusing to give in to the weak temptation to feel sorry for herself.

'Because you shouldn't be.' The words left Dante's mouth, a silky murmur that was as dangerous as a dark incoming tide. 'The likes of Luisa Sofia Moore can't hold a candle to you.'

He raked his fingers through his hair. He'd broken eye contact but he was still alive to her warmth, the feel of her next to him.

'It's not just about how you look,' he breathed, reluctantly turning back to her, ensnared by the pure crystal green of her eyes. 'So why is he with you? That's what I find so puzzling. You're not background, Caitlin. You might not stalk into a room like Luisa, but you still know how to make your voice heard. Nobody has ever talked to me the way you have. So, you and my brother, Alejandro, who has never been known to say boo to a goose? No. I'm just not getting it.'

Caitlin didn't say anything and, into the silence, Dante continued roughly.

'Me,' he breathed, 'I'm the sort of man who could handle you. Not my brother.'

Those words hung in the air between them and then he leaned forward and so did she, without even realising it.

Her body moved of its own volition. A fractional movement. Her eyes closed drowsily and there was a buzzing in her ears as his mouth hit hers, hard and hungry and demanding. His fingers curled into her hair and she didn't want to, knew she shouldn't, but she returned that devouring kiss as though her life depended on it and then, just like that, he was pulling back.

She looked at him, horrified.

'If I had any questions,' Dante said in a flat, hard voice, 'trust me, they have now been answered.'

With which he vaulted out of the water, his bronzed muscular body glimmering with droplets that glistened in the glare of the sun, while she remained frozen in place, like a block of ice.

Watching and barely breathing as he walked away.

CHAPTER SIX

DANTE DIDN'T KNOW who repelled him more. Himself, for his lack of control that had propelled him into crossing lines that should never have been crossed, or her, for crossing those lines with him when she was engaged to his brother.

He didn't glance back as he strode away from the pool back towards the house.

All those questions that had been buzzing in his head ever since he had found out who she was now raged inside him, an angry swarm searching for answers.

Work.

He would bury himself in his work because that always did the trick. He hadn't made it to the house before he realised that no amount of work was going to do the trick this time. He didn't know what Caitlin was doing. He didn't want to know. His mouth still burned from where her cool lips had opened beneath his and so, much to his rage, did his body.

He'd never responded to any woman the way he'd responded to her.

Was it because she was off limits? Maybe there was some deeply buried need to take what belonged to his brother. Was that it? Dante didn't think so. He had never wanted anything Alejandro had possessed. In fact he had no idea what women his brother had dated in the past, but he was quite sure he would never have dreamt of lusting after any of them. It just wasn't in his nature. He'd never lusted after any man's woman in his life before. Hadn't come close. He was a red-blooded male with a healthy libido and he enjoyed the pleasure of sex but, even in that faraway place where mistakes had been made, he couldn't recall having experienced this fury of attraction that wiped out everything in its path.

What the hell was going on here?

He dressed fast, shrugging out of his swimming trunks, replacing them with jeans and the first tee shirt that came to hand, and then back out he went, to his car, which was parked at an angle in the courtyard.

Where the hell was she? He hated himself for even wondering.

He arrived at the hospital with no idea where he was going with this, but he had a driving need to confront his brother, which was ridiculous given the fact that Alejandro was dead to the world.

Dante had kissed her. She'd kissed him right back. No coercion on his part! She'd melted in his arms and he had enjoyed every second of it. He just had to think about the piercing sweetness of her mouth, the way her soft, small, luscious body had curved towards him, and he could feel the stirring of an erection. Her clear green eyes, as they had fastened on him with smouldering hunger, had woken a sleeping monster in him he hadn't known existed.

Dante was rarely confounded by anything or anyone, but he was confounded now.

The hospital was quiet as he made his way to his

brother's ward. They knew him at the desk so, when he nodded at the little cluster of nurses and medics chatting by the reception desk, they smiled and gave him the go-ahead to enter the room.

He was going to have to tell Alejandro what had happened. He was going to have to find answers to the questions rolling around in his head. He was going to have to try to find out what, exactly, was going on.

He had no idea how he was going to accomplish this because his brother wasn't going to be answering anything any time soon, but he had to get things off his chest.

Dante pushed open the door and let it swing on quiet hinges behind him, then he pulled one of the visitor chairs next to the bed and looked at his brother.

Now that everything had been stabilised, Alejandro could have been peacefully sleeping. His breathing was gentle and even.

'We need to talk,' Dante began.

He smiled at the incongruity of the statement, then the smile disappeared and he thought, out of the blue, when had he ever said that to his brother? When had he ever met up with him just so that they could talk? About everything and nothing? Without a sense of duty hanging over both their heads, aware only that, as brothers, meeting up now and again, however uncomfortable, was just something they should do?

'Something has happened, Alejandro...' He structured his thoughts. Caitlin's image popped into his head, and he gritted his teeth together because never had his body been so relentlessly disobedient. How was he going to break this to his brother? Was it even right to try? He couldn't be sure that Alejandro would hear a word he said and, even if he did, who knew whether he would remember any of the conversation?

Many of Dante's doubts stemmed from his inter-action with Caitlin. He had listened and watched and everything inside him had questioned the relationship she was purporting to have with Alejandro. Her reac-tion to Dante earlier by the pool…that kiss…was just the icing on the cake.

She wasn't some besotted lover, starry-eyed over his brother, counting down until the wedding bells began ringing.

Nor did his brother seem to be head over heels, like a swooning hero in a fairy tale.

But what if he was wrong about Alejandro? It wasn't as though he knew how his brother thought. It wasn't as though they had the sort of bond that might allow him any insight into what went on in Alejandro's head and in his heart.

Was Dante willing to say what he had to say, to risk Alejandro taking everything in under that serene lack of consciousness and remember that the woman to whom he was engaged was not what she seemed?

Was Dante willing to break his brother's heart?

His jaw clenched. This sort of truth, he thought, was worth imparting. He wished to God someone had saved him months of pointless infatuation with a woman who had turned out to be as pure as mud, by setting him straight at the very outset.

Haltingly, expecting nothing in response, he began to explain.

Alejandro would sleep through it all. Dante was one hundred per cent certain on that point.

He was, however, wrong.

* * *

It took ages for Caitlin to get her act together because he had kissed her...no, they had *shared* that kiss...and everything inside her had gone into free fall.

She had felt his mouth on hers long after he'd disappeared back into the house and it was only when he'd gone that her brain had begun functioning and she'd remembered, with sickening horror, what he had flung at her when he'd walked off.

If he'd had any questions, then they'd been answered.

You didn't have to be a genius to get the drift. She'd kissed him and the sham of her relationship with Alejandro had been revealed. In a handful of seconds, she had done the one thing she'd been determined not to do. She'd given the game away. Nor could she now be honest. How could she? Alejandro's secret was his to reveal, so she would have to accept that Dante would now see her as the worst possible candidate for the role of his brother's fiancée.

She hurried back to her bedroom, fearful that she might bump into Dante somewhere in the house, but she didn't. Just in case, however, she dressed quickly, and called a taxi to take her to the hospital. While she waited for it to arrive, she remained locked in her bedroom.

She had no idea what was going to happen next, but, playing it out roughly in her head, it involved her going to see Alejandro, where she would just have to explain what had happened and tell him, whether he could hear her or not, that she had no option but to return to London.

She could always leave a text on his mobile phone and he would pick it up as soon as he came to, and, naturally, she would phone the hospital daily, but leaving was her only option when the alternative was to run slap bang into Dante at some unspecified time in the future.

She felt very bad about his parents, but what choice did she have?

On the spur of the moment, she wrote a note, which she left in her bedroom, to be given to his mother, apologising for her abrupt departure and blaming work demands.

She would have some appreciation of what that meant considering at least one of her sons had sold his soul to the workplace.

The minute she thought of Dante, her mind began shutting down and her heart picked up pace and she had to close her eyes and breathe deeply so as not to feel faint.

That kiss.

There had never been anything like it in her life before. Jimmy…solid, reliable, steady Jimmy had never made her heart beat fast. She had liked him and they had fumbled around a bit but neither had had the slightest urge to take things to the ultimate conclusion.

He'd lived with his dad and she'd been living with her parents and it was a small village where everyone knew everyone else. Renting a room in their one and only hotel would have been ridiculous.

They would look forward to really enjoying making love when they were married, they had vaguely told one another. Actually, she wasn't even sure they had discussed it at all, simply assumed that that would be how things worked out between them.

Afterwards, when he had dumped her for the improbable model, she had been realistic enough to conclude that he hadn't pushed for sex because, as much as he'd liked her, he hadn't been attracted to her. Not really.

She hadn't stopped to ask herself whether *she'd* been attracted to *him*.

She'd nursed her wounded feelings and escaped.

Now, Dante had kissed her and it had been a thunderbolt. *That* was what passion felt like. *That* was the sort of aching and yearning that would have been impossible to ignore. She felt as though she had been sleepwalking and now she was fully awake, for better or for worse.

The taxi driver took his time getting to the hospital. On the way, he insisted on having a long conversation with her in Spanish, even though her responses were limited to an array of vaguely interested expressions and non-committal murmuring.

In her head, she was working out how she might get a flight back to London. Bye-bye to yet more money she didn't have. She would just have to go to the airport with her bag in hand, get to a ticket desk and pay whatever it cost for the first flight out.

Funny thing, she mused, hurrying into the hospital and pausing for a few seconds to get her bearings because the place was just so huge and she couldn't seem to keep a mental tab on which lift she needed to take to get to his ward, Alejandro would have understood her dilemma.

They would have spent hours laughing and talking about the mess she'd got herself into.

She hit the ward and was heading towards the reception desk when she saw Dante.

His face was grim, drawn. Given half a chance, Caitlin would have fled in the opposite direction, but two things stopped her. The first was the sight of Dante striding towards her, a man on a mission, eyes firmly pinned on her hovering figure even though he was on his phone, talking urgently to someone at the other end.

The other was the fact that there was a commotion happening outside what seemed to be Alejandro's room, even though it was hard to be completely sure.

It was the latter that fired her forward and she reached Dante just as he shoved his phone back in his pocket.

'What's happening?' Caitlin breathed, trying to peer around his body but not getting very far. 'Is Alejandro okay? All those people… Is that his room or someone else's?' Her eyes were already filling up at the thought of her friend having some kind of unforeseen setback.

'My brother is awake.'

'What?'

'It is as if he's been having a nap and now he's up and ready to start the day.'

'That's…that's amazing. I have to go and see him, talk to him…' She took a step to the left and Dante reached out and blocked her from stepping forward with a hand on her arm.

Caitlin froze. Her mind emptied of everything. All she could feel was the burning touch of his fingers on bare skin.

'He's going to be wheeled off for a battery of tests,' Dante was saying, while she desperately tried to focus on something, *anything*, other than his hand on her arm. 'There's no point in you trying to get to him.'

'But—'

'I've just been on the phone to my mother and said exactly the same thing to her. As you can imagine, she is as keen to see Alejandro as you are.'

Caitlin finally looked directly at Dante and inwardly quailed because all too clearly she could remember the inappropriate kiss that had galvanised his appalled withdrawal and damning judgement.

Should she bury the memory and pretend that nothing had happened between them? Or bring it out into the open, get rid of the elephant in the room before it started wreaking havoc? Or did it matter anyway, considering she was planning on clearing off as soon as she got back to Dante's house?

The decision was taken out of her hands when Dante said, coolly and firmly, leading her away from Alejandro's room towards the double doors back out into the main body of the hospital, 'You and I need to have a little chat.'

'About what?' At that very moment, Caitlin decided that pretending nothing had happened was definitely going to be the best option. 'I really think I should stick around here for a bit…see what's happening with Alejandro before I go—'

'Before you go?' Dante pulled to an abrupt halt and stared down at her with a veiled expression.

'Work is beginning to get a little impatient, Dante. I honestly can't stay over here indefinitely. My parents are also… They're anxious about me…'

'You're a big girl,' Dante gritted. 'I'm sure your parents will understand why you've stayed on.'

Caitlin didn't say anything. She had spoken to her mother the evening before and had detected the stress in her voice with a sinking heart. Her parents were clinging to their composure by the skin of their teeth and, more than ever in their lives, relying on her to steady them in stormy times.

Soothing, long-distance conversations were just not the same as seeing them face to face, being able to have a cup of tea, to hold her mother's hand and assure her that everything was going to be just fine.

Her father was doing his best, but he had always been the easy-going one between the two of them and now that her mother was on the verge of cracking up, her father was fighting his own battle with low-level panic, paralysed by the fear that everything he had worked for, what little remained, would somehow be wiped out from under his feet, and plagued with guilt at the thought that he had been the one responsible for all their problems.

How much longer could she just hang around?

'Don't tell me what my parents can or cannot understand,' she said sharply. 'I'm overjoyed that Alejandro has regained consciousness. I had planned on leaving later today but now I'll see him when he's up to visitors and I will leave for London as soon as I do afterwards.'

Dante didn't say anything. He had no intention of having any kind of showdown inside a hospital, so he spun round on his heels, making sure to keep his fingers firmly locked round her arm, and began leading her quickly towards the exit, ignoring the bank of lifts in favour of the stairs.

His car, in the underground car park, was waiting for them and they made their way there in complete silence.

There would be enough to talk about in due course, he thought.

'Where are we going?'

'To a café I know in the Plaza Mayor.'

'But can't you just tell me what you need to tell me right here?' She knew what he was going to say. He was going to mention that wretched kiss. He was going to

voice all the suspicions that had been playing around
in his head ever since he had set eyes on her. As far as
he was concerned, she had offered up conclusive proof
that he had been right to have been suspicious. He was
going to call her to account and she couldn't blame him.

But it surely wasn't going to be a long conversation!

Was it even going to be a conversation at all? Or a
full-frontal attack, which she would deal with by being
as unresponsive as possible?

Judging from the way she had been frogmarched to
his car, she was going for the full-frontal attack.

But at least they would not be having it at his house.
At least, in the public arena, she wouldn't feel quite so
overwhelmed.

And the Plaza was just a wonderful place, a beautiful
rolling arcade ringed with stunning sepia-and pastel-
coloured buildings, a tribute to history and the stunning
architecture of the period.

She might just be able to sideline his attack by absorbing her surroundings, a sort of displacement therapy.

The café was nestled in one of the sepia-coloured
shops. From the outside, it looked as though it might
be on the verge of collapse. Inside, it was a marvel of
modernity, with a long steel counter behind which five
chic young girls catered for the needs of the most dis-
cerning of coffee drinkers and pastry consumers.

'I had no idea my brother would come to when I went
to see him,' Dante opened. 'I had to go because of what
happened between us at the pool.'

Caitlin cringed. 'About that...' she said faintly. She
couldn't look at him. She couldn't meet those arrest-
ing dark eyes that were pinned to her face. For the first

time, she wondered whether he had kissed her because he had been caught up in the moment, just as she had been, or whether he had kissed her as some kind of test to find out whether she really was the adoring fiancée she claimed to be.

She felt sick. Her stomach churned. All her insecurities pointed her in the direction of that kiss being nothing more to him than a means to an end. Why else would a guy like Dante, a guy who could turn his back on a woman who looked like Luisa, look at *her*? Yes, he had said something about her being *sexy*, but of course he would say that to butter her up and lower her defences for the moment when he leaned into her for that kiss, testing the ground, feeling his way to the answers he had been seeking.

'Yes?' Dante enquired coolly. He sat back as his double espresso was put in front of him, the attractive waitress taking her time as she positioned the cup *just so*. His eyes remained fixed on Caitlin's face, keenly noting the delicate bloom of colour in her cheeks. A guilty conscience would do that to a woman, he thought tightly.

'I never meant for that to happen.'

'I'm sure you didn't,' he responded smoothly. 'Engaged to one brother but happy to get into an intimate clinch with the other? Not exactly an example of a woman with sterling moral principles, is it?'

Trapped by a secret that wasn't hers to share, Caitlin could only bow her head in silence.

She would accept the full force of his condemnation. She would be gone in a heartbeat and she would be able to put it all behind her, except she knew that that would be easier said than done. Idiot that she was, she actually *cared* about what he thought of her.

Somehow, she had been incapable of locking the man away in a convenient one-dimensional box. She'd tried, but he'd broken out of it and come right at her with all those complexities that had turned him into a living, breathing, fascinating guy who had fired her up in ways she would never have dreamt possible.

That was why she had kissed him. He stirred a crazy attraction inside her and she just hadn't been able to resist, but she knew how it looked on the outside. Kissing him had boxed her in as a two-timing woman who was happy to fool around behind her fiancé's back.

'You don't understand,' she said, without much hope of him paying a blind bit of notice to what she had to say. 'I know what it looks like, but I'm not that kind of person.'

'Thank you for telling me that. That answers all my questions.'

'There's no need to be sarcastic.'

'Then try coming at me with something a little better.'

'What do you want me to say?'

'What about the truth?'

'I'm telling you the truth. I'm not that kind of girl. I don't...' She looked away and fell silent because there was nowhere to go with an explanation.

'I told my brother about that kiss and you'll never guess his response.'

Caitlin was pretty sure she could.

'Actually, I had no idea my conversation would prove to be the thing that would rouse my brother from his deep and peaceful sleep, but it was. I started to talk to him...'

Dante paused and recalled the way he had felt, opening up to a sleeping Alejandro. For the first time he had felt something strong and bonding. It had been the one and only meaningful conversation he had ever had with Alejandro. The fact that Alejandro had been unconscious at the time had made it easy, had removed the inhibitions born over time.

Dante met her eyes and sucked in a sharp breath. So green, so crystal clear…so full of a disingenuous innocence that was way off mark. 'I started to talk to him and *bang*. He opened his eyes and was as with it as though he'd never been dead to the world at all. Funny thing, he didn't seem all that perturbed by what we did. I had expected some kind of forceful reaction, had braced myself for his disgust and loathing for my weakness. I didn't get any of that. Does that surprise you?'

Faced with that direct question, Caitlin frantically tried to compose an answer that would make sense. The truth was off the table. She stared down at her empty coffee cup and licked her lips nervously.

'He's…er…a very understanding kind of guy, as I'm sure you'd know if you'd ever taken the time to find out about him.'

Dante could only admire her attempt to divert him from her non-answer by launching a missile at him.

'Nice try but it won't work.'

'Maybe we don't have a conventional relationship.' Caitlin didn't bother to ask him what he'd just meant by that because she knew.

'What do you mean?' Like a shark sensing blood, Dante felt on the verge of a revelation. If his head had temporarily been elsewhere, he was now once again committed to the task at hand. He pushed his cup to one side and leaned forward, resting his forearms on the table.

'I know what you were trying to do when you kissed me,' she said, swerving round his question.

'Come again?'

'You wanted to see if I would respond. You pretended to be attracted to me, you said lots of stuff you didn't mean, because you knew that if I responded then you would have all your suspicions confirmed. You want to push me into a corner and paint me black, but leading me on? That's sly.'

'You think I'm *sly*?'

Caitlin looked at him in stony silence.

'You couldn't be further from the truth,' he gritted brusquely. 'I'm not a man who plays that kind of game.' This was getting off point and he dragged his runaway thoughts back to the matter at hand.

'You and Alejandro. You were telling me that what you had wasn't a conventional relationship. Explain.' He shifted in the seat and tried to focus. He wasn't going to let her derail the conversation by veering off at random tangents, but he couldn't help but admire the antics. She was a match for him and he liked that.

'We were both great friends.' She was going to have to tiptoe round all manner of minefields, but Dante wasn't going to let up. 'Things went from there.'

Dante waited. Nothing further seemed forthcoming. He was very happy to play the long game, but eventually, he said, 'You *drifted* into a relationship because you happened to be good friends?' He looked at her with rampant incredulity.

'Friendship is a very good basis for a relationship,' Caitlin said defensively.

'And you would have married him? He would have married you? I find that hard to believe. For starters, you're young. Why would you abandon the one thing most women seem to want? Love, passion and a belief in fairy stories about happy-ever-afters? Nor do I understand why my brother would do the same.' But Dante knew that *he* had no faith in the institution of marriage. Love and fairy stories? No way. His own experience had taught him that any permanent relationship should always have a solid basis in reality. He'd fallen for the wrong woman once upon a time and his guard was permanently up. Maybe Alejandro was fashioned from the same cloth. Maybe he, too, had had an unfortunate experience that had taught him that a marriage of convenience was the way forward. Who knew?

And his parents *had* been getting quite vocal on the subject of their eldest son settling down.

Maybe he'd decided to opt for the friend knowing that he wouldn't be troubled by a demanding or jealous woman who might end up wanting more than he was prepared to give.

That was certainly the lens through which he, Dante, viewed relationships...

He felt as though he was clutching at straws, but what else could explain his brother's nonchalant reaction to what had happened at the pool between himself and Caitlin?

But why would Caitlin have gone along?

'I had a terrible experience once upon a time,' Caitlin said softly, severing any further conclusions he might have been formulating on the subject of her and his brother. 'I was engaged to a guy. We'd known each other for ever, and in a small village like the one I grew up in that counts for something. Getting married was expected. Except no one—not me, not Jimmy, none of our family or friends—could foresee a five-foot-ten model swanning into his life and sweeping him off his feet.'

Reliving the moment, Caitlin realised that she felt next to nothing thinking about it now.

'He felt sorry for me. That was the toughest part. I suppose everyone did. I left for London and I put men behind me. I wasn't going to get involved with anyone ever again. Alejandro,' she tacked on truthfully, 'made sense.'

'Well, I hate to burst the bubble, but you might have to start rethinking that scenario,' Dante gritted. 'Alejandro's feathers weren't ruffled at the thought of me kissing you. Are you happy to settle for someone who doesn't really give a damn what you do and with whom?'

'I've talked enough,' Caitlin muttered, rising to her feet. She felt hemmed in and suffocated by Dante's oppressive presence and the sheer force of his personality. 'I'm going to see Alejandro...'

'No point.' Dante stood up, dumping money on the table, more than enough to cover the coffee they had ordered. 'Like I said, he's having a battery of tests. You won't be able to see him until tomorrow.'

'I'd planned on leaving this evening,' Caitlin reminded him, digging her heels in and refusing to be bullied.

'That's the thing about plans. They often have to change.'

For a moment, they stared at one another, and then Caitlin broke eye contact and began walking towards the door, only to stop because she was going to have to return to the house and with Dante, unless he decided to hang around in the city centre for no apparent reason.

'I'm very sorry about what happened at the pool,' she said in a stilted voice as they began leaving the city, heading out towards his house. *Clear the air*, she thought. He had and so should she. 'I think it's best if I pack my bags when I get back. Don't worry about me. I've got stuff to do. Tomorrow, I can easily take a taxi in to the hospital and then I can leave for the airport straight from the hospital. I don't know if I'll get a flight immediately but…but…' She ran out of steam and stared straight ahead at the scenery whipping past.

For a while, Dante didn't say anything.

He could sense her nerves. She had every right to be nervous. She also had every right to apologise about what had happened by the pool. He wasn't proud of himself, but he wasn't the one with a ring on his finger, even if the engagement was a complete sham from the sounds of it.

'I expect,' he said smoothly, 'that the touching engagement will now be a thing of the past? Our parents will be bitterly disappointed.'

Caitlin glanced at him.

This engagement was a charade but it was one that had suited both of them. So what happened next? It was something she would have to discuss with Alejandro. Did he still want to buy time? Dante might believe that theirs was just a convenient arrangement but many unions were based on less. She certainly wasn't going to commit to one thing or the other until she had spoken to Alejandro.

'Well?' Dante prompted sharply. They were nearing his house, all signs of habitation falling away to open land with the occasional manor to be glimpsed through imposing gates.

'I don't know what's going to happen.'

'You don't love my brother, Caitlin.'

'But I do.'

Dante killed the engine and swivelled so that he was staring at her with brooding intensity. Frustration soared through him. He'd thought he'd got what he wanted but had he? What did she mean by that?

'Love without passion is the recipe for an empty marriage. And then there's us...let's not forget about that...' His voice was lazy now and pensive.

'There's no *us*.'

'No,' he agreed, 'there isn't, but you went up in flames when I kissed you. Don't worry. It was a mistake to touch you but I won't be succumbing to the temptation again. It's not in my nature to pursue any woman who belongs to someone else.'

Caitlin laughed shortly. *'Belongs to someone else? What era are you living in, Dante? I don't belong to anyone.'*

'Oh, but you do. Friends or no friends, you're my brother's lover—'

'I'm not!'

Stunned silence greeted this. For a moment, Dante was lost for words. The idea that two people could be engaged without having consummated their relationship beggared belief.

'And on the subject of lies...' Did she think he was born yesterday? Was she hoping to airbrush away their little moment of intimacy by pretending that fidelity to Alejandro wasn't imperative because they weren't lovers?

'I'm not lying,' Caitlin whispered.

'Tell me my brother isn't a substitute for your ex-lover,' Dante said sharply. 'No man wants to bed a woman who's thinking of some love she had and lost.'

'You don't get it, Dante!'

'*What* don't I get?'

'I'm not some scarlet woman! I haven't slept with your brother and…and…'

'And?'

'And I don't have any ex-lovers tucked away in my head, demanding my attention and messing up my life! I don't have any *ex-lovers* at all!'

'I don't get what you're saying.'

'What do you *not* get?' Caitlin finally snapped. 'I don't have any ex-lovers because I'm still a virgin!'

CHAPTER SEVEN

CAITLIN DIDN'T KNOW who was more stunned by that admission, Dante or herself.

She didn't wait to find out either, pulling open the car door and leaping out, heading at speed towards the front door.

Dante, on the other hand, took his time getting out of the car, grasping the roof and swinging his long body out.

Virgin? *Virgin?* Could she possibly be lying about that? No. He had seen the mortified embarrassment wash over her face in a red tidal rush, and he had known that she'd been telling the truth.

But her confession left him more confused than he already was.

Why was she engaged to his brother? What was going on? But then, the cogs in his brain began to crank back into life and he knew that there could be only one conclusion.

Alejandro was very kind, one of the world's gentle souls. Growing up, he had been the one in the kitchen helping the housekeeper cook while Dante had been kicking a ball outside or climbing a tree. Later, when rugby and black-run skiing had replaced the ball kicking, Alejandro had remained in the kitchen, but this time enjoying the business of preparing food and eating it, happy to read and pursue isolated hobbies. Dante had never really been able to get it.

What he was getting now, though, was the reality that his brother had doubtless found himself in a pickle. Their parents had become increasingly anxious to see their eldest son settle down and produce a few heirs to the throne.

And into this scenario, cue stage door to the left, came Caitlin, wounded by heartbreak, disillusioned with the whole business of love, and yet still desirous of having a family.

Two and two had made four and although she and his brother weren't in love, they liked each other well enough to do a sensible deal.

Hence Alejandro's lack of reaction when he, Dante, had mentioned that kiss by the pool.

He truly didn't fancy Caitlin. That was something Dante simply couldn't understand because he had never in his life found any woman more alluring.

A virgin!

He looked at her for a second, pausing. She was standing by the front door, every part of her body trembling with the urge to escape as fast as she could after her admission.

She couldn't have been dressed in an outfit less appealing to Dante. Somewhere along the line, she'd bought two long flowered skirts that harked right back to some distant hippie era. She was wearing one of these now. The mesh of swirling colours would give anyone a headache were they to make the mistake of staring for too long. Twinned with this was a short-sleeved tee shirt that was neither loose nor tight.

And yet nothing could disguise the intense sensuality of her body. He clenched his jaw hard.

Okay, so maybe the situation was a little more blurred than he'd first thought. Maybe what was an engagement, given the weird circumstances, couldn't be called *a relationship* at all. Doubtless it was just a matter of time before she broke it off, because all that rot about love and friendship counted for nothing when the shimmer of passion hovered in the background like a steady haze, and he had shown her that shimmer of passion.

Would she easily be able to go back to the empty dryness of a situation in which affection was the sum total of what she felt?

She was glaring at him, her face tight with the strain of suppressing her emotions, her hair all over the place. She looked like a wild cat and he marvelled that Alejandro could ever have thought that such a fiery creature could submit to a non-relationship indefinitely.

Heartbreak or no heartbreak.

Dante strolled towards her. She didn't have a key or he was pretty sure she would have been firmly locked in her bedroom by now.

He slotted his key in the door, pushed it open and stood aside as she brushed past him.

'Caitlin.' His voice was rougher than he'd expected and he felt suddenly awkward.

'What?' She spun to look at him, her body taut and straight as an arrow, every nerve in her body still shimmering with heightened emotion. What had possessed her to share that most intimate of secrets with him? What?

'Join me in the kitchen for something to drink. Maybe eat. It's been quite a day.'

Caitlin opened her mouth to tell him that she would

rather not but then she thought, so she had let slip that detail about herself... What of it? She had simply tried to defend herself against the slur of being a two-timer without a conscience. What was wrong with that? And what was the big deal with being a virgin? Why should she be embarrassed? It was her body to give when she wanted, not when the world deemed it suitable. She would far rather live a life being choosy about the person she chose to share herself with than sleep with any and everyone just because...

Besides, on a more pedestrian note, she didn't want to spend the remainder of the day hiding away in her bedroom. Why give Dante the satisfaction of thinking that he had got to her?

She could either allow herself to be swept along on a fierce tide of helpless reaction or else try hard and fast to emulate his cool control.

She nodded and forced her reluctant legs to follow him into the kitchen.

Every gadget was high-end and polished to gleaming perfection, including the extraordinary coffee maker, which was a work of art in itself, but Dante bypassed that and headed for the fridge, which was concealed behind the banks of glossy grey cabinets.

It wasn't quite yet six but he offered her a drink, a glass of wine. Desperate to calm her nerves, Caitlin accepted with alacrity and finished glass number one at speed, instantly relaxing as the alcohol began coursing through her veins. It was easier to talk to Dante when she wasn't battling low-level panic and sickening awareness of his intense physicality. The wine lowered her defences and muted her nerves and, after a while, she knew that she was relaxing into normal conversation

about Alejandro, now that he had regained consciousness, so she was unprepared when Dante suddenly sat
forward, his dark eyes pinning her to the spot, his body
angled forward so that she felt the heat he emanated.

'So talk to me. Tell me. I'm curious...' he said softly.

'Talk to you about what?' She had already finished
two glasses of wine but as her eyes sought out the nearly
empty bottle of Chablis, Dante relieved her of that easy
route to Dutch courage by gently moving her glass out
of reach.

'Why you've never slept with a guy.'

Instantly Caitlin stiffened. 'I should never have told
you that.'

'But you did and I'm glad you did. The pieces are
falling into place. So talk to me, Caitlin. Tell me why.'

'I already told you. I was hurt. I picked up the pieces
and moved on.' She looked at him narrowly, alert for
any show of mocking cynicism, but he was listening
intently, his lean, beautiful face interested and non-
judgemental, and she had a sudden fierce urge to confide. When she had left for London, she had locked
away her past but now it was clamouring at the door,
begging to be released. 'I just lost faith in relationships.'
She paused. 'You wouldn't understand.'

'You might be surprised. I had a bad experience myself once upon a time.' Dante was shocked by an admission he had never shared with another living soul.

'Really?' Caitlin had never been more curious. 'Was
it Luisa?'

That made Dante laugh, banking down his natural unease with sharing anything of a personal nature
with anyone.

'I was nineteen,' he mused, 'and she was...older.

With a child. I foolishly flung myself into something I thought had legs only to find out that she was not who she claimed to be. She was after my money and I had a lucky escape because I found out before I'd committed to something that would have ended up more than just a major headache. Nevertheless, I managed to squander a substantial amount of money in the process.'

Caitlin nodded, instantly understanding that, for a man as proud as he was, such a miscalculation would have been a source of bitter humiliation, even though he would never admit as much.

A low stirring began deep inside her. She felt hot and restless, her senses heightened in a way they never had been before in her life.

'But it wouldn't have occurred to me,' he continued, without breaking stride, 'to have given up on sex.'

'We're all different,' Caitlin said quietly.

'Know what I think?'

'I don't think I want to know what you think.' But she was frightened at just how much she really did.

'You know you do.' Dante tipped his finger under her chin so that she would focus on him and that simple gesture felt like something way more intimate, daringly intrusive even. Mesmerised, she could only stare at him. 'I think you're scared,' he said softly. 'I think my brother was the easy way out for you. Maybe you want a family and you can just about see your way to coupling with a man who couldn't possibly hurt you because you've handed nothing over to him, at least not the searing passion of real, complicated love. And perhaps my brother, who knows the weight of parental expectation, is prepared to buckle and accept what is on the table... Is that it?'

Caitlin said nothing. He had fumbled his way towards an explanation and, while he had hit the spot with certain assumptions, he was way off target with others, but then he was not to know the complexity of the situation.

One thing she was realising, though, was there was no way she could continue the pretence of an engagement to Alejandro, not to Dante or his family. He had forced her to recognise that passion was there; she had tasted it. The only problem was that the fruit she had tasted was forbidden. Dante was not the man for her.

'Stop asking me to talk about this,' she whispered.

'Are you really going to go ahead with a farcical engagement and a marriage that is going to eventually end in tears, whatever your reasons for instigating it?'

Caitlin could look at him now and say, truthfully, 'No.' She sighed. 'Are you satisfied?'

'Are *you*?'

'I need to go up now. I... I'm tired. I just want to have a long, hot bath and go to sleep.' She stood up because if she remained sitting, remained in his orbit, she knew that the urge to reach out and touch would be too powerful. 'I'm going to talk to Alejandro tomorrow and then...then... I'm going to head back to London...'

She talked to Alejandro. She'd thought that she might bump into Dante the following morning, and after the conversation they had shared she had been dreading that, but when, at a little after nine, she stepped into the taxi she had ordered to take her to the hospital, he was nowhere to be seen.

She wasn't sure what to expect but Alejandro was subdued, though very much with it and itching to leave the hospital. He was going to recuperate at his parents' house, he told her. The bones would heal and he would be on crutches within a week. Mobile. They got past the formalities of two people circling what they both knew was going to be the main event.

'I know you must have feelings for him.' Alejandro was the first to cross the Rubicon. 'You forget how well I know you. You need to be careful. He has a terrible reputation when it comes to women.'

'I'm not about to get involved with him, Alejandro.'

'But you'd like to?'

'No.' She'd thought of the way her body went up in flames whenever Dante was near her. She thought of those taboo images that had flashed through her head at regular intervals, hot and sharp and leaving her weak.

They'd spoken, Alejandro had said awkwardly. Dante had talked to him, openly and honestly, thinking him to be out of it. He had talked about how much he regretted the passing of time when they had had so little to do with one another. Caitlin could see that the Alejandro who had emerged from his deep sleep was a different Alejandro.

The engagement was no more. He would, he told her, break it to his parents and hang the consequences. But he was still going to send her the money he'd agreed on, even though Caitlin was horrified and downright forbade it.

'I've already emailed my guy at the bank,' he warned her. 'A deal's a deal. Now, you go.' He smiled wryly. 'People are queuing to visit, including Luisa, for reasons best known to her. Can't remember her paying me a scrap of notice and I've known the woman since she was twelve.'

Something stirred in Caitlin. She remembered the

venom on the other woman's face when she had bumped into them on the hospital ward not long ago, and shivered. Why would Luisa still be hanging around? Not her business. She was an old family friend. Did those ever really go away?

'That fall,' Alejandro's parting words were, 'might just have saved my life, Caitlin.' His voice was pensive. 'You should do what you feel you have to do. Take it from me, when you have a scare it makes you realise that life is precious and you only get to live it once...'

Her mind was on so many things when, much later, she let herself back into the house, having remembered this time to take a spare key. Two were kept in a metal safe in the kitchen and she had had to sign it out.

Having not seen Dante before she left for the hospital, she had taken it for granted that he would be similarly absent when she later returned.

He wasn't. Just as she was about to enter her bedroom to pack her bags to leave, he appeared at the opposite end of the corridor. Coincidence or not? Was he intending to continue his interrogation? Hadn't they both said enough? She desperately wanted a surge of inner strength to accompany those bracing thoughts, but it failed to materialise as he strolled towards her.

'How was he?' Dante asked quietly. He was holding his laptop under his arm, on his way to the important business of catching up on work, she thought. And it was pure coincidence that they had collided in the wide corridor. She could tell because he was in a rush, stopping only because politeness dictated that he did. That was the feeling she was getting. Their intimate conversation of the evening before had been buried for him. Maybe he felt that too much had been shared.

'Good,' Caitlin returned. 'I think he's going to get bored of being in hospital very soon. Apparently the broken bones are healing nicely. He'll be hobbling about before you know it. He's going to go stay with your parents and then, I guess, in due course, he'll return to London.'

'A single man...' Dante looked at her as her eyes shifted from his. He'd had time to think overnight. He couldn't remember a time when he had ever had as open a conversation with anyone as he had had with her and that, he had concluded, wasn't a good thing. Telling her... about that incident in his past had felt like a weakness, but it was too late to retrieve confidences shared and he wasn't going to waste time beating himself up about it.

He'd also had time to think about what she had told him about herself, her startling confession that she had never slept with anyone. She had been neither ashamed nor proud of her virginity. It was as it was, her attitude had implied and, while he admired her for that, he was in no doubt that she wasn't nearly as casual about her relationship status as she claimed to be.

She was so...fiery...so full of personality...so *opinionated*. How could she really be the sort to accept the reality of a relationship that delivered on all fronts except the single one that mattered, which was passion?

She might kid herself that she had squashed any romantic streak she might have had because of some broken heart back in the day, but she hadn't, and Dante had firmly made up his mind that, temptation or not, and whether she was now a free woman or not, he wasn't going to go there. Wasn't even going to think about it. She lacked the experience to deal with a sex-with-no-strings-attached situation.

Yet the delicate flush in her cheeks, the nerves she was trying hard to conceal, the intensely feminine *smell* of her...were all beginning to wreak havoc with his high-minded, well-intentioned resolutions.

'I'm keeping you. I was just about to pack my bags.'

'Pack?' That felt like a punch to the gut. Wrong reaction on every front.

'I told you, I intend to head back to London and the sooner, the better.'

That single sentence clarified everything in Dante's mind. It was one thing to be sensible when temptation wasn't staring you in the face. It was quite another when...it was.

She would leave and he wouldn't be seeing her again. He would be left wondering *what if...?* whether he liked it or not. The woman had got under his skin, and if she walked away now she would remain under his skin for ever. A burr he would not easily be able to yank free. An annoying itch that he would regret not having tried to scratch.

'Don't.'

That single word hung suspended in the air between them. Caitlin marvelled that a single one-syllable word could have such a dramatic effect on her senses. Her heart sped up. Her mouth went dry. Her pulses began to race.

'Yet. Don't leave yet.'

'What do you mean?'

'You know exactly what I mean.'

She did.

'There's no *you and Alejandro* any more,' Dante breathed thickly. 'Once upon a time, there was a convenient charade. That's over. You're a free woman.'

'It wouldn't work.'

'What wouldn't? Are you telling me that when you look at me…you don't want to touch?'

His voice had sunk to a husky murmur that felt like feathers brushing against her skin. She shivered. So many things were going round in her head right now, but top of the list was—*I want you… I don't know why, or how I could feel so attracted to you, but I want you…*

'That's not the point,' she responded, angry at the telltale weakness in her voice.

'Why?' All his natural aggression and instinct to pursue what he wanted surged to the surface, wiping out every mental obstacle in its path.

'How could a relationship work between us? Your parents…your friends…your relatives…all those people who had gathered there for the engagement party… what would they think?'

'Why would they know?'

'I don't understand.'

'I'm not talking about a relationship, Caitlin,' he husked. 'This would be sex. Pure and simple. I want you and you want me and one and one makes two. I'm not interested in getting involved with anyone with a view to anything other than having some fun. Yes, you have to get back to London, but you don't have to get back *just yet.*'

Every shred of heartfelt romanticism in Caitlin rebelled against the unadorned brashness of his proposition. There was no attempt to wrap it up as anything other than what it was—two people having sex for a few days before they parted ways, a ripple in both their lives, gone before it had had time to become anything bigger.

Caitlin was an unintentional virgin. She hadn't been saving herself for the right guy to come along. She hadn't slept with Jimmy for reasons that had become blindingly clear after he had fallen for the model, and since then she had retreated into herself. No one, not a single guy, had broken through the wall she had erected around herself. She'd pretty much come to the conclusion that she was frigid.

Sure, she wanted kids and a family and one day, she had vaguely thought, a guy would come along and she would be attracted to him and things would fall into place. It was a thought that barely registered on her radar, because she was just so busy building a career and, lately, stressing out about her parents. When it *had* registered, she had assumed the guy who eventually showed up would tick all the usual boxes. Nice, thoughtful, good sense of humour, non-smoker.

And yet here was Dante, all dark and dangerous, and definitely *not* Mr Nice and Thoughtful... And she wanted him so much it made her feel weak.

'I'm gathering from the prolonged silence,' he said wryly, interrupting the frantic racing of her thoughts, 'that sex without a *relationship* label attached to it isn't something you would be prepared to sample.' He lowered his eyes and her heart raced even faster. 'Although you'd be shocked at just how much fun it would be...'

He straightened. Somewhere along the line, they had moved close to the wall and he had been lounging against it, a long, lean, powerful jungle cat prepared to have a bit of fun with the antelope.

Antelopes, Caitlin thought in confusion, never came off well in any encounter with powerful jungle cats.

He was strolling away when all of a sudden she was galvanised into action.

He wanted fun. He wasn't relationship material and he hadn't bothered to hide that fact.

What was so wrong if she wanted a bit of fun, as well? There hadn't been much of that around for the past few months. She was here and she was only going to be here for a matter of a few days if she decided to stay on. After that, she would return to the reality of life on the other side of the ocean, back to the stress and the worry.

'Dante!' Crunch moment. She took a deep breath and was suddenly filled with a wave of pure, fizzing excitement.

He'd stopped, turned round and was looking at her with lazy interest.

He hadn't expected her to stop him but now that she had, he was aware of a soaring sense of relief. He hadn't realised just how much it had meant for her to come to him, and not because he had kissed her or tried to seduce. He hadn't wanted her to be swept away in the moment. He'd wanted her to make a conscious decision in the cold light of day.

He looked at the sexy sashay of her rounded hips and banked down the fierce ache of an erection.

'Yes.' Caitlin cleared her throat and looked at him without flinching.

Dante didn't say anything for a couple of seconds, then he reached out and cupped the side of her face, his long fingers soft and tender, stroking the satin smoothness of her cheek.

When he kissed her, she finally discovered what it felt like for the earth to stop spinning.

CHAPTER EIGHT

THEY MADE IT to his bedroom, fingers entwined. He nudged the door, which was slightly ajar, with his foot and, instead of turning on the overhead light, he just wrapped his arms around her in the gathering darkness in the bedroom and held her close.

'Would you listen to me if I told you not to be nervous?'

It was the one thing guaranteed to calm her nerves and it did. She visibly relaxed and settled into the embrace, her head resting on his chest so that she could hear the faint beating of his heart.

She tentatively wrapped her arms around him, then slid them underneath the polo shirt and shivered at the feel of muscle and sinew under her fingers. Very gently, he mimicked what she was doing. Without making a big deal of it, he expertly unclasped her bra.

Caitlin gave a soft whimper as he curved his big hands under her breasts, stroking the crease beneath them and then, very slowly, working his way up until he was massaging both her breasts, and as he massaged them he rubbed the pads of his thumbs over her stiffened nipples.

'You have no idea how long I've wanted to do this,'

he murmured. 'I'm hard like steel for you. One touch and I don't know what the outcome will be. I might embarrass myself by not being able to hold back... If I make you nervous then, rest assured, you make me nervous, as well...' He wasn't kidding. The gentle, shyly faltering sweep of her hands along his body made him wonder whether he would be able to last long enough to actually get inside her.

'No, I don't,' Caitlin breathed. She was hopelessly drifting on a current of such pure, delicious sensation. Her nipples were tingling and, between her legs, her panties were wet. Her clothes felt like an impediment. It was as if, slowly but surely and without attempting to remove a single article of clothing, he was somehow managing to get her to a place where she wanted to rip them all off.

Dante laughed softly. He looked down at her upturned face and lowered his head to kiss her. It was a long, leisurely, lingering kiss, and he didn't stop touching her nipples, playing with them, teasing them so that she was squirming, her whole body hot and restless.

He made no attempt to touch her anywhere else. Just that kiss that went on for ever and the light, lazy caress of her breasts. It was driving her crazy.

She broke free and began tugging him towards the bed. She could hear her own breathing and then a low laugh from him.

'I'm taking my time,' he husked.

'You're driving me nuts,' Caitlin responded with staccato jerkiness, and he laughed again.

Through the window, the declining sun was casting long shadows into the bedroom. The open shutters turned the light into stripes. It was still very warm outside, but here in the bedroom it was beautifully cool. Thick walls, she assumed. A fortress of a mansion that could withstand the heat of summer and the cold of winter.

She was pulling him towards the bed and when she felt the side of the mattress against her knees, she sank down and then looked up at him. He was standing over her and, very, very slowly, he began to undress.

Nervous? No way could this man ever be nervous when it came to making love but, she thought, he'd been kind to have said so because he'd have known that she would have found it endearing and a little funny and it would have relaxed her even more.

Everything he was now doing spoke of self-assurance and complete confidence in himself.

Of course, she'd seen him in his swimming trunks, but it was different now because, this time, this was going somewhere. She was appreciating the broad, naked chest and the muscled width of his shoulders in an entirely different way.

He flung the polo shirt on the ground and then his hand hovered for a few seconds on the zipper of his trousers.

Caitlin's breath hitched in her throat.

'You're so perfect,' she breathed, and he burst out laughing.

'And you're so honest. I like that.' He stepped out of the trousers but kept the boxers on. 'You don't play games in bed. It's refreshing.'

She could see the bulge of his erection and it made her feel faint.

She was sitting on the side of the bed and he nudged her legs open so that he was standing between them.

'I want to see you.'

With a few words, her excitement was ratcheted up a few notches and she hooked her fingers under the baggy tee shirt and pulled it over her head, taking the bra with it at the same time.

Her instinct was to cover her nakedness with her hands, but Dante was far too expert a lover to allow her to hang on to her natural reserve and, with a few adept touches, she shed her nervous apprehension and began to relax.

Dante stared. He couldn't help himself. He'd seen some of the most beautiful women on the planet and yet this one...got to him in all sorts of places no one else ever had. That was a mystery to him, but then the circumstances were completely different from any he'd ever been in before and, beyond that, he had shared more of himself with her than with any other woman. Another mystery.

Her breasts were full, more than a handful and tipped with perfect pale brown discs, large and succulent and inviting.

He stifled a groan and reminded himself that he had to go slow. It was going to be a feat of willpower.

He lowered himself, boxers still in place, and knelt between her, urging her to sit up so that he could suckle her breasts one at a time.

Caitlin arched back, eyes shut, rocked to the very core. She curled her fingers into his dark hair. She needed to get rid of the rest of her clothes. When she'd walked towards him in the corridor, when she'd made that momentous decision to sleep with him, she'd braced herself for all the nerves she'd known would accompany her first time making love, but her nerves had disappeared, overridden by fierce, burning *need*. It cut through everything.

He pushed his hand under her skirt and skimmed her thighs. Her skin was satiny soft and smooth. He nudged his knuckles against her crotch and felt her dampness. For a second, he had to empty his head because the whole situation was far too erotic, from her soft moans to the pliancy of her sexy body. She was giving him the gift of her virginity and for a moment he was filled with doubt, then he wiped that clean from his head because they were both adults and choices had been made, eyes wide open.

And in a way, wasn't he doing her a favour? As time went on, her virginity would surely become an albatross round her neck, a prize to be given to Mr Right, except would there ever be a Mr Right? Did that person exist? Or would she end up trusting some guy like her ex, only to be let down? Wouldn't her heartache be a thousand times worse because she would have opened herself up to that person, expecting all the fairy stories peddled by the rest of the world? At least, with him, he wasn't selling her stories or making promises he couldn't keep. Theirs was a straightforward arrangement.

Dante pushed the skirt up and she wriggled so that it was ruched and gathered at her waist. It felt wildly decadent. He was still there, between her legs, and modesty slammed into her when he inserted his finger underneath the stretchy fabric of her underwear, but he gently eased her hand away.

He linked his fingers through hers and kept her hands still at her sides, then he nuzzled against the damp underwear, breathing in her musky smell. He tasted her through the silky barrier. He was going to go further, going to feel her wetness on his face, but not yet.

The need to be gentle, to take his time, to make sure she enjoyed this first experience felt crucially important. She never hesitated when it came to speaking her mind, and she'd had more to say on the subject of him and his lifestyle than anyone else in living memory, but, emotionally, he sensed a curious vulnerability and that vulnerability, now, was bringing out in him a protective streak he hadn't known he had.

He unclasped their hands and waited until he knew that she was ready, then he eased the underwear off and parted her legs.

No underwear now as a barrier and the honeyed sweetness between her thighs was a powerful aphrodisiac. Dante licked and sucked. Easily finding the throbbing nub of her clitoris, he began to tease it until she was writhing with mounting pleasure.

His own erection was a steady, pulsing ache in his groin. No problem. The second he entered her, he knew that he was going to come very quickly. For the moment, he would devote all his attention to getting her to that place where she was desperate for him to sink into her.

He continued to feast on her wetness until her cries became more demanding.

'Please… Dante…' Caitlin said brokenly. 'I'm going to… I won't be able to help myself…' She didn't want to come against his mouth. She wanted to feel the closeness of him inside her.

Never in her wildest dreams had she ever imagined that sex could be this good.

When he stood up, it left a cool void, and in the ever-darkening room she followed his progress to the dressing table, where he found his wallet and very quickly spun round, ripping off the tin-foil wrapping of a condom.

Protection. Of course. And in his wallet. A man who was not prepared to take chances.

She sat up and pulled down the skirt just as he did the same with his boxers. She gave a sharp intake of breath and a prosaic thought flitted through her head... *Will he fit inside me?*

He was impressively big. She watched as he walked slowly towards her. His eyes were pinned to hers but he was absent-mindedly holding himself with his hand. Watching as he stroked himself was an incredible turn-on.

Her eyelids fluttered. She shuffled into a horizontal position, barely able to keep any part of her body still, busily drinking in the truly beautiful sight of his nudity. Where she was milky white, he was so sexily bronzed, and when he joined her on the bed she could only marvel at the difference in colour between them.

He manoeuvred her so that they were facing one another and ran his hand along her side, enjoying the dip of her womanly waist and the flare of her hips.

It was incredibly intimate looking deep into his eyes from this close.

'Are you relaxed?'

'I wasn't to start with.'

Dante half nodded and smiled. He slipped his hand between her legs and cupped her. He didn't go any further than that. He just cupped her there and moved his hand until she wanted so much more, until she was quivering, her fingers digging into his shoulders and only then, when he had roused her to fever pitch, did he move over her and gently begin to insert himself.

He felt her nerves, the way she stiffened, and he began whispering into her ear, soothing her as he eased himself in.

She was so wonderfully tight, scared and nervous now but, oh, so eager for him.

Dante had to grit his teeth not to push hard and satisfy himself. Bit by bit he entered her, her wetness easing a path, her groans escalating in volume the deeper he was and when, at last, he had that final thrust, Caitlin was ready for him and her body responded with enthusiasm. He moved and she moved as well, their bodies in total harmony.

It felt so good. Unbelievably so. Dante came with an explosion that shocked him in its intensity.

Her own orgasm followed his. She arched up to him and cried out, all inhibitions gone in that moment.

Afterwards, it was like swimming back up to the surface having been underwater. Caitlin sighed and shifted so that they were belly to belly. Never had she felt closer to anyone and yet, even as she knew that, she also knew that that was an admission she should never make.

'That was the best,' she said with honesty. 'At least,' she added, even more honestly, 'for me. I don't suppose it was much of a deal for you.'

'Don't even think of saying something like that.' Dante kissed the side of her mouth and ran his fingers through her tangle of colourful hair.

Dante had become jaded over time. In business, he got what he wanted. He was single-minded, focused, ambitious and feared. Born into wealth, he had continued climbing up that ladder, unimpeded. The sense of satisfaction he had felt when he had first started diversifying and doing his own thing, setting up his own empire, had become a dull, background acceptance of success. Winning deals, absorbing companies, the thrill of being the first to spot the gold mine waiting in the wings…the shine had worn off. Thinking about his brother and his dislike of the job he had inherited, his forays into other worlds that had nothing to do with money but were adventures to be had and nothing more, Dante felt a sharp pang of envy.

He was the younger but a lot more cynical.

And when it came to women…

Dante gazed at the woman lying next to him, warm and drowsy post-sex.

He would tire of her. He always did. He wondered whether his defence mechanisms against becoming too involved with any woman were so finely honed that it made it impossible for him to have anything approaching a normal relationship. No sooner had he slept with a woman than his attention began to stray. It was something he had long accepted. It was why he found the idea of marriage so inconceivable and why, if it ever hovered at the back of his mind, it was in the shape of something convenient, without the exhausting, futile and complicated shenanigans associated with emotion.

'Penny for your thoughts,' Caitlin said lightly, her clear green eyes not shying away from him.

She had her life to get on with. He had his. She would find someone eventually and her belief in love would be rekindled.

'You could stay awhile,' he murmured.

Caitlin looked at him seriously. 'I have a job to go back to.'

'Jobs can wait.'

'That's fine for you to say. You're your own boss and you can afford to do what you want.'

But that invitation was so tempting, even though she could read the corollary... *Stay awhile because pretty soon I'll get fed up anyway...*

'Don't you want to...to do this all over again?'

She hesitated, and in that pause he smiled slowly.

'Because I really want to.'

'I have responsibilities.'

'I'm not talking about a long-term arrangement, Caitlin. I'm talking about a few days of uncomplicated fun before we go our separate ways.' He stroked her side and her eyelids fluttered. 'Your responsibilities will be waiting for you when you get back to London, I'm sure.'

They would, Caitlin thought. Her parents...the stress...the uncertainty...none of that would be going anywhere any time soon. Alejandro had told her that he had instructed his bank to deposit the promised money into her account. She had no intention of keeping any of it so she would be back to square one when she returned to London.

But was she really the sort of person who could enjoy a few days of guilt-free pleasure without consequences? She'd shrugged off the whole business of relationships but, looking back at it, she hadn't been tempted into any anyway, so shrugging them off hadn't been an issue.

But she and Dante had slept together.

Lust.

That was what it had all been about. Lust and maybe the allure of being in a different country, where grim day-to-day reality could be kept at a distance... It was as real as stardust.

He wanted days. She could do days. Lust faded. And what was wrong with snatching a little time out?

His parents wouldn't know. Alejandro would probably suspect but he would be amused. They would live in a little bubble for a week and then the bubble would burst and that would be that. No harm done.

'Okay.' She blushed. She reached out and did what he was doing to her: she stroked him, her fingers sliding over taut sinew and muscle, then lower to where his stirring erection left her in no doubt that what he felt for her was very, very genuine. 'You're right. Responsibilities can wait awhile...'

His parents wouldn't know. They would be spared the bewilderment of thinking that she had been engaged to one brother only to move on to the next. Without the complexities of the situation being explained, how could they think otherwise? They lived some distance away so it wouldn't be an issue. Somehow, Caitlin had managed to avoid another dinner invitation and she suspected that that was because they were too wrapped up with events to even think about entertaining their son's fiancée, however much they might have wanted to.

Dante, perhaps, had engineered things so that they could have time to themselves, in that very special bubble where the past and the future didn't exist, just a very physical and very exciting present.

'It's extraordinary,' he had told her the evening before, when they had lain together, their limbs entangled so that they were almost a single unit, 'but this is the best sex I've ever had.'

Caitlin had laughed and quelled the unexpected hurt she had felt. *The best sex...* Maybe there were women who would have seen that as a compliment. She could understand that. Dante was a man of experience, a man who could have any woman he wanted at the snap of an imperious finger, so doubtless when he'd said that, it had been said as a compliment.

But for Caitlin…since when had that ever been her dream? Since when had she ever thought that she would end up snatching time with a guy who wasn't interested in anything beyond a romp in the sack? Had she ever thought that she would be helplessly sucked into the sort of non-relationship she had been schooled to avoid at all costs?

And yet, those words had filled her with a guilty pleasure.

She had to keep reminding herself that none of that really mattered because she would soon be gone.

Alejandro would soon be leaving hospital. She had visited him first thing this morning and he had been upbeat. He had shrewdly asked her about Dante and she had not committed to any kind of answer, but he had gone ahead and warned her off him again anyway, as if she had needed that warning.

Right now, Dante would be on his way back from the hospital. He had gone to work—an urgent meeting, he'd said, but he would much rather have lazed in bed with her—and would be stopping on the way back to his house.

Caitlin had already been there for an extra three days. Mentally, she had dealt with extending her stay by a week. That gave her four more days to bask in their short-lived relationship. When she thought about boarding that plane back to London, her mind skittered away from the unpleasant feeling that that was the last thing she wanted to do and, she told herself sternly, that had nothing to do with the fact that she hated the thought of never seeing Dante again. It was simply because she was having a holiday from all her stress and who ever wanted a holiday to come to an end? No one.

Standing in the kitchen now, with a bottle of wine chilling in the fridge and a meal in the oven, prepared by one of the three members of staff permanently employed to make sure that no need of Dante's ever went untended, including the need to eat extremely fine food and drink extremely fine wine, Caitlin glanced down at her outfit.

She had forgone the usual uniform of loose skirt and loose top, which Dante referred to as her *hippie chick outfits*, and was wearing a pair of skinny jeans and a fitted top, which she had bought the day before. Huge extravagance and she had no idea why she had done that, except she'd been out with Dante and he had practically shoved her into the shop and then had declared the outfit an amazing fit when she had grudgingly paraded it for him. She'd been squirrelling every spare penny into an account for her parents and hadn't spent anything on herself for ages and suddenly, for no reason, she'd felt reckless.

Regrettable, considering her arrangement with Alejandro had bitten the dust, even though, up to this morning, he'd pressed her to take the money, which he didn't need and she desperately did, and not be silly. He'd refused to give her his bank details. She would sort that out as soon as he was out of hospital, she'd decided.

And she had to agree with Dante—the outfit suited her.

An uneasy thought surfaced. Was she, subconsciously, dressing to please him because she wanted to somehow persuade him into a relationship he had declared he didn't want? Did she want a week to stretch into a month? A year? Longer?

If that were the case, which she wasn't even going to give houseroom in her head, then she had obviously lost her mind.

She didn't hear him enter.

She'd been lost in her thoughts. Then she looked up and there he was and her heart skipped several beats.

He was so breathtakingly beautiful, so spectacular in every possible way, that she could only stare and blink for a few seconds, like a rabbit caught in the headlights. He was magnificent naked but no less so when he was kitted out in his handmade leather shoes and the designer suit that would have cost the earth.

He'd dumped his jacket somewhere along the way and unbuttoned the top three buttons of his white shirt, which was cuffed to the elbows. His trousers, pale grey and hand-tailored, were a beautiful fit and somehow managed to make him look businesslike yet crazily sexy. Quite an achievement, she thought faintly.

Eventually, their eyes met and she blinked.

'What's wrong?' How quickly she had become used to his eyes darkening when they rested on her, to the slow, unfurling smile that could make her toes curl and bring a surge of heated colour to her face.

Right now, as he remained standing by the kitchen door, his face was grave and that sent a chill of foreboding through her.

'We need to talk.' Dante didn't take his eyes off her as he walked directly to the fridge to pour them both a generous glass of Rioja.

'You think I might need a drink to cope with whatever you have to say?'

He'd moved to sit at the table and she followed suit, although adjacent to him with a chair between them. Close enough to lean into whatever conversation was about to take place but far enough for her to remove herself from the suffocating effect he had on her senses.

She tried to read what he was thinking but he was adept at concealing what he wanted hidden.

'It's about my brother.'

'But…' she half rose '… I was with him this morning and he was absolutely fine.'

Dante tilted his head to one side. 'He told me.'

'He told you…?'

'Caitlin…you should have said. No, scratch that… of course, you couldn't have broken the promise you made him but…' Dante rubbed his eyes wearily. 'I wish I had known.'

'Alejandro *told* you?' Shocked, Caitlin leaned towards Dante, her urgent green eyes colliding with his weary dark ones. He looked drained. More than that… he looked *saddened*.

She reached out and covered his hand with hers and breathed a sigh of relief when he curled his fingers into hers. He slumped back in the chair for a few seconds, eyes closed, then he opened his eyes and looked at her.

'We spent years growing more and more distant from one another. I had no idea how he felt about working for the company until you told me. I had no inkling that he was gay and the worst of it was that he felt so damned apprehensive about telling me. Yet he had every right to keep it to himself. When have I ever given Alejandro any indication that I was interested in his personal life? We were ships that crossed in the night, exchanging as little as possible of any significance.'

'That's sometimes how it goes,' Caitlin told him gently. 'But there is an opportunity now for things to change between you. He's your brother and you're so lucky to have a sibling.' She thought of the cares and troubles she was having to manage single-handedly. 'Alejandro is one of the kindest people I've ever met and I know he would be so happy, so thrilled and excited, to have you in his life. I mean, properly in his life.' She paused. 'Has he…er…broken this news to anyone else?'

'He's going to tell our parents later today. He's wary, he tells me, but it's something he said he should have done a long time ago. I think coming here under those false pretences, his fall…brought home to him the need to come out and be honest.'

'I'm really glad he has,' Caitlin admitted. 'You have no idea how hard I've tried to persuade him that living a lie wasn't a good idea.'

'You agreed to the charade,' Dante mused softly, 'because he was so desperate to do what he thought he needed to do, didn't you? He talked you into pretending to be his fiancée and you agreed because that's just the kind of person you are…'

Uncomfortable with this summary of events, Caitlin shuffled in the chair and wondered whether she should launch into the full account of the hare-brained scheme they had agreed upon.

She remained silent. What would be the point? The main thing was that all the hiding behind closed doors was over for Alejandro and a new chapter in his life was about to begin.

'Yes, I'm a saint,' she quipped. 'If you'll excuse me, I'll just vanish upstairs for a minute so that I can polish my halo.'

Dante burst out laughing. His eyes darkened with appreciation.

There was something *special* about her. The fact that she had stepped up to the plate and done something as dramatic as she had, for the sake of friendship, struck him as almost noble.

Would she have carried on with the pretence? And for how long? Yes, she had been hurt in the past, but would that hurt have propelled her into a permanent arrangement with Alejandro if events had not played out the way they had?

He also admired the fact that she could have told him. She could have broken that confidence, knowing that it would have put a completely different slant on things. She must have known, after that kiss they had shared at the pool, that his opinion of her would have been in the dirt when he'd walked away. But she hadn't followed him. She had remained true to the promise she had made his brother.

Self-serving she was not, and he really liked that.

And now…

Dante had truly thought that her novelty value would have worn off by now. Here they were, playing truant from reality like a couple of heady teenagers, and he had assumed that the sheer *difference* about her, the very thing he figured had got to him in the first place, would have worn thin by now.

Yet he saw her and he wanted her. He touched her and he had to stop himself from shaking. He heard that infectious laugh and he smiled.

And now everything had changed and a forbidden thought crept into his head like a thief in the dark.

What if they carried on for longer than the week prescribed? He wasn't looking for permanence and neither was she. He'd half feared that she might have begun to view what they had as more significant than he had told her it was destined to be, but there had been no hesitant forays into a future beyond the coming weekend. She had not hinted at wanting any more than what they had agreed upon. She had been as casual as him, living in the moment and enjoying it.

'I like your sense of humour,' Dante confessed, his thoughts still running unchecked. 'Women have always been way too eager to do what they think I might like. You're not like that…'

'You live in a different world, Dante.' But Caitlin was inordinately pleased by the compliment. 'I guess people suck up to you because of who you are and you've become accustomed to that. I don't live in that world and it's not how I've been brought up.' She smiled. 'We're all different.'

'And I like that. More than I thought I would.'

'What do you mean?'

'Things have changed with Alejandro's revelation. My parents, for better or worse, will find out that the engagement they had such high hopes for was all a pretence. Well intentioned, but still a pretence. Alejandro is terrified that they will pass judgement and he will be found wanting. I like to think that that is not going to be the case. At any rate…' he looked at her, his lean, handsome features decisive '…you will be able to face them for who you really are.'

'I won't be facing them, Dante,' Caitlin said with

alarm. 'I'm leaving in a few days. There's really no need for me to meet up with them again.'

Still accepting of her departure, Dante thought with appreciation. Not going beyond the brief. A first. He was accustomed to having his freedom threatened sooner or later by women who wanted more longevity than he was prepared to give.

He shrugged and smiled. 'You can go at the end of the week,' he concurred, 'or you can stay on. Better still, I can arrange to temporarily transfer to London, sort things out in my brother's absence...'

'You want to *carry on*?'

'For a while,' Dante said hurriedly.

He isn't bored yet, Caitlin thought. *But soon he will be.*

He wanted everything on his terms, but what about hers? She was in danger of forgetting them, and she couldn't afford to do that because every day something deep inside was being chipped away.

'I don't think so.' She didn't wait for temptation to start interfering with common sense. 'Let's have fun and then, at the end of the week, let's do what we agreed to do. Let's say goodbye.'

CHAPTER NINE

IT WASN'T DIFFICULT to find out where Caitlin lived. Far more difficult had been Dante's decision to travel to London and search her out, because it just wasn't in his nature to pursue anyone. Pursuit equated to weakness, but, after more than two weeks without her, Dante had managed to convince himself that the real weakness would be in staying put, in ignoring the perfectly reasonable desire to finish something that had not quite reached its natural conclusion. How could he live with himself if he remained where he was, pointlessly thinking about her and having nightly cold showers? Did that make any sense at all? If she turned him away, then so be it. He would shrug it off but at least he would have tried, and you couldn't do more than that. The not trying would have been the less courageous option.

As promised, she had remained in Spain for the remainder of the week, daily visiting Alejandro, who, having awakened from his deep sleep bright-eyed and bushy-tailed, had been frustrated at not being able to get out of hospital as fast as he had hoped, thanks to the small detail of broken bones that needed to rest awhile.

Part of his urgency to leave had been sheer relief at

having come out. He had told the world and the world had been a lot more forgiving than he had anticipated.

What his traditional and old-fashioned parents had made of the whole thing was a mystery to Dante. Outwardly, at least, they had been supportive and that had been the main thing.

And now that barriers had broken down between himself and his brother, they had begun the rocky but well-intentioned road of making amends for the silent relationship that had developed between them over the years.

Between building bridges with Alejandro, engaging with his parents and all those family members now on the receiving end of what would have been, at the very least, pretty startling revelations, and focusing on some major deals in the pipeline, he should have found Caitlin's easy disappearance from his life barely left a ripple in its wake.

It had been a source of constant frustration that he couldn't get her out of his head. He had been forced to conclude that it hadn't been just about the sex. He had enjoyed her company and he didn't much like that recognition, because it wasn't something he had factored into their short-lived relationship.

So here he was.

He could have asked Alejandro for her address, but he knew, instinctively, that his brother would have cautioned him against prolonging a relationship with someone he obviously cared about. Deep and meaningful conversations he and Alejandro might not have had, but that didn't mean that Alejandro was ignorant of Dante's womanising lifestyle choices. He wouldn't have understood that he and Caitlin were on the same page when it came to their relationship. She wasn't going to lose her head over him. She wasn't going to get hurt. Why else would she have found it so easy to walk away? There hadn't been so much as a hint that she'd been looking for more than what had been put on the table.

He'd asked his PA to get hold of her address and, lo and behold, it had taken under half an hour.

He hadn't known what to expect of her living arrangements and was shocked to discover himself standing, now, outside something that looked as though an act of kindness would have been to take a wrecking ball to it. But then, he acknowledged grimly, his background had not prepared him for the reality of living on the breadline.

It was a squat, rectangular block of flats, all connected by outside concrete walkways. Washing lines groaning under the weight of clothes only partially concealed chipping paint. Bikes were leaning in front of most of the flats. The lighting was poor and Dante concluded that that was probably a good thing, because in the unforgiving light of day the sight would probably be twice as depressing. He had never been anywhere like this in his life before and he was shocked and alarmed that she lived in a place like this.

Was she going to be in?

He'd taken a chance. It was after nine on a Wednesday evening. He was playing the odds.

He took the steps two at a time. There was a pervasive odour in the stairwell but he didn't dwell on that as he headed up to the third floor, then along the walkway, brushing past the washing, dodging the bikes and random kids' toys and finally banging on her front door because there was no bell.

And then, suddenly nervous, Dante stepped back and waited to see what would happen.

Caitlin heard the banging on the door and assumed it was Shirley three doors down. She had a good relationship with the much older woman. Too good, in some ways, because Shirley was a lonely seventy-something and, for her, Caitlin was the daughter she'd had but who now never visited.

Caitlin slipped on her bedroom slippers, pulled open the door and then stared.

The whole hit her before the detail. She knew it was Dante. Half lounging against the wall, hand poised to bang once again on the door. Yes, she registered that, then she absorbed, numbly, the detail. The faded black jeans, the grey polo shirt, the weathered bomber jacket because summer was morphing into autumn and the nights were getting cooler.

'What are you doing here?' she asked faintly, hovering by the door, so shocked that she could barely think straight.

She'd been thinking about him and he'd materialised like a genie from a lamp, as beautiful and as cruelly mesmerising as she'd remembered. She'd stayed those last few days and stuck fast to her insouciant *this-is-fun-but-it's-got-to-end* routine, but every second had been filled with the wrenching pain of knowing that she would never see him again, and since she'd returned to London the pain had not subsided. He'd filled her head every waking moment, obliterating everything, even the ongoing anxiety about her parents. And now, shockingly, here he was. They'd had a straightforward deal and she'd spent the past weeks reminding herself of that baldly unappetising fact, but now he was here and she felt the electric buzz of awareness zip through her body like a toxin.

Dante lowered his eyes, his long, dark lashes brushing his slanting cheekbones and shielding his expression.

The nerves had gone. She was standing in front of him and the nerves had been replaced by a racing excitement. She was in some loose, hanging-around, *who-cares-how-I-look?* clothes. Baggy jogging bottoms, baggy sweatshirt, weird fluffy slippers. Her hair was loose, a riot of vibrant curls spilling over her shoulders and down her narrow back.

He'd never seen anything quite so beautiful in his life before.

She'd asked him a question. What was it? His breathing had slowed and when he raised his eyes to meet hers, it was like being hit by a sledgehammer.

He said the one and only thing that came to mind.

'I've missed you.'

If it hadn't been for those three words…

Caitlin looked at the man sprawled in her bed with the stamp of lazy ownership embedded in the very core of his lean, elegant body. He was as addictive as the finest of Belgian chocolate and she couldn't peel her eyes away from his reflection in the mirror as she brushed her hair.

It was eight thirty. It was Sunday. They'd been talking about Alejandro and his rapid recovery. He had left the hospital a mere six weeks previously, but only now was he really fit to travel and he was packing up to return to London.

He was a changed man, light of heart and easy of spirit. Friends and family had been so supportive, he had repeatedly told Caitlin, in between preaching to her about the dangers of going out with his brother.

'Although,' he had mused only three days previously, 'he does seem to have changed. Very understanding about the whole work thing. I'm going to be heading up a team overseeing a new direction with the company. Boutique hotels. Three of them. Much more my thing than pretending to be interested in the financial side of things. He seems relaxed and I'm not the only one to have said that. He's been in touch with our parents several times since he went to London to take over, and off his own bat, which has always, it seems, been a rare occurrence. He's less stressed out. You've obviously removed a couple of his high-energy batteries when he wasn't looking.'

As a postscript, he had added, mischievously, 'At any rate, it's put Luisa fully in the picture. I had no idea she'd been that set on Dante.'

'Luisa's spending lots of time with your brother,' Caitlin said now, standing up and blushing because she recognised the brooding, sensual appreciation in his gaze as his eyes rested on her, naked and fresh from a shower.

'Poor Alejandro. The woman has always clung to our family like a limpet. Come to bed.'

'I know you said that that's because she has no family of her own.' Why was she worried about Luisa? Caitlin didn't know and her run-ins with her had been few, but she didn't trust the woman and her hands were tied when it came to saying anything to Alejandro because he never saw the bad in anyone. Besides, there was no way that she could set her sights on brother number two, bearing in mind that Alejandro had come clean about his sexuality! But the other woman's name had cropped up time and again, indicating a presence on the scene that felt vaguely threatening.

'Come to bed...' Dante repeated, and Caitlin smiled, their eyes still locking in the mirror on the wall.

Her breasts ached and her limbs felt languorous and there was a familiar ache between her thighs.

She'd never been so uninhibited. He did that to her. He'd shown up on her doorstep a month ago, had uttered those three words, and she'd been his. Her determination not to be swept away on a tide of pointless emotion had bitten the dust in record time.

He'd missed her. There had been a naked honesty in that statement of fact and it had echoed her own feelings. She had opened the door to him and even as she was doing so, she had been helplessly aware that the common sense that had driven her departure a fortnight previously was going to be ditched.

'I have things to do.'

'With me.'

'I have a deadline to finish a layout on that shoot I did last week...'

She was smiling, though, and not moving as he eased himself off the bed, splendid in all his proud, masculine, impressive and very turned-on glory.

He absently held himself as he strolled towards her, then he was standing behind her, so much taller and broader, his bronzed skin such a striking contrast to her own smooth, milky pallor. Two naked lovers, looking at one another in the mirror, eyes tangling. There was something wildly erotic about the way they were standing, her back pressed against his chest. He reached to cover her breast with one hand and she arched back, eyelids fluttering as he caressed it. Through half-closed eyes, she followed the motion of his fingers as they played with her pulsing nipple, teasing it, rubbing the stiffened peak. When he licked his finger and touched her again, she groaned and squirmed. He leant down to kiss her neck but he wouldn't let her turn around.

'I like you watching what I'm doing to you,' he murmured in a husky, shaky voice. 'Can you feel how hard I am for you right now?'

In response, Caitlin reached back to lightly touch him. She stroked the tip of his erection, a feathery caress, one she knew he liked. She felt him stiffen and smiled drowsily.

'You were saying something about work...' Dante breathed.

'I was...'

'Then I'd best not keep you and if we climb into bed, then you won't be getting much work done any time soon.'

Caitlin had to acknowledge that this was, indeed, very true. Dante never rushed things. When they lay in bed, he took his time. He touched her slowly, exploring every inch of her body until she was begging him for release. He was a man who could put his own desires on hold for as long as it took to satisfy hers. It showed a lack of selfishness when it came to making love and she had dimly registered, somewhere along the line, that underneath the sometimes ruthless and always sweepingly self-assured exterior was a guy who was, essentially, not driven at all by ego.

There was an overriding sense of fair play about him

that was admirable. Both Dante and Alejandro had so many admirable qualities, in fact, that it was shocking that their relationship had disintegrated so much over the years, and she knew that one of the really great things to have emerged from the situation had been the slow meeting of ways between them, a gradual journey discovering themselves as brothers and appreciating that the bond that had been lost could be rebuilt with effort and goodwill.

She looked at Dante in the mirror, the incline of his dark head as he nuzzled her neck, and she was filled with a wave of such tenderness that she was, momentarily, disoriented and terrified.

'We'll just have to be quick,' he was saying, his voice muffled because he was talking against her neck.

As he said that, he slipped his finger against the wet crease between her legs, and that momentary jolt of *awareness*, a feeling that something inside her was changing somehow, was lost as pure sensation took over.

She clutched his wrists with her hands, then they fell slack to her sides for a second, before she balled her hands into tight fists, straining against the rhythm of his finger as he stroked, delving deeper with each stroke, building up a tempo that left her breathless.

Their reflection in the mirror was unfocused because her eyes were half closed. She was dimly aware of their bodies pressed tightly together, her body at the forefront, partially concealing his. One big hand rested on her breast, the other was moving between her legs. Their eyes collided and she licked her lips in a gesture that was unconsciously erotic.

He'd said quick. She was going to oblige because she

could feel the rise of her orgasm, starting as a ripple then growing in intensity until it was taking over and she spasmed in a rush against his hand, crying out and arching back, her whole body stiffening as she came.

For a while, her mind was a complete blank, then gradually she came down from that peak and swivelled so that she was facing him. She touched his sides lightly, running her hands up and down and delighting in the feel of muscle and sinew. She stroked his inner thigh, then she knelt in front of him and teased him with her mouth and her tongue.

Dante curled his fingers into her hair.

She could turn him on like no one else on the planet, turn him on to the point where he lost the ability to think. He gave a guttural sound of satisfaction as she remorselessly pleasured him with her mouth and when he could hold out no longer, he came with a shudder that ripped through him, sending him rocking back on his feet.

And she still had work to do, she thought!

But he could do this to her, point her in a direction, knowing that she would follow because, with him, she was helpless.

Caitlin didn't get it because she had never been a helpless person. Even in the aftermath of her break-up with Jimmy, she had moved on, keeping herself to herself and picking up all the pieces without fuss. If London had overwhelmed her when she'd first arrived, then she had, likewise, taken it in her stride and faced down the unknown because what was the worst that could happen? She had her health.

But Dante…this man…

He made her feel helpless. She knew that she had

ended up doing what she had told herself she would never do, had ended up caving in to her emotions and that cowardice had made her vulnerable. Very vulnerable.

A world imagined without him was no world at all.

She had gone and done what she had been cautioned against. She had fallen in love with him and as she dithered and wondered what to do about it, the days went by, each one making her more dependent than the one before.

Meanwhile, loose ends piled up around her. She was saving hard, steadfastly ignoring Dante's insistence that she move in with him, move in to the vast penthouse apartment in Mayfair that he had used as a base in the past whenever he'd happened to be in London. That final step, she knew, would be a huge mistake. At least her little one-bedroom flat was hers and he had given up trying to persuade her out of it. His solution was to avoid it at all costs because the area made him feel uncomfortable and, gradually, Caitlin had grown accustomed to a life largely led in his rarefied part of the world.

The money Alejandro had transferred was still sitting in her account, untouched.

He refused to give her the details of his bank account so that she could transfer it back to him.

He'd told her that it had been thanks to her that he had finally moved forward with his life and was no longer trapped in a cage of his own making.

He owed everything to her, he had confided the last time she had telephoned him and brought it up.

She would give him back the cash, she decided, just as soon as he was back in London, which would be in five days' time.

Face to face, he would have to cave because she would just refuse to leave him alone until he did.

Looking back on everything, she understood why she had agreed to the arrangement and yet, somehow, when she thought of that cash, she was overwhelmed with a feeling of guilt and unease.

She knew that she was enjoying life with a desperation that could only end in tears, so when, the day before Alejandro was due to arrive back in London, she glanced up from the kitchen table where she was meticulously looking at a series of photos she had taken two days previously, to see Dante framed in the doorway to the kitchen, she was almost resigned to the axe about to fall.

It was there in his expression. She realised that she had become accustomed to him strolling in to greet her with a smile that was part pleasure, part desire. Without even consciously thinking about it, she had been lulled into a state of security that had always been fragile at the very best. God, she was in *his* kitchen, as comfortable as though it were her own! She had fallen into the trap of thinking that she could tame a tiger.

Even in the depths of passion he had never, not once, offered anything other than what had been put on the table from the very start. Impermanence. Passing enjoyment. Lust.

His expression was cool. He stared at her until she fidgeted, angry with him for his silence and with herself for the fear that was filling up inside her.

'Too good to be true,' he rasped stonily, 'is what comes to mind when I look at you.'

He clenched his jaw and for a moment he was catapulted back to Luisa, her unexpected knock on his office door less than an hour and a half ago. He hadn't welcomed her in. In fact, he had risen to his feet to escort her out but as he had moved impatiently towards her, she had extended her hand with a piece of paper grasped in her fingers.

'Before you throw me out—' she had halted him in his tracks '—you need to have a look at this.'

'You need to leave my office, Luisa.' But his eyes had already been drawn to the single piece of paper and he had snatched it because it had seemed the fastest way of getting rid of the woman. He had listened to Caitlin's intermittent noises about Luisa and had played them down, omitting to tell her that he had fended off an unpleasant phone call from the other woman shortly after he had arrived in London. Why open a can of worms? The minute Luisa had accosted him in his office, he had assumed that she was going to pursue her plea to think about their long family connection and the value of resurrecting their defunct relationship.

This time, he'd thought, he wasn't going to bother with politeness.

He had half looked at that damning sheet of paper and then had looked more carefully.

Now, standing in his kitchen, he could still feel the cold fury that had swept through him when he had registered what was written.

But before the fury...

The devastation of realising that, once again, he had been sucked into a relationship with a woman who had not been what she had seemed.

Worse, he had realised, with shock, that there was

something beyond devastation, beyond rage at his lack of judgement.

There had been the raw pain of knowing that what he'd felt for Caitlin had been far deeper than he could possibly have imagined, and on the back of that pain had come icy rage.

The self-discipline that was so much a part of his personality had masked all emotion as he had politely frozen Luisa out of the satisfaction of engineering the outcome she had anticipated, but his rage had not abated.

And now...standing here...

'Where did you get this?' Colour drained away from her face and her hand was shaking.

If ever there was a picture of guilt, he thought bitterly. What had he expected? Really? Some crazy explanation that might make sense?

Unfortunately, he knew exactly what he had expected. He had expected her to be different. When he looked back, he knew that he had thought her different from the very first moment he had clashed with her as she had skulked up the long avenue that led to his mansion. She had intrigued him, and she had continued to intrigue him, and when everything had come out in the wash about his brother he had done the unthinkable. He had dropped his guard and given her the benefit of the doubt.

For the first time in his life he had begun to play with the crazy notion of longevity.

He should have stuck to the brief and he was paying for straying from it now.

'Where?' she repeated. The beautiful lean lines of his face were unforgiving and she could understand why. She had come to know this man in many little ways, and for him to have proof positive that there had been more to her relationship with Alejandro than an altruistic desire to help him in his hour of need by pretending to be his fiancée would signal the death knell to whatever he might have felt for her. Not love, no. But affection, yes, and certainly desire.

The email to the bank was brief, simply giving Alejandro's private banker instructions to transfer a hefty amount of money to her account.

'Does it matter?' Dante asked with glacial indifference.

Naturally it would have made zero difference if she had tried to blag her way out of this, but he was still enraged that she was making no effort to even try, and angry with himself for caring one way or the other.

The game was up and she was showing her true colours. No more eager desire to please.

'I don't suppose it does,' Caitlin said in a low voice. She couldn't meet his eyes. She couldn't bear the cold accusation there, the *disappointment*.

'Is that all you have to say?' Dante gritted. '*"I don't suppose it does"*? For the record, Luisa came by it and very thoughtfully decided to hand it over.'

'Of course she did,' Caitlin said wearily.

'Luisa may be many things but her faults have always been out in the open. She happened to be helping my brother pack his things and when he was out of the room, she accidentally refreshed his computer when she went to pick it up and curiosity got the better of her when your name popped up on the heading along with an account number. Quite a substantial sum of money, I must say. A good day at the office, wouldn't you agree?' He breathed in deeply and watched as co-lour suffused her. 'What were your plans for the money? Well-deserved spending spree? And did you decide that I might have been a more lucrative bet than my brother because if you managed to hook me, you might just have yourself a permanent passport to wealth instead of a one-off? Did you start as a fake fiancée only to imagine that you could become a real one but with the other heir to the throne?'

'How could you say that?' This time she *did* look at him, and with distress. 'Don't you know me at all?'

'It would seem not,' Dante grated harshly.

The truth was that he'd felt as though he *did* know her and even now, with the evidence of his own stupid-ity right in front of him, he *still* felt as if he did. It was an act of wilful self-delusion that enraged him further.

'Would you even make an effort to believe me if I told you that…' she sighed and blinked away a rush of miserable tears '…that it's not what you think, despite what it looks like?'

'It looks like you had a financial arrangement with my brother to cover your agreement to pose as his fi-ancée for the benefit of friends and family and to get our parents off his back on the business of marrying him off. How am I doing so far?'

Caitlin stared at him mutely.

'I'm gathering from your silence that I'm doing pretty good. Except you got here, and things didn't quite go according to plan. I should have paid a bit more attention to your striking lack of luggage when you arrived. I'm assuming the jaunt was supposed to be short-lived? A one-night charade then back to nor-mal with a much-inflated bank account?'

'You're seeing it all in black and white…' But actually, every single word was spot-on and there was nothing she could do to defend herself. Her own sense of guilt would have stopped her anyway.

'No wonder you were so panicked at the thought of hanging around. Until, that is, you discovered that a little hanging around might work in your favour.'

'You know that's not true. You're making it out like I'm some sort of…of…*tramp*…some sort of…*sexual predator*…' She looked him squarely in the eye. 'You were my first, Dante.'

Dante had the grace to flush but then he aggressively told himself that that counted for very little when hard evidence of her mercenary nature was in front of him.

'Why are you still continuing with…' he waved his hand at the pile of photos spread across her side of the kitchen table '…*that*?' He vaulted forward, too restless to stay still any longer, and prowled the room before coming to stand in front of her, a towering and intimidating figure. 'And why are you still living in that dump? What was the money for, Caitlin? Debts?'

'Something like that.'

'What debts?' Dante didn't understand and he didn't like the feeling. 'Forget it,' he snapped, slashing the air with his hand in a gesture of conclusion. 'I'm going to go out for an hour. In that time, I want you to pack whatever things you might have here and leave. Put it this way, when I get back I don't want to find you still here.'

Dante was never going to listen to what she had to say, Caitlin realised. He had made his mind up. The only way he would ever have entertained hearing her out would have been if he had loved her, because if he had he would see what she saw, that it wasn't black and white but a thousand shades of grey, and he would have understood.

She was realising now what the fundamental difference between lust and love was.

Lust was essentially self-centred. It went so far when it came to seeing the bigger picture, to listening and forgiving, and no further.

Love was what bridged the gap, jumped over the chasm, having faith that you would reach the other side and being willing to take the risk.

She loved Dante and she knew that, had the shoe been on the other foot, she would have listened because she would have known, in her gut, that there was no way he could be the person circumstances were portraying him to be, that there would be another explanation, however things might look on the surface.

Well, there was no point hanging around and hoping for the impossible.

She nodded quietly. 'I'll be gone by the time you get back.'

CHAPTER TEN

IN THE EVENT it was two days before Dante returned to the penthouse apartment.

One hour? There was no way he intended to risk returning to find her still there, hunting around for the last of her things and, frankly, considering the fact that she had refused to move in with him, she had managed to find homes for a lot of her personal possessions. A couple of photography books here and there…spare bedroom slippers because she had to have something on her feet when she walked around…a selection of novels, all started and not one finished because she always lost interest somewhere between Chapter Three and Chapter Four…

He hadn't wanted to head back even after a day just in case she had forgotten something and had decided to return to collect it. He had forgotten to ask her to hand over the spare key he had insisted she have. She might have kept it. Who knew? She would leave it behind her in the apartment. He knew that without having to ask himself how.

So Dante had gone off grid for the first time in his life, dumping London altogether and heading to the coast for a couple of days to clear his head.

She was gone. She'd pulled the wool over his eyes and she was gone. End of story.

He would pick up where he had left off because the world was full of beautiful women and he knew, without a trace of vanity, that he could have any of them.

Including Luisa, should he so choose, but the very thought of her made his teeth grind together. Like the messenger carrying a poisonous communication, she had been sliced out of his life for good, whatever the long-standing family connections. What she had done had been done with the worst of self-serving motives. He would wait until she tried to get in touch, which she inevitably would, to tell her exactly what he thought, but right now he just couldn't be bothered.

He couldn't be bothered with anyone or anything. He escaped London thinking that he would escape Caitlin. It had been a remarkable failure on that front.

Dante spent the first night drinking way too much at the Michelin-starred restaurant in the hotel where he had booked for the two nights.

Then he spent the second night wondering what the hell he was going to do because things seemed as clear as mud.

But by the time he began the journey back to London, clarity was imposing itself.

Without the benefit of distractions, he could think, and in the confines of his Maserati, as he drove back to London, he finally began to see what had been lurking on the sidelines of his mind for so long now. Like wisps of smoke, warning him of a conflagration. He should have paid attention.

The warning bells should have started sounding the very second he'd decided to cross that ocean and meet her again. Then he had entered a comfort zone without even realising it. He had become accustomed to the way she laughed and looked at him, to the comfortable silences between them.

He hadn't been fazed by the sight of her toothbrush next to his or her photos spread across his kitchen table, as they had been when he had confronted her about that damned email.

Dante began joining all the dots on his way back to London and by the time he hit the crowded outskirts of the city, he was frantic to do what he should have done a long time ago. He had to be honest. He had to stop pretending that he was an island.

He had to move on from hard and fast notions that had dominated his life and kept his emotions under lock and key.

But first and foremost, he had to convince her to hear him out. He stopped at his apartment only to dump his bag and have a rushed shower.

All evidence of her had been carefully removed.

The place was immaculate, wiped clean of her presence. Not even the faintest of smells lingered. That flowery, clean smell that followed her wherever she went? Gone.

He knew the way to her apartment like the back of his hand, even though he had, very quickly, refused to go there, preferring the comfort of his penthouse.

At a little after midday, there were signs of life, with kids out and about in front of the block of flats, aimlessly cycling around. He headed up to hers, nodding a greeting to some elderly lady with whom Caitlin had developed a firm friendship.

'She's not there.'

Dante stopped dead in his tracks. 'I have a key. I'll wait.'

Shared keys…something else that should have set those bells ringing in his head. Since when had he ever come close to handing a key to his place over to any woman, far less having a key for hers?

'You'll be waiting a long time, son.'

'Why?' Panic gripped him, like a vice.

'She's gone to her parents'. Told me to keep an eye on her place because she might be a while.'

'Her parents'?' He realised that, despite his knowing so much about her, she had singularly failed to talk to him about her parents. She had told him about her ex, about where she had grown up, had passed occasional remarks about her childhood, but her parents…? No, she hadn't mentioned them and suddenly that failing felt significant. 'Would you happen to have their address?'

She did. She handed it over. There were a lot of questions, most of which Dante answered as honestly as he could and to the best of his ability, given that he was inept when it came to disclosing how he felt about anything with a complete stranger.

But he realised that he would, frankly, have done whatever it took to know how he could find the woman he had fallen hopelessly in love with.

He would climb a thousand mountains and walk a thousand miles, but on a more pressing level there was, he now realised, just one more thing he had to do first…

Caitlin heard the buzz of the doorbell. It was irritating, really, because this was the sixth night at her parents' house and the first evening she had had in on her own. The previous nights had been spent doing the rounds, as she had had to do the minute she'd appeared, unannounced, on her parents' doorstep.

It was a small village and people would have been offended if she hadn't immediately dropped by. Where her parents lived, being a recluse was practically a punishable offence, and it had been pretty reassuring visiting a couple of her parents' friends, knowing that they knew about the dire situation and were supportive.

The local vicar, another on the list of people she had seen and the first person who had shown up within hours of her arrival, was also fully in the know and very sympathetic.

They were all trying to keep spirits upbeat.

Everyone was rallying around.

Notwithstanding, that still left the matter of the finances that needed sorting out and this was her first evening in when she could really get down to seeing what was going on.

Her parents were out for the evening, dinner at friends'.

So the buzz of the doorbell, which she knew heralded another well-intentioned visitor, was…*irritating*.

She took her time getting to the door. She hoped that whoever was there might slink off, thinking that the house was empty.

But there was another buzz and so she pulled open the door and…

Déjà vu.

Hadn't she been here before? Staring at muscular legs encased in faded black jeans? At a body she had touched a million times? A face whose lines she knew from memory?

Hadn't this guy shown up, unannounced, on her doorstep once upon a time?

All those thoughts flashed through Caitlin's head in the seconds it took for her to register Dante's shocking appearance at the door.

'I know.' He tried a smile on for size. 'You're going to tell me that we've been down this road before.'

His voice was lazy and controlled but his heart wasn't. He was standing on the edge of a precipice, gazing down at a sheer drop and he wasn't sure whether there would be a safety net for when he took the plunge.

Rendered speechless, Caitlin could only gape.

'I went to your apartment.' Dante filled in the silence. He had to because he didn't want her to slam the door in his face. He could have inserted himself into the house, but that he didn't want to do because he was here with a begging bowl and he wasn't about to forget that. 'I met your neighbour. She told me where you were. She gave me your parents' address...so here I am.' He shuffled uncomfortably and flushed. Desperation bloomed. She wasn't saying a word and her expression told him nothing.

'Caitlin...'

'Stop right there!'

Why was he here? He had kicked her out of his life without giving her a chance to say her piece. He hadn't been interested then so...had he come bearing more tasty damning morsels? She didn't know and she didn't want to find out.

'You have *no right* to just show up at my parents' house! You should *never* have been given the address.'

'I've made mistakes...' He looked down, then raised his eyes to meet hers.

'Is that what you've come to tell me?'

'Please let me in.'

'I already did,' Caitlin said bitterly. 'I let you in and it was the biggest mistake I ever made.'

'Don't say that. I don't want to have this conversation out here, on the doorstep. I know your parents are probably in and... I am happy to talk to you with them present.'

'What?'

'What I have to say, I would be happy for them to hear.'

Caitlin hadn't been expecting that and she hesitated. If he was here about the wretched money, then she might as well get it over and done with. She pulled open the door with marked reluctance and stood back as he walked past her into the house.

He looked around and she saw what he did, but through his eyes. A small but tidy house. Her mother had always been house-proud, and her dad had never minded a bit of DIY, and the house reflected this. In her mind's eye, she saw his magnificent estate, the vast mansion shrouded in privacy, the acres of marble that told a tale of impossible riches, a penthouse with a priceless and exquisite Chagall painting hanging in the cloakroom, just the sort of casual afterthought only a billionaire could ever afford. Anger tasted like bile in her throat when she imagined him writing her off as a cheap, nasty gold-digger.

She walked towards the kitchen and was aware of him following in her wake.

'My parents are out at the moment,' she offered tersely, 'but they'll be back soon and I don't want you around when they get back. I don't want to have to explain...anything.'

'The last time I showed up unannounced,' Dante

said, declining the cup of coffee she offered although he knew he could do with a stiff drink in its place, 'I told you that I missed you.'

Caitlin blushed a furious red and waited in silence for him to get on with it. She'd been a sucker once and she wasn't about to repeat the exercise.

He was still standing but he sat down now and so did she, like two strangers facing one another in a board-room, not quite sure how the meeting was going to go. Her spine was rigid and her fingers were curled over her knees in a defensive, vice-like grip.

'When I saw that email,' Dante plunged right in, still very much conscious of the fact that he could be chucked out at any given moment and he wouldn't blame her, 'I... I felt like the bottom of my world had dropped out. I couldn't have been more shocked and I reacted in just the way I was programmed to react.' He held up one hand because he could see that she was on the point of interrupting and he just needed to carry on saying what he had to say, had to gather momentum and run. It was the only way he was going to be able to hurl himself off the edge of that damned precipice.

Caitlin was riveted. He shouldn't be here. She shouldn't be listening to him. But there was a gut-wrenching, despairing honesty about him that held her rapt.

'I'd been let down once and, after that, I built a wall around myself. There was no way that I was ever going to be let down again. Then I got that email and read it and realised that I'd done the unthinkable. I had dropped all my defences. It was the only thing that could account for the sickening feeling in the pit of my stomach, the feeling that my world had stopped turning.' He breathed in deeply and realised his heart was racing. 'You don't believe me?'

'You've never said anything like this before.'

'I didn't…know how.'

'I'm not drifting back into some sort of relationship with you because you still want me in your bed.'

'When I said that I missed you, I should have said the bits I miss most aren't the ones where you occupy my bed. Not that I don't miss those.'

'I don't know what you're trying to tell me.'

'I'm trying to tell you that I don't care. I don't care about whatever financial arrangement you had with my brother. I don't care whether you needed the money to cover a lifestyle of fast cars and gambling dens.'

Caitlin raised both eyebrows. She was still clutching her knees, but the white-knuckle ride was abating and something inside her was melting.

'You didn't even hear me out,' she said painfully. 'You just went ahead and assumed the worst.'

'I did and I will regret that for the rest of my life.'

'You searched me out once, Dante, because you felt that what we had should have carried on. I'm not that same person any longer.' She really wasn't, she thought. She was way too involved to risk having her heart broken all over again.

'I don't expect you to carry on with what we had,' Dante told her seriously. 'It wouldn't be what I wanted. I don't want a fling with you, *querida*. I want the rest of my life with you.'

Caitlin blinked and gaped.

'You're kidding…'

Dante reached into his pocket. The black box had been burning a hole there since he had entered her house. That thing he'd had to do, the final step he'd had to take.

The box sat in the palm of his hand, then he opened it, his dark eyes firmly pinned to her face, registering her tremulous disbelief, then the dawning smile that told him that everything was going to be just fine.

'Far from it. I'm deadly serious. I love you and I can't envisage a life without you in it. I want you to wear this ring and then I want you to wear my wedding ring next to it.'

Caitlin stared then she smiled and tentatively reached out to touch the ring with one finger. It was the most beautiful thing she had ever seen, a solitaire diamond glittering in its bed of white gold, and on the band were tiny diamonds, like perfect tiny stars paying homage to that single, glittering and much bigger one that nestled in the centre.

'Am I dreaming?' she murmured to herself. She raised her eyes, barely able to breathe.

'You're not dreaming.' He took a chance and slipped the ring onto her finger and then stared in silence because this was the biggest thing he had ever done in his life before. It literally rendered him speechless. He gently stroked her finger before continuing gravely, 'I had a few days away from everything after you left and I came to my senses. It took me a while. But how could I recognise the symptoms of something I'd never felt before?'

'You want to spend the rest of your life with me?' She couldn't stop staring at the ring, now on her finger, the perfect fit.

'Why do you think I told you that I would have this conversation in front of your parents? I want to marry you, Caitlin Walsh, so will you say yes?'

'Just try and stop me.' She breathed unsteadily, then went over to him and curled herself onto his lap, her arms flung round his neck, loving the tightness of his embrace.

'The money thing…' She pulled back and looked at him and sighed.

He reached to shush her but she held his finger in her hand and squeezed it.

Then she stood up and pulled a chair right up next to his so that her legs were pressed between his and she could rest her hands on his thighs. The gleaming diamond, so much a tangible statement of intent, so much *Dante*, who was a man of such intent, gave her the strength to come clean and broach the topic that had severed their relationship.

'Where to start? I knew that Alejandro was terrified about coming out. I think he felt that he had gone as far as he could resisting his parents' efforts to marry him off and, in his desperation, he came up with the idea of me posing as his fiancée, basically to bide time until…until you decided to settle down, which would take the heat off him. It was a crazy idea, really, and I didn't want to go along with it but I felt sorry for him. He said that it would be a business deal and I refused.'

She felt tears trying to leak out of the corners of her eyes as she thought back to the train of events that had led to her changing her mind.

'I kept refusing and then two things happened in very quick succession. My parents ran into some terrible financial debt. My dad had been scammed and he'd been keeping it quiet. I found out and basically… he'd been conned out of all his savings. I won't go into the details, but it was very clever. He was mortified.

His pension isn't huge, and those savings were going to be the foundation for their old age. Of course, I told them that I would help, but shortly after my mother had a heart attack. Stress induced, the doctor said.' She sighed. 'And there was Alejandro, with that plan still at the back of his mind. I caved in. I took him up on his offer. So you see, there were debts but not mine and not of my making.' She paused. 'Only thing was I hadn't banked on the guilt. I couldn't take the money in the end. Maybe if it had all stayed as a business arrangement, but then things happened and I got involved with you... The money is untouched and I intend to force it back to Alejandro as soon as he gets to London. He refuses to let me have his account details so I might just have to show up with a few sacks of coins and bills.' She smiled. 'I don't blame you for suspecting the worst.'

'You should blame me for everything,' Dante told her gravely. 'Most of all for being a fool and almost letting you go. Trust me, I intend to spend the rest of my life making you happy.' He leant forward and drew her towards him and kissed her.

It felt as if he was coming home. It was just where he wanted to be.

There was a lavish wedding in Spain. Tradition, Dante had told her wryly, was tradition and his parents were finally getting the wedding they had wanted for a while. Both sets of parents hit it off and there was so much parental involvement on both sides that Caitlin wasn't quite sure just how vital her contributions were.

But it all went off without a hitch. The dress was spectacular, as was the awesome cathedral. Her heart fluttered and her mouth ran dry the minute her eyes found Dante waiting for her with his brother to his right, the very proud ring bearer.

Then, a mere handful of days later, there was a far smaller do close to her parents' home, where family and friends celebrated the union over a home-cooked meal prepared by the caterer at the one and only hotel in the village.

The honeymoon was wonderful. Two weeks in the Maldives, where all those problems that had afflicted her once upon a time seemed very long ago.

But then, she was living a new life now, with the man she loved.

That very man was right at this moment pouring her a glass of wine while she relaxed on the sofa, a lovely vantage point from which she could appreciate him.

The honeymoon had come and gone. Reality of life with Dante was even sweeter than she could possibly have imagined.

'We need to sort out where we're going to live.' He handed her the glass and Caitlin dutifully rested it on the low coffee table next to her.

'Now that my brother is jet-setting in his new role, I think London will be my base. Naturally we can return to Madrid whenever we wish, but I feel that this would be more suitable for us, as a couple.'

Caitlin nodded and tried to imagine bringing up a family in a penthouse. Glass and toddlers were not a happy mix. Should she mention that now?

'And not here.' He grinned.

'Since when did you become a mind reader?'

'It's called being in love.'

She was wearing some comfy track pants and a

baggy top and when she shuffled along the sofa to snuggle against him, the warmth of her little body suffused him with the sort of deep contentment he had never envisaged for himself.

'Where were you thinking?' she asked, inclining her head so that their eyes met.

'To be decided. We can discuss where but I'm thinking within commuting distance from London but far out enough to be surrounded by some open land. And, of course, more in the direction of your parents.'

'That's a good idea,' Caitlin murmured, 'because we're going to need a bit of space and a bit of land and less sharp corners and glass surfaces.'

'We are?' Dante stilled, his sharp eyes noticing that the wine, her favourite brand, was untouched.

'I only found out this morning and I wanted to surprise you, my darling...'

'You've succeeded.' He angled her so that he could kiss her and kiss her he did. Then he looked at her and stroked her face with such tenderness that her heart expanded until it wanted to burst.

'A baby on the way.' He couldn't stop grinning. 'I love you, my darling. You make my life complete and a baby to come? It couldn't get any better...'

* * * * *

ONE NIGHT
ON THE
VIRGIN'S TERMS

MELANIE MILBURNE

To my editor and shadow editor, Nic Caws
and Hannah Rossiter.

Thank you both for being so supportive
through my at times (more times than I'd like!)
difficult writing process.

Your faith and confidence in me is so appreciated.

Bless you! xxxx

CHAPTER ONE

IVY KENNEDY WAS at the hairdresser's when she found a solution to her virginity problem. The answer was in the very first gossip magazine she flicked through. Truth be told, the answer had been under her nose for years, but it hadn't been until now that she'd had her *Aha!* moment.

Louis Charpentier—the king of one-night stands and her older brother's best friend. Her problem solved. Who knew that getting highlights could be the highlight of your week? Your month? Your year?

Sarina, the hairstylist, glanced over Ivy's shoulder at the magazine article and whistled through her teeth. 'Gosh, isn't Louis Charpentier enough to stop your heart? I swear that man should come with a warning. He's so gorgeous, I'm getting a hot flash just looking at his photo. I hear he's won Hottest Bachelor of the Year again. How many times is that now? Three?'

'Four.'

Ivy turned the page over but surreptitiously used her left thumb as a bookmark. She wanted another look at Louis without the hairdresser drooling over her shoulder.

She gave what she hoped would pass as an indifferent shrug and added, 'He's okay, I guess.'

For years Louis had been nothing more than her brother Ronan's best friend. Handsome enough, but not enough to 'tempt her', to borrow a phrase from Jane Austen. But, with her thirtieth birthday rapidly approaching, and her status as a virgin unchanged, she had to do something—and soon.

How was she ever going to find a partner in life unless she did something about her embarrassing intimacy issues? She'd spent most of her adult life finding any excuse she could to avoid dating, out of fear. Fear of being naked with a man and him finding her not good enough. Fear of being hurt. Fear of falling in love with someone only for them to dump her.

But she was about to turn thirty, and she had to push past this road block in her life. Thirty. *Eek!* Who'd ever heard of a thirty-year-old virgin these days?

And who better to fix her little problem than Louis, who was super-experienced at seduction. How could her inhibitions around sex be solved any other way? It would be awkward and cringe-worthy, asking him, but she couldn't bear the thought of asking anyone else.

She wanted someone she knew and trusted to help her, not some casual hook-up who might laugh at her or mock her for still being a virgin at her age. Or make rude comments about her body, like one of her erstwhile dates. Louis wasn't a stranger, he was a friend... Well, perhaps a 'friend', inverted commas, would be more accurate.

Now that her brother had emigrated to Australia to

be with his partner Ricky, Ivy only saw Louis for a coffee or lunch now and again. And she'd had to cancel the last time due to a large shipment of antiques arriving from France at the store where she worked as a curator.

Ivy knew that if she didn't act on her decision this very afternoon she might lose her courage and not act at all. She only had a month until she turned the big Three O, but she wanted to experience the Big O well before then. The birthday clock was ticking like a bomb.

She took a deep breath, opened the magazine again and studied Louis' distinctive features. Tall and dark, with his smoky blue-grey gaze brooding in an I-don't-quite-know-what-he's-thinking kind of way, he was the epitome of heart-stopping gorgeousness. She traced the firm line of his mouth in the photo and began to imagine how it would feel pressed to her own. Her eyes went further down the photo to his strongly muscled thighs and a soft flutter of nerves wafted through her belly.

She closed the magazine with a definitive snap. Yep. He was The One. Not as in a happily-ever-after The One, but the perfect solution to her embarrassing problem.

All she had to do was convince him.

Louis Charpentier was doing the final drafts of a major architectural project in his London office when his secretary buzzed him on the intercom.

'Louis? There's—' she began.

'I said no interruptions this afternoon, Maureen.' He injected his tone with stern authority. Why couldn't his temporary secretary obey his simple instructions, for

God's sake? He was on a tight deadline and the client was difficult and demanding. Story of his life. What was it about him that attracted the most demanding clients? No doubt the same bad-luck fairy that had given him difficult and demanding parents.

'I'm sorry, but there's a Miss Ivy Kennedy here to see you. She hasn't made an appointment but she insists it's important she sees you as soon as possible. She says she's the sister of a close friend of yours. Will I send her in or tell her to come back some other time?'

Louis pushed his computer mouse to one side and scraped a hand through his hair. What could be wrong? Ivy had cancelled the last time he'd suggested they have lunch. Her brother Ronan had asked him to keep an eye on her when he'd emigrated to Australia. Louis enjoyed his occasional catch-ups with Ivy, but he tried not to notice her in any way that could be even loosely described as sexual. Not easy to do when she looked so damn sexy without even trying. But messing with his best mate's kid sister was a no-go zone. Ivy was the hanging out for the fairy tale, the forever love. She was the wanting-to-have-babies type. He was the sleep-with-them-once-and-move-on-without-looking-back type. They had zilch in common other than her brother Ronan. Besides, his best mate had experienced enough trouble coming out to his family without Louis adding more to the mix.

Louis pressed the button on the intercom. 'Send her in. And hold all my calls until she leaves. Understood?'

'Got it.'

The door opened and Louis rose from behind his

desk, his eyes scanning the pint-sized whirlwind that came in. With almost waist-length wavy red-gold hair, periwinkle-blue eyes, Celtic alabaster skin and a full-lipped mouth, Ivy Kennedy looked as if she had stepped out of another era—apart from her clothes, of course. He tried not to stare too long at her slim legs encased in blindingly white jeans, and the way her black V-neck cashmere sweater outlined the firm up-thrust of her small but perfect breasts. She was wearing burgundy heeled, pointy-toed ankle boots that highlighted the daintiness of her ankles. But even with the boost of her heels she still didn't make it up to his shoulder.

'Hello Ivy.' His voice came out a little huskier than he'd intended, and he was conscious of the effort it took to keep his gaze away from the ripe, plump curve of her mouth. 'What can I do for you?'

'Louis, I hope you don't mind me coming to see you like this, but I have a problem and I think you're the only one who can help me.' Her voice was breathless and twin circles of colour formed on her cheeks.

Louis was never sure whether to greet her with a kiss on the cheek or a hug but, given the way his groin was stirring just now, a hug was very definitely out.

Maybe his self-imposed celibacy was a mistake. Mr Amazing One-Night Stand was taking a much-needed sabbatical. How long had it been? Three, or was it four, months? He stayed behind his desk and waved a hand to the chair in front of the desk reserved for clients. 'Please, sit down.'

'Thanks. I won't take up too much of your time.' Ivy plonked herself down on the chair, her dangling silver costume-earrings swaying against her heart-shaped face. He caught a whiff of her perfume—white lilacs and lily-of-the-valley—which danced around his nostrils in an intoxicating vapor. Her small, neat hands were clasped around a rectangular bag only big enough to carry a mobile phone and the bare essentials. She ran the tip of her tongue across her cherry-red lips and then gave him a dimpled smile that almost knocked him off his feet. Small white teeth with an adorable overbite and those luscious lips were a bewitching combination that sent his pulse up another notch. 'It's good to see you, Louis. Sorry I had to take a rain check last time.'

Stop staring at her mouth. And don't even think about looking at her breasts.

'That's okay. I had a lot on that week anyway.' He cleared his throat and sat down, resting his forearms on the desk. 'So, what can I help you with?' He used his let's-get-down-to-business tone, but he was aware of a strange energy in the air—a subtle tightening of the atmosphere that made the black hairs on his arms tingle at the roots.

She rolled her lips together, her gaze lowering to the Windsor knot of his tie as if she found it the most fascinating thing in the world. 'Erm… Well, it's kind of difficult to explain…' Her cheeks went two shades darker and her fingers picked at the stitching on her bag as if she was determined to dismantle it then and there. He automatically checked her left hand for rings. Nothing.

He let go of a breath he hadn't realised he'd been holding. He lived in silent dread of her getting involved with the wrong man. It would be just his luck to have her fall for some totally unsuitable guy on his watch. Her brother had told him she'd been dreaming about getting married since she'd been given her first doll. He'd also heard she'd been unlucky in the dating game, no doubt because she was way too generous and trusting and not at all street-smart.

Louis leaned back in his chair and reached up to loosen the knot of his tie. 'Would you like a drink? Coffee? Tea? Something stronger?'

Ivy glanced at him, her small white teeth snagging her bottom lip. 'Do you have any brandy?'

He frowned. 'Since when do you drink brandy? I thought you only drank white wine or champagne.'

Her lips twitched in a self-deprecating smile, her cute dimples appearing. 'This is kind of a brandy situation.'

'Now you've got me intrigued.' Louis rose from his chair, walked over to his drinks cabinet and poured a small measure of brandy into a tumbler. He came over to where she was sitting and handed the brandy to her. Her fingers brushed his in the exchange and a current of electricity shot from her fingers to his and straight to his groin with lightning-bolt speed. What was going on with him today? He was acting like a hormone-mad teenager. Maybe his sex sabbatical wasn't such a great idea. It was messing with his head, messing with his morals, messing with his boundaries.

Louis perched on the corner of his desk in front of her chair rather than go back behind his desk. He told himself it would make her feel more at ease, less intimidated without the barrier of his huge desk between them, but deep down he knew it had more to do with wanting to be close enough to study every nuance of her face. He watched her lips move against the rim of the crystal tumbler, imagined them closing around him and a wave of heat swept through his body.

Yep, he really needed to break his sex drought. Getting the hots for his best friend's sister would be crossing a line he had sworn he would never cross. Ronan had issued him with the task of keeping an eye on her. Nothing else. Eyes on. Hands off. What else could there be between them? He wasn't her type in any shape or form. Ivy was the sweet, homespun type who couldn't walk past a jewellery-shop window without gazing at diamond engagement rings and wedding rings. The type of woman who tried on wedding dresses in her lunch hour. The type of woman who drooled over prams and puppies and dreamed of promises of forever love. He had no faith in that kind of love. How could he when he had watched his parents' forever love turn into forever fighting over the years?

Ivy took three eye-watering sips, coughed twice and then leaned forward to put the glass on Louis' desk with a grimace. 'Gosh, how do people drink this stuff? I'm not sure I can finish it.'

'Probably a good thing.'

She hunted up her sleeve for a tissue and, taking one out, mopped at her eyes, giving him a sheepish look from beneath eyelashes as long and spiky as spiders' legs. 'I'm sorry for interrupting you when you're so busy. Is that a new secretary? She seems awfully nice.'

It was typical of Ivy to see the best in everybody. It was an endearing quality but not one he possessed.

Maybe he was more like his father than he realised. *Shoot me now.* 'Yes, she's only been here a couple of months. My usual secretary, Natalie, is on maternity leave.'

Ivy leaned forward in a conspiratorial manner and continued in a stage whisper. 'I think she's a little bit in love with you.'

Louis coughed out a laugh and pushed himself off the desk with his hands. Maybe it wasn't such a good idea to sit so close to her. Her perfume was doing strange things to his senses—not to mention the glimpse he got of her delightful cleavage when she leaned forward. He moved back around behind his desk, sat on the chair and crossed one ankle over his bent knee in a casual pose he was far from feeling.

'I never mix business with pleasure, and dating staff is a recipe for disaster.' Dating anyone for longer than twenty-four hours these days was a disaster. He'd once been fine with a week or two with someone, even a month, but that was before his most recent lover, who'd had trouble accepting the end of their three-week fling. Being stalked for weeks on end by a woman who'd fancied herself madly in love with him had been no fun. His new rule was one night and one night only. It gave no time for feelings to develop on either side.

Ivy rolled her lips together, her eyes briefly dipping to his mouth. 'Are you…seeing anyone at the moment?' Her voice had a tentative, breathless quality to it and the pink in her cheeks darkened.

Louis swivelled his chair in slow sideways movements, his gaze holding hers. 'Not at the moment. Why?'

She gave a one-shoulder shrug, her eyes skittering away from his. 'Just asking…'

He lowered his crossed ankle to the floor and leaned his arms on the desk again. 'Ivy.' He used his parent-to-child tone, because right then he was having way too much trouble seeing her as his mate's sister. He was seeing her naked in his bed, those gorgeous breasts in his hands, his mouth on hers, his…

Stop. Do not go any further. Just stop.

Ivy slow-blinked like a little owl. 'Can I ask you something?'

Louis sat back again and rubbed a hand over his late-in-the-day stubble. 'Yeah, sure. Go for it.'

She gave an audible swallow, the tip of her tongue sneaking out to deposit a layer of moisture on her lips. Lips he couldn't stop thinking about kissing, to see if they were as soft and pliable as they looked. To see what they tasted like—sweet or salty or a sexy combination of the two? 'Louis…what do you find most attractive in a woman? I mean, you date a lot, so I guess you'd know what's hot and what's not, right?'

What was hot was sitting right in front of him, with her small white teeth pulling at her lower lip. What was hot was thinking about peeling those skin-tight jeans and sweater off her and planting kisses on every inch of her body. What was hot was thinking about her legs wrapped around his hips while he drove them both to oblivion.

Louis suppressed a shudder and gave himself a vigorous mental shake. Anyone would think he was the one who'd drunk that brandy. 'Confidence is enormously attractive in a woman.'

Ivy slapped one of her thighs and sprang to her feet; her bag dropped to the floor with a thud but she didn't even seem to notice. 'I *knew* it. That's exactly what I think and it's why I'm here to ask for your help to gain some.'

Louis raised his brows a fraction. 'Me?'

She came around to his side of the desk, standing close enough for him to touch her. *Do. Not. Touch. Her.* The temptation to do so was painfully difficult to resist. Her hair was a red-gold cloud around her neck and shoulders, and every time she moved her head he could smell the fruity fragrance of her shampoo. Her eyes were so bright they could have auditioned for a position in the Milky Way. And her lips... Dear God, her lips were plump and shimmering with lip-gloss, and it was all he could do not to lean forward and kiss her.

'Yes. You,' Ivy said, her smile triggering those cute dimples again. 'I wouldn't feel comfortable with anyone else. I need someone I know and trust. It would be too hard for me to do this with a stranger.'

Do what with a stranger? And why did she trust *him*? Louis wasn't so sure he deserved her trust, given where his mind was leading him—straight into the gutter. He pushed his chair back and stood, putting a little more distance between them. He went over to the drinks cabinet and poured himself a neat whisky. He wasn't a heavy drinker—thankfully that was one way in which he was different from his father—but right then he could have drained the bottle and followed it with a brandy chaser.

He took a measured sip and turned back to face her. 'I'm not sure I'm following you. What exactly do you want me to do?'

Ivy shifted from foot to foot, her hands interlaced in front of her body, her cheeks blooming again with colour. 'I have a problem with…with sex…'

Louis sprayed most of his second sip of whisky out of his mouth on a choked splutter. He wiped his mouth with the back of his hand. 'Are you sure I'm the person you should be talking to about this?'

Her mouth was down-turned at the corners, her shoulders slumped. 'I'm still a virgin and I'm almost thirty. I need to do something to fix myself otherwise I'll never find a partner—especially today, when everyone's so adventurous and open about sex. I'm a pariah. An uptight prude who can't even get undressed unless the lights are out.'

To say he was shocked was an understatement. Almost thirty and still a virgin? He'd lost his in his teens. Didn't most people? She wasn't particularly religious, so deliberate abstinence could not be the issue. Had something happened to put her off doing the deed? His skin crawled at the thought of some pushy guy pressuring her or abusing her. Anger rose in his gut and climbed into his throat with acid-laced claws. Louis put down his glass of whisky and took a deep steadying breath.

'Firstly, Ivy, you don't have to fix anything. You should only do what you're comfortable doing when, and only when, you're comfortable doing it.'

'But I might never be comfortable if I don't do something sooner rather than later. I can't go on like this. It's beyond embarrassing going on a date with a new guy and then bolting out the door as soon as he touches me.'

Louis rapid blinked. Tried to ignore the little stab of unease in his gut about her hooking up with some guy she barely knew. 'Let me get this straight... You want *me* to *sleep* with you?'

Her cheeks darkened but her eyes contained a single-minded light that was more than a little unsettling. 'No one is never going to be interested in me unless I get over my inhibitions. There's no point me trying to date anyone unless I feel more confident. And I don't think I'd be comfortable with anyone but you. I know you. I've known you for years. Plus, you know what you're doing with sex, and I think you'd be the best person to teach me.'

A trap door creaked open in his mind, a narrow gap revealing a host of erotic possibilities he had locked down there, out of sight. Getting naked with her, doing all the things he'd been trying not to think about for the last couple of years. Gliding his hands down her beautiful body, exploring her breasts, discovering all the sweet contours of her feminine frame. Kissing her, touching her, their limbs entwined...

Louis held up his hand like a stop sign. 'Whoa there, Ivy. You're talking like a crazy person. I'm an architect, not a sex therapist. And, besides, we're friends. The friends-to-lovers thing never works.'

'But in this case it would work, because I'm not after anything other than a one-night stand. That's what everyone calls you, right? Mr Amazing One-Night Stand. I'm not asking you to marry me. I just want you to have sex with me one time so I can say I'm not a virgin any—'

'I heard you the first time,' Louis cut in quickly. 'I'm not interested.' If he heard her ask him to have sex with her one more time, he'd be a goner. There was only so much self-control he could muster at a given time.

She looked like a puppy that had been refused a pat. Her teeth sank back into her bottom lip and she bent down to pick up her bag from the floor, where it had fallen earlier, and then straightened and levelled him with a wounded look. 'Is it because I'm not attractive enough? You find me a turn-off?'

Louis tried to keep his gaze away from her cleavage. Tried but failed. 'You're one of the most attractive women I've ever met but—'

'Prove it.' She put her bag on his desk and approached him. He had forgotten how tiny she was until she was toe-to-toe with him. She had to crane her neck to maintain eye contact. Her eyes were clear and her expression determined, and his self-control had a panic attack.

Louis cleared his suddenly tight throat. She was so close, if he moved half a step her breasts would brush his chest. He could see every pore of the creamy perfection of her skin, the only blemish a tiny white two-centimetre scar above her left eyebrow. Her blue eyes were an intricate mosaic of deep blue, purple and indigo with wide jet-black pupils as infinite as outer space. Her lower lip was twice the size of her top one, the shape of her mouth a perfect Cupid's bow. *And don't get me started about those adorable dimples.*

'Don't be ridiculous. I don't have to prove anything.'

His tone was curt and cold but his blood was hot. Smoking hot. He placed his hands on her upper arms, ostensibly to keep her from him, but somehow his fingers sank into the softness of her cashmere sweater and the distance between their bodies closed. Had he moved or had she? Her hips brushed against his, her breasts poking into his chest, and a wave of hot, tight longing barrelled through him like a tornado.

'Kiss me, Louis.' Her voice was just shy of a whisper, her vanilla-scented breath dancing across his lips. 'Prove to me you don't find me a total turn-off.'

He'd kissed lots of women and had always been able to walk away. Always. It was his modus operandi. No strings. No follow-up dates. Just plain and simple one-night sex. But if he kissed Ivy he would be crossing a line he'd sworn he would never cross. He kept his relationships short—if you could call them relationships. Those 'relationships' were easy to walk away from without regret. But he already had a long-term relationship with Ivy. Not a sexual one, but a friendship that would be completely changed if he acted on her wishes. The last thing he wanted to do was rush into a one-night stand with Ivy until he understood exactly what she wanted from him.

His conscience leaned indolently against the back wall of his mind and smirked. *Oh, so you're actually going to consider sleeping with her?*

Louis summoned every bit of self-restraint he possessed and stepped back from her, dropping his hands from around her arms. He schooled his features into suave city playboy. 'If I kiss you, things could get hotter than you can handle. Are you sure you're ready for that, *ma petite*?'

A flicker of uncertainty passed over her face. 'Not completely, but if you won't do it then I'll have to resort to my Plan B.'

'Which is?'

Her small chin came up to a defiant height. 'I'll have to ask a stranger to do it.'

He held her gaze for a throbbing moment, his mind whirling with images of creepy strangers taking advantage of her guilelessness, and his guts churned with bile. No way was he going to let some filthy jerk touch her. There were some real weirdos out there these days, men who wanted to fulfil their darkest pornographic fantasies without considering their partner's wishes. Ivy wouldn't have the experience to handle something like that. It would totally destroy her.

'No, you will not do that.' He channelled his best schoolmaster voice, throwing in a deep frown for good measure.

Her expression became hopeful. 'So, you'll agree to help me?'

Louis speared a hand through his hair, then stood with his hands on his hips in a braced position. 'We'll come to that later. For now, I want to know why you got to the age of almost thirty with your virginity intact.'

Her gaze drifted away from his, her cheeks firing up again. 'I've always been a little bit uncomfortable even talking about sex, mostly because my mum has always been so out there about it—especially since she and Dad got divorced.' She glanced up at him. 'Did you know she's studying to be a sex therapist now? Sex is all she talks about.'

'Yeah, I heard about her new venture. But why not talk to her about…?'

A look of horror passed over her face. 'No way! I want to fix this on my own… Well, not quite on my own…with your help.'

He went back behind his desk and pulled out his office chair. 'Look, I'm on a tight deadline, but can we talk about this over dinner tonight? I'll pick you up at eight.'

Dinner? His conscience smirked again. *Dinner and then what? Dinner and nothing, that's what. Nothing to see here, as the saying goes.*

'Are you still in the flat in Islington?'

'Yep. My two friends Millie and Zoey have moved in with me now. The rent on my own was killing me.'

'Why didn't you say something? I could have helped you.'

A glimmer of pride entered her gaze. 'You've done enough for my family already—helping Mum with the mortgage last year when she got behind with the payments. She'll never be able to repay you, you know. She's always been hopeless with money.'

Louis' frown was back. Harder. Deeper. Seemed no one kept a promise these days. He'd insisted Deirdre Kennedy keep quiet about his offer to help her out of yet another financial hole because he genuinely hadn't wanted Ronan or Ivy to suffer any more stress than they already had. He'd been particularly worried about Ronan. Finally coming out to your divorced parents and then being rejected by your father was enough to set off an existential crisis in the most stable of people. It had taken the best part of two years for him to feel comfortable Ronan was out of danger.

Louis sat in his chair and absently straightened some papers on his desk. 'She told you about that?'

Ivy nodded, her look grim. 'I forced it out of her. Ronan doesn't know, does he?'

He leaned back in his chair, picked up his fountain pen and rocked it back and forth between his thumb and index finger. 'It wasn't a big deal to me. It's just money. And I didn't want to worry you or Ronan. You had enough going on with your father's reaction to Ronan's situation.'

She gave a tight-lipped smile, but it was at odds with the shadow that passed through her gaze. 'All the same, it was nice of you to step in like that. Mum would have lost the house if it hadn't been for you.'

Louis let the pen drop back on the desk with a little clatter. 'Have you told Ronan about this hare-brained scheme of yours?'

Ivy brought her gaze back to his. 'No. But he's hardly likely to find out now he's in Australia with Ricky. Anyway, he'd worry too much. He's been warning me for years about not getting fanciful ideas about you.'

'What fanciful ideas?' Louis knew he shouldn't ask.

'He said you weren't the marriage-and-babies type. But I told him not to worry about me because I would never be interested in a man who didn't want marriage and babies.'

If she mentioned 'marriage and babies' one more

time he was going to blow a fuse. Not his most favourite words in the English language. His parents had married and had one baby and look how that had turned out. Thirty-five-plus years of misery for all concerned. 'I'm not sure falling in love works quite that way,' Louis pointed out. 'People fall in love with the wrong people all the time.' His parents being a case in point. Totally unsuited to each other but they soldiered on regardless. 'Soldiered' being a pertinent word, since every day was a battleground of injured egos, resentments, grievances and bitterness.

Ivy tilted her head and studied him for a moment. 'Have you ever been in love?'

'No.'

Her eyebrows rose. 'Not even once? Like when you were a teenager or…?'

'Nope.'

'But surely you must have felt a flicker of something for someone along the line?' She looked at him quizzically. 'You've had heaps of lovers. Have you just been using them all for sex?'

'Ahem, you're the one who wants to use me for sex, so don't go jumping up on your high horse just yet,' Louis said, holding her gaze.

She shifted her nose from side to side like a cute little bunny. 'It's not the same thing at all. I have an established relationship with you. You're like an older brother to me.' Her forehead creased in a tiny frown and she added, 'Well, maybe not so much a brother figure—because that would be kind of creepy and weird, having sex with you—but a good mate. Someone I can always rely on.'

A good mate would have stopped this conversation before it had got started. Drawn a thick black line through it. Frogmarched her out of his office and told her to go and get some therapy. Talking about this scheme of hers was like allowing a dangerous mind-altering vapour to infiltrate the air-conditioning. It was fuelling his forbidden fantasies, making it harder and harder to find a reason to say no. 'Have you told anyone about this plan of yours?'

'No. I wanted to ask you first.'

Louis leaned forward again and straightened the same papers next to his computer. 'I can't believe we're even having this conversation.' He glanced back at her with a stern frown. 'Are you sure you know what you're doing?'

Ivy picked up her bag from his desk and smiled so brightly she could have been advertising toothpaste. 'But that's the whole point—I don't know what I'm doing, but you're going to teach me.'

The scary thing was... Louis was seriously, danger-ously, tempted to do exactly that.

CHAPTER TWO

Ivy put the last touches to her make-up in the bedroom at her flat before her dinner date with Louis. Dinner date. Such strange words to be using when it came to her relationship with Louis. Normally they had a quick catch-up over coffee or lunch. Dinner sounded a lot more…intimate. But she wasn't actually *dating* him. She was going to convince him to take her virginity, which would entail getting hot and sweaty with him.

A flutter of nerves erupted in her belly like a swarm of bumble bees. *Getting naked with him.* She smoothed a hand down her stomach. She hadn't got naked with anyone. She'd come close a couple of times but had freaked out. But any reservations she had would have to be put aside. She *had* to do this. How else would she gain the experience she needed? She couldn't face yet another dating disaster where a date wanted to take things to the next level and she bolted out the door like a Victorian prude.

The humiliating shame of her previous dates made her cringe on a daily basis. It had stopped her from venturing further into the dating world out of fear of further embarrassment. She'd had five dates and given up accepting any other invitations. Five dates! How pathetic was that? She didn't know why she had become so sensually locked down but, ever since she'd hit puberty, the thought of sharing her body with someone had paralysed her with fear.

What if they didn't like her body? What if she wasn't the right shape or size? What if she didn't do or say the right thing and they thought her a freak? What if she fell in love and got rejected like her mother had got rejected by her father?

Every time she went on a date those fears would flap through her brain like a swarm of frenzied bats. *What if? What if? What if?* It made it impossible to think of anything else but escaping as soon as she could. Not exactly the best way to find the life partner you'd been dreaming of finding since you'd been a little girl.

But her plan to get Louis to help her was a masterstroke of genius. He was exactly the right person to help her overcome this hurdle of intimacy avoidance. Then she would be free to search for Mr Right.

One of her flatmates, Millie, peered round Ivy's bedroom door. 'Woo-hoo. You look gorgeous. Are you going on a date?' She waggled her eyebrows meaningfully.

'Don't get too excited. It's not really a date.' Ivy put her lip-gloss back in her cosmetics bag. 'I'm going out for dinner with Louis Charpentier.'

Millie came further into the bedroom, eyebrows raised. 'Your brother's friend? The four-times-and-counting hot bachelor of the year? For dinner? How is that not a date?'

Ivy adjusted her little black dress over her hips. 'We're just…catching up.'

Millie's gaze ran over Ivy's outfit and make-up. 'Mmm, methinks you've gone to a lot of trouble for a simple catch-up with a friend. Are you sure nothing's going on?'

Ivy flicked an imaginary piece of lint off her shoulder. 'Of course, I'm sure. It's not a big deal. Louis likes to check up on me now and again now that Ronan's living in Sydney.'

Millie gave a light laugh. 'Gosh, I would love someone as hot as Louis Charpentier to check up on me every now and again. What do you two talk about when you get together?'

'Just…stuff. Movies, books, work—that sort of thing.' A trickle of fear slithered its way down Ivy's spine. What had she got herself in to? She was actually *going to have sex*. With her brother's best friend. *Eek.* Ivy felt bad about not being totally truthful with her friend. Why should it matter if she told Millie about her plan? But surely the less people who knew, the better? It was a one-off thing with Louis. No point allowing her friends to think it was anything else.

Millie leaned down and peered into Ivy's face. 'Why are you blushing?'

'I'm not blushing.' Ivy might as well not have bothered with using blusher, the way her cheeks were feeling.

Millie straightened and folded her arms. 'Come on. Fess up. What is going on with you and Louis?'

Ivy should know it was virtually impossible to keep a secret from Millie. Her friend was like a sniffer dog for secrets. The trouble was, she wasn't so good at keeping them. Ivy met her friend's gaze and released a sigh. 'He's helping me with something.'

Millie frowned. 'What something? Has your mum been leaning on you for money again?'

'No. It's about me. About my...problem.'

Millie's eyes widened to the size of light bulbs. Football-stadium light bulbs. 'The V problem? Seriously—you're asking him to do what, exactly?'

'I'm going to have a one-night stand with him. Then my problem will be solved.'

'And he's agreed to that?'

'Not in so many words, hence dinner tonight. But I'm not going to let him talk me out of it. He's the only person who can help me. The only person I *want* to help me. I'd be too embarrassed or shy with anyone else.'

Millie's expression was etched in concern. 'But what if you develop feelings for him? I mean, different from what you have for him now?'

Ivy laughed, picked up her hairbrush and began stroking it through her hair. 'You mean like fall in love with him? Not a chance. He's not the settling down type. It would be stupid to fall in love with him, knowing he doesn't want the same things in life that I do. Louis only has one-nighters. I want someone who's there for the long haul. Someone who'll stick around no matter what—unlike my father. Not that Louis is anything like my father, but you know what I mean. Once a playboy, always a playboy.'

Millie's expression was so sceptical she could have been keynote speaker at a sceptics' conference. 'What your father's done really sucks, but have you actually looked at Louis lately? I mean, *really* looked at him? The man is traffic-stopping gorgeous.'

'I know, but I don't think of him that way,' Ivy said, spraying perfume on her pulse points. She wasn't sure why she didn't see Louis the way other women did... although there had been a strange little flicker of something when their hands had touched that afternoon. A tingle travelled up her arm like a current of electricity. And when he'd used a French term of endearment, well, what girl wouldn't have got a shiver down her spine? But her preference had always been for blond men and Louis, with his Anglo-French ancestry, had pitch-black hair. Not her type at all.

'You might think of him that way once you get naked with him.'

Get naked with him. The words made her skin lift in a delicate shiver. Ivy put the perfume bottle down with a definitive clunk. 'Not going to happen. This is just about sex, nothing else.'

'So how long are you going to be sleeping with him?'

'Just for one night.'

Ivy picked up her evening bag and smoothed her hand over her fluttering stomach. *If I can convince him and then have the guts to go through with it.*

'Wish me luck?'

Millie gave her a long, searching look. 'You're going to need more than luck. You're the last person on earth—apart from me, of course—who's a one-night stand sort of person. People are always telling me to move on from losing Julian but it's too hard these days to find someone who doesn't expect you to put out before you even get to know them.'

Millie had tragically lost her fiancé, Julian, to brain cancer only weeks before their wedding three years ago. His battle to fight it had been long and gruelling and it was heartbreakingly sad Millie hadn't got to marry her childhood sweetheart before he died. Apart from a disastrous blind date set up by another friend a couple of months ago, Millie had point-blank refused to think of finding room in her heart for anyone else.

Ivy took Millie's hand and gave it a squeeze. 'What you had with Jules was really special, and I don't blame you for finding it hard to think of moving on. But don't you see? I want that sort of love one day too, but I won't find it spending yet another weekend at home alone watching box sets.'

Millie touched Ivy on the arm, her expression serious. 'Are you sure you're doing the right thing? This might change your relationship with Louis for ever. Are you prepared to risk that?'

Ivy straightened her shoulders. 'I have to do this, Millie. I want to be able to date a guy without my inexperience hanging over me and this is the best way to do it.' She leaned forward and kissed her friend on the cheek. 'But thanks for being concerned about me.'

The doorbell sounded at that moment and Ivy's stomach pitched. 'That'll be Louis.' She waved a hand on her way out of the bedroom. 'Don't wait up!'

Louis had lost count of the number of times he'd taken a woman out to dinner, so there was no reason why this time he should be feeling as if this date was something special.

Date? Is that what this is?

No. It. Was. Not. He hadn't committed to anything. One part of him was determined to talk Ivy out of her plan to have him initiate her into the joy of sex, the other part of him was mentally stockpiling condoms and scented candles. What had got into him? Where were his set-in-stone boundaries?

Louis adjusted his tie and then pressed the doorbell on Ivy's flat. The sound of heels click-clacking on floorboards sent his pulse up. Was it his imagination or could he already smell her perfume? The door opened and Ivy stood there in a little black dress that clung to every delicious curve on her body, the vertiginous heels she was wearing showcasing her slim legs and ankles. Her hair was loose around her shoulders, and his fingers itched so much to reach out and touch it, he had to shove his hands into his trouser pockets.

'Hiya.' Her lips curved around a smile and desire coiled hot and tight in his groin. Her smoky eye make-up made her periwinkle-blue eyes look all the more stunning, and her shimmering lip-gloss highlighted the perfect shape of her mouth. Her utterly kissable, sexy-as-hell mouth. Heaven help him.

'Good evening.' Louis stretched his mouth into one of his carefully rationed smiles. 'You look amazing.'

Amazing, sexy, gorgeous, stunning, beautiful... The words piled into his brain as if he had swallowed a thesaurus. She didn't look like his friend's sister any more, which was a problem, because he needed to get those boundaries firmly back in place. And fast.

'Thank you.'

There was a funny little silence.

'Right. Well, then.' Louis took his hands out of his pockets and gestured towards the street where his car was parked. 'Shall we go?'

Ivy stepped down the three steps to the footpath but almost stumbled on the last one and Louis shot out one of his hands to stabilise her. 'Whoa, there. Take it easy in those shoes. How on earth do you walk in them?' His fingers moved from grasping her wrist to curl around hers and another punch of lust hit him in the groin.

'I like wearing heels. It makes me taller. Otherwise I'd end up with neckache trying to look up at people all the time, particularly people as tall as you.'

He kept hold of her hand on the way to his car. Her fingers were soft as silk and her hand so small it was completely swallowed up by his. 'I'll have to get you a stepladder or something when you're with me. I don't want you to break your ankle on my behalf.'

She gave a tinkling-bell laugh and playfully shoulder bumped him. 'Don't be silly. So, where are we having dinner? I'm starving.'

'A French restaurant.'

She grinned up at him. 'So you can dazzle me with your fluent French?'

'Something like that.' Louis was the one being dazzled. Big time. He knew he was crazy even to take her out to dinner, let alone contemplate anything else. She was exactly the type of girl he avoided—the type who wanted the husband, the house and the sleepy hound in front of the cosy fireplace. He'd missed out on the settling-down gene, or had had it pummelled out of him through witnessing the marital misery of his parents. These days the sense of claustrophobia at being in a relationship longer than twenty-four hours was suffocating. He enjoyed sex for the physical relief it gave but, since his stalker, the thought of a longer relationship made him break out into hives.

In his opinion, long-term commitment was a dirty word.

Louis helped her into the passenger seat and tried not to notice how her black dress revealed a tiny shadow of cleavage and a whole lot of her shapely thighs. Tried to ignore the way his pulse shot up and his blood thickened.

He strode to the driver's side and gave himself a stern talking to.

It's just dinner. Nothing else. You're going to talk her out of her crazy plan, remember?

'Louis?'

He flicked her a quick glance as the engine turned over. 'Yes?'

Her fingers were fiddling with the clasp on her evening bag, her cheeks a faint shade of pink. 'Do you carry condoms with you all the time?'

He stared blankly at her for a moment. 'Ah, well, yes, but we're not going to need them tonight.'

'But why not?'

His hands gripped the steering wheel so hard his

knuckles threatened to burst out of his skin. And that wasn't the only part of his anatomy fit to burst. The stirring in his groin sent hot tingles down his legs at the thought of making love to her. He met her gaze. 'We're not going to have sex, Ivy. Not tonight, not tomorrow, not—'

'Why not? I bet you have sex with other women on the first date.'

'This isn't a date,' he said through tight lips. 'It's a meeting to discuss your…situation.'

'My situation is that I want you to take my virginity. Why are you being so…so difficult about this?'

He sent her a sideways glance. 'You're not the one-night-stand type. You've got no experience of how to do this sort of hook-up.'

'Which is why I want you to give it to me.'

Louis clenched his jaw so hard, he thought he was going to crack his mandible. 'Look, I think we should talk about it some more before we go rushing into something with so many pitfalls. If we sleep together, it will change everything. We will never look at each other the same way again.'

'Does it matter? I mean, you have sex with heaps of women and it doesn't seem to be a problem.' She let out a whooshing sigh. 'Maybe it's *me* that's the problem. I'm so undesirable you can't bear the thought of touching me.'

If only it were that simple. He'd been fighting the temptation to touch her since she'd come into his office that afternoon. He was fighting it now. She was the most desirable woman he'd met in a long time. 'Feeling desire for someone doesn't mean I'll act on it. Not unless I'm convinced it's the right thing to do.'

'How else can I convince you? Do you know how embarrassing it is for me to be the only person in my circle of friends who's still a virgin? I can't imagine asking anyone else to help me. I would be too embarrassed—or at least more embarrassed, because it certainly wasn't easy asking you this afternoon. Hence the brandy. Imagine if I had to ask a stranger!'

His gut roiled at the thought of her going out with a stranger. Doing *anything* with a stranger. Louis forced himself to relax his grip on the steering wheel. 'I don't think we should rush into this without some proper checks and balances done first.'

'Fine. But let's not take too long about it—because I turn thirty in a month and no way am I going to celebrate my birthday as a flipping virgin.' She blew out a breath and continued, 'I know this has come as a shock to you, but I've been struggling with this for years. I hate it that I can be so confident at work but this area of my life is so stuffed up. I need to get past this in order to move on with my life. It's like there's a big fat pause button on my future. Solving this will press the go switch, I'm sure of it.'

Yes, but it was the 'go' switch he was most worried about. Worried about removing the boundaries he had set up. Relaxing his self-control. Doing things with her he had only done in his most wicked dreams.

She suddenly flashed him a teasing smile. 'Are you worried you might fall for me? Is that where your reluctance is coming from?'

He gave her the side-eye. 'I know how to keep my feelings in check.' He'd been doing it most of his life. Controlling his reaction to his father's acid tongue and overly critical eye. Ignoring his father's repeated digs about his choice of career and how he had let everybody down by not joining the family accounting business as expected. Ignoring his mother's incessant nit-picking over every aspect of his life, knowing deep down it was her way of compensating for her lack of power in her marriage, and her bitter disappointment at only having one child after several miscarriages.

He had witnessed way too many of his parents' fights in which bitter words had been exchanged, but one in particular had stuck in his mind as a ten-year-old child, so too the harrowing aftermath. His mother's admission into a mental health clinic for months on end after a suicide attempt. Louis had shut down his feelings at seeing his mother inside the walls of a locked mental-health unit. Her blank, flat look—as if someone had pulled out the power cord to her personality. He had suppressed his own despair in order to cope with his father's. When his mother had finally come home, his father had grovelled, begged, over-adapted and promised things he could never deliver.

That was forever love? Louis wanted nothing to do with it.

'I sometimes wish I could keep my feelings in check...' Ivy's tone contained a self-deprecating note. 'Ronan's always telling me I wear my heart on my sleeve. Both sleeves, actually.'

Louis glanced at her. 'Have you heard from your father lately?'

She sighed and looked down at her hands in her lap. 'No. I think he's blocked me on his phone. It's much worse for Ronan. The things Dad said to him were unforgiveable. I was really worried about him there for a bit.'

'Yeah, so was I.' Louis pulled into a parking spot near the restaurant and turned off the engine. 'But he seems happy now with Ricky.'

She swivelled in her seat to look at him. 'Louis?'

'Yes?'

Her eyes went to his mouth and a small frown settled on her forehead. The tip of her tongue came out and licked her lips, and scorching heat flooded his groin. The air tightened and the space between them shrank, his self-control wavering like a slab of concrete on a building site held by a gossamer thread. It would be so easy to reach for her hand, to stroke the creamy curve of her cheek, to lean forward and press his lips against the plump ripeness of hers. He could feel the magnetic pull of attraction drawing him closer, every cell in his body poised, primed for contact. In his mind he was already doing it—kissing her until they were both breathless, his tongue tangling with hers, his blood pounding like a tribal drum.

Go on, do it. You know you want to.

Her gaze met his and she gave one of her dazzling, dimpled smiles. 'Hey, for a moment there I thought you were going to kiss me.'

Louis traced the curve of her mouth with a lazy finger, fizzing sensations shooting through him. 'I was definitely thinking about it.' His voice was so rough it sounded as if he'd been snacking on gravel.

'Then why don't you do it?' Her voice was not much more than a breathy whisper that sent a wave of hot tingles across his scalp and down his spine.

He leaned across the gear shift and lowered his head until his mouth was barely an inch from hers. Her breath was milk and honey with a dash of cinnamon-sweetness, innocent, addictive. 'Once I kiss you, I can't *un*-kiss you.'

Her fan-like eyelashes came down over her eyes and her right hand came up and slid along the side of his face, the soft skin of her palm and fingers catching on his light stubble like fine silk on sandpaper. 'You worry too much.' She closed the distance between their mouths and touched his lips with the rose-petal softness of hers. It was the barest of touchdowns, but an explosion of sensation erupted in his lips. She eased back to look at him, her eyes dark and luminous. 'See? No harm done. It was just a kiss.'

Just a kiss? Her lips were a drug he hadn't known he had a weakness for until now. Before he could stop himself, Louis put a hand behind her head, splaying his fingers through the wild curls of her hair. Her mouth opened on a soft little gasp, as if his touch electrified her the same as hers did him.

He lowered his mouth to hers in achingly slow motion, drawn by a force as old as time. An irresistible force that sent his blood roaring through his veins and his willpower flying out the window. His lips finally met hers and incendiary heat charged from her mouth to his. He gave a low, deep groan and increased the pressure of his lips on hers, fuelled by an uncontrollable need for closer, firmer contact. Her mouth opened beneath the insistent pressure of his, her tongue brushing shyly against his. He cradled one side of her face, the other hand still buried in the red-gold tresses of her fragrant hair, his kiss deepening, his desire rising, his self-control wavering.

Ivy whimpered against his mouth, her hands coming up around his neck, her fingers playing with his short-cropped hair.

Every hair on his head tingled at the roots, every nerve in his body was on high alert, every reason for not sleeping with her retreating to the back of his mind. He breathed in the scent of her—spring flowers with an undertone of heady, intoxicating musk. Somehow, he sucked in some much-needed air before taking the kiss a step further, his tongue duelling with hers in a sexy tango that made his blood thunder through his body. Every time his tongue touched hers, a zapping lightning bolt of lust fired through him. Her lips were velvet-soft and he could taste her strawberry lip-gloss and his own salty, earthy and raw desire—a lethal blend of temptation. He knew he would never be able to eat a strawberry again without thinking of their first kiss.

Without thinking of *her*.

The thought was sobering enough to give him pause. He pulled back from her, lowering his hands from her cheek and the back of her head, his breathing still out of order, his body still roaring with lust. She looked as dazed as he felt—her eyes shining, her lips cherry-red and swollen, her cheeks tinged with pink.

'Well, that was a surprise.' Her tone was light, but a small frown appeared between her neat eyebrows and her gaze drifted back to his mouth. She moistened her lips with a quick dart of her tongue, her gaze coming back to his. 'I didn't think it would be as…as nice as that.'

'What? You haven't enjoyed being kissed before?'

'Not really, but with you it was…something else.' She touched her fingers to her lips as if she couldn't quite believe what had happened. Her fingers fell away and she added, 'Is it my imagination or was that kiss kind of off the charts?'

Louis fought not to smile. 'It was pretty damn good. You certainly don't need any tutoring in that department.'

She cocked her head like an inquisitive little bird. 'Hey, is that a smile you're trying to hide?' Her own mouth was curved in a smile that made something warm spread through his chest. But he could and would keep his emotions out of this. He did it all the time. A kiss was just a kiss. He wasn't going to commit to anything else that could have more troubling consequences. He unclipped his seatbelt and took the wireless car-key out of its slot on the dashboard. 'Come on. Let's eat. I'm starving.'

But it wasn't a physical hunger gnawing at him.

It was good old-fashioned, rip-roaring lust.

Ivy was still reliving every moment of their kiss when they were shown to their table in the fancy French restaurant in Soho. Their table was in a secluded part of the restaurant and she wondered if Louis had requested it especially to avoid public scrutiny. She knew he wasn't fond of the attention his high-profile career as an award-winning architect occasionally attracted from the press. She herself had been guilty of poring over articles about him online, but mostly in a he's-my-brother's-best-friend-and-I'm-proud-of-his-achievements sort of way. Nothing else. She had zero interest in him romantically…although that kiss had certainly been a bit of an eye-opener. Her lips were still tingling, along with other parts of her body that had rarely, if ever, tingled before.

Louis looked up from his perusal of the menu. 'Is there anything that you particularly fancy?'

You. Ivy was a little shocked at how much she fancied him. Up until recently, he had simply been her brother's best friend—the person she could always rely on to help her, which was why she had approached him with 'the V plan'. But that kiss had changed something inside her. Maybe Louis was right—they wouldn't be able to go back to the way they'd been. Changing the dynamic of a relationship—any relationship—was something that could be risky.

She wasn't the greatest fan of change. She'd been in the same job since university, she'd had the same friends since school. She hadn't coped well with her parents' divorce when she'd been a teenager. She hated moving house. She couldn't pack a bag for a weekend away without worrying she might leave something behind that she needed.

But hadn't things already changed between them? How could she see Louis as anyone other than the first man who had set her mouth on fire? Lust was a new experience for her. Her previous dates hadn't stirred anywhere near the same sensations in her body—she hadn't felt a thing from any of them. She had learned from her parents' divorce that the last thing she wanted to do was develop feelings for someone who couldn't love her back. But all Louis had done was kiss her and she was hot for him. She could still taste him in her mouth, could still feel the brush of his hand against her face, his fingers buried in her hair.

She shivered and buried her head in the menu, wondering if her cheeks were as warm as they felt. 'Let me see, now... Snails? Frogs' legs? Steak tartare?'

'Tell me you're joking.' His tone was so dry it could have mopped up an oil spill.

Ivy gave him a cheeky smile. 'I'm joking. But, hey, what sort of Frenchman are you to turn your nose up at *escargots*?'

'I'm only half-French. My mother is English.' He picked up the wine list and opened it. 'The only time I ate snails was when my father insisted on it when I was six years old.'

'And?'

He didn't stop looking at the menu, but she had a feeling he wasn't registering a single word written there. His features tightened as if he was trying to keep an unpleasant memory contained. 'I was violently ill.'

'Are you allergic to them or something?'

Louis put the menu down and met her gaze with a

now bland expression. 'No. But, since they're my father's favourite dish, I was left in no doubt of how much I'd disappointed him.' He tapped the wine menu with his fingers. 'Champagne or white wine…or how about some brandy?' His grey-blue eyes glinted and something between her legs fluttered like the wings of a moth.

Ivy shifted in her seat, winding her mind back to his earlier comment rather than examine too closely what her body was currently doing. 'I'll have white wine. What are your parents like? You've never told me anything about them before. Are you close to them?'

He gave a soft grunt that said everything that needed to be said. So too did the bitter twist of his mouth and the ripple of tension along his jaw. 'I have very little in common with either of them other than DNA.'

The waiter came for the drinks order at that moment and it gave Ivy a chance to surreptitiously study Louis. It occurred to her that she had known him for years—close to a decade—and yet there was still so much about him she didn't know. He was a reserved type of man, similar to her brother Ronan, which had strengthened the bond between them during her brother's difficult time in finally embracing his sexuality. But she hadn't known anything about Louis' relationship with his family other than he was an only child and that his father ran a large international accounting firm with branches throughout Europe. The unknown aspect of Louis' character was a timely reminder not to allow her feelings to get involved. But, perversely, it made her all the more fascinated by him. Who was he behind the Mr Amazing One-Night Stand persona?

The waiter left and Ivy picked up the conversation again. 'Do your parents live here or in France?'

'They split their time between the two,' Louis said. 'My father inherited my grandparents' chateau in the Loire valley when they died a few years ago. It's been in our family for five generations.'

'So, being their only child, you'll inherit it one day?'

He gave her an inscrutable look. 'Perhaps.'

Ivy wrinkled her forehead in a frown. 'Perhaps? What does that mean?'

He let out a slow breath and moved his water glass a quarter turn. 'It means my father is likely to change his mind after some perceived slight from me, so I don't have any expectations in that regard. I've made my own money. I don't need his.'

Ivy picked up her own glass of water. 'Gosh, and here I was thinking my father was a pain in the butt.' She took a sip of water before putting the glass back down. 'Not that he was always like that…'

Louis met her gaze. 'Do you miss him? Ronan told me you used to be really close to him before your parents divorced.'

She found it hard to hold his gaze and looked at the small flower arrangement on the table instead. Her parents divorcing when she was thirteen had been tough, but her father's rejection of her because of her loyalty to her brother had been the hardest thing she had ever faced. Her father's love was something she'd thought she'd always be able to rely on, but she'd been wrong.

His ultimatum that she cease all contact with Ronan otherwise never see him again had totally blindsided her. To be made to choose between her adored older brother and equally adored father was beyond cruel.

'I thought he loved me. I really did. I thought he loved both of us, and Mum too back in the day. He used to say Mum's quirkiness and out-there personality was what attracted him in the first place, but where was his love for her when he had that affair when I was thirteen? Their divorce was bad enough but at least I still got to spend time with my dad on weekend access visits. I never doubted his love for me and Ronan. But, since Ronan told us he was gay two years ago, Dad turned off his love for us like turning off a light switch. I still can't quite get my head around it. I mean, we're his flesh and blood, and yet he refuses to have anything to do with us. I feel like I've loved someone all my life that I didn't really know at all.'

Louis reached across the table and covered her hand with the broad expanse of his. The skin on the back of her hand tingled, the hairs on the back of her neck standing up, the soft flutter between her legs returning. His eyes were an intense smoky blue—clouds and sky, shadows and sunlight, unknowable depths and shifting shallows.

'I'm sorry you've been so hurt by him. But it's his problem, not yours. You have to remember you and Ronan did nothing wrong.'

Ivy gave him a wry smile. 'You should have been a therapist.'

His gaze dipped to her mouth for a brief moment, his

own mouth twisting in a rueful half-smile. He removed his hand from hers and sat back in his chair. 'Yes, well, I've been handling difficult people all my life.'

Ivy wanted to ask more about his family, but just then the waiter came back with their wine and, once it was poured, he took their meal order before discreetly melting away again.

Ivy picked up her glass and raised it in a toast. 'What shall we drink to? One night without strings?' On the surface she sounded cool and calm about sleeping with him but on the inside her nerves were going haywire. What if she freaked out just as she had the other times? But then she recalled their kiss and thought maybe she wouldn't freak out. Maybe making love with him would be like kissing him—wonderful, amazing. But how would she know without convincing him to do it?

Louis' mouth flattened. 'Here's the thing—it's never without strings. It's rare for two people to want the same thing out of a fling, no matter how short it is.'

'But as long as we're clear on the rules from the outset why should it be a problem? I mean, we're not strangers—we're friends who will continue to have a relationship once our night together is over.'

One of his ink-black eyebrows rose in a sceptical arc. 'Will we?'

'Of course,' Ivy said. 'Why wouldn't we? You're Ronan's best friend. I will never forget how much you've supported him over the years. You were the first person he came out to, years before he told anyone else. I truly think he wouldn't have made it without your support and acceptance.'

'Which is why I'm concerned about this plan of yours.' His expression was etched in lines of gravitas. 'What if it proves too awkward to go back to being friends?'

Ivy let out a gusty sigh. Was this going to be the story of her life? Constant rejection? 'I think you're looking for excuses not to sleep with me. All right. You win. Forget about my plan. I'll find someone else.'

There was a tight silence.

Louis reached for her hand again, his fingers warm and strong over hers. 'No. Don't do that.' His eyes held hers in an unwavering lock. 'I'm still getting my head around what you want from me.'

'Why? Because I have sexual needs just like anyone else?' Ivy asked, pulling her hand out of his. 'I'm not a child, Louis. I'm a fully-grown woman and I want to feel like one in bed with a man. But how can I if I freak out at the thought of undressing in front of a guy?'

'Have you gone on any dates in the past?'

'Four.' Ivy mentally cringed at her paltry number of dates. No doubt Louis' dates numbered six figures by now.

'Only four?'

'Yep, and they were all disasters.'

His dark brows drew together, a shadow of concern backlighting his gaze. 'Why?'

Ivy released a heavy sigh. 'The first one of my dates asked me out for a drink. That was fine until he said he forgot his wallet and he suggested we swing by his house and…'

'You didn't go with him, did you?' His frown was deeper, almost savage in its intensity.

Ivy wasn't sure how to answer. How could she tell him she was afraid of trusting someone enough to let them get that close to her? As physically close as two people could be? Not just physically close but emotionally close. That was even more terrifying. 'Well, I was so new to dating, I didn't really know what else to do. He asked me out, so I went with him out of politeness. But once we got to his flat he tried to kiss me and touch me and I found it all a bit too much too soon. The second date was a bit better but ended much the same. We met for a drink and then went to a nightclub and then went back to his place.'

'Did he pressure you to go home with him?'

'Not really. I wanted to go. I actually liked him more than the other guy. I thought there was some potential there for a proper relationship. We kissed a bit, but I can't say I enjoyed it. And as soon as he started to undress me I freaked out. It was so embarrassing. He must have thought I was a crazy person. I bolted out the door and caught a cab home. The other dates were much the same. I'd be sort of fine until it came to the kissing and touching part and then I would freeze or run. I haven't dated anyone since. I'm rubbish at it, which is why I have to do something about it before it's too late.'

'It sounds to me like you've had a bunch of crap dates. You shouldn't let it put you off dating again.'

Ivy's shoulders slumped on a sigh. 'I'm not confident enough to date someone I don't know. But how can I get to know someone if I don't date them? It's an impossible situation.'

There was a silence.

He picked up his wine glass but didn't raise it to his mouth. 'Maybe I can help you with that.'

Ivy's eyes flicked back to his. 'How?'

His eyes drifted to her mouth once more. 'We could go on some dates together, to help you build your confidence around men.'

'You mean sleep with me? You'll actually do…?'

He held up his hand like a stop sign. 'Wait. Hear me out.' He lowered his hand to the table. 'I think what's happened with your last dates is, you felt pressured the whole time about having sex straight up. What might help is spending time with me—for instance, where sex is a possibility rather than a given.'

Ivy frowned. 'Sex as a possibility? Seriously, is that what you think every time you go on a date, Mr Amazing One-Night Stand?'

He gave her a mock glower. 'Not usually, but neither do I pressure a woman to have sex if I don't think she wants the same thing. You and I can spend a bit of time together to help you feel more in control.'

Maybe he had a point. The possibility of sex might somehow be less threatening than the certainty of it… And yet strangely, because it would be Louis and not some other guy she was randomly dating, she wanted certainty. 'Okay. So, where will we go?'

'Look, if we're going to do this, then I think we need to keep a low profile. I don't want the press sniffing around and it getting back to Ronan.'

Ivy could understand his guardedness on one level but another part of her wondered if his reluctance to be seen in public with her had more to do with her looks. She wasn't his usual type. He went for tall and tanned leggy blondes, and she was short and curvy, her hair was red and her skin as white as milk. Not exactly billboard model material.

'Fine. We can do that. When do we start?'

He took a deep sip of his wine before he answered. 'Are you free this Friday night?'

Ivy rolled her eyes. 'I'm free *every* Friday night. That's the whole problem.'

A smile played at the edges of his mouth. 'I don't know what's wrong with the young men in London to overlook you for all this time.'

She gave him a rueful glance. 'It's not the young men that's the problem. It's me. I've refused heaps of offers of dates. But hopefully you'll be able to fix me.'

His smile faded and a frown appeared on his forehead. 'You don't need fixing, Ivy. There's nothing wrong with you.'

'What if I'm frigid? What if I can't get over my inhibitions?'

'We'll work on building your confidence first and I bet the rest will sort itself out.'

Ivy grasped his hand across the table. 'Thank you.'

He picked up her hand and brought it up to his lips, holding her gaze with the grey-blue intensity of his. He pressed a soft-as-air kiss to her bent knuckles, sending a wave of heat through her entire body. Electric fizzes and tingles that made her acutely aware of the throbbing pulse deep and low in her pelvis. She couldn't break his gaze even if she'd wanted to. She was transfixed by the naked need she could see reflected there, the same need she could feel vibrating in her body.

But he still hadn't fully committed to sleeping with her and the clock was ticking as she approached her thirtieth birthday. *Tick. Tick. Tick.* What if he refused to do as she asked? What if his 'possibility of sex' became an impossibility for him? The thought of hooking up with a stranger was even more distressing to her now, especially since she had been kissed by Louis. His kiss had surprised and delighted her in a way no other kiss had. Her previous dates had kissed her, but those kisses hadn't been a patch on Louis'. He'd suggested spending time together first, and that sounded all fine and dandy, but what she wanted—needed—was to offload her inhibitions. And the only way to do that was to get the deed done. With him.

The moment was broken by the waiter turning up with their entrée but, all through the rest of the meal, Ivy was conscious of Louis' every movement. It was as if her body's radar had a new setting, aware of him in a way it hadn't been before. His hands as he operated his cutlery. The movement of his lips as he took a sip of wine. The way his crisp ice-blue business shirt framed his broad shoulders and muscular chest. The tan of his skin that hinted at the amount of time he spent outdoors. The long, straight blade of his nose, the aristocratic contour of his cheekbones, the dark slash of his eyebrows above his sharply intelligent eyes.

As far as the male package went, he had everything—looks, wealth, stability, sex appeal. Why hadn't she noticed that brooding sex appeal before? Or maybe she had but had dismissed it, thinking he would never be interested in her.

But he *was* interested in her. His kiss had proved that without a doubt. The chemistry between them was unmistakable, obvious even to someone with as little experience as her.

Ivy picked up her napkin and dabbed at each corner of her mouth. 'Just out of interest—have you ever made love to a virgin before?'

Louis blinked as if her question had startled him out of a private reverie. 'No.' He put down his knife and fork in the 'finished' position on his dinner plate.

Ivy picked up her wine glass, a strange tickly sensation trickling down the back of her legs. 'Does the thought of doing so make you nervous?'

His eyes came back to hers and another jolting sensation pulsed through her body. 'No. I can see now how much your virginity is troubling you.'

She studied him for a moment. 'So, you're really serious about helping me?'

'One thing you should know about me, *ma chérie*. Once I commit to a goal, I always see it through. Always.'

Ivy suppressed a delicious shudder. *Lucky me.*

CHAPTER THREE

'SO HOW DID your dinner with Louis Charpentier go?' Zoey, her other flatmate, asked the next morning. 'I hope you don't mind, but Millie told me about "the plan". Did he agree to it?'

So much for keeping her plan a secret. One thing was certain, Millie would never cut it as an undercover agent. 'Yes and no. I think he's stalling but I'm going to change his mind. I have to. I've only got a month to get this done.' Ivy reached for a coffee pod and popped it in the machine. 'We're going out on Friday night.' Saying those words out loud made her body tingle all over in anticipation. Louis hadn't touched her again after he'd dropped her home the night before, and it surprised her how much she'd wanted him to.

'Ooh! Where's he taking you?' Zoey leaned on the counter near the coffee machine, her own steaming cup cradled in her hands.

'I don't know. He didn't say.' Ivy spoke over the noise of the coffee machine. 'Do you think I'm crazy to ask him to help me?'

'Not really,' Zoey said. 'You're friends, so you already trust him. That's huge when it comes to physical intimacy.'

'He's not actually agreed to sleep with me, or at least not on the first date. He just wants to spend time with me first with sex being a possibility rather than a given. He thinks it will help me to gain more confidence around men.'

'Listen, honey, if a man wants to spend time with you he wants to sleep with you.' Zoey's tone was dry.

Ivy was still in two minds about what Louis wanted. On the one hand, she was certain he wanted to make love to her, but on the other hand, she suspected he was feeling too conflicted to act on his desire. Her job was to change his mind one way or the other. 'Millie thinks I might fall in love with him and get my heart broken.'

Zoey studied her for a moment. 'Do you think that's a possibility?'

'I don't think so. I'm not attracted to love-them-and-leave-them playboys.' She chewed at her lower lip and stirred her coffee. 'I've known Louis for close to a decade and never once felt anything for him other than friendship.'

Apart from the moment she'd walked into his office. And at dinner. Not to mention *the kiss*. And every time he dropped a French endearment her way.

'Why should that change if we did have a one-night stand?' Why should that change after one kiss? But, niggling doubts aside, she couldn't back out now. She wanted to see this through no matter what. It was imperative she get herself sorted out and no one could help her better than Louis.

Zoey plonked her cup down and pushed herself away from the bench. 'It's a risk, I guess. Good sex can have a potent effect on your emotions. Not that I've had any lately, but nor do I want any. I'm completely over men.'

Ivy knew her friend was still getting over the betrayal of her long-term boyfriend who had cheated on her while she'd been away with her father on business. Zoey was still in a man-hating phase even though it had been over a year since she'd found out about the affair. 'How did your dinner with your dad go?'

Zoey sighed and picked up a piece of toast. 'He drank too much and I had to bundle him into a taxi. Same old.' She bit into the toast as if she wanted to hurt it, her stunning violet eyes shadowed with decades-old pain.

'Oh, dear.'

Ivy knew all about embarrassing parents. Her mother had struggled, self-medicating with alcohol and casual affairs with multiple partners, after Ivy's dad had left when she was a teenager. Her mother had only ever had one lover until then—Ivy's father—so it had been weird seeing her mother with a host of men she'd met in a pub or wine bar. Ivy had never known who she would meet on her way to the bathroom or what sounds she would hear coming from her mother's bedroom. None of the men had stayed around longer than a night or two before someone else would appear.

'I'm worried it's going to affect the business,' Zoey went on. 'I've had to cover for him so many times lately.' She speared a hand through her thick, glossy black hair, her expression troubled. 'It's like he's self-sabotaging what he's worked so hard for all his life.

I can't stand by and watch him destroy the company. It's my company too—or it would be if he'd change his mind and make me a partner.'

'Oh, Zoey, I wish I could say something that would help. It must be so awful for you.'

Zoey stretched her mouth into an on-off smile. 'Don't mind me, I'm just venting. The thing that gets me is the blatant sexism. If I was the son he'd wanted, he would've handed the partnership to me years ago on a golden platter. But, no, I'm just a frivolous, empty-headed girl like his three ex-wives. What would I know about advertising?'

'You know heaps,' Ivy reassured her. 'That dog food commercial you worked on last month was absolutely brilliant. And, if your mum was still alive, I know she would be proud of you.'

Zoey twisted her mouth and picked up her coffee cup again. 'Maybe, but I still lost the pitch to one of our biggest competitors. But I'm determined to win next time we're vying for the same account.' Her eyes began to sparkle with determination. 'I can't wait to wipe that arrogant smirk of victory off Finn McConnell's face once and for all.'

'You go, girl,' Ivy said, holding her coffee mug up in a toast. 'To achieving our goals—no matter what.'

Louis was not normally a thank-God-it's-Friday person. Call him a hard-nosed workaholic, but the weekends were when he got a sense of satisfaction from ticking off the long list of jobs he had to do that couldn't be done during the week. He often preferred to work at weekends rather than socialise, especially since his last lover had had trouble accepting he wasn't interested in taking things further than a short fling. But, as the weekend approached, he found himself thinking less about work and more about his 'date' with Ivy.

It was faintly disturbing how *much* he was thinking about her. Hardly an hour went by without him recalling the taste and velvety texture of her mouth. And he'd developed a sudden craving for strawberries. Every time he thought of what she'd asked him to do, he got aroused. He was distracted, daydreaming when he should have been working, mentally dwelling on what it would feel like to bury himself deep inside her and take them both to heaven.

But, while he could allow himself the odd daydream, what he couldn't allow was making those daydreams a reality. Ivy wasn't a one-night-stand type of woman and he'd had nothing but one-night stands. How could doing the deed with her be a good thing?

Louis had hours before he had to pick up Ivy, so he sat at his desk and worked on a project that needed some final adjustments before it was sent to the builder. His mind kept drifting to his date with Ivy. He blinked, sat up straighter in his chair and locked his gaze back on the design on the screen.

Work. Work. Work. He chanted the words to himself, but it wasn't long before his mind was going off on another tangent.

The possibility of sex.

A hot tingle ran down his spine and he shifted in

his chair, cleared his throat and spoke out loud just to
drive the point home.

'You can do this. You work ten to twelve hours a
day. Get on with it.'

So now he was talking to himself as well as daydreaming about Ivy. He was well aware of the risk of
spending more and more time with her. It might raise
her expectations that he would solve her virginity problem. And he hadn't signed up for that—only the possibility of it which, weirdly, was making it even harder
to resist her.

But he refused to think any further than spending the
evening with her to help her feel more at ease. He was
good at cordoning off his emotions, especially when it
came to sex. Sex was a physical experience he enjoyed,
like any other full-blooded man. He didn't associate any
feelings with sex other than that of lust and pleasure.
He had never been in love and never intended to be. He
wasn't even sure the concept existed outside of novels
and Hollywood movies. The chances of finding one
person who complemented and fulfilled you in every
way and would continue to do so throughout a lifetime
was a fantasy in itself.

And one he *never* dabbled in.

But taking Ivy out a few times to help her build her
confidence was certainly doable. There was no harm in
kissing and fooling around a bit. No harm in that at all.
His conscience rolled about the floor laughing.

*Ahem. Mr Amazing One-Night Stand is going on a
few dates with the same woman with only the* possibil-

ity *of having sex? The man who doesn't date anyone longer than a day, and then only for sex?*

Louis leaned one elbow on his desk, pinched the bridge of his nose and tried to block the taunting of his conscience. He was thinking of Ivy, not himself. She needed to be more relaxed without the pressure of sex hanging over her. That was his plan and it was a good one. A safe one. To hang out together on a few dates without the expectation of intimacy. Easy.

Louis continued to stare blankly at his computer, but then his phone suddenly rang and Ivy's number and name popped up on the screen. A stone landed in his gut with a sickening, organ-crushing thud. What if she was calling to cancel? What if she had changed her mind because he hadn't committed to her request? What if she'd decided to go with the stranger plan instead? Maybe someone else had already volunteered to take her virginity. Maybe she'd done it last night with a stranger she'd found online or even one of those male escort services.

He was ambushed by the host of unfamiliar emotions assailing him—disappointment right at the top of the list. He hadn't realised how much he was looking forward to being with her tonight until the possibility of it being cancelled became possible. She'd cancelled lunch a couple of months ago, and even now he didn't like admitting how disappointed he had been.

He snatched up his phone and answered it. 'Ivy.' He was pleased with how cool and collected he sounded when his heart was thumping as though he'd just consumed three energy drinks.

'Hiya, Louis, I just wanted to know what type of clothes to wear. You didn't say where we were going tonight. Do I need to dress in anything fancy?'

He hadn't said because he hadn't decided until that morning. But he'd managed to secure box-seat tickets to a popular musical he knew she'd always wanted to see. He wanted their 'date' to be special and memorable. There was a risk of drawing press attention by being in such a public place. While he'd thought of taking her to his house in Chelsea or his place in the Cotswolds to afford them more privacy, he knew it wouldn't be wise to spend time completely alone with her. Tempting, yes, but definitely not wise. 'I've booked tickets to a West End musical. We can have supper afterwards.'

'Oh, what fun! I haven't been to the West End in ages. Shall I meet you there or—?'

'Ivy, when I date a woman I pick her up and I take her home. I'll see you at seven.'

Ivy was putting the last touches to her make-up when the doorbell sounded, announcing Louis' arrival. She pressed her lips together to set her lip-gloss, quickly snatched up her evening bag and went out of her bedroom to greet him. When she saw him standing there in a dark charcoal suit, with a crisp white shirt and blue-and-grey-striped tie, her breath caught and her heart did a funny little skip. He was the epitome of a handsome, successful male in his prime.

'Hiya. Do you want to come in for a minute? No one else is home.'

'Sure.' He stepped over the threshold and she closed the door.

Suddenly her flat seemed too small to accommodate his six-foot-four frame. She could smell the citrus and woodsy notes of his aftershave and his eyes looked darker than normal—more pupil than iris. His gaze swept over her black cocktail dress and high heels and then back to her face.

'You look stunning.' His voice had a rusty edge that did strange swoopy things to her stomach.

Ivy smoothed her hands down her hips. 'I bought it this afternoon. I thought I'd better treat myself since this is my first proper date in months.'

'How many months?'

She could feel her cheeks warming and leaned down to pick up her bag from where she'd put it when she'd answered the door. 'Ten.' She cast him a sideways glance. 'I've been out with girlfriends and stuff but not alone with a guy for close to a year.' She twisted her mouth in a rueful grimace. 'Kind of weird for an almost-thirty-year-old, huh?'

He came over to her and took one of her hands in his, stroking his thumb over the back of her hand, his eyes locking on hers. 'It's a little unusual but definitely not weird.' He gave her hand a light squeeze and released it, slipping his hand in his suit pocket as if determined not to touch her.

Ivy was aware of the grey-blue intensity of his gaze, aware of the tightening of the air, aware of the faint tingling of her skin where his thumb had stroked. 'So, how was your day?' Nothing like a bit of inane conversation to recalibrate the atmosphere.

Louis glanced at her mouth and her stomach swooped and dived again. 'Boring until now.'

She moistened her lips, her pulse fluttering. 'Are you flirting with me?'

He stepped closer, his hands taking both of hers, his thumbs doing the spine-loosening, stroking motion again. 'Isn't that what a man does when he takes a woman out on a date?'

Ivy's stomach fluttered and she couldn't stop staring at his mouth. 'If I was one of your normal dates, you would sleep with me at the end of the evening, wouldn't you? How do I know if you will or you won't?'

His eyes moved between each of hers—back and forth, back and forth—each time making her heart beat a little faster. Then they dipped to her mouth and he slid a hand along the side of her face until his fingers were entangled in her hair. 'It's always a possibility, but let's wait and see.' His tone contained a relaxed go-with-the-flow note but his eyes communicated something else. The flared pupils, the concentrated focus, all spoke of a man who was tempted, seriously tempted, to act on his primal desires.

Ivy didn't know whether to be relieved or disappointed. She was stuck in a strangely exciting limbo of 'would he or wouldn't he?'. She began to step back, but before she could take even half a step he caught her by the wrist, his fingers overlapping.

'It's not that I don't want to, *ma petite*.' His voice had dropped even lower in pitch and it sent a wave of goose bumps tiptoeing over her skin. He brought her wrist up to his mouth and pressed a kiss to her leaping pulse, his eyes holding hers. 'I've been thinking about little else all day.'

Ivy swallowed. 'Really?'

He gave a rueful slant of a smile. 'Really.' He released her wrist and stepped back to open the door. 'We'd better get going. They won't let us in until after the interval if we show up late.'

Ivy followed him out of her flat to where he had parked his car half a block up the road. He helped her into the passenger seat and pulled down the seatbelt for her. She clipped it into place and watched as he strode around to his side of the car, the lines and planes of his face so familiar and yet so strange. It was as if she were seeing him for the first time, not as her older brother's friend but as a virile thirty-four-year-old man with primal drives and desires. A man who was attracted to her and, unless she was very much mistaken, tempted to do as she asked. A tiny frisson passed over her flesh and her breath hitched at the thought of him being her first lover. Maybe even tonight.

Louis slipped into the driver's seat beside her and sent her a glance. 'Relax, *ma petite*. We're just hanging out together to see what happens. Okay?'

Ivy could feel a blush rising to the roots of her hair. 'How did you know what I was thinking?'

He gave a slow smile and started the engine with a throaty roar. 'Because I'm thinking it myself.'

He backed out of the parking space and deftly wove into the traffic, and for once in her life Ivy was lost for words.

* * *

Musicals weren't really Louis' thing, but he enjoyed watching Ivy being captivated by the songs, the costumes and stage set of the popular musical. She looked captivating herself in a dress that hugged her breasts and thighs, her impossibly high heels showcasing her legs and ankles. Every now and again he caught a whiff of her flowery perfume and, every time she glanced his way with her shining gaze, his heart would trip like a foot missing a step on a ladder.

The theatre was packed, and he was dreading being noticed, but it was worth it to see Ivy having such a good time. During the interval, once they had their drinks with them in the private box, she leaned closer to point out something in the programme he'd bought her. 'Hey, isn't that the actor in that BBC drama you recommended a few months ago?'

Louis looked at the name and nodded. 'Yep. That's her.'

'Did you ever date her?'

'No.'

Ivy swept her gaze over the audience below. 'On balance, given you've slept with so many women, there must be a few of your past lovers here, don't you think?'

'It's highly unlikely.'

'Why's that?'

He turned his head to look at her. 'The press grossly overstates my sexual proclivity. If I'd slept with as many women as reported, I'd never have been able to build such a success of my career.'

'Why are you driven to work so hard? Ronan told me you hardly ever take holidays and you often work weekends and public holidays.'

Louis leaned back in his seat and picked up his glass of champagne from the holder on his seat. 'I run an architectural business. I have people depending on me, clients and staff, and I'm committed to doing a good job of everything I take on.' He took a sip of champagne, savouring the pear and honey notes.

'Do you enjoy it?'

'Of course I enjoy it.' He put down his glass and glanced at his watch to see how much longer before the second half of the show. 'It sure beats the hell out of being an accountant.'

'Is that what your father wanted? For you to work in his accountancy firm?'

Louis was conscious of his jaw automatically tightening. 'In my father's mind, I let the family line down by pursuing architecture instead of accountancy like him and his father before him. The Charpentier accountancy firm will end with my father and for that he will never forgive me. Nor, I suspect, will my mother, mostly because she desperately wants grandchildren and I'm not interested in providing them.'

He picked up his champagne again and took another sip. That was another feeling he suppressed— the guilt he felt about his mother's hopes and dreams being dashed by his decision.

Ivy's small white teeth sank into the pillow-softness of her lower lip and her eyes lost their sparkle. 'Oh, Louis, that's terrible. You have to live your own life—

fulfil your own dreams and aspirations instead of those
of your parents'.'

'Try telling them that.' Louis gave a twisted smile
and put his champagne glass down again before he
spilled any more family secrets.

'Maybe you'll change your mind about having kids
one day,' Ivy said after a small silence. 'Lots of men do.
Even Ronan is considering having a child with Ricky
via a surrogate. He'll be a great dad, and so would you
if you'd—'

'I won't change my mind.'

Just then the bell rang to announce the end of the
interval and people started filing back into the theatre.

Louis was relieved the conversation was halted by
the bell. He rarely spoke to anyone about his family. Not
out of a sense of disloyalty to his parents but rather because it was nothing short of depressing to know how
much of a disappointment he was to his family. The
strange thing was, his grandfather had been exactly
like his father—nit-picking, pedantic and overly critical
of anyone who didn't follow his orders to a T. Another
good reason for Louis to resist the biological drive to
procreate. The last thing the world needed was another
difficult Charpentier.

Ivy left the theatre with Louis after the musical came
to an end. She had enjoyed it immensely but found she
could barely recall what'd happened in the second half
because she'd been mulling over what Louis had told
her about his family. And his adamant stance on never
having children. Even though she knew it was none of

her business what choices he made about his life, a part of her felt sad he would never experience the joys of parenthood, not to mention the satisfaction of a long-term relationship with a partner. He said he had never fallen in love, but she wondered if he would never allow himself to, closing off his emotions so he wasn't made vulnerable by anyone. She, on the other hand, longed to be loved and supported by a lifelong partner, someone who wouldn't reject her or give up his love for her the way her father had done so easily.

Louis led her to a wine bar that served cocktails and light meals, a short walk from the theatre. Their table was upstairs in an exclusive and private section that overlooked the bustling street below.

Ivy sat on the plush velvet wing-back chair opposite Louis and looked around the room with avid appreciation. 'This is gorgeous. I've never been here before. I feel like royalty or a celebrity or something.'

'A friend I went to university with owns it,' Louis said, handing her the cocktail menu. 'What would you like to drink?'

Ivy looked at the array of exotic cocktails. 'Let me see, now… Gosh, so many to choose from. What do you recommend?'

'How about a strawberry gin cocktail?' He pointed to the one on the menu.

'Sounds good. I love strawberries.'

His eyes flicked to her lips and one side of his mouth curved upwards. 'I've developed rather a fancy for them myself lately.'

Something about his wry tone sent a light shiver over her skin.

Their drinks soon appeared, and soon after that a light tapas-style supper followed, with a host of flavoursome delicacies both savoury and sweet. Once she had eaten her fill, Ivy dabbed at the corners of her mouth with her linen napkin and, setting it aside, sat back in her chair. 'That was amazing. Thank you for taking me out tonight. I've had the best time.'

'My pleasure. I enjoyed it too.'

She twisted her mouth. 'You don't seem like the West End musical type. I thought you'd rather go to a classical symphony concert.'

Louis shrugged one broad shoulder and then leaned forward to pick up his cocktail. 'You're making me sound staid and boring.'

'You're definitely not that.'

His eyes locked on hers and a faint prickly sensation ran down her spine and down the back of her legs. She ran the tip of her tongue over her lips and drew in a wobbly breath. Either that strawberry gin cocktail was going to her head or Louis was making her feel things she had never felt before. The energy in the air shifted, a subtle tightening, as if all the oxygen particles had been disturbed.

A band was playing in the background and Louis leaned forward to put his cocktail back on the table. He pushed back his chair and stood, offering his hand to her. 'Would you like to dance?'

'Sure. Why not?' Ivy took his proffered hand and went with him to the small dance floor. They moved in perfect time to the sweetly cadenced ballad, and she was conscious of every point of contact with him. One of his arms was around her, his other hand holding hers, her cheek resting on his chest right where his heart beat so steadily. Her heart was doing an Irish jig in her chest, and when he tipped up her face to meet his gaze it did a backflip.

His arm around her tightened just enough to bring her closer to the heat of his pelvis, his mouth slowly, ever so slowly, coming down to hers. His lips were warm and gentle, but then his pressure increased, sending shooting sparks of pleasure through her body. His tongue stroked for entry—a lazy let-me-play-with-you stroke that sent a lightning bolt of lust straight to her core. She suddenly remembered they were in a public place, on a dance floor surrounded by other people, and she pulled back, biting her lip where his tempting tongue had just been. 'Sorry. A bit public for me.'

He gave both her hands a squeeze and smiled. 'You're right. Now is not the time or place.' He led her back to the table and they each took their seats.

Ivy aimed her attention at his mouth rather than hold his gaze. 'But when and where will be the time and place?' He didn't answer for so long, she brought her gaze up to meet his.

His expression was difficult to read, but somehow she sensed he had come to a decision in his mind. 'What are you doing next Friday night?'

'I haven't got anything planned. Why?'

'I have a place down in the Cotswolds. I thought we

could spend the night there and drive back on Saturday morning.'

Ivy blinked. 'Does that mean you're going to…?'

'You have a one-track mind.' His tone was playfully reproving. 'No, it doesn't necessarily mean we're going to sleep together.'

'But what is the point of us hanging out together if you don't do what I asked you to do? I've only got three weeks now until my birthday. Time is rapidly running out.'

'Why the big hurry to do it before your birthday?'

She opened her eyes wide. 'Why the hurry? Because I made a promise to myself that I wouldn't still be a virgin by then. If you're not going to help me, say so, Louis. It's not fair to string me along if you've no intention of—'

'I would do it in a heartbeat if I was confident we both wouldn't regret it in the end.'

'You know what I think?' Ivy shot him a heated glare. 'I think you're the one who's worried about getting hurt in the end. You spend your life sleeping only once with women you'll never see again because you're worried about feeling something for someone.' She snatched up her bag from the table. 'Thank you for this evening. I'll make my own way home. And I'll find someone else to help me, so you're off the hook. Goodbye.'

'Ivy.' His voice had a commanding note. 'Wait.'

She turned from the door to face him. 'I've wasted enough time waiting. I get it. You don't want to help me. You're not attracted to me even though you give a very good impression of it. But I'm a big girl. I can handle the rejection. God knows, I've had plenty of practice.'

He came over to her and took both her hands in his. A battle played out on his features, a war of conflicting emotions he was clearly trying to hide, but she could see it in the shadows in his eyes and the tightness in his jaw and the thinning of his lips. 'Okay. Here's the deal. One night and one night only. I'll pick you up on Friday after work. And on Saturday we go back to being friends as normal.'

Ivy wanted to refuse his offer out of pride but the thought of anyone else sleeping with her turned her stomach. It *had* to be him. 'Okay.'

He gave her hands a quick squeeze and then tucked one of her arms through his. 'Come on, Cinderella. Time to get you home.'

Louis spent the following week wondering if he needed his head read for agreeing to Ivy's plan. He'd been at war with himself from the moment she'd put it to him. He'd been dragging his heels, not so much because he didn't want to do it but because he did. Badly. The more time he spent with her, the more he wanted her.

Normally his week at work flew past but this one dragged as if someone had slowed down time. He had deliberately delayed going down to the Cotswolds for another week to give her a cooling-off period. Didn't all good business deals involve a cooling-off period? And the only way to approach her plan was to keep things businesslike. One night was all she wanted. One night was all he ever gave. But Louis became so restless and on edge, he finally caved in and called Ivy on her mobile just after two on the Friday.

'What time will you be ready? A client cancelled a meeting, so we can go earlier to get ahead of the traffic.' It wasn't exactly a lie—a client had cancelled, but it had been earlier that morning. Louis had plenty of work he could have seen to if he'd wanted to but he couldn't wait to whisk Ivy away to his own private little paradise.

'I'll be ready in half an hour.'

'Perfect. See you soon.' Louis clicked off his phone and took a deep, steadying breath. If his secretary, Natalie, could have seen him now—leaving work in the middle of the afternoon and taking most of the weekend off—she would have raised her brows until they disappeared under her fringe, or reached for a thermometer and threatened to call a doctor. He smiled and pushed back his chair to stand, grabbing his keys and phone off the desk.

For once, work could wait.

CHAPTER FOUR

IVY WASN'T THE best packer on the planet for an over-nighter. All the weekend access visits to her father after her parents had divorced during her teens had ramped up her anxiety to the point where now she couldn't pack a bag without worrying about all the things she might need, so she took everything just in case. Her bedroom looked as if it had been done over by a burglar. Her wardrobe had turned into a 'floordrobe' and she couldn't find the matching knickers to her favourite black bra.

Why hadn't she bought some new underwear? What if Louis was turned off by her lingerie? But there was a new level of anxiety in packing this particular bag. She was actually going to do it.

She was going to have sex. With Louis.

The doorbell sounded and her stomach dropped. He was here and she wasn't properly prepared. The day was finally here and she was stuffing around, trying to de-cide what underwear to take. She went to the front door and opened it, her heart doing a funny little hopscotch when she laid eyes on Louis, still dressed in his busi-ness wear, although he'd removed his tie.

'I'm almost ready. Do you want to sit down while I finish packing? Or shall I make you a coffee or something? A juice or—?'

'Don't be nervous, *ma petite*.' His husky tone almost made her swoon, so too the look of concern in his eyes.

Ivy could feel a blush stealing over her cheeks. 'I'm sorry to be so flustered. I'm just hopeless at packing. I always take too much stuff and then end up without the things I most need.'

He gave one of his slanted smiles and her heart tripped again. 'You look good in anything you wear.'

A pool of heat swirled in her lower body and her pulse went off the charts. 'So do you.'

A twinkle came into his eyes. 'Are you flirting with me?'

She gave him a coy smile. 'I think I might be.'

He stepped across the threshold and closed the door, taking her by the upper arms and bringing her close to his body. His eyes darkened and became hooded, his head bending down so his mouth was just above hers.

'I told myself I wouldn't do this, but I've been thinking about nothing else for days.' He closed the distance between their mouths in a kiss that threatened to blow the top of her head off. Desire flared and ran like hot flames through her body. His tongue entered her mouth on a silken thrust that had distinctly erotic undertones and she shivered in delight. His hands moved from her upper arms and went around her body, drawing her closer to his hard frame. She could feel the thickening of his body, the signal of his arousal, and another wave of incendiary heat swept through her. One of his hands came up to cradle the back of her head, his fingers splaying through her hair. He groaned against her mouth, a deep, guttural sound that sent a shudder of need right through her body. It was beyond thrilling to hear and feel his response to her. It made her confidence grow, like a plant starved of water finally receiving a life-saving drink.

Louis eased back to look down at her. 'Are you still sure about this?'

Ivy was getting off just being held in his arms. Never had her body felt so warm and tingly, especially with his erection pressing against her feminine mound. Why wasn't she freaking out and trying to put some distance between them? Or was it because Louis' body spoke to hers in a way that made her feel more confident in her sensuality? 'Yes. It feels like you are too.'

His pupils flared like black holes in infinite space. 'I've been thinking about nothing else all week.'

Ivy could feel heat stealing over her cheeks. 'I hope I'm not a disappointment. I'm such a prude, I can't even watch sex scenes in movies without blushing.'

He stroked a gentle finger down the curve of her hot cheek. 'I think it's cute how you blush all the time. Don't ever apologise for it.' The timbre of his voice made her legs feel weak. Or maybe it was the tender look in his eyes.

Ivy patted his chest with one of her hands. 'I'm holding us up. Give me five minutes to finish packing?'

He bent down and brushed her lips with his. 'Go for it.'

* * *

Louis had to stop himself from following her into her bedroom and finishing what he'd started. Yes. What *he'd* started. So much for his boundaries. He'd promised himself he would keep his hands off her until they got to his place in the country, yet as soon as he'd seen her he'd crushed his mouth on hers like a magnet attracted to metal.

He scraped a hand through his hair, trying to get his breathing back under control. Every time he kissed her, it made him want her all the more. It was as though a switch inside him had been flicked and there was no turning it off again. Kissing her at the wine bar had nailed it for him. A kiss here or there was never going to cut it. Not now. He was too far gone for that. He wanted her with a fervour that was unlike anything he had felt before.

Desire pounded through him with an unstoppable force, a need so raw and primal he felt it in every cell of his body. He wanted to think it was because he hadn't had sex in four months but, deep down, he suspected it was more to do with Ivy. She was someone he cared about, someone he respected, someone he would continue to see long after their physical relationship ended. It made their alliance dangerous in a way none of his previous encounters had been. But he was a master at putting emotions to one side when he needed to. This would be no different. Their little secret tryst in the country had all the makings of a hot-blooded fantasy. *If* he allowed it.

The thought wandered about his mind like a stray

guest in a mansion looking at things he shouldn't be looking at, touching things he shouldn't touch. Trespassing into areas he had never allowed himself to go before. They would be spending the night doing all the things he'd told himself they weren't going to do...

Louis pulled himself out of his reverie and wandered over to the sideboard in the sitting room where a group of photos was displayed. There was one of Ivy and Ronan at his graduation, another of Ivy with two attractive young women he presumed were her current flatmates. His gaze landed on another one of Ivy as a child at an Irish dancing contest. He picked up the photo frame and couldn't hold back a smile. The red-gold-haired cherub in that photo was enough to make anyone's heart melt.

He put the photo down and his gaze went to the one of her rescue dog, Fergus, who had died a couple of years ago. Ronan had told him Ivy had been inconsolable and on an impulse Louis had sent her flowers and a card. She'd sent him a neatly written thank-you note that he still had in his filing cabinet. He couldn't quite explain why he'd kept it.

Ivy came back into the sitting room lugging two overnight bags. 'I'm ready.'

'Here, let me take those for you,' Louis said, reaching for them. 'What have you got in them? A full set of encyclopaedias?'

Her cheeks pooled with twin circles of pink. 'I hate people who can go away for a weekend and fit everything in one bag. My make-up and toiletries fill one bag on their own.'

Louis gave a soft laugh. 'Come on. Let's get going before we get stuck in traffic.'

He wanted no time wasted until he could kiss her again.

About two hours after leaving London, and after driving down a long, winding hawthorn-fringed lane and over a narrow bridge across a small river, they arrived at a traditional Cotswold-stone manor house. Ivy leaned forward in her seat in excitement, struck by the beauty of the gardens surrounding the house that had been recently renovated, with an extension that perfectly suited the old bones of the house. 'You said it was a little place in the Cotswolds. This is huge!'

'Only ten bedrooms,' Louis said. 'I could have bought one with fifteen but thought that was a little over the top for one person.'

She glanced at him as he brought the car to a halt in front of the house. 'But don't you want to have a family one day to share this with? I mean, this would be ideal for—'

'No.' His tone was blunt. Emphatic. Decision made and will not be changed. 'I don't.'

Ivy unclipped her seatbelt, more than a little intrigued as to why he was so adamant against settling down one day. 'How often do you come down here?'

'Not often enough.' He got out of the car and came around to her side to help her out. 'I have a caretaker and housekeeper and a couple of gardeners who keep things in check. I try to spend a couple of weeks here in the summer and the occasional weekend throughout the year.'

'Is that all?' She looked at him in surprise. 'If this was my place, I would never want to leave. It's so private and peaceful.'

'Speaking of private—we're keeping our time together a secret, right? I don't want anyone speculating that we're an item. The press would have a field day.'

'Sure...' Ivy avoided his gaze, pretending an avid interest in a garden sculpture near the front of the house.

'Ivy.' His tone was commanding. 'Look at me.'

She sucked her lower lip inside her mouth and turned to glance at him. His gaze was probing, the line of his mouth firm. 'I'm sorry, I wasn't going to tell Millie, but then...but it kind of slipped out the other week when we first went out for dinner, and then she told Zoey.'

'Oh, God.' His despairing groan was a shattering blow to her self-esteem. Was it so embarrassing for him to be associated with her, even for a weekend? 'And who else will they tell? Will it be all over social media by now?'

'Don't be ridiculous, they would never do something like that.'

'Who else have you told? Your mother? Or Ronan?' His frown was savage, his eyes as piercing as a detective honing in on a suspect.

'No, of course not.' Ivy sent him a glowering look. 'Do you really think I'd crow to all and sundry that you're helping me with my intimacy issues? It's embarrassing enough for me without broadcasting it to the world.'

He released a rough sigh that had a note of resignation on its backdraft and turned to pop the boot open. 'Okay. Fine. But don't tell anyone else.'

She looked down at her feet and kicked at a pebble with her toe. 'Is this embarrassing for you too? I mean, being here with me?' She somehow found the courage to meet his gaze once more.

His expression was unreadable. 'No. Not at all.' He turned and took her bags out of the boot as if they weighed nothing more than a couple of pillows. 'Come on. I'll show you round.'

Ivy breathed in the scents from the herbaceous border—stocks and lupins and foxgloves and hollyhocks, the colourful array attracting busy bees and fluttering butterflies. The early-summer sunshine was surprisingly warm and was a stark contrast to the greyness of the London sky they had left behind close to two hours ago. Birds twittered in the shrubbery and the neatly trimmed hedges, and in the distance, she heard the eerie call of a peacock on a neighbouring property. She followed Louis to the front entrance of the grand manor house, wondering how many other women he had brought here. Should she ask or would it seem too intrusive?

He put down her bags, deactivated the alarm system on his key fob and unlocked the front door, pushing it open for her. 'In you go. I'll take these up to your room and then come and show you around.'

'Why separate rooms? Aren't we supposed to be—?'

'I'm a restless sleeper, and I often get up to work at night. Besides, you won't be up to marathon sessions just yet.'

Ivy stepped into the house and turned to face him once he'd brought the bags in and closed the door. 'How many women have you brought here for marathon sessions? Or have you lost count?'

He placed his keys in a glass bowl on a polished hall table—a beautiful Regency piece that was in perfect condition. 'I've never brought anyone here before.'

She raised her eyebrows. 'Really? Why not?'

'I come down here to chill out and relax. I find relationships—even temporary ones—hard work.'

Ivy shifted her gaze, her teeth savaging her lip. 'I hope my presence isn't going to spoil your precious idyll for you.'

He stepped forward and trailed his index finger down her cheek, his expression softening. 'It won't. I'd thought of asking you and Ronan down some time anyway. I just didn't get round to it before he emigrated to Australia because the renovations took a little longer than I expected.'

Ivy was conscious of her heartbeat increasing at his proximity. Aware of the tingle in her cheek from his faineant touch. Her gaze drifted to his mouth and something in her stomach fell off a shelf with a soft little *kerplunk*. His jaw was peppered with late-in-the-day stubble and, before she could stop herself, she lifted her hand to his face and stroked it down the sexy prickles, the sound overly loud in the silence. 'Thanks for bringing me here. It's so beautiful and I already feel relaxed.'

His hand came up and encircled her wrist, and for a moment she thought he was going to remove her hand from his face and set her away from him. But then his eyes darkened and he brought her inexorably closer, until she was flush against his rock-hard body. She smothered a gasp, her heart thumping so loudly she wondered if he could feel it pounding against his chest.

'I have this insatiable desire to kiss you.' His voice was so deep and rough, it made her skin lift in a delicious shiver.

'Same here.' Her voice was barely more than a hoarse whisper.

His eyes went to her mouth and he muttered a swear word and brought his down to hers. It was a kiss of fervent passion that made every hair on her head lift off her scalp. Desire flooded her being, giant waves of it coursing through her body in scorching-hot streaks. His hands skated down the sides of her body and then settled on her hips, bringing her even closer to the jutting heat of his. He lifted his mouth off hers, his eyes glittering with unbridled lust. 'I'm finding it hard to believe you need any tutoring from me. You turn me on so much I can barely stand it.'

Ivy glowed at his compliment and her damaged ego crawled out of the corner and unfolded itself from the foetal position. 'I didn't realise it would be this way between us.' She stroked his lean jaw again. 'But I'm worried you'll be disappointed when it comes to having sex with me.'

His eyes darkened to a midnight-blue. 'You won't disappoint me.' He brushed the pad of his thumb over her lip where her teeth had just been. 'Now, let's get you unpacked, and we'll have a drink in the garden before dinner.'

Ivy followed him up the stairs with her body still buzzing from his passionate kiss. If she'd had the confidence, she'd have insisted he make love to her right now. Why wait when they were alone for the whole weekend?

But maybe he was right not to rush her. She needed to take things slowly, to be more in control of what happened with her body. Her previous dates had pressured her, and it had made her panic, and they hadn't taken the rejection well. One had made insulting comments about her body that she had been fretting over ever since. She wanted it to be different this time. To be able to enjoy every moment without embarrassment, or feeling pressured and on edge, or fearful of being body shamed.

Louis led her to a room on the second storey that had a beautiful view of the back garden and the rolling fields beyond the estate. Her bedroom was decorated in cream and white, which gave the room a spacious and luxurious feel that would rival that of any top hotel. Her eyes went to the queen-sized bed and molten heat pooled between her legs at the thought of lying in it with Louis, his body buried deeply in hers...

He placed the bags on a velvet-covered linen box at the end of the bed and straightened to look at her. 'There's an *en suite* bathroom through there.'

'Where's your room?'

'Further down the hall.'

'How much further?'

He released a heavy sigh and reached to tuck a loose

strand of her hair back behind her ear. 'Don't take it personally. I often get up at night and tinker away on my computer. I wouldn't want to disturb you.'

Ivy searched his features for a crack in the firewall of his self-control. He kept glancing at her mouth as if unable to pull his gaze away. And there was a doggedness about the line of his jaw, as if he was calling on every bit of willpower to stop himself from acting on the desire she could see shining in his eyes. 'You work too hard.'

He gave a lop-sided smile and released her. 'I'm going to rustle up some dinner. Come down when you're ready.'

Louis left her to unpack and went downstairs to check if his housekeeper had followed his instructions to leave supplies for dinner. Yep. Done, and done well. Who said you couldn't get good help these days?

The dining room was set up, the fridge and pantry stocked, the champagne and wine on chill. A casserole was in the slow cooker, filling the kitchen with the fragrant aroma of chicken and herbs. There were even flowers from the garden on the table and throughout the house, filling the air with a summery smell.

The garden was bathed in golden early-evening sunlight, making him wonder why he didn't come down here more often to relax. Like 'commitment', 'relax' was another word he'd shied away from in his quest to succeed as an architect. The thing was, he now had the success he'd always aimed for, but he still kept striving. He was stuck in work gear, always going at full throttle, because that was all he knew now. It was all he wanted, right? Work. Achievement. Success.

Louis opened the fridge and took out the champagne. He got two glasses from the cabinet and placed them on a tray, along with cheese, crackers, fruit and pâté. He heard Ivy's footsteps coming down the stairs and along the passage to the kitchen and something deep and low in his pelvis tightened. *Sheesh.* Even the sound of her footsteps got his blood roaring.

She came into the kitchen wearing a long, summery, Bohemian-style off-the-shoulder dress that highlighted the creamy perfection of her neck and shoulders. Her hair was bundled up in a makeshift up-do with some loose tendrils cascading about her heart-shaped face. She glanced at the champagne and smiled, making her eyes sparkle. 'That's my favourite.'

'I know.' Louis picked up the tray and nodded towards the French doors leading to the garden. 'Let's take this outside and enjoy the sunlight before dinner.'

Ivy walked ahead of him and opened the door, then followed him out to the garden. 'I love your garden. Was it already like this or did you design it?'

'I made some changes, along with the house.'

Louis put the tray down on the outdoor table under the wisteria trellis, the sweet fragrance of the pendulous blooms as heady as a drug. Or maybe he was feeling a little intoxicated by the way Ivy looked and the fact she was here. Alone with him.

'How long have you had this place?'

'Three years.' He uncorked the bottle and poured

out two glasses. He put the bottle down, handed her a glass then picked up his own.

Ivy took the glass from him, her fingers brushing his, and a jolt of electricity shot through him. 'I really like the way you've blended the old with the new. You didn't think of designing a new house from scratch like you do for most of your clients?'

Louis shrugged one shoulder. 'I saw this place and liked it. It had good bones, so I didn't see the sense in changing it too much, just enough to put my stamp on it.'

'I think you've done an amazing job,' she said, turning back to look at the house. Now that her back was towards him, Louis had an uncontrollable urge to press a kiss to the back of her neck where red-gold curls dangled like miniature corkscrews.

She turned around again and smiled. 'Your parents must be so proud of you. How many awards have you won now? Dozens?'

Louis held his glass to hers. 'To achieving goals.'

Her brow furrowed, her blue eyes searching his. 'They *are* proud of you, aren't they? I mean, you're one of the most talented architects in the world. Ronan told me you have a long waiting list of clients desperate for you to work for them.'

'I don't like talking about my family. It's too depressing to be reminded of how much of a disappointment I am to them, especially to my father.' He handed her the plate of cheese and fruit. 'Want some?'

She took a grape off the plate and popped it in her mouth. After she'd swallowed it, she took a portion of cheese and placed it on a cracker. 'I'm glad my parents never really interfered with Ronan's or my career plans. I love working in antiques and can't imagine doing anything else.'

'What do you love about it?'

'So many things…like the fact that generations of people have used a piece of furniture or crockery, or glassware or jewellery, before. The sense of history fascinates me.' Her face shone with enthusiasm, her tone almost reverent as she went on. 'My pet love is Victorian crockery. I sometimes just hold a piece of it in my hand and imagine the people who have used it before. I'm going to Paris next week to see a collection from a deceased estate.'

Louis reached out and tucked one of her loose tendrils behind her ear. 'It's not ridiculous to be passionate about something.'

Her eyes dipped to his mouth and back again, the tip of her tongue darting out to moisten her lips. A rocket blast of lust hit him like a sucker punch, and he took the champagne glass off her and set it down beside his on the table. He took her hands in his and brought her closer to his body. 'And while we're on the topic of passion…'

He lowered his mouth to her upturned one, her lips flowering open to the gentle pressure of his. She made a soft whimpering sound and rose up on tiptoe, her hands creeping up to link around his neck, the action bringing her even closer. Dangerously, temptingly, tantalisingly closer. He entered her mouth with a bold stroke of his tongue, shivers coursing down his spine as her tongue mated shyly with his. The playful little darts and flickers of her tongue sent his pulse soaring, the delicious press of her breasts against his chest making him wild with primal want. Heat poured into his lower body—hot, hard heat that threatened to engulf him.

Louis placed a hand at the small of her back, just above the sweet curve of her bottom, his senses reeling at the way her mouth responded to him with such passionate fervour. He brought his other hand to the curve of her breast, cradling it through her dress, allowing her time to get used to being touched so intimately. She made another sound of encouragement and leaned her pelvis further into him, moving against him in an instinctive fashion. He lifted his mouth off hers and placed it on the exquisite softness of her neck, trailing slow kisses from below her ear, over her shoulder and to the upper curve of her breasts. She drew in a hitching breath, gasping in pleasure, and he stroked his tongue over the exposed part of her breast, aching to explore her in more intimate detail. He began gently to tug her dress down to reveal more of her breast, but she suddenly froze and then pushed his hand away.

'I'm sorry...' She bit her lip, her cheeks bright pink.

Louis placed his hands on her hips. 'Too soon for you?'

'It's not that...'

'What is it? Talk to me, Ivy. Tell me what's worrying you about me touching you like that.'

She swallowed and brought her gaze back to his. 'My breasts are small. I'm worried you won't find them attractive.'

He stroked a lazy finger down the curve of her blushing cheek. 'I find everything about you attractive.'

A tremulous smile flirted with the edges of her mouth, but the shadows hadn't gone from her eyes. 'One of the dates I had made a comment about my breasts when I told him I didn't want to sleep with him, and I've never really got over it. I can't look at my body without thinking how unappealing it must be to men.'

Louis had to suppress a wave of anger so intense it threatened to boil his blood at what that jerk of a boyfriend had said to her. 'Ivy, that idiot guy needs to be taught a lesson and I wish I could be the one to teach him. You have no reason to be ashamed of any part of your body. I've been trying not to notice for years how damn attractive you are.'

Ivy peered up into his face as if she couldn't quite believe what he'd said was true. 'Really? You never gave me any indication.'

He played with a loose curl of her hair, winding it around his finger and releasing it again. 'Yes, well, your brother might have had something to say about it if I had, knowing my playboy reputation with women.' He frowned and added, 'I can't help thinking he won't be too happy about us spending the night together. I promised to keep an eye on you, not to sleep with you.'

Ivy pursed her lips, eyes flashing. 'It's time my brother accepted I'm not a child any more. I want to sleep with you, Louis.' She took one of his hands and placed it back on her breast. 'Now, where were we?'

Louis smiled. 'Well, I was about to do this...' He gently peeled her dress down to uncover half of her bra-less breast and then lowered his mouth to the ripe curve. She gave a soft sound of approval and he pulled the dress a little lower to uncover her nipple. He rolled his tongue over and around her peaking flesh, delighting in the exquisite softness of her skin and the way she was responding to his caresses.

'Oh...oh...*oh*...' Her voice was a breathless thread of sound and she gave a little shudder.

Louis lifted his head to look at her, his hands going to her hips to steady her. 'Okay so far?'

Her eyes shimmered with the same desire he could feel thundering through his body. Hot. Urgent. Desperate. 'More than okay. It feels so good to have you touch me like that.' She sounded almost surprised that she enjoyed it. 'Do it again. Please?'

'Your wish is my command.' *And my most wicked fantasy.*

Louis bent his head and placed his mouth over her right breast, sucking softly, teasing her with his lips and tongue and the gentle tether of his teeth. Her skin was like silk and she smelled of flowers and vanilla and musk, sending his senses haywire. He moved his mouth to her other breast, exploring it in the same thorough detail, delighting in the sounds of encouragement she was making, thrilled by her avid response to his touch.

She quivered under his hands, her eyelashes at half-mast, as if drunk on the sensations he was triggering in her. Powerful, intense sensations that were erupting vicariously through his own flesh. His erection was so tight and heavy it was painful, the desire for completion a pounding primal force in his blood. But he needed to be in control and, right now, his control was slipping away, pushing every thought aside for the goal of intense physical satisfaction.

But this wasn't like any other one-nighter. This was Ivy and he had to take things slowly. Painfully, agonisingly slowly. With a strength of will he didn't know he still possessed, he eased back from her, breathing heavily. 'Let's take a breather. I said I wasn't going to rush you and I'm not going back on my word.'

Disappointment spread over her features, her cheeks darkening to a warm shade of pink. 'Did I do something wrong?' Worry was threaded through her voice and her teeth captured her lower lip.

Louis framed her face in his hands, holding her troubled gaze. 'You did nothing wrong, *ma chérie*. I want your first time to be perfect and making love out here in the open is probably not the way to do it.'

'So, you're not going to change your mind about making love with me?'

He brushed her mouth with a light kiss. 'If I were a better man, then perhaps I would.' He gave a rueful twist of his lips and added, 'You've done strange things to my moral compass.'

A small frown formed a tiny crease in the smooth perfection of her forehead. 'What's immoral about two consenting adults having sex? We're not doing anything wrong or illegal.'

'I know, but we'll only be having sex tonight,' Louis said, watching her steadily. 'I don't want there to be any confusion about that. This is not happening after we leave here tomorrow, okay?' He wasn't sure if he was saying it for her benefit or his. But it needed to be said. And underlined.

Her eyes drifted to his mouth and her tongue poked out to wet her lips. 'I understand the terms, Louis. You don't have to spell them out all the time. I only want this night with you. After that, we go back to being friends as normal.'

He had a feeling nothing would ever be normal again. He bent down and pressed another kiss to her soft mouth. 'Stay here and finish your drink and enjoy the garden while I sort out dinner.'

And get my self-control back in order.

CHAPTER FIVE

IVY WATCHED HIM go back into the house and wished she had the courage to go in after him to distract him from cooking dinner and make him take her straight upstairs to bed. But she knew he was determined to take things slowly and a part of her was grateful he wasn't rushing her. She had been rushed before and it hadn't ended well.

In a strange way, his go-slow approach was making her want him all the more. Her body felt alive and tingling with anticipation, reacting to every look he cast her way, every touch of his hand or brush of his lips. She picked up her champagne glass and took another sip, listening to the sounds of the birds settling in the shrubbery, the throaty croak of a frog on the bank of the pond and then the resounding *plop* as it went below the silvery surface. She rose from the garden chair and wandered over to the nearest flowerbed, bent her head to smell the heady clove-like scent of night stocks.

She glanced towards the house and caught a glimpse of Louis in the kitchen, preparing their food. As if he sensed her gaze on him, he looked up from what he was doing and locked gazes with her. A hot rush of longing travelled through her body and she began walking towards the house as if drawn by a powerful magnet. She *did* have the courage to go to him. His touch had awakened it in her. The needs raging in her body refused to be put on hold. It was as if a fever had gripped her—a fever of longing to feel Louis' mouth on hers, his arms holding her close to his body.

When she got to the kitchen, Louis wiped his hands on a tea towel and smiled. 'Too cold out there now?'

Ivy stepped up to him and looked up into his grey-blue eyes. 'I kind of like the heat in here more.'

His pupils flared and his gaze dipped to her mouth, his hands settling on her hips. 'You're not making this easy for me, Ivy. I'm supposed to be giving you dinner before we do anything else.'

She moved closer, winding her arms around his neck, her breasts pushing against his chest. Any shyness she might have felt was gone, obliterated by the overwhelming need powering through her body. The need he had brought to life in her flesh. 'I'm not hungry for food. I'm hungry for you.'

He groaned and covered her mouth with his in a long, drugging kiss that made her senses go into a tailspin. His tongue mated with hers and her spine loosened and her knees wobbled. One of his hands cupped her breast, his touch light and yet sending thousands of shivers through her sensitive flesh. He pulled her dress down a fraction and began to caress her breast with his lips and tongue, teasing her nipple into a tight peak, tantalising her with the sensation of his stubble against her soft skin.

Ivy whimpered with longing for more of his touch, the passionate need in the core of her body pulsating, pounding. He moved to her other breast, exposing it to his hungry, smouldering gaze and placing his mouth on the upper curve, then trailing his tongue over and around her nipple, taking it into his mouth and gently sucking on it. The nerves in her tender flesh rioted with ecstasy, triggering even more flutters and flickers and flames in her lower body.

Louis lifted his head to look at her with eyes dark and glittering with lust. 'Dinner can wait. I want you.' His voice was low and deep and gravelly, sending a shiver whispering down her spine.

'I want you too, so, so much,' Ivy said. 'I've never experienced anything like this before. It's like my body hasn't been alive until now.'

He framed her face in his hands, his expression serious. 'I won't do anything you're not comfortable doing.'

Ivy stroked his stubbled jaw and gazed into his eyes. 'I know you won't. That's why you're the only person I could ask to help me. I trust you.'

A fleeting shadow went through his gaze before it lowered to her mouth once more. He drew in a ragged breath and took one of her hands, his fingers warm and strong around hers. His eyes met hers and he smiled a slow smile that made her heart slip sideways. 'Let's go upstairs.'

Ivy went with him up the grand staircase and he led her to his master suite at the other end of the wide corridor from her bedroom. Her skin was tight all over, her heart rate picking up, her senses on high alert. She was attuned to his every movement, not out of fear but out of excitement. The twilight was still filtering into the room, giving it a muted and intimate glow, and when Louis didn't reach for the light switch she wondered if he'd remembered her confession about not being comfortable undressing unless the lights were out. It touched her that he was being so patient and understanding with her.

He stood with her next to the king-sized bed, his hands loosely holding hers. His gaze roved over her face, lingering on her mouth and then coming back to her eyes. 'Remember, you're the one in control here. I want this to be perfect for you.'

'Everything's been perfect so far.' Ivy slipped her hands out of his and began to unbutton his shirt. 'I want to feel your skin on mine.' Her heart was fluttering, but with excitement rather than nerves. It was empowering to know he would be patient with her, not rushing or pushing her to do things she wasn't ready to do. Somehow it made her feel more emboldened than she had ever felt before, the needs of her body overtaking the paralysing fears in her mind. Funny how those fears were retreating further and further into the background, every magical touch of his melting them away.

Louis shrugged himself out of his shirt and then reached to undo the clip holding her hair on top of her head. It cascaded down around her shoulders. He swept her hair to one side and lowered his mouth to the soft

skin just below her ear, and she shivered as his lips and
tongue subjected her to feather-light caresses.

'You smell beautiful—like flowers and summer—
and I can't wait to taste you all over.' His tone had a
roughened edge, as if he was fighting to keep his control in check.

Her own control was facing a similar battle. The shy
part of her nature wanted to put the brakes on before he
could act on his erotic promise but the sensually awakened part of her relished the thought of him caressing
her in such an intimate way. 'I want to taste you too.'

She brought her mouth to his neck in the shallow
dish between his clavicles and pressed her lips to the
saltiness of his skin. He shuddered under her touch and
brought her closer to the jutting hardness of his body.
Ivy grew emboldened by the impact she was having
on him and kissed his neck again, this time using her
tongue in kitten-like licks.

He made a sound at the back of his throat and, with
one hand pressed to the small of her back, brought the
other to cup her breast. 'I want to see you. All of you.
Do you want me to undress you or would you feel more
comfortable doing it yourself?'

Ivy was touched that he'd asked rather than assumed
he could go ahead. 'I want you to do it.' She could
hardly believe she was saying it, but it was true. She
felt totally comfortable with him peeling the clothes
from her body. Besides, the room was even darker now,
so she didn't feel as exposed as she might have done.

Louis slowly slid her dress down her body, his eyes
glinting in the low light as her breasts were finally

uncovered. Ivy resisted the urge to cover herself and watched as his gaze lingered on her curves. Her dress went to a puddle at her feet and she stepped out of it, standing in nothing but a tiny pair of knickers.

'You are every bit as beautiful as I imagined…' His voice had a raw, earthy quality to it that made her desire for him go up another notch. His hands cradled both her breasts and he bent his head to caress them with his lips and tongue. Ivy shivered as she watched his dark head lower to her naked flesh, the sheer eroticism of his action making her inner core contract with want. He knelt down in front of her and kissed his way down her body—below her breasts, over her ribcage, her abdomen, and then to the top of her lacy underwear. Ivy stiffened, suddenly shy at revealing the most intimate part of her body.

Louis steadied her with his hands on her hips, his eyes meeting hers. 'Don't be shy, *ma chérie*.'

She bit her lip and stepped out of his hold, covering her breasts with her hands. 'I'm sorry. I don't think I can go any further.' Her feverish body screamed, *No! Don't stop now!* But she couldn't overcome the fear he might find her repulsive.

He straightened and came over to her, resting his hands on the top of her shoulders. 'Look at me, Ivy.'

Ivy slowly brought her gaze up to his, her cheeks so hot they felt like they were going to explode. 'See? I told you. I'm an uptight prude.'

He gave her shoulders a gentle squeeze. 'Tell me what's worrying you. Did that jerk say something to you about this part of you too?'

She looked at his chin rather than meet his gaze. 'No, but I'm... I'm worried you won't like the way I look down there. You sleep with so many women. What if I'm a freak compared to them?'

He placed a finger beneath her chin and brought her gaze back to his. 'Women's bodies come in all shapes and sizes. You're perfect just the way you are. You don't need to be ashamed of any part of your body.'

'I know, but I am, and I can't seem to help it.'

Louis stroked his finger over her bottom lip, his eyes shining. 'I love everything I've seen so far.'

'Really?' Ivy lowered her hands from covering her breasts, aching to feel them pressed up against the naked skin of his muscular chest.

'Really.' He devoured her breasts with his gaze and a hot spurt of longing shot to her core.

She moved closer so her breasts were against his chest, her arms going back around his neck. 'Thanks for keeping the lights off.' In semi-darkness she could hide her secret thoughts and feelings...she could feel less exposed, less vulnerable. She was ready to give herself to him physically but she wanted her emotions kept in the shadows where they couldn't be seen.

'That's fine. I can make love to you by Braille.'

Ivy laughed, shivering at the thought of his hands and lips and tongue reading every inch of her flesh. 'You mean you haven't given up on me yet?'

His eyes held hers in a heart-stopping lock. 'Do you want me to give up?'

'No,' she said, standing on tiptoes to press a kiss to

his mouth. 'I want you to make love to me. That's why we came here tonight. I need to do this.'

'Then let's do this,' Louis said and brought his mouth down to hers.

Ivy sighed with pure pleasure as his mouth subjected hers to a passionate exploration. His tongue playfully teased hers into a sexy tango, one of his hands coming up to cradle her face, the other to hold the back of her head, his fingers splaying through her hair. Desire flared and flamed in her lower body, longing coursing through her flesh like lashing tongues of flame. She was pressed so close to him she could feel every hard ridge and contour of his body, the heat and potency of his arousal against her stirring her female flesh into a frenzy of want. She could feel the secret preparation of her body, the dewy wetness of female arousal and the low, deep pulse in her core.

Louis raised his mouth off hers and led her to the bed. He whipped off the covers, then his shirt and trousers, and drew her down beside him on the bed. He was still wearing his underwear, but she couldn't take her eyes off his aroused length tenting the fabric, but was too shy to reach for him. What if she did something wrong? What if he didn't like her touch?

'You can touch me if you want.' His voice was deep and rough with desire.

'What if I don't do it right?'

He took her hand and placed it on his erection over his underwear, a ripple of pleasure passing over his face at her touch. Then he peeled his underwear out of the way and placed her hand on him, skin on skin. 'You won't hurt me. That's it, hold me in your hand.'

He was so thick and strong, like velvet-covered steel, and her intimate muscles quivered at the thought of him entering her. She stroked him harder, enjoying the guttural sounds he was making, enjoying the power it gave her to tantalise him with her touch.

'My turn now.' He removed her hand from his body and gently pushed her back down on the mattress, propping himself up on one elbow, the other hand stroking her from her breasts to her belly and back again in long, slow strokes until her back was almost arching off the bed. He went lower with his hand, cupping her mound over her knickers. She moaned against his hand, wanting more but unsure how to ask for it. He left his hand where it was and kissed her mouth again, long, slow and deep. It gave her time to get used to feeling him touching her, holding the most sensitive part of her body without pushing her to go any further. But she wanted to go further, she wanted to go all the way. Her body was hungry and aching for his possession.

'I want you.' Her voice came out breathless.

'Patience, *ma petite*.' His tone had a sexy, raspy edge that made her shiver all the more with longing. 'There's no rush.'

Ivy took his hand and placed it on her female flesh. 'I want you to touch me. I need you to.'

His eyes darkened until there was only a narrow rim of grey-blue visible around the bottomless black of his pupils. 'How about we take these off, hmm?' He peeled away her knickers and she lifted her hips to help him, way beyond shyness with her body raging with such unstoppable lust. He stroked the seam of her body, slowly, torturously slowly, and every nerve in her pelvis fizzed like a firework. Hot streaks of sensation ran down her legs, a warm pool forming at the base of her spine and spreading to her core. He brought his mouth down to her and stroked his tongue where his finger had just been. It was shockingly intimate and yet she didn't flinch or shy away from it. She was too far gone for that. She whimpered, gasped and throbbed with longing.

He lifted his mouth off her and separated her folds with his fingers, his gaze devouring her female form as if it was the most beautiful thing he'd ever seen. 'You're gorgeous…' His voice was husky, his touch exquisitely gentle.

Ivy sucked in a much-needed breath and instinctively spread her legs wider, her heart racing with excitement. 'Are you going to do what I think you're going to do?' Her voice was so breathless it came out like a strangled whisper.

'Only if you want me to.'

She swallowed. 'I want you to.' Never had she wanted anything more. Her body was on fire and flickering with delicious sensations.

Louis brought his mouth to her again, his lips and tongue playing with her female flesh, finally triggering a powerful rush that seemingly came from nowhere and everywhere at once. Waves and ripples of pleasure washed through her pelvis, making her writhe and cry out as if she was possessed by a paranormal entity.

Ivy gasped and flung her head back against the bed,

her chest heaving, her body limp as the aftershocks gradually faded. 'Oh, God, that was... I don't know how to describe it.'

Louis came up on one elbow and smiled down at her. 'It will get better.'

She had no idea how it ever could. She had never experienced anything so earth-shattering. She tiptoed her fingers down his sternum all the way to his rock-hard abdomen. 'Aren't you going to...?'

He captured her hand before it could go any lower and pressed a kiss to the middle of her palm. 'Not right now.' His expression became unreadable and she could sense him pulling away as if an invisible drawbridge had come up between them.

She blinked at him in surprise. 'But aren't you...?'

He pressed a finger to her lips to halt her speech. 'This is about your pleasure, not mine.'

Ivy brushed his hand away and grasped him by the shoulder. 'But isn't making love meant to be a two-way thing?'

'Yes, but there's plenty of time. We've got all night.' He rolled away and picked up his shirt and trousers from the floor and proceeded to put them back on.

Ivy pulled the bed sheet up over her nakedness, wondering why he'd called a halt when it was so obvious he desired her. *We've got all night.* But wouldn't most guys want to make the most of it?

She was starting to wonder if one night was going to be enough for her. He had awakened needs and desires in her that thrilled and delighted her. But what was going to happen when this night was over? Back to being friends only. 'Is this about your one-night-only rule? You can't bring yourself to sleep with me more than once? Why do you even have such a dumb rule?'

Louis' jaw tightened. 'I've always been a fan of the casual one-nighter—hence my moniker, Mr Amazing One-Night Stand. Brief hook-ups are less complicated, given my work commitments. I don't like being tied down in a relationship when I have other demands on my time. But a few months ago I allowed a hook-up to stretch out to three weeks. Big mistake. The woman became increasingly attached and started dropping hints about moving in with me. I broke things off as gently as I could but it didn't go well.'

He speared a hand through his hair and blew out a breath before continuing, 'She was clearly heartbroken and I felt awful about causing her that much pain, especially as we'd both agreed at the beginning it was only a short-term fling. She stalked me for weeks on end. I had to block her on my phone and email, to stop the bombardment of calls and texts and emails. It was embarrassing when she'd show up at work in tears, desperate to talk to me. Once she turned up in another city where I was presenting at a conference. Since then, I made a promise to myself never to date anyone longer than twenty-four hours.'

Ivy got off the bed, bringing the sheet with her as a sarong around her body. 'So, you're letting one woman who didn't know how to deal with rejection ruin your chance to ever be in a proper, fulfilling relationship?'

'But I've never wanted anything more than casual

relationships.' His tone was curt. 'I've seen the way fulfilling relationships change over time into full-on war.'

She frowned. 'Your parents?'

His lip curled. 'My parents and yours and numerous others.'

Ivy could hardly argue with that. Her parents had seemed happy enough until her father's affair had been uncovered. The affair had been going on for close to a year. No wonder her mother had gone off the rails once she'd found out. 'I know not everyone ends up happy forever, but at least it's worth a try. Falling in love with someone and building a life together is all I've ever wanted.'

'Good luck with that.' Cynicism laced his tone.

Ivy chewed her lip for a moment. 'So, why did you date that woman for as long as you did?'

Louis blew out a breath, his brow creased in a frown. 'She was good company, easy to get along with and—'

'Good in bed?'

He gave her an unreadable look. 'It's not a habit of mine to discuss previous lovers with other people.'

'That's very reassuring.'

His eyes held hers for a beat or two. 'What happens between us stays between us. You have my word on that.'

Ivy went up to him and placed a hand on his forearm. 'Thank you. I sometimes lie awake at night worrying what those guys I dated are saying about me to their friends. It's one of the reasons I haven't gone on any other dates.'

He placed his hand over hers, his fingers warm and

strong. His grey-blue eyes drifted to her mouth and back again. 'You don't kiss like a Victorian prude.' His other arm came around her body, drawing her closer to his deliciously hard frame. Every female cell in her body rejoiced at the contact, her breasts tingled, her lower body contracted and her heart began to pick up its pace.

Ivy reached up and stroked her hand over the prickly stubble of his lean jaw. 'How many Victorian prudes have you kissed?'

His eyes became sexily hooded, his hand going to the small of her back, bringing her even closer. 'I don't kiss and tell, remember?'

'Good to know.' Her voice dropped to a whisper, desire beating with an insistent pulse between her legs. She breathed in the male scent of him, the salty hint of perspiration and the sharp citrus notes of his aftershave. 'Louis…about the Victorian prude thing…'

She glanced up at him again. 'Remember when my parents got divorced in my early teens? Well, Ronan probably told you how crazy our mother went, although he didn't see a lot of it, as he was at boarding school and then university. She had so many boyfriends coming and going. It was like she was trying to outdo my father, to punish him for having that affair for so long. She wasn't choosy in who she brought home either. It was terrifying at times to suddenly confront a strange man on his way to the bathroom or in the kitchen, helping himself to stuff.'

Louis frowned. 'Did anyone touch you or…?'

She shook her head. 'No, thankfully not, but I felt creeped out by it all. And then, I'd visit Dad at his flat, where he was living with his new girlfriend. He would act all lovey-dovey, the way he used to act with Mum. I felt so angry, but I couldn't say anything, as I didn't want to lose him out of my life. But I did in the end, anyway.'

'It must have been a terribly confusing time for you,' Louis said, still frowning.

'It was... I feel a bit silly about it now. I mean, I'm almost thirty and I've let something that happened so long ago stop me from living the life I want to live. But I truly couldn't bear the thought of having sex with someone I didn't know and trust like my mother did after Dad left.'

His look was long and thoughtful, as if her words resonated with his own situation. 'You coped the best way you could. Don't be so hard on yourself.'

She gave him a crooked smile. 'But all that's going to change now you've helped me embrace my sensuality. I don't know how to thank you.'

He brought his mouth to the right side of her forehead, his lips moving against her skin in teasing little brushes that made the hairs on her head stand up and a warm, treacly sensation flow down her spine. He moved his lips down her face—the sensitive spots in front of and below her ear—and she shuddered with the tickling pleasure of his touch. He kissed the edges of her mouth without actually touching her lips, ramping up her desire for his kiss to a frenzied, fiery ache in her flesh.

Ivy gripped him by the shoulders, her body so close to his she could feel every hard ridge and solid plane, sending a wave of intense longing through her. 'Kiss me, Louis. Don't make me beg.'

He framed her face in his hands, his eyes as dark as outer space. 'If I kiss you, I might not want to stop.'

She licked her lips and held his gaze. 'Why would that be a problem if I don't want you to stop?'

He leaned his forehead on hers, their breaths mingling intimately in the space between their faces. 'I thought I had the willpower, the self-control, to talk you out of your crazy plan to lose your virginity to me.' He eased back to look down at her. 'But it seems I overestimated the limits of my control.'

Ivy traced the outline of his mouth with her finger, her heart beating a tattoo in her chest. 'I want you to make love to me. I want you to be my first lover. It feels right for it to be you and not someone I don't care a fig about. Or someone who might talk about me to their friends.'

He brushed her hair back from her forehead, his eyes dark and serious. 'It's only for tonight. After that, we go our separate ways. I can't offer anything else.'

'I don't want anything else.' Ivy wrapped her arms around his neck and stood on tiptoe as his head came down. His mouth covered hers in a fireball kiss, sending sparks shooting through her body. She opened to him and his tongue teased hers into a dance that mimicked the most erotic of connections two humans could have with each other. Desire leapt and burned and blazed in her flesh as he increased the pressure of his lips on hers. She pushed herself against him, hungry for his touch, aching for his possession.

His hands skated down the sides of her body, peeling the bed sheet away like a skin and covering one of her breasts with the broad expanse of his hand. His touch was gentle and yet electric, sending hot sparks through her flesh. Her nipple went to a tight bud, the soft flesh of her breast tingling. He removed his hand and replaced it with his mouth, exploring her in intimate detail. He rolled his tongue over and around her nipple, then took it into his mouth, gently sucking on it, releasing a shower of pleasurable sensations through her body. He moved to her other breast, subjecting it to the same passionate exploration until she was gasping and writhing with the need to feel more.

Louis brought his mouth back to hers in another drugging kiss, his arms going back around her body, one of his hands cupping the naked curve of her bottom. He groaned against her lips, his kiss deepening, his breathing as hectic as hers. 'God, I want you so badly. How did I ever think this wasn't going to happen eventually?'

Ivy stroked his jaw and leaned into the throbbing pulse of his lower body. 'I want you too.'

He held her from him and locked gazes. 'By the way, are you using any contraception?'

'I'm on a low-dose pill.' She twisted her mouth in a rueful manner. 'Not that I've needed it until now. It was just wishful thinking on my part.'

'I always use condoms in any case but it's good to be doubly sure there won't be an unwanted pregnancy. That's a complication both of us could do without.'

'Okay. Sounds good.' Ivy had wanted children since

she'd been a child herself. The thought of never having a family of her own was her worst nightmare. But she could hardly tell Louis that. He was so adamant about not settling down and she was not going to compromise on something so important to her. Besides, she was not involved with him with the goal of happy-ever-after. Louis wasn't the answer to her fairy-tale fantasy—he was just the answer to her V problem. She was engaging his services to help her get in the dating game with more confidence. Why would she be interested in a future with a renowned playboy? That wasn't a future—that was a recipe for heartbreak. And she wanted no part of it.

Louis sourced a condom from his wallet in the pocket of his trousers and then, stepping out of his clothes, led her back to the bed. The moon had risen and cast the room in a silvery glow. Strangely, her shyness about being naked in front of him wasn't an issue. All she could think about was finding release from the tender ache between her legs. An ache he had triggered with his magical touch. Ivy drank in the sight of his fully aroused body, all the strong planes and contours of male flesh in its prime. Her desire for him rose again like an unquenchable thirst. 'How many condoms did you bring?'

'Enough.' His eyes glinted and he tore the packet open and applied the condom.

Ivy stroked him with her hand, enjoying the sensation of his powerful flesh quivering from her touch. 'I never thought I'd feel comfortable doing this but with you it feels so…so right.'

He pressed her back down on the bed, his expression clouding. 'It feels better than it probably should, given our situation.'

Ivy frowned. 'What do you mean?'

His eyes went back and forth between each of hers and then drifted to her mouth. He drew in a deep breath and gave a half-smile that looked a little forced. He brushed her hair back from her face, his eyes dark and unreadable. 'Is one night going to be enough for you?'

Ivy licked her suddenly dry lips and aimed her gaze at his chin. 'That's what we agreed, right? Those are your rules and I'm fine with that.' Was she, though? A niggling doubt wormed its way into her mind. The exquisite pleasure he'd made her feel so far had made her hungry, ravenous, greedy for more. How was one measly little night going to satisfy her?

He lifted her chin with his finger and meshed his gaze with hers. 'Yeah, that's what we agreed. One night and one night only.'

Ivy pulled his head back down to hers. 'Then we'd better get on with it.'

He covered her mouth in a kiss that spoke of desperate passion only just held in check. His tongue flickered against hers, erotically mimicking the full possession of her body she craved so much. Ivy moved against him, silently urging him to assuage the throbbing ache of desire in her flesh. One of his legs hitched over hers, the sexy tangle of their limbs arousing in itself.

'I want you so much.' He groaned the words against her mouth, his body hot and hard against her.

'Me too.' Ivy could barely speak for the rapacious hunger vibrating in her body.

Louis brought himself to her entrance, nudging her with his tip but not going any further. 'If you don't feel comfortable at any point, let me know.'

'Okay.'

His first thrust was shallow and gentle, but Ivy was too impatient to wait and lifted her hips to receive him, her hands going to his taut buttocks to urge him on. He gave an agonised groan and went a little deeper, the slickness of her body welcoming him. He stilled his movements, his breathing hectic. 'Are you okay?'

'Don't stop. Please keep going.' Her body was on fire, flickers and, flames and fizzing sensations travelling throughout her pelvis and down the backs of her legs.

Louis continued to thrust, but she sensed he was holding himself back out of consideration for her. But her body was enjoying every inch of his powerful length and was crying out for more. She gripped him harder by the buttocks and lifted her hips to meet each downward thrust. He sucked in a harsh breath and his rhythm increased, the thrusts becoming deeper and faster, sending her senses reeling. Her body wrapped tight around him, his intimate invasion not quite enough to send her over the edge into the abyss. But then he began to caress her with his fingers, giving her the extra friction she needed to soar. She threw her head back and gasped out sobbing cries of release, her body shaking, quivering, thrashing with the sheer force rocketing through her.

Ivy was still suffering the aftershocks when Louis

found his own release and she held him through it, enjoying the way his body tensed and then finally broke free from the restraints he'd put on it. There was something so deeply primal about his groans and almost savage about his orgasm. It thrilled her that she had brought him so undone by her touch, her body, her caresses.

Louis rolled away, disposed of the condom and then lay back and flung an arm across his eyes, his chest still heaving. 'Dear God in heaven...'

Ivy propped herself up on one elbow by his side, her hand stroking down his chest. 'Was it good for you?' She couldn't quite remove the note of uncertainty in her voice.

He turned his head her way and smiled a lopsided smile, and something in her chest turned over. He covered her hand with his, anchoring on the thud-thud-thud of his heart. 'Better than good— amazing.'

She leaned forward and pressed a soft kiss to his lips. 'Thanks for making it so special for me.'

He tucked a wayward strand of hair back behind her ear, his gaze locked on hers. 'I didn't hurt you?'

She smiled and tiptoed her fingers across his toned pectoral muscles. 'Not a bit. I read somewhere that the only way you can tell if a woman is a virgin is if she tells you and you believe her. All that stuff about broken and bleeding hymens is a bit of a myth. Most women and girls damage their hymen doing sports during childhood or using tampons when they get their periods.'

'True, but sex can still be uncomfortable for a woman if her partner isn't considerate.'

Ivy lifted her hand to his head and toyed with his short-cropped hair. 'But you were very considerate.'

His expression was warm with tenderness, his hand going to her hip and rolling her towards him. 'If I was truly considerate, I'd take you downstairs and feed you the delicious dinner my housekeeper prepared.'

'I'm sensing a "but" at the end of that sentence.'

He grinned and swiftly turned her over so her back was against the mattress, his body half-covering hers. 'But I want to do this first.' And his mouth came down to hers.

Louis kissed her slowly and leisurely at first, but then a storm of need began to barrel through him, and he deepened the kiss with a commanding thrust of his tongue. She opened to him like a flower and he groaned at the back of his throat and explored her sweet mouth as if it was the last kiss he would ever have. Her lips were soft and yielding, passionate and responsive, and his blood pounded with renewed desire. Making love to her had shocked him to the core. Not in a bad way, but in a way he hadn't been expecting. Normally sex was just sex, a physical thing he enjoyed like any other man. But with Ivy something felt different. Not just because it was her first time, although he had to admit that had made it rather special—memorably special. But the taste of her skin, the response of her body, stirred him in a way no other lover had done before.

Louis rained kisses down her body, lingering over her breasts before going to the silk of her inner thighs. He teased her with his lips and tongue, working his way to the feminine heart of her body. She gasped as he anointed her with his tongue, her body shuddering through an orgasm, his own body desperate for intimate connection with the tight slickness of hers.

Ivy reached for him and he only just had time to put on another condom in his haste to bury himself in her honeyed core. The tumult built to a crescendo inside him, her movements so in tune with his, sending his senses reeling. The heat, the musk of mating, the glide of aroused male flesh against velvet female flesh, sent him into the stratosphere where no thought could reside, only pleasure...mind-blowing, skin-tingling bliss...

In the quiet, restful moments afterwards, a stray thought managed to get through the firewall of Louis' mind.

One night, huh? Are you sure that's going to be enough?

He tried to think of something else but, with Ivy's soft hand gently stroking the flank of his thigh, he knew the hunger he had for her was not going to be satisfied by one night. But he would have to accept that and stick with the plan. Continuing this any longer than a night was tempting but too dangerous. It was a physical hunger, nothing else, and it would fade as long as he didn't fuel it. He didn't *do* anything else. Couldn't do anything else. *Wouldn't* do anything else.

But, oh, how he wanted to.

CHAPTER SIX

IVY WOKE TO find herself alone in bed early the next morning. Louis had told her he was a restless sleeper who often got up during the night to work but she hadn't seen him bring a laptop with him—although she had noticed a well-appointed study downstairs. Perhaps he had put in a few hours on his latest project or gone for a run or something.

She pushed aside the sense of disappointment that Louis hadn't woken up beside her and instead focussed on the positives. She was no longer a virgin. Her mission was accomplished with two weeks to spare until she turned thirty. Her body felt different, somehow, more alive and sensitive than ever before. Even the sensation of the sheets against her skin was heightened. It was as if her nerves had shifted position.

She pushed the bedcovers off and slipped on the satin bathrobe she'd brought with her. The smooth fabric on her body felt as delicious as a caress and she couldn't wait to feel Louis' touch again. She squeezed her thighs together. Her inner muscles gave the faintest of protests and a frisson passed over her flesh. How wonderful would it be to spend the rest of the weekend together, making love again—and not just this weekend, but the one after and the one after and...

Ivy was pulled away from her thoughts as if by the sudden tug of a marionette's strings. *One night and one night only.* That was what she'd agreed on and it was all Louis was offering. She knew enough about him to know he could be stubborn when his mind was made up.

Wouldn't it be better if she avoided the 'morning after the night before' scene she was dreading? How could she look at him now and see him as only a friend and not the most amazing lover a woman could ask for? Her body was already craving him. How would she hide her longing from him? It was better to leave before he came back from wherever he'd gone during the night. Before he saw how much she wanted him to continue their fling. Before her feelings got involved any more than they already were. Before she made a complete and utter fool of herself by begging him to extend their fling beyond the one night they'd agreed on.

She reached for her phone and organised a taxi back to London.

Hopefully she would be halfway home before he even knew she had gone.

Louis hadn't slept so soundly for years—even if it had only been until just before dawn. Maybe it was the Cotswolds air. Maybe it was breaking his sex drought. *Maybe it was Ivy...*

He'd left her sleeping in the early hours, not trusting himself to wake up beside her without wanting to make love to her again. Or tweaking the rules so they spent the rest of the weekend down here. But he had no business tweaking the rules. He had done as she requested and there was no need to take things any further.

Weird, but he had no regrets about last night. How could he when it was the best sex he'd ever had? Sensual, meaningful, memorable, tender…and yet racy. His body tingled at the thought of Ivy's touch. His lips remembered the taste and texture of hers. Every cell in his body wanted her with a grinding hunger.

But their night together was over.

It was Saturday morning and their relationship had to go back to normal. Normal? How normal was it that every time he looked at her now he would recall the softness of her mouth under his, the stroke of her hands, the warm, velvet grip of her body? He shuddered and groaned as desire swept through him like a tide, heating and hardening his flesh to the point of pain.

He went for a long run along the country lanes, trying to summon his self-control. Maybe he should tweak the rules. Maybe she needed more than one night to gain even more confidence. She'd told him how her parents' break-up had contributed to her uneasiness with intimacy, and it had made him realise even more how stressful and difficult her adolescence had been. Hadn't he carried his own hang-ups from his childhood?

You're rationalising—you just want to continue your fling with her.

Louis knew the danger of extending their fling. It was one of the reasons he'd been reluctant to start it in the first place. Ivy wasn't like the other women he dated—not because they hadn't been nice women, with lots to offer. But he could always switch off his feelings when he had casual dates. He was a master at it. But with Ivy those unwanted feelings had a habit of slipping under his guard, making him hunger for things he had so long suppressed or told himself he didn't really want.

And then there was the other complication of his friendship with her brother. Ronan would never forgive him for hurting Ivy. And how could he avoid hurting her if he continued to sleep with her without offering her the whole package she yearned for—marriage, babies and forever love? A package he had no intention of offering to anyone. Ever.

Louis came back from his run and showered and dressed before going to Ivy's room. The door of her room was closed, so he gave it a gentle tap.

'Ivy? Are you up? Time for breakfast before we head back to London.'

There was no answer, so he opened the door and went in. The bed had been stripped and the duvet neatly folded back to wait for fresh sheets to be placed on later. It took him a moment to register what he was seeing—or not seeing. There was no trace of Ivy in the room. Her luggage was gone and when he checked the *en suite* no trace of her toiletries remained. All that was left was the faint trace of her perfume lingering in the air.

There was something strangely mocking about that bare and empty bed. He was the one who normally left before his casual dates woke on the rare occasions he spent the whole night with anyone. He assiduously avoided the morning-after scenes where a date would drop hints about wanting to see him again. Why had Ivy left? *How* had she left?

And then he saw the note propped next to the bedside lamp. He walked across the room and snatched it up, unfolding the rectangle of paper to read:

> *Thanks for last night. I didn't want to wake you, so caught a cab back home. I have to get ready for Paris next week.*
> *Your friend, Ivy*

He stared at the word 'friend' for so long, he became cross-eyed. He sucked in a harsh breath, scrunched the note into a ball and tossed it on the bed. The bed where he had made love to her last night. Not simply had hookup sex, but actually made love. Her first time had been *his* first time feeling more than needing an itch to be scratched. His first time feeling more than lust, feeling something far more complicated.

Why had she left without seeing him face to face? Was she feeling uncomfortable? Embarrassed? Regretful? He took out his phone and called her number, but it went through to voice mail.

'Call me.' He spoke more curtly than he'd intended, annoyed with himself for not anticipating her leaving. He was rarely blindsided by people these days. He never got close enough to anyone for them to surprise him. It didn't sit well with him to be the one left behind, staring at the empty bed where he'd had the best sex of his life.

One night not enough for you, huh? His conscience jeered from the sidelines.

Louis ground his teeth so hard, he thought he'd be taking his meals through a straw for the next month.

No, one night wasn't enough—so he was going to do something about it.

Ivy was tidying up the back office of the antiques store for her elderly boss, Mr Thornley, when she heard a customer come into the shop. She glanced at the CCTV monitor on the desk and her heart missed a beat— and then raced, as if it needed an emergency dose of beta blockers. Louis had only once before come in to the shop and her heart hadn't threatened to go into overdrive then. But that had been before she had slept with him, experienced for one night the phenomenal magic of being in his arms.

She wiped her suddenly damp palms on the front of her skirt and went out to greet him, painting a smile on her face. 'Hiya, Louis.'

She was proud of how normal she sounded. Who said she couldn't switch back to being friends with him without a stumble? Even if every cell of her body was acutely aware of him and longed to feel his arms go around her to hold her close.

His grey-blue eyes ran over her skirt and blouse and she wondered if he was recalling every inch of her naked flesh and how it had felt against his own. His mouth was set in a firm line and there was a muscle twitching in his jaw. 'Why did you leave without saying goodbye on Saturday, or calling me as I asked?' His tone was as curt as the short message he had left on her voice mail the other day. A message she had chosen not to obey.

Ivy raised her chin, sending him a tiny flash of her gaze. 'You didn't ask—you demanded.'

His eyes warred with hers for a long moment. Then his tense features softened a fraction and his voice lowered to a rich, deep burr. 'I was worried about you. I thought you might be feeling some regret about our night together.'

Ivy schooled her features into 'Ms Modern Hook-Up' mode. 'Why should I be feeling regret? We spent the night together as agreed. It went well and I went home. End of.'

A frown pulled at his brow and his mouth flattened once more. 'But why not wait until I drove you back?'

She turned to straighten some papers on the cluttered desk. 'I thought it was better to go before you talked me into staying the whole weekend with you.'

There was a silence so intense, the soft ticking of the French carriage clock on the desk sounded like hammer blows.

Louis gave an incredulous laugh. 'You thought I was going to ask you for an extension?'

Ivy turned back to face him, her look pointed. 'Weren't you?'

A shutter came down at the back of his gaze, screening his thoughts, hiding his feelings, locking her out. 'I only do one-night stands, remember?'

Ivy folded her arms across her body and lifted her right hand to her mouth, tapping against her lips as if studying a particularly interesting artefact. 'Then why are you here now? It's too late for lunch or even coffee. Besides, I'm flying to Paris early tomorrow, so—'

'So am I.'

Ivy stared at him. 'You are?' She disguised a tight swallow. 'Are you seeing a client or…?' She couldn't complete the rest of her sentence. She didn't want to know if he planned to hook up with someone while he was in France. He often travelled for work, and was rarely in London for more than a week at a time. He would no doubt go back to his playboy lifestyle now and she would have to suffer seeing him in the gossip pages with a host of other women who were happy with the brief encounters he offered them.

'I have a couple of projects going on in Paris that I need to check,' he said. 'Where are you staying?'

'I haven't had time to book my accommodation yet,' Ivy said, unfolding her arms. 'My boss normally organises it when I go away on a business trip for him, but his wife had a fall on Sunday night, so he's been a bit distracted. I was going to find a room tonight.'

'Stay with me at my apartment.' His expression was still difficult to read but something about the incredible stillness of his posture made her suspect he was holding his breath.

She ran the tip of her tongue over her lips, not sure what to make of his invitation. Wanting to accept it but not sure if it was wise to do so. Stay with him in Paris. The most romantic city in the world. The city of love. 'Why do you want me to stay with you?'

His eyes darkened and he crossed the distance to where she was standing in two or three strides. He took one of her hands in his and stroked his thumb over her racing pulse. 'You know why.' His voice was so deep it could have come from the centre of the earth.

Ivy decided to play it cool. 'Do I? Last time we spoke you made it clear we were a one-night thing. Are we going to be friends or lovers in Paris?'

His thumb stroked over the fleshy part of her thumb, triggering a storm of sensations that travelled from her hand to her core in a fizzing fire trail. His eyes held hers in an unwavering lock, making her spine tingle, as though sherbet were slowly trickling through her vertebrae. 'We can be both.'

'But I thought—'

'How long will you be in Paris?'

'Wednesday till Friday.'

'Can you stay until Sunday?' he asked.

'I guess so… But I thought you said—'

'Five days in Paris. That's all I'm offering. Take it or leave it.' His tone was so businesslike and clinical, yet his hand holding hers seemed to communicate a more desperate plea. A plea that her own body was communicating with a raised pulse and a skipping heartbeat and bated breath.

Ivy chewed one side of her lip and looked down at their joined hands. She recalled his hands on her most intimate flesh and something turned over in her stomach. One night was never going to be enough but would another five cure this sweet, torturous ache he alone triggered in her body? Probably not, but she would at least have more memories to keep when the time was over. She slowly brought her gaze back up to his. 'I'll come with you to Paris.'

His smile was lazy, but it ignited a flare in his eyes that made her heart skip another beat. 'Good.' He brought her hand up to his lips and kissed her bent knuckles, still holding her gaze. 'I'll see you in the morning.' He released her hand, his expression turning rueful. 'I would have suggested dinner tonight but it's my mother's birthday. I wouldn't want to give her the wrong impression about us.'

Ivy would have liked to meet his parents in an effort to understand him better, but she was reluctant to voice it out loud. They were having a fling, not a relationship that followed a more traditional pattern of dating, courtship, marriage. She had no right to be offended that he didn't offer to introduce her to his family. She wasn't a permanent fixture in his life or at least not in a romantic sense. She had never envisaged him as a romantic partner, never allowed herself to think of him in any way other than as her brother's friend. But one kiss had changed something inside her, which was faintly worrying. She was meant to have kept her emotions out of their arrangement. The last thing she needed was to complicate her life by falling in love with a man who had locked his heart away.

'I totally understand. Just imagine if I brought you home with me to see my mum. She'd book a wedding planner on the spot and she'd probably beg to be my bridesmaid.'

Louis' smile didn't quite reach his eyes. 'Then it's best we keep this trip to Paris to ourselves.'

'Fine. Good plan.'

He moved closer again and leaned down to press a soft kiss to her lips. When he pulled back, her lips clung to his like silk snagging on something rough. His mouth came down again, firmer, warmer, more insistent, and her senses skyrocketed. She opened to him and wound her arms around his neck, her body pressing against the hard planes of his frame.

His tongue met hers in a silken thrust that set off fireworks in her blood. Molten heat flared in her core and her legs trembled with the effort of keeping upright. He made a rough sound at the back of his throat and brought her even closer, one of his hands pressed against the curve of her bottom, the other buried in the tresses of her hair. The slight tether of his fingers in her hair felt almost primal, possessive, and a shiver coursed down her spine like a shower of champagne bubbles. Louis angled his head to change position, deepening the kiss even further. An intense ache spread through her flesh, centred in her core where a heavy pulse thrummed.

He lifted his mouth off hers, his breathing heavy, his eyes glinting with desire. 'Hold that thought, *ma chérie*. I'd better not be late for my mother's birthday dinner. I'll finish this in Paris.'

'Is that a promise?'

He smiled a sexy smile that made her inner core shiver in anticipation. 'Damn right it is.'

'So, Paris this week with Louis, huh?' Millie said, watching Ivy pack her bag in her bedroom later that evening. 'What happened to the one-night-only rule? Who changed it? You or him?'

Ivy folded a silk evening blouse and placed it in her bag on the bed. 'He did.'

'Woo-hoo. You go, girl. You must have some serious chemistry going on between you.'

Ivy put a matching skirt next to the blouse in her bag. 'It's just a fling, Millie. Don't get too excited. He's not the falling in love type.'

'Maybe not, but you definitely are. Are you sure you're not falling a teensy weensy bit in love with him?' Millie pressed her thumb and index finger together in a tiny pinching gesture.

'It would be crazy for me to develop feelings for him.' Crazy, crazy, crazy—so she had to try even harder to ignore those soft little flutters in her heart every time he looked at her.

Millie picked up a pendant she'd designed for Ivy's last birthday and ran the fine silver chain through her fingers. 'Let me know if you want me to design your engagement and wedding rings for you. Mates' rates and all.' Her friend might not be able to keep a secret, but she was excellent at spotting a white lie when she heard one.

Ivy turned to pick out some underwear from the wardrobe. 'Don't be silly. There's not going to be an engagement or wedding. We're calling it quits after Paris.'

She gripped the edge of the drawer and tried to imagine going back to being friends with Louis instead of lovers. How would she be able to do it? How could she look at him and not think of how it felt to be in his arms? To have his mouth clamped to hers, his body buried deep inside her? To feel the stroke of his hand down her spine or to feel his arm slip around her waist and draw her closer? Her body literally ached when she wasn't with him. She had relived his love-making hundreds of times since coming home from work that evening. Her body was still humming and thrumming with the need he awakened.

Millie put down the pendant and met Ivy's gaze. 'But you don't want it to end it, do you?'

Ivy sat on the bed with a sigh. 'No. Not yet.'

Millie sat beside her and slipped an arm around her shoulders. 'I won't tell you I told you so.'

Ivy gave her the side-eye. 'Thanks.'

'I'll save that phrase for my mother. Did I tell you she's getting divorced again?'

'Again? How many times is that? Three?'

Millie flicked her eyes upwards in a despairing manner. 'Four. And each time she's been royally screwed over.' She bounced off the bed and turned to face Ivy, her expression determined. 'I'm not going to watch her get done over again. I'm saving up to get the best lawyer for her I can.'

'They don't come cheap. What about asking the guy you went on that blind date with a couple of months ago... Hunter Addison? Isn't he a celebrity divorce lawyer? I've heard he's brilliant. He might do it pro bono for you. It can't hurt to ask him.'

Millie's cheeks went as pink as the silk shirt in Ivy's weekend bag. 'Erm...well... I kind of burned my boats with him.'

'Oh, really? What happened that night? You've always been a little cagey about talking about it.'

Millie shrugged one shoulder in an off-hand manner. 'Nothing happened other than we both decided our mutual friends got it wrong in thinking we might ever hit it off. We had nothing in common and spent the whole ghastly evening annoying each other.'

Ivy wondered if her friend had deliberately sabotaged the date out of her unwillingness to move on from the death of her fiancé. 'Hmm, well, all I can say is, he might be the worst blind date but word has it he's one of the best divorce lawyers in London. If you don't get him for your mum, then her ex will get him and, believe you me, you don't want the best in the business working for your enemy.'

Millie chewed at the corner of her mouth; her eyes were troubled. 'Gosh, I hadn't thought of it that way...' She straightened her shoulders and painted a bright smile on her face that didn't fool Ivy for a second. 'I'd better let you finish packing. Enjoy Paris.'

'I will.'

It didn't matter where she went with Louis, it would be impossible not to enjoy herself. The only trouble was...what would she have after Paris?

Memories. That was all.

CHAPTER SEVEN

THEY FLEW TO PARIS the following morning and a short time afterwards Louis took her to his apartment in the Sixteenth Arrondissement in Saint-Germain-des-Prés. The historic architecture was stunning, and many of the beautiful old buildings had been turned into modern apartments—including Louis'.

Ivy stepped over the threshold and stood for a moment, struck speechless by the elegance and design. The crystal chandeliers overhead tinkled from the slight draught from the door opening and closing. The marble floor was covered in places with hand-woven silk rugs that were so soft to step on, she thought her ankles were going to be swallowed. The pieces of antique furniture were priceless and came from various periods—from as early as the Renaissance, through to Louis XIV, Louis XV, Regency, Art Deco and Art Nouveau to modern times.

'Oh, my God.' She stepped further into the foyer, touching various pieces with worshipful fingers. 'Your taste is amazing. And your budget. Some of these things must've cost a fortune.'

'If I like something, I buy it. I don't allow the expense to influence my decision.'

'Lucky you.' Ivy leaned down to look more closely at a Louis XV rosewood and gold-inlaid writing desk she was sure she had seen before at work. 'Hey, I'm sure we had this piece in the show room last year. I seem to remember a French interior designer bought it with a whole shipment of other stuff.' She straightened and looked at Louis. 'Did she buy it on your behalf?'

His expression was indecipherable. 'I told her to buy from your shop because I know you have good quality, genuine antiques.'

Ivy gave a rueful smile. 'It's not my shop, it's Mr Thornley's and I have a horrible feeling he's going to sell it now that his wife's health is going downhill.'

'Would you like to own your own business rather than work for someone else?'

Ivy ran a lazy finger over the gold inlay on the writing desk. 'I don't know... I want to keep working in antiques, but I want to have a family one day, and running a business is hard work and very time-consuming.' She lowered her hand from the table and glanced at him. 'And I certainly don't have the money to buy Mr Thornley's business. Not with Mum needing financial top-ups all the time.'

A frown settled on his brow. 'Your mother's financial problems are not your responsibility.'

She gave him an ironic look. 'And nor are they yours, but you still bail her out from time to time.'

He gave a crooked smile. *'Touché.'* His smile faded and he continued, 'But it's hard not to feel sorry for her. She's never really got over your father leaving, has she?'

Ivy shook her head and sighed. 'No. They were child-hood sweethearts. He was her first lover. She thought they'd be together forever and then he traded her in for someone half her age.'

'Marriage doesn't suit all men.'

Ivy had come to realise, since sleeping with Louis, how much her mother's lifestyle choices had affected her while growing up. The fear of being rejected by someone you thought loved you was too terrifying.

'Remember how I told you how my mother was so out of control with her drinking and flings with men she'd met at the pub? Well, it embarrassed me so much, and I think it's why I locked down my own budding sexuality. Mum was so open about sex that it made me all the more uncomfortable. She would talk about her latest lover and what they'd got up to and I'd cringe with embarrassment. *I* became the disapproving, prudish parent rather than the young teenage girl I really was.

'And I couldn't talk to Dad about it, because it might have made him fight for full custody, and no way did I want to live with him and his younger girlfriend. I'd then have to watch him acting like a born-again teenager with her every day instead of only the occasional weekend. And I didn't want to worry Ronan because he was having enough trouble dealing with his own issues. I'm sure he would have come out about his sexuality a whole lot sooner if it hadn't been for my parents breaking up and carrying on the way they did.'

Louis squeezed both her hands. 'You've both done an amazing job of surviving what was and still is a difficult time. Parents can be so annoying when they let us down. But we let them down too, I guess. And those of us who choose to be parents will one day do the same to their children.'

Ivy tilted her head at him. 'Have you ever been unfaithful to a partner?'

'I'm never with them long enough to think of straying.'

'But would you, if you were?'

'No.' There was a firm edge of finality about his tone. 'An affair hurts everyone in the end. No one wins. I admire people who can move on from it but I'm not sure I could.'

'Nor me. It's a deal breaker for me. One of my flatmates, Zoey, was cheated on by a long-term boyfriend over a year ago. She's still not over it.'

Louis picked up their bags from where he'd left them on the floor. 'I'll take these upstairs. Have you got to be somewhere by a certain time?'

'This afternoon I have to meet with the daughter of the man who died at the villa in Montmartre, where the deceased estate is being housed. Mr Thornley wants me to check the quality and authenticity of the Victorian china before we commit to buying anything.'

'Have you got time for a quick lunch?'

Ivy glanced at her watch. 'Sure. But don't you have meetings too?'

'They can wait.'

A short time later, Louis took Ivy to one of the cafés nearby. He watched her work her way through a crispy baguette and soft, creamy cheese, marinated olives and a glass of white wine, her enjoyment obvious with the little 'Mmm' sounds she made. She caught him looking at her and her cheeks turned a light shade of pink.

'Why are you looking at me like that? Haven't you seen a woman eat before?'

Louis smiled and reached for his barely touched wine. 'It is indeed a rare occurrence for me to be with a woman who really enjoys her food.'

'That'll teach you for dating supermodels all the time.' She picked up another olive and popped it in her mouth. She chewed and swallowed, then added, 'I forgot to ask you how your mother's birthday dinner went.'

He took a slow sip of wine before answering. 'It was…bearable.' He put his glass back on the table and leaned back in his seat. 'At least they didn't bicker the whole time I was there.'

Ivy grimaced. 'If they're so unhappy, why do they stay together? Surely it would be better to call it quits or get counselling or something?'

'They were happy once.' Louis leaned forward to take a couple of olives off the plate between them. He put them on his side plate and then wiped his fingers on his napkin. Talking about his parents always ruined his appetite. 'But my mother's disappointment at not being able to give my father the large family he wanted ate away at that happiness.'

'That's so sad. But at least your dad didn't trade your mum in for someone who could give him what he wanted. That's something to be grateful for, I guess.'

Louis' mind flashed back to his mother's blank face and deadened personality while she'd been in the mental health clinic. His gut—even after all this time—tightened into hard knots and his skin went ice-cold. 'Yes, that's true.'

Ivy leaned forward across the table and placed her hand on his wrist. 'What's wrong?'

Louis rearranged his features into a blank mask. 'Nothing, why?'

She leaned back and sighed. 'I don't know...it just looked like you were really upset about something but trying not to show it.'

He must be slipping. He had no idea he had become so transparent. Another good reason only to spend this week with her before she got even further under his guard. 'Talking about my parents isn't my favourite pastime.'

She looked at him for a long moment. 'You care about them, don't you? Even though they are difficult and annoying, deep down you love them, otherwise you wouldn't make time for your mother's birthday.'

Louis picked up his wine glass again. 'You're becoming quite the little psychologist, aren't you?' He kept his tone playful and accompanied it with an indolent smile.

She twitched her nose in her cute bunny way. 'I'm always banging on about my parents, but I really love Mum. Dad, not so much. I guess I've taught myself not to care any more about him. It's less painful.'

Louis waited a beat before responding, 'My father suggested separating to my mother when I was ten years old, but she had a mental health crisis as a result. A serious one. She ended up in a clinic for months. He has never mentioned the words separation or divorce since in case she took another overdose.'

Ivy blinked at him in shock. 'Oh, I'm so sorry. How terribly distressing.'

Louis flicked a baguette crumb off the table with his

fingers. 'I used to hate going to see her at the clinic. I don't know if it was the heavy drugs the doctors gave her, or whether she had completely shut down, but she was blank and motionless, just a body lying on the bed. She didn't talk, she didn't smile, she didn't even seem to know who I was most days.'

Ivy reached forward again and grasped his hand. 'Oh, Louis, how frightened and confused you must have been. Does Ronan know about this? He's never said anything.'

'No, I didn't tell him. It's not something I ever talk about with anyone.' He gave a rueful twist of his mouth. 'It happened a long time ago. I've almost forgotten about it now.' Almost. But every now and again his mother would get a vacant look in her eyes and a wave of dread would swamp him. Was it happening again? Was she thinking of taking another overdose? The torturous thoughts circled his brain for hours as he remembered the anguish he'd felt and his utter powerlessness at being unable to do anything to help her.

'I'm not sure anyone could forget such a harrowing time,' Ivy said, softly stroking the back of his hand. 'Has she ever had a relapse?'

'Thankfully, no.'

'But you must be living in dread of it anyway.' Her insight was spot on, which shouldn't have surprised him. But he wasn't used to being close enough to a person for them to see the structural cracks in his façade. His childhood foundation had been compromised like a building that had suffered a destabilising earthquake tremor. He had reinforced where he could but there were still hairline cracks if you looked close enough. And he had a feeling Ivy was looking very closely indeed. Too close for comfort.

Louis glanced pointedly at his watch. 'I hate to break up the true confessions party, but I have to see a man about a house.'

Ivy pulled her hand away from his and looked at the time on her phone. 'Goodness, is that the time? I've got to dash too.'

Louis rose from the table to help her with her chair, resisting the almost uncontrollable urge to turn her in his arms and kiss her. He breathed in the fragrance of her perfume instead. But then she turned around, stepped up on tiptoe and brushed his lips with hers in a soft kiss that sent a shudder of longing through him.

'Thanks for lunch. And thanks for telling me about your childhood. I know it was hard for you to do so.'

She knew way too much but, strangely, it didn't bother him as much as he thought it would. A weight had come off him in revealing his childhood drama. A weight he hadn't even been conscious of carrying. He brushed a wayward strand of hair away from her face, his chest feeling as soft and mushy as the creamy Camembert on the table.

'*De rien.* You're welcome. I'll book somewhere nice for dinner.' He leaned down and kissed her on both cheeks, and then on the plump cushion of her mouth. '*Au revoir, ma chérie.*'

She clutched at her chest in a pretend swoon. 'If you're going to speak French to me the whole time we're here, I'll melt into a puddle at your feet.'

Louis smiled and playfully touched her cheek with his finger. 'I hope your meeting goes well.' He reached into his trouser pocket and handed her the spare key to his apartment. There was another first for him—he had never given anyone a key to his apartment before. He was crossing a line he had never crossed before, but he reassured himself it was only for five days. 'I'm not sure how long I'll be, so just make your way home and I'll meet you there.'

'Okay.' She took the key and popped it in her bag, snapping it shut with a resounding click. Her eyes were clear and bright as she met his gaze. 'Louis?'

'Yes?'

'Thank you for asking me to come with you to Paris. I was kind of dreading coming on my own.'

He leaned down and pressed another kiss to her lips. 'I was too.'

On her way home from her appointment Ivy was still ruminating over Louis' revelation about his mother's breakdown. It explained so much about his guardedness with relationships. The fear he must have felt over seeing his mother in such a state, not to mention the suicide attempt itself. It was a lot to handle for a child of ten, especially a deeply sensitive and intuitive one like Louis.

Until recently, Ivy hadn't realised how truly sensitive he was, but as she had come to know him better she could see how it had played an important and significant role in helping her brother Ronan finally gain the courage to come out as gay. Louis had been the steady, stable friend who had never once wavered in his support.

And he had sent her a gorgeous bouquet of flowers after her elderly dog Fergus had died, understanding how devastated she was at losing her beloved pet.

He had been sensitive to her mother's financial issues, taking it upon himself to give her a loan that Ivy knew for a fact he wouldn't want to be repaid.

How could she stop her admiration for him turning into something bigger, broader, more consuming than a simple friendship? It had happened almost without her realising it.

Louis wasn't incapable of love. She could sense the deep care and concern he had for his parents even though it was tempered by his frustration with them. He resisted long-term love out of fear, just as she had resisted dating and becoming intimate with someone in case they hurt her, like her mother had been hurt. Like she had been hurt when her father had claimed to love her and yet abandoned her because of her loyalty to Ronan.

Of course there was a risk she would get hurt by Louis. But didn't all relationships carry some element of risk? Even Millie and Zoey let her down occasionally, as she did them. It was part of the deal with caring about people—investing in their lives, sharing the highs and lows and everything in between.

But Louis was only offering her five days in Paris. He wasn't offering forever. He wasn't offering her the fairy tale she longed for.

Five days.

How could she have thought it would ever be enough?

CHAPTER EIGHT

LOUIS MET WITH a couple of clients in his Paris office, as well as catching up with two of the junior architects he was mentoring, but the whole time his thoughts kept drifting to Ivy. Just knowing she would be waiting at home for him made his body tingle in anticipation. He wished now he hadn't promised to take her out to dinner. He would much prefer to have had a simple meal at home and make love to her for hours. He wanted this week to be special for her, a time she could look back on with pleasure instead of regret.

If anyone had told him a few days ago he would ask her to be with him for five days in Paris, he would have laughed out loud. But, ever since the Saturday morning when he'd woken to find her gone from his Cotswold house, he had been obsessed with spending more time with her. His work was taking a back seat when usually it was front and centre. His mind was full of images of her beautiful body, his desire for her a constant background ache that tortured him relentlessly.

But it wasn't only the physical attraction that drew him to her. She was open emotionally, he was closed, and yet somehow he felt drawn to revealing more of himself to her. Telling her—telling *anyone*—about his childhood would have been unthinkable, even days ago. But revealing his pain over his mother's breakdown had released a tight knot inside him. A knot that had formed when he'd been ten years old and never once eased its tension.

He had never been a fan of talk therapy—what words could ever undo things that had been done? Things he had witnessed and never wanted to see again? But somehow Ivy's gentle empathy had soothed a raw ache in his heart, like a cooling salve does to a scalding burn. His body was hungry for her touch in a way it had never been for anyone else's.

There was a corner of his mind that raised a red flag. One day someone else's touch would have to satisfy him because he wasn't prepared to risk falling in love with her. His parents had once been in love, madly in love, yet they had done nothing more than make each other miserable since.

He couldn't bear the thought of Ivy one day looking at him or speaking to him the way his mother did to his father. So few long-term relationships lasted the distance with both parties happy and contented. Why would he think he and Ivy had a chance? He had never been good at romantic relationships. He got bored so quickly. Desire flared and then just as quickly faded.

But so far it hadn't faded with Ivy. In fact, it was flaring and flashing and firing all the time. He only had to stand next to her for his blood to pound. He only had to touch her and his senses went wild. He only had to kiss her for a tsunami of lust to blast through him.

Louis walked back to his apartment and stopped on the way to buy flowers and some chocolates from a specialty chocolatier. But then he walked past a jewellery store and found himself turning back to have a look in the window. Sparkling diamonds, midnight-blue sapphires, blood-red rubies, forest-green emeralds and milky-white pearls were displayed in a glorious array.

And then his eye caught sight of a rare pink Argyle diamond from the Kimberley region of Australia. The pink hue reminded him of Ivy's cheeks when she blushed.

You're thinking of buying her jewellery? A diamond? Seriously?

Louis ignored the voice in his head and listened to the one in his heart. It was her thirtieth birthday soon and he wanted to buy something special for her. It was an early birthday gift. Nothing else.

When Ivy got back to Louis' apartment, she expected to find her luggage in one of the spare bedrooms but instead found it in the master suite. Did that mean he intended to spend the whole night with her? Or maybe it was because he didn't trust her to disappear again without saying goodbye.

She opened her bag and began unpacking her things, feeling a little awkward about hanging her clothes next to his in the walk-in wardrobe. But she didn't want to drape her clothes over the back of a chair or dressing table and, as they would be in Paris for five days, what else was she supposed to do?

She found some spare coat hangers and hung her

clothes on the opposite side of his. He had an assortment of expensively tailored suits and crisp shirts, ties, Italian leather shoes and belts, and cufflinks in a glass-topped drawer. There were casual clothes as well—jeans, shirts and T-shirts, shorts and leather loafers. She found herself trailing her hand along his clothes, breathing in the faint trace of his aftershave and the smell that was unique to him.

'Have you found enough space for your things?' Louis' deep voice spoke from the door of the walk-in wardrobe and Ivy jumped and spun round, her cheeks feeling hot enough to iron her clothes.

'I wasn't sure if you wanted me to sleep in the spare room or—'

'I want you with me.' His eyes were dark—more inky-black pupils than grey-blue irises. They drifted to her mouth and back again in a slow perusal and a frisson passed over her flesh.

'So you can stop me running away without saying goodbye?'

He came closer, placing his hands on her hips and shifting her so she was flush against his body. The possessive warmth of his hands sent a flare of molten heat to her core and the unmistakable jut of his erection sent her heart rate soaring. His thighs were like columns of steel, while hers felt like soggy noodles as desire shuddered through her body. 'I'll have to find a way to entice you to stay with me.' His tone was deep, smoky, sexy, and another delicate shiver coursed down her spine.

Ivy stood on tiptoe and placed her arms around his neck, the elevation in height bringing her breasts into closer contact with his rock-hard chest. She gave him a playful look. 'I wonder how you'll do that? I'm not easily enticed.'

He glided his hands up from her hips to her ribcage, close to her breasts but not touching them. The desire to have him do so was a tingling ache that was both pleasure and pain. His gaze went to her mouth, his lips tipped up at the corners in a slow smile that heated her blood to boiling.

'And I'm not easily bewitched but somehow you've achieved it.'

His mouth came down to hers in an explosive kiss that sent a shockwave of lust through her body. She opened to the demanding thrust of his tongue, relishing the erotic play that made her tingle from head to foot. His lips were firm yet gentle, teasing her into a response that was almost feverish. She gasped, she whimpered, she clung to him, desperate to take in more of him. He tasted of mint and male heat and mad passion and she couldn't get enough. His kiss was like a drug to her senses, sending her into a frenzy of need that spiralled through every inch of her flesh. Her most intimate flesh swelled with blood, moistened with excitement, lava-hot and hungry for his possession.

He lifted his mouth off hers, gazing at her with glittering eyes. His hands moved up to cup her breasts through her clothes and she gave another desperate whimper. 'Let's get these clothes off you, shall we?'

'Do let's.' Ivy began to unbutton her top, but her fingers wouldn't cooperate, so he took over. Slowly, torturously slowly, leaving a kiss on each section of her skin as he exposed it.

'Your skin tastes so good.' His voice was deep and rough, his lips warm and sending sparks of heat to her core. He peeled off her blouse and bent his head to her breasts, still encased in a balcony bra. He gave each upper curve a lazy lion-like lick that made her gasp with pleasure. He deftly unclipped the fastening on her bra and it fell in a silky silence to the floor. He drew in a shuddering breath and stroked his tongue over and around her right nipple, then he gently sucked on her, drawing her into the heat of his mouth. He released her nipple and then ever so lightly took it between his teeth. The soft tether of his teeth to her sensitive flesh sent a wave of tingly warmth through her pelvis.

Ivy clutched at his head, arching her spine, her body raging with need. 'I want you. Now.'

Louis straightened and gave her a slow smile. 'I like hearing you beg. It turns me on.'

Ivy shivered at the dark glint in his gaze. She tugged at his shirt, pulling it out of his trousers, and began to undo the buttons with more haste than competence. A button popped off and landed nearby. 'Let's even this up a bit. I'm not going to bare all unless you get naked too.'

'Good plan.' He shrugged off his shirt but left her to undo the waistband of his trousers, sucking in a breath when her fingers skated over his erection. 'Your touch drives me crazy.' He stepped out of his trousers and underwear and came back to work on the rest of her clothes, unzipping her skirt and peeling away her knickers. He feasted his eyes on her naked body, making her feel like the most beautiful and sexy woman on the planet. 'Everything about you drives me crazy.'

'Right back at you,' Ivy said, barely able to speak for the sensations rushing through her body. Urgent needs begged to be assuaged. Needs she'd had no idea she possessed until his touch had awakened her.

Louis scooped her up and carried her out of the walk-in wardrobe to his bed, laying her down before joining her. He glided one of his hands down from the top of her shoulder, over her breast and ribcage, over her stomach and lower abdomen, down the flank of her thigh and then back up again. A slow, sensuous glide that made her aware of every millimetre of her skin, every pore responding to his touch, every nerve tingling. His eyes drank in every curve of her body, making her feel utterly feminine and desirable.

'So, so beautiful—every part of you.' His voice had an almost reverential note to it, and it made it all the harder to ignore the way her feelings for him had intensified. Going from a platonic admiration to full-blown passionate adoration—a mature and lasting adoration that she had longed to feel for someone all her life.

Ivy placed her hand on the side of his face, enjoying the masculine texture of his skin so different from her own. 'You make me feel beautiful...' Her voice caught on the words, so intense were her emotions. She didn't want to spoil the moment by blurting out her feelings. They weren't part of their arrangement. But holding them in, keeping them hidden, made her heart ache with the pressure of keeping them contained. She spoke them with her hands instead, stroking each of his eyebrows, down the length of his nose, around his mouth.

He brought his mouth down to hers, kissing her deeply, lingeringly, his tongue playing with hers in a dance as old as time itself. A primal dance, erotic and playful, yet with deadly serious intent. His intention was clear—she felt it in every stroke of his tongue, every glide of his hand, every erogenous zone he touched. He wanted her. He was going to have her. She would enjoy every heart-stopping second of it.

Ivy breathed in the scent of him, the musk and salt and aroused male smell that so tantalised her senses. He lifted his mouth off hers to work his way down her body, leaving branding kisses that sent her pulse skyrocketing. He went from her breasts to her belly and beyond, her skin tightening in anticipation. He parted her with his fingers, exploring her most intimate flesh with his lips and tongue. The tension gathered in her swollen tissues, a delicious tension that built to a crescendo. And then the storm broke and she was flying, falling, swirling and spinning in a vortex of intense, spine-tingling pleasure, the ripples and aftershocks spreading throughout her pelvis. 'Oh, wow…oh, wow…oh, wow…' Her breaths came in stuttering gasps, her limbs feeling spent and useless.

Louis kissed his way back up her body, holding her gaze when he got close to her mouth. 'I love watching you come. You hold nothing back.'

Ivy was holding far more back than he realised. Love flowed through her as passionately as her orgasm had just done. She could feel it fill every part of her being, a deep attachment to him that was going to be hard to ignore for much longer. But how could she tell him? It wasn't something he wanted to hear from her. It wasn't something he wanted to hear from anyone. He'd been a playboy for a long time, and he would go back to being one once their fling was over.

Her heart contracted at the thought of him moving between lovers in the future. One after the other, each one a fleeting encounter that meant nothing more than a temporary relief of lust. And back in her normal day-to-day life she would be grieving the loss of his intimate touch, mourning the end of their passionate fling. How would she bear it? She ran her fingertip over his sensual bottom lip, her gaze carefully avoiding his. 'I hope I can be just as responsive with someone else when the time comes.'

The silence thrummed with an unusual energy as if each and every oxygen particle had been disturbed by her comment. Even *she* was disturbed by her comment. How could she ever make love with someone else? Who would make her flesh sing the way Louis did? It was unthinkable. Impossible.

By the time Ivy brought her gaze back to his, Louis' expression was masked, all except for a camera-shutter-quick movement at the back of his gaze. No more than a rapid blink—a reset, an unwelcome thought swiftly, ruthlessly blocked. 'I seem to remember I promised to take you out to dinner, but I got a little waylaid.' His tone was mildly playful but it was at odds with his screened features.

Ivy stroked her hand down his lean jaw, one of her

legs hooking over his. 'How can you think of food at a time like this?'

His mouth came down to just above hers. 'Believe me, *ma chérie*, I am definitely not thinking of food right now. I'm only hungry for you.' His kiss showed her just how hungry, his hands urgently moving over her body even more so.

Ivy pressed herself closer, drawn to the heat and power of his hard male body, her smooth legs entwined with his hair-roughened ones, her body on fire. He moved away only long enough to get a condom and she watched him smooth it over himself, her pulse racing with excitement, her inner core heated with longing. He positioned himself over her, balancing his weight so as not to overpower her, his entry swift, sensual, sense-spinning. Tingles shot through her sensitive tissues, her body gripping him, welcoming him, pleasuring him as his pleasured her. His guttural groans were music to her ears, his deep, rhythmic thrusts ramping up the coil of tension in her core. She was climbing a mountain, higher, higher, the pinnacle just out of reach. She wanted. She wanted. She wanted. The aching throb in her body was accompanied by the chant in her head.

'Please…please…*please*…' She didn't care that she was begging. She didn't care that she was thrashing beneath him like a paper boat in a storm-tossed sea.

'Come for me.' Louis' voice was husky. 'Don't hold back. Don't be frightened of it. Let it take you.'

He slipped his hand between their bodies and slowly caressed her moist and swollen flesh. The delicious sensations came from far-off places in her body, gathering to a feverish point in her female centre. And then they exploded in a shower of sparks and tingles and spasms that carried her to another plane of existence. An exquisite existence of sheer mind-blowing, planet-shifting ecstasy. It was bigger and better than anything she had experienced before, the monumental force of it almost terrifying. How could her body split from her mind in such a way? How could her body contain so many nerve endings? So many pleasurable settings that fired with such heart-stopping intensity?

Louis kept moving within her, taking his own pleasure with deep thrusts and guttural groans until, finally, he tensed all over and then gave one last shuddering groan as his orgasm hit. Ivy held him through the storm, feeling completely undone by the way his body responded to hers. So powerful, so potent, so primal and passionate. She moved her hands up and down his back in smooth massaging movements, listening to his breathing quietening, enjoying the relaxed weight of him lying over her.

'Am I too heavy for you?' His lips moved against the sensitive skin of her neck where his head was buried, and she shivered.

'No...' She gave a long blissful sigh and stroked her hand over the taut shape of his buttocks. 'If anyone had said a few weeks ago I'd feel comfortable with a naked man sprawled over me after making mad, passionate love to me, I would have laughed. Or fainted.'

He leaned up on one elbow, a smile tilting one side of his mouth, his eyes dark and lustrous. He traced his finger from her chin to her sternum and then back to her lower lip, teasing it with a feather-light caress. 'It's good you feel comfortable with me.' His smile slowly faded and his gaze grew serious. 'But neither of us can get too comfortable with this arrangement. The time limit still stands.'

Ivy had to work hard not to show her disappointment. She was conscious of her every facial muscle, of trying to control the micro-expressions that might betray her emotions.

The time limit still stands.

He wasn't budging from his rules on their fling. In spite of the fabulous sex, in spite of their friendship and the increasing closeness she felt was growing between them, he was determined to keep things temporary.

'I know.' She gave a little forced laugh. 'Just think what Ronan would say if he knew we were having a fling. Or Mum.'

The frown between his eyebrows deepened. 'Yes, well, all the more reason to stick to the rules. I don't want anyone's expectations raised and then dashed when our...fling ends.'

His slight hesitation over the word 'fling' made her wonder if perhaps a part of him—a secret, well-buried part—was already compartmentalising his involvement with her as something completely different from his normal flings. He rolled away from her, got off the bed and disposed of the condom in the bathroom.

Ivy used the opportunity while he was in the bathroom to wrap herself in a plush bathrobe. His bathrobe that contained the tantalising scent of him on its soft fibres. It completely swamped her, but at least it covered

her nakedness. But it wasn't really her physical nakedness she was most worried about covering—it was her
emotional nakedness. The raw hope filling her heart
more and more each day that he would come to love
her. A hope that refused to give up even though it was
hanging by a silken thread.

She desperately hoped he would want more than a
scratch-an-itch fling. That the chemistry between them
would prove to him that what they'd experienced together was special, unique, something to be treasured
and not put aside as a distant memory.

Louis disposed of the condom and gripped the edge of
the basin in front of the mirror. He looked at his reflection and wasn't sure he liked what he saw. A man who
was seriously questioning if he'd done the right thing
in sleeping with Ivy. Not because he didn't enjoy every
moment of having her in his arms—he did. Too much.
Way too much. So much, he was finding it harder and
harder to think of their involvement as a fling. As a
casual fling, like any other he'd experienced. It wasn't
and it could never be. It was in an entirely different category. Not just because he was her first lover. Not just
because the sex was so fulfilling and mind-blowingly
pleasurable and made his body hum for hours afterwards. But because it was Ivy. Sweet, cute, adorable
Ivy, with her dimples and her curls and her curves and
her funny little bunny twitch.

But one day, in the not too distant future he would
have to see Ivy move on with someone else. Someone
who would give her the things she wanted—love, mar-

riage, babies, commitment for a lifetime. And she had every right to want those things. She deserved no less than wholehearted commitment and love.

His gut twisted like writhing snakes. One day, he would even have to attend her wedding or think of a very good excuse not to accept the invitation, thus hurting her, her mother and her brother in one fell swoop. God, how had he got himself into this mess? A beautiful mess he didn't want to end.

Not yet.

CHAPTER NINE

Ivy WANDERED OUT to the salon, still dressed in Louis'
bathrobe, where there was a huge bunch of pink roses
wrapped in white paper and tied with a black satin bow
resting on the coffee table. There was a box of chocolates from a Parisian chocolatier next to them, as well
as a flat, rectangular black velvet jewellery box.

Her breath stalled, her heart tripped, her stomach
flipped. Flowers. Chocolates. Jewellery. Gifts a man
in love gave to the woman he adored. Hope spread
throughout her chest, lifting her spirits, sending a burst
of happiness through her.

But then a doubt slipped into her mind like a curl
of toxic smoke wafting under a door, slowly but surely
poisoning her fledgling hopes. For all she knew, he
might buy all his lovers gifts. Consolation prizes, trin-
kets to remember him by when their fling came to its
inevitable end.

She wanted more than memories. She had been trying to ignore it from the first time he'd kissed her, but
she could ignore it no longer. Her love for him had
been in the background for so long, she hadn't recog-

nised it until it had moved to centre stage. The passion he awakened in her had turned a spotlight on her emotions. Emotions she had shied away from at first, keeping them in the shadows in case she got hurt. But they were out of the shadows now, spreading light over all her self-delusions, revealing the truth at the heart of her involvement with Louis. She loved him. She wanted him, not just during a fling, but forever.

Louis came out from the bedroom and she turned to face him. He was still naked, apart from a white towel wrapped around his lean hips, and his hair looked as if it had been recently combed with his fingers.

'Are these for me?' She pointed to the items on the coffee table, keeping her expression neutral... Well, as neutral as she could, which wasn't saying much.

'Who else would they be for?' His tone was guarded, as if he sensed the undercurrent of tension in her face and body that she was so desperately trying to hide.

Ivy turned back to the coffee table and leaned down to pick up the roses, lifting them to her face to breathe in the sweet fragrance. She put them back on the table and turned sideways to look at him again. 'You don't have to buy me gifts, Louis. You've spent enough money helping my mother without going to any more expense on me as well.'

He came further into the room to stand on the other side of the coffee table. 'I have plenty of money, and if I want to spend it I will.' His tone had a clipped edge, as if he was annoyed at her attitude to his generosity.

Ivy elevated her chin, locking her gaze on his inscrutable one. 'I don't want you buying me hideously expensive gifts. I don't need compensation for when our…fling is over.'

A savage frown divided his brow. 'Compensation? Is that what you think this is?' He waved a hand at the gifts on the table between them, his grey-blue eyes glittering with something that very much looked like anger. Good, because she was angry too. Furiously angry that he was paying her off. Softening the blow with fancy gifts when all she wanted was his love. Not his money, just his love.

Ivy arched her eyebrows in a haughty manner. 'Isn't it?'

He muttered a swear word in both French and English, his hand reaching up to rub the back of his neck, as if to relieve sudden tension. He dropped his hand back by his side, every muscle in his body rigid. Unyielding. As though he was putting up a physical barrier as impenetrable as his emotional firewall.

'No. It is not that at all.' Each word was bitten out, his mouth set in a tight line. 'The flowers and chocolates are to thank you for coming with me to Paris. The jewellery is for your birthday—I thought I'd give it to you early in case I don't see you on the day. If you want to read anything else into it, then fine, go right ahead.'

Ivy's anger deflated like a pricked party balloon. 'Oh, Louis, I'm sorry. I almost forgot about my birthday.' He had made her forget everything but how wonderful it was to be in his arms. And how, within a matter of four impossibly short days, she would be out of them and alone again.

He shrugged one broad shoulder in a dismissive

manner. 'Forget about it.' His tone was gruff, offhand, but she could read a thread of lingering hurt in it too.

She stepped around the coffee table and placed her hand on his leanly muscled forearm, meshing her gaze with his screened one. 'I'm sorry for being tetchy when you've been so generous. Forgive me?'

He made a soft grunting sound and wrapped his arms around her and brought her close against him, his head resting on the top of her head. 'There's nothing to forgive.' His deep voice reverberated against her cheek where it was resting against his broad chest. She wanted to stay there forever, just like this, in the warm, protective shelter of his arms.

After a long moment, Ivy tilted her head back to look at him. 'Can I open my present now?'

He smiled and gave her bottom a playful pat. 'Go for it.'

She slipped out of his arms to pick up the jewellery box, holding her breath as she flicked the little gold latch and opened the lid. Lying on a cream velvet bed was a pink diamond pendant on an exquisitely fine white-gold chain with a matching pair of droplet earrings. 'Oh, my goodness...' She stared at them in amazement, struck by their beauty and his thoughtfulness. 'They're just divine. Thank you so much.'

'Do you want to try them on?'

She gave him a rueful smile. 'I'm not sure they'll be shown off to their best advantage while I'm wearing your bathrobe, as expensive and luxurious as it is.'

His grey-blue eyes smouldered. 'There's an easy solution to that.'

He reached for the waist ties of the bathrobe and slowly, deliberately, untied them, all the while holding her gaze in an unwavering lock. Then he slipped the bathrobe off her shoulders, his eyes hungrily travelling over her naked flesh. The garment fell to the floor at her feet and he took the jewellery box from her.

'Turn around.' His commanding tone made a shiver run up and down her spine, so too the brush of his fingers as he fastened the pendant around her neck. He placed a warm, firm hand on one of her shoulders to turn her back round. 'You'd better put the earrings on yourself.'

He handed them to her and she slipped them through her pierced earlobes. 'How do I look?'

His gaze swept over her again. 'Ravishing.' He placed his hands on her hips and brought her up against him. She was left in no doubt of how ravishing he found her—he was as hard as stone—and her lower body responded with hot little flickers of lust. He brought his mouth down to hers in an incendiary kiss that set off fireworks and bombs in her blood. Heat raced through her system, molten heat that made every cell in her body throb and ache with rampaging need. He deepened the kiss with a silken thrust of his tongue, calling hers into intimate play, teasing, cajoling, captivating her senses until she was whimpering with delight.

Somehow his towel fell to the floor, but she couldn't remember if she'd tugged it off or he had. All that mattered was it was off, and she could feel him rising against her belly, the velvet and steel of his form inciting her to even greater dizzying heights of arousal. Her body was slick, her legs trembling, her spine loosening.

'I want you so damn much.' He growled against her lips, his hands moving from her hips to cup her breasts. He brought his mouth to each breast in turn, licking and circling each tightly budded nipple with his tongue. The sensations rioted from her breasts throughout her body on intricate networks of sheer pleasure.

Ivy grasped his head in her hands, bringing his mouth back to hers. 'I want you too. So much it's like a pain.'

His eyes gleamed with erotic promise, his lips tilted in a smile that sent another wave of heat through to her core. 'Then let's do something about that, shall we?' He picked her up and carried her back to the bedroom, placing her on the bed and coming down beside her.

Ivy waited with bated breath as he reached past her to get a condom. He applied it and came back to her. He stroked her from shoulder to thigh and back again, his eyes smoky with lust. 'I think we're going to lose that dinner booking. Do you mind?'

She linked her arms around his neck and smiled. 'Not one little bit.'

As it turned out, they didn't lose the dinner booking, in spite of the mind-blowing sex they'd shared. Louis was nothing if not ruthlessly efficient when it came to giving her pleasure. Her body was still tingling and her lips still swollen from his passionate kisses.

Later that night, Louis sat opposite Ivy at an intimate table in the window of the restaurant a short walk from his apartment. The current of electricity between them seemed to have followed them to the restaurant. Every time she glanced at him, she felt the zap and crackle of energy pass from his gaze to hers. When he reached for her hand across the table, her inner core spasmed with a pleasurable ache.

Ivy picked up her champagne glass and took a sip, conscious of Louis' gaze steadily watching her. She put her glass back down. 'What are you thinking?' It was a bold question to ask but the mood seemed right. Their earlier lovemaking had shifted something in their relationship. Or maybe it was she who had shifted. She felt more confident in her sensuality, more at ease in expressing herself sexually.

His eyes darkened. 'You can't guess?'

A shiver coursed down her spine and sent a soft flicker to her core. 'You're not the easiest person to read but I'm guessing you're thinking about what happens after dinner.'

A slow smile spread across his face and he reached for her hand across the table and held it in his. 'Those diamonds look fabulous on you. The colour reminds me of your cheeks when you blush.'

Ivy touched one of the droplet earrings before placing her hand back in her lap. Her other hand tingled where it was encased in his. 'I'm not sure what Millie is going to say when I come home wearing diamonds from a high-end jeweller. Did I tell you she's a jewellery designer? She lets me wear her stuff for free.'

He pulled his hand away and picked up his glass of champagne, his expression difficult to read. 'They're a birthday gift, that's all.' He took a sip of his drink and placed the glass back on the table with a little thud that seemed to serve as an underline to his statement.

Ivy chewed one side of her mouth. 'Are you cross with me?'

He sighed and gave a forced-looking smile that faded almost as soon as it appeared. 'No. It's just I don't want your friends to get the wrong idea about us. I would have preferred they didn't know about our…arrangement.'

'Well, I get that, but what am I going to say to Ronan or Mum when they see these?' She touched the pendant hanging around her neck.

His mouth tightened. 'I've bought you birthday presents before. What's the big deal?'

'Book and cinema vouchers aren't quite in the same league as diamonds, though, are they?'

Louis picked up his glass and drained it, placing it back down again with a heavy sigh. 'Just for the record, I don't give my ex-lovers diamonds, or any other jewellery when it comes to that.'

'Maybe that's my point.'

A frown settled between his brows. 'And your point is?' His tone was guarded, and his gaze had 'keep away' written in its smoke and sky hues.

Ivy wished she hadn't started this conversation but felt compelled to continue it regardless. The clock was ticking on 'their arrangement', as he called it. An arrangement that was passionate, exciting and thrilled her senses but was doomed to bring her heartache in the end.

Why hadn't she realised that before now? She was on a road that came to a dead end. It would be crazy to keep driving along it knowing she would never get from Louis what she most wanted. Yes, he'd bought her diamonds and treated her like a princess. He'd made love to her as if she was the only woman in the world he ever wanted to make love to. But he was not willing to open his heart to her.

She took a prickly breath, her heart thumping, her stomach bottoming out. 'My point is I want more than you're offering.'

Not a single muscle moved on his face, but something shifted at the back of his eyes like a furtive shadow at the back of a stage. 'What? Diamonds aren't enough?' His tone had a sarcastic edge.

She sent him a reproving look. 'Louis, I think deep down you want more too, but you're not ready to admit it. You wouldn't have bought me such a beautiful gift if you didn't feel something for me.'

He signalled for the waiter to settle the bill. 'Now is not the time or place to have this conversation.'

'I think it's a perfectly good time,' Ivy said. 'What's the point of us being here together in Paris if we go our separate ways in four days? We have only four days now, Louis. Do you realise how clinical that sounds? You can't put a time limit on your feelings, or at least I can't.' She swallowed and continued, 'I have feelings for you that can't be turned off by a date on the calendar.'

His mouth was so tight, white tips appeared at the corners. 'Look, you're getting confused by the sex. You're new to physical intimacy. People can fancy themselves madly in love with a lover but what they're in love with is the endorphins that good sex sets off. You'll see that I'm right in a few days. Once we stop having sex, you'll—'

'What? Forget how you make me feel? Pretend none of it happened? Come on, Louis, don't you see how much I care about you? It's in every kiss and touch. Every time we make love I give all of myself to you, not just my body, but all of me. I love you.'

He grimaced, as if suffering a deep pain. 'You don't know what you're saying, Ivy. You'll be embarrassed by this in the weeks ahead. I can guarantee it. You're seeing me through oxytocin-tinted glasses—it's the sex hormone that makes people feel bonded to a lover. We have no bond other than friendship. This fling we're having—'

'It's not a fling to me!' Ivy interjected, her heart contracting with anguish at his constant use of that horrible word. 'It's never been a fling or an arrangement. I think on some level I always knew that it could never be that. I think I asked you to help me with my intimacy issues because I loved you. I wouldn't have asked you if I didn't. I see that now. It had to be you because it's always been you I loved.'

'Look—one of the reasons I only have flings is because of this sort of thing happening,' he said. 'I let people down without even trying. I told you from the start what I was prepared to give. It upsets me to see you hurt, knowing I have caused it.' He rubbed a hand over his face and shook his head as if he couldn't believe how he had got himself into this situation. 'I'm sorry, Ivy, but this is all I can give you right now.'

Diamonds. Memories. A clock ticking on their fling. 'It's not enough. And I don't think it's enough for you either. You feel bad about this situation because it clashes with how you think of yourself and the way you really want to be. That's the source of your pain, not the fact you've let me down or any number of other people down. You've let *you* down. The true you.'

The waiter approached with the bill and Ivy was forced to contain her emotions until the transaction was processed. Louis silently led her out of the restaurant, his expression going into lockdown. It wasn't the way she wanted their evening to end but, now she had come to her senses, she had no choice but to see this through. She could not keep driving down a dead end until she crashed into Louis' emotional stop sign.

They walked back to his apartment in silence. His expression might have been closed but Ivy could feel Louis' frustration coming off him in waves. Even the sound of his key stabbing into the lock and the way he opened the door hinted at his brooding tension. He closed the door with a snap and tossed his key onto the hall table with a careless flick of his hand. The key landed into a ceramic bowl with a noisy clatter.

'I told you from the start how uncomfortable I was about this whole plan of yours,' Louis said. 'You have only yourself to blame for how it's turned out now.'

Ivy pressed her lips together, trying to gather her composure. She didn't want to end their fling in a slanging match. But their fling *had* to end. Tonight. Now.

Not another day could go past with her continuing to fool herself their relationship would turn into something else. He had made it abundantly, blatantly, brutally clear it wouldn't. 'Louis, this is not easy for me to say, but I want to finish our fling now. It wouldn't be right for me to sleep with you again, not under these terms. I don't want to cheapen what we've shared.'

'I could hardly call what we've shared cheap.' His tone was cruelly sardonic, his glittering gaze cutting as he glanced at the diamonds in her ears and around her neck.

Ivy stiffened as anger spread through her. So, that was the way he wanted to play it, was it? She purposefully removed each earring and placed them in the ceramic bowl with his keys. She placed her hands behind her neck to undo the fastening of the pendant, glaring at him with icy disdain. 'I've decided I prefer book and cinema vouchers after all. Maybe you can find some other fling partner to give these to. I don't want them.'

His top lip curled, and his eyes flashed. 'What? You don't want to take home a souvenir of your first love affair?'

She ground her teeth so hard, she thought she would crack a molar. 'Love affair? On my part, maybe, but not yours. You've hardened your heart out of fear, the same way I avoided intimacy out of fear for all those years. You won't allow yourself to get close to anyone in case they hurt you or make you feel vulnerable. You've got intimacy issues, Louis. You won't ever be happy unless you address them. You're not at heart a playboy. You remind me of Ronan, pretending all those years to be

something he's not and could never be. You are a man
who wants to love and be loved but you're too frightened to give anyone the power to hurt you.'

Louis threw his head back and gave a cynical laugh
that grated on her already shredded nerves. 'Stick with
antiques, *ma petite*. You'd make a lousy therapist.' His
laughter lines faded and his expression tightened. 'I'm
perfectly happy with my playboy lifestyle.'

She raised her chin, giving him a level stare. 'Then
you won't mind going back to it sooner rather than later.
I'm going home tomorrow morning. There's no point
me staying here in Paris with you any longer. Our relationship was always coming to a dead end and I should
have seen your emotional stop sign at the end of the road
a whole lot earlier. I'll sleep in the spare room tonight.'

'Fine. You do that.' His voice was clipped, his expression tightly drawn. He reached for his keys in the
ceramic bowl and added, 'I'm going out. I'll see you
in the morning.'

No, you won't, Ivy decided on the spot. *I'll be long
gone by then.*

Louis walked several blocks, trying to get his emotions
in some sort of working order. *His emotions.* What a
joke. He didn't possess the emotions Ivy wanted him
to feel. Of course he cared about her—why else had
he bought her such an expensive gift for her birthday?
Why had he been so reluctant to enter into their fling
in the first place?

Hurting her was the last thing he wanted to do. He
should have known it would end this way—with her

upset with his lack of commitment. But he couldn't change what was an essential part of his character. He wasn't the marriage and babies type. He could think of nothing more claustrophobic than ending up in a marriage like that of his parents.

His father had promised 'in sickness and health' and got more sickness than health. His mother had promised 'to love and to cherish' and ended up loathing and criticising. Ivy's own parents had done the same, along with numerous others. Love, when and if it even existed in the first place, never lasted. It had never lasted for him. He had occasionally felt flickers of something for the odd partner, and he had definitely felt more than a flicker for Ivy, but it didn't mean it would last the distance.

It would pass. It always did.

And it would again.

CHAPTER TEN

Ivy QUICKLY PACKED her things and then called a cab to take her to a hotel closer to the airport. Within the space of minutes, she was out of his apartment and on her way back to her old life. But her life would not be the same as before. She had changed, and those changes had come about through her relationship with Louis. She had seen sex as something to get out of the way, a box to be ticked. But he had shown her how pleasurable sex could be with a partner you trusted. Sex for her was never going to be a simple scratching of an itch, a purely physical response to stimuli. She needed more, she wanted more, she ached for more.

She *deserved* more.

She was not just a body that had needs and desires. She was an adult woman who craved intimacy that went beyond the physical expression of lust. An emotional intimacy. A deep and lasting bond that would only be enhanced by physical passion. She had hoped Louis felt the same way about her. Hoped and dreamed he would open his heart to her, but where had those hopes taken her?

To a dead end.

It was time to do a U-turn and get on with the rest of her life. Without Louis. Without the love she so desperately craved. Without her happy-ever-after fairy tale.

Louis came back to his apartment an hour or so later and immediately sensed Ivy was gone. The atmosphere was dull, listless, as if the energy had been taken out of the air, leaving it stale and empty. His bedroom door was open, the bed where they had made passionate love only hours ago neatly made, the sheets and covers drawn up, as if to remove any imprint of her having been there. He ruthlessly pulled the covers back off the pillows and picked one up and buried his face in it, breathing in the scent of her fragrance.

Go after her. Bring her back. Don't let her leave like this.

His conscience prodded him from a place deep inside where he never visited. A place where he hid away all the feelings he forbade himself ever to feel. A place that contained a sliver of hope that he could have a different life other than punishing hours of work and transient relationships that left no impression on him other than a vague sense of dissatisfaction. He thought of a life with Ivy—a life where he could be the knight in shining armour she longed for. But how could he guarantee his armour wouldn't lose its shine some day, as his father's had done for his mother? How could he guarantee he wouldn't hurt her or disappoint her the way he'd hurt and disappointed his family?

The only thing he lived for was his work. It was the

only thing that satisfied him. It gave him money, loads of money, and numerous accolades that proved his decision to become an architect had been the right decision.

Letting Ivy go was another difficult decision that he knew would prove to be the right one. Four more days in Paris with her might have been the biggest mistake of his life to date.

Yes, it was better that she was gone, even if it felt like hell. It wouldn't feel like this forever.

But, hey, he didn't feel anything forever, right?

This too would pass.

'Hey, why are you back so early?' Millie asked when Ivy came into the flat the following day. 'I thought you were going to be away until—'

'Don't ask.' Ivy slipped her tote bag off her shoulder with a despondent sigh.

'Okay, but judging by the redness of your eyes I'd say you've recently spent a considerable amount of time in tears. Am I right?'

Ivy nodded. 'Yep. I ended things with Louis. I told him I loved him and wanted more than a fling, but of course, he didn't say it back.'

'Oh, honey, I'm so sorry.' Millie enveloped Ivy in a bone-crushing hug. After a moment, she eased back to look at her. 'I was worried from the outset this was going to happen. But are you absolutely sure he doesn't feel the same way about you?'

Ivy slipped out of her friend's embrace. 'I know you did, and I stupidly didn't recognise it until it was already too late. I think I've always been a bit in love with him. And when he bought me the pink diamonds…'

'He bought you pink diamonds?' Millie's eyes were as big as saucers. Satellite-sized saucers.

Ivy shrugged one shoulder. 'He bought them for my birthday, but I mistakenly thought they somehow signified he was falling in love with me. I was wrong. Big time.' Heartbreakingly wrong.

Millie nibbled at one side of her mouth. 'I guess that means he won't be coming to your party, then.' She suddenly clamped her hand over her lips. 'Oops, forget I said that.'

Ivy frowned in puzzlement. 'What party?'

Millie's cheeks were pink, her grey-blue eyes troubled. 'I'm sorry. It was supposed to be a surprise. I'm rubbish at keeping a secret. Zoey and I planned to have a party on your birthday, and we sent Louis an invitation last night via email. We told him it was a secret. We thought you'd like him to come.'

'How did you get his email address?'

'Off his website.'

Ivy couldn't think of anything worse than Louis turning up at her birthday party, especially when she had nothing to celebrate other than getting a year older and having her heart broken in the process. 'Cancel it. I don't want a party. I've never felt less like celebrating.'

Millie looked horrified. 'Oh, Ivy, you can't let a milestone like this pass by without some sort of celebration. We've gone to a lot of trouble, and a lot of people will be disappointed if you don't show up. You can still pretend to be surprised. Please don't tell Zoey I let it slip.

She'll roast me alive. She's done a lot of the planning and would be so upset if she thought—'

Ivy sighed. 'Okay, let's go ahead with the party.' She just hoped that Louis wouldn't spoil it even further by showing up.

Louis was so distracted by what had happened in Paris that he didn't check his emails until he was on the flight back to London the following afternoon. Which was frankly weird and totally out of character for him. He could normally set a world record for the amount of daily screen time he used. But, no, he had pushed work aside to ruminate over the disaster of the end of his fling with Ivy. An end he'd known was coming from the start but had allowed himself to think wouldn't hurt *him*. How misguided had he been? But he was only feeling this searing pain in his gut because he had disappointed her. It had nothing to do with anything else. What else could it be?

He scrolled through the dozens of emails and saw the invitation to a surprise party for Ivy's thirtieth birthday. He mentally groaned. No way could he show up and cause any more hurt to her. He would ruin the party for her. He would have to stay away and send a present, hoping she wouldn't throw it back in his face.

But not pink diamonds.

Definitely *not* pink diamonds.

A couple of days later, Louis was on his way to work when he got a call from his mother, informing him his father had been rushed to hospital during the night with a heart scare. Louis dropped everything to meet her on the cardiac ward. When he arrived, his father was lying asleep on a bed, hooked up to various monitors, and his mother was sitting white-faced and pinched-looking beside him.

'Oh, Louis, I was so frightened I was going to lose him,' she choked.

Louis went over to her and enveloped her in a hug. He suddenly realised it had been years since he had last hugged his mother. Their usual greetings and farewells were little more than impersonal air-kisses. Not full-on hugs where you could feel the other's heart beating against your own. How had their relationship got so distant? 'I'm here now.' He slowly put her from him but kept hold of her hands. 'How is he?'

She blinked back tears. 'The specialist said it was a mild heart attack. He's booked in for some scans with the possibility of surgery, but we have to wait and see. He's sleeping now. He was awake most of the night complaining of chest pain but he wouldn't let me call an ambulance. He kept saying it was indigestion, but in the end, I rang anyway.'

'Good decision. At least he's safe here now,' Louis said, and released her hand to glance at his sleeping father. That was another sudden realisation—his father was his mother's world. She would be shattered if she lost him. And, when he thought back to the time when she had been in the clinic, his father had been equally distraught at the prospect of losing her. Who could figure out love in all its guises?

'Yes, he's safe.' She gave a little shudder and tried to

smile but it didn't quite work. 'I'm sorry for calling you in such a state. I know you're frightfully busy.'

'Not too busy to be here for you when I'm needed.'

Her eyes watered up again. 'Louis, I know your father can be difficult at times, but he's not had it easy. I'm wondering now if the stress of his work has contributed to his heart condition. He never wanted to be an accountant, but he felt pressured by your grandfather. Deep down, I think he's a bit jealous of you—that you had the courage and grit to find your own pathway in life. He's proud of you, in his way. As indeed I am. Your dad is a good man. Oh, I know he finds fault far more than favour, but he's never been unfaithful, in spite of all my mental health struggles. I haven't been the easiest wife to live with, but I love him. He's the only man I've ever loved—apart from you, of course.'

Louis enveloped her in another tight hug. 'Thank you. I love you too.'

A couple of days later, after his conversation with his mother, Louis was working on a new design for a hotel in New York and trying not to think about Ivy. Every hour of the day he tried not to think of how unhappy he had made her, not to mention himself.

But at least he had other things that had gone better for him just lately. His father was back home after having had a stent inserted and was recovering well, even talking of retirement. Louis had seen a remarkable change in how his parents spoke to each other. The health scare had helped each of them realise the deep care and affection they still had for each other. And he liked to think he saw a change in how they spoke to him. Each time he visited, he enveloped both of them in a hug, enjoying their new-found closeness. He had come to understand his father's sacrifice of his own dreams and aspirations, and it humbled Louis to think of how difficult and painful that must have been for him, and why it had impacted his relationship with his only son.

Louis recalled Ivy's comments about him not being true to himself about what he really wanted. He had been true to himself about his desire to pursue architecture. He hadn't let anything or anyone get in the way of his hopes and dreams. But his personal life had suffered. He had fixed things with his parents but his relationship with Ivy was still a sore point. He kept revisiting it, mulling over each moment he'd spent with her, wondering if he could have done anything differently and not ended up with this infernal pain burrowing into his chest. It wasn't indigestion. It wasn't a heart attack…or maybe it was. Not a genuine, medical heart attack, but his heart was definitely hurting in a way it never had before.

But he would have to get over it. Work would have to go back to filling the hole Ivy had left in his life. A hole *he* had foolishly allowed to open.

Louis was thinking about how much he needed a coffee when his office door opened after the briefest of knocks. He looked up to see Natalie, his secretary, who was currently on maternity leave, standing there with a baby strapped to her chest in a sling carrier.

'Hi, Louis. How come no one's manning the desk? Where's the temp—Maureen?'

Louis pushed his computer mouse aside and scowled. 'She called in sick.' He didn't wish ill health on anyone, but he was relieved he didn't have to deal with any more of Maureen's questions about why he'd come home early from Paris.

Natalie's brows rose and she came further into the room, one of her hands carefully cradling her baby's downy head. 'Do you want me to call for a replacement? You look busy as usual, and more than a little frazzled, to be perfectly honest.'

His scowl deepened. 'You're supposed to be on mat leave.'

'And you're supposed to congratulate me on the birth of my baby and gush over him like everyone else does.'

'Didn't you get the flowers and presents I sent you?'

'Yes, they were lovely. You're great at buying presents.'

'Glad somebody thinks so.' His tone was so dry, he could have offered his services as a nappy for the baby. He still had those wretched pink diamonds. He looked at them every day just to remind himself of his foolishness in agreeing to Ivy's plan.

He moved a little closer to Natalie. She could have been carrying a bomb strapped to her chest by the way he was feeling. Babies freaked him out a bit. More than a bit. They were so tiny and needy and…and cute. Yes, heart-squeezing cute, even if he said so himself. 'What's his name?'

'Thomas Charles,' Natalie said, unclipping the carrier, taking the sleeping baby out and handing him to Louis. 'Want to have a cuddle?'

Louis wanted to say no but didn't want to offend her. Mothers had a thing about their babies. His mother had told him recently about her utter devastation as each of her subsequent pregnancies since his birth had failed— how she had loved and grieved for those unborn children, even though she had only been a few weeks along. Somehow, he found himself holding the baby, not as expertly as he would have liked, but the kid didn't seem to mind. Thomas opened his tiny mouth and yawned, and one of his little starfish hands came out. Louis offered his index finger and the baby grasped it. His chest felt as if the baby had grasped onto his heart as well. 'Oh, wow, he's really cute. I can't believe how tiny he is.'

'He didn't feel tiny when I was pushing him out.'

'Spare me the details.' Louis couldn't stop staring at the baby's tiny features and thought about how amazing it must be to see a part of yourself in the next generation. The baby broke wind loudly and Louis quickly passed him back to his mother with a grimace. 'You'd better take him back. This suit is expensive.'

Natalie crooned over the baby as she strapped him back into the sling carrier. 'So, how have you been, Louis? Seen any more of Ellen?'

He stared at her blankly. 'Ellen?'

'Stalker Ellen. Has she been hassling you any more or has she finally got the message?'

Louis raked a hand through his hair, went back behind his desk and sat in his chair with a thump. 'Haven't heard a peep, thank God.' He hadn't thought of anyone but Ivy. She filled his thoughts every hour of the day and most hours of the night.

Natalie studied him for a moment. 'Are you all right? You don't seem yourself at all. You look like you've had no sleep for a week.'

Was he all right? Not really. And, yes, he hadn't slept for a week, and not just because of his dad's health scare. He hadn't been right since Ivy had left him in Paris. But then, maybe he hadn't been right since the first time he'd kissed her. Making love with her had changed him and he couldn't change back to who he had been before. He couldn't slip back into his old life as a carefree, freedom-loving playboy because, damn it, holding his secretary's adorable little baby had shown him a part of himself he had strenuously denied existed until now. He had refused to acknowledge these past few days, even though it was there in how he had come to his parents' aid, supporting them both through a harrowing time.

He was capable of love—more than capable.

He loved Ivy.

How had he not realised until this moment? Why had he shied away from the core of who he was as a person? He adored her. Worshipped her. Missed her so badly it was destroying him day by day.

Louis sprang out of his chair and swept past Natalie. 'Sorry, Nat. I have to go.' He stopped at the door, came back over to her, kissed her on the cheek and dropped a kiss to the baby's head as well. 'Thank you for making me see what a stupid fool I've been.'

Natalie's smile spread over her face and her eyes twinkled. 'Well, look at you. If I'm not very much mistaken, I'd hazard a guess and say Mr Amazing One-

Night Stand has fallen for someone and fallen hard. Am I right?'

Louis grinned. 'You're right.' And then he shot out the door.

Ivy was home alone on Friday night watching a box set—story of her life —when the doorbell rang. Millie and Zoey were supposedly both working late, but she knew from Millie it was a ruse—they were doing last-minute party preparations for tomorrow night. She clicked off the TV and tossed the remote back on the sofa. She went to the front door and opened it to see Louis standing there with a huge bunch of pink roses and a box of chocolates. But, sadly, no black velvet jewellery box.

'May I come in? I have something to say to you.' His expression was tightly set and she mentally prepared herself for another argument. Why did he have to come here and rub it in?

She held his gaze, raising her chin a fraction. 'I think you said everything back in Paris.'

He handed her the roses and the box of chocolates, the tension around his mouth loosening. 'Please, Ivy, hear me out. I wish I could rerun that night and do everything differently.'

Ivy wasn't brave enough to pin too many hopes on his coming to see her. It had been a week since she'd left him in Paris. Over a week with not a single word from him. Why should she think anything had changed? She took the roses and chocolates from him and stepped aside to let him in. 'All right. But make it snappy because it's my birthday party tomorrow and I—'

He frowned. 'You know about the party?'

She blew out a breath and closed the door. 'Millie let it slip but I'm pretending I don't know for Zoey's benefit. She's gone to a lot of trouble and I don't want to ruin it for her.'

'I got an invitation, but I wasn't sure if you'd want me there.'

Ivy moved further inside her flat and put the roses and chocolates on the coffee table. 'I can't imagine how you'd want to be there now.'

'Ivy. Look at me.' His tone had a note of desperation about it, his expression etched in remorse. 'I can't begin to tell you how much I regret how I handled things in Paris. I was a fool to let you go like that. I don't know why it took me all this time to see what has been staring me in the face from the start. You were right when you said I wasn't being true to myself. I wasn't. I was living a lie, denying any feelings in case they made me vulnerable. But, over the last few days, I've come to understand how little I knew myself—the real me. I had stopped listening to my heart for so long, I didn't recognise the signs that were there all along. I love you. I adore you. I can't imagine my life without you in it—not just as a friend but as my lover, my partner. My wife.'

Ivy stared at him, speechless, for long, heart-stopping seconds. Was she hearing him correctly or was her mind and the foolish hopes it contained conjuring up the words she longed to hear from him? 'I don't know what to say…'

He came to her and grasped her by the shoulders, his

eyes pleading. 'Say yes, *mon ange*. Say you'll marry me. Say you'll have babies with me and build a life together.'

Ivy's eyes filled with happy tears, joy bursting out of every cell in her body. She threw her arms around him and hugged him close. 'Oh, Louis, you can't imagine how wonderful it is to hear you say those words. I love you so much. I've been so unhappy, so desperately miserable since I left you. I'd given up hope that we could be together.'

He tilted up her face to gaze into her eyes, his face wreathed in a smile. 'I love you to the depth of my being. I can't bear the thought of another day without you by my side. Marry me, *ma chérie*? I need to hear you say yes otherwise I won't believe you're really mine at last.'

Ivy pressed a kiss to his lips. 'Yes, I will marry you. I can think of nothing I'd love more than to be your wife. You've made me so happy I can barely stand it.'

He cradled her cheeks in his hand, his eyes so full of love it made her heart contract. 'I love everything about you. Your goodness and kindness, your ability to always see the good in people instead of focussing on the bad. You have opened my heart like I thought it never could be opened. I feel I can cope with anything with you by my side.'

Ivy stroked his lean jaw. 'I love everything about you too. You're kind and generous and hard-working to a fault. You're everything I've ever dreamed of in a partner. I know we'll be happy together. I will do everything in my power to make you the happiest man on earth.'

'You made me that by saying yes just now.' He

reached into his jacket pocket and took out the flat rectangular jewellery box she'd left behind in Paris. 'I want you to have these. They'll match the pink diamond I've purchased to go with them. I thought Millie might like to design our engagement ring.'

Ivy took the velvet box off him and peeped inside to see the pendant, earrings and beside them a loose pink diamond. 'Oh, Louis, that's so thoughtful of you. She'll be tickled pink. Ha ha.' She closed the box and put it to one side so she could return to his warm and loving embrace. Back where she belonged. 'But what changed your mind about being with me?'

'My dad had a heart scare a few days ago. I spent a fair bit of time sitting with my mother while he was being attended to in hospital. I came to understand the dynamic between them a little better. They don't always show it but they truly care about each other. And something you said a while back really started to resonate with me. You said at least my father hadn't run off with someone else but had stayed loyal to my mother. I'd always seen that he'd stayed out of fear of her trying to take her life again, but he stayed with her because he loved her and didn't want to lose her. He'd only suggested a separation all those years ago because she was so unhappy after a miscarriage. He thought she might be better off with someone else. I've been looking at all the things that were wrong in their relationship instead of all the things that are right.'

'Oh, I'm so glad you understand them both a little better. Do you think I can meet them some time? I'd really love to.'

He grinned. 'Of course. I can't wait to show off my beautiful fiancée.' He pressed another kiss to her lips. 'I don't want a long engagement. I want to be married to you as soon as possible. And let's not leave it too long before we start on making a baby.'

Ivy smiled up at him. 'You really mean it? You want to have babies with me?'

He kissed her again. 'Yes. A baby or two, and we'll get a dog too. And I'm going to make your boss an offer on his business. I think you'd be great at running your own antiques business. Or would that be too much?'

Ivy wrapped her arms tightly around his waist, leant her head on his chest and sighed with pure joy. 'That would be perfect.'

EPILOGUE

LOUIS DIDN'T NEED to drink champagne at Ivy's birthday party the following night to feel tipsy. He was drunk on the sight of her dressed in a scarlet velvet dress that clung lovingly to every sweet curve of her body. She was wearing the earrings and pendant he'd given her, and her friend Millie was already working on a design for the engagement ring.

Ivy had done a brilliant job of acting surprised when she'd come into the venue where the party was being held, but ended up being completely surprised by the presence of her brother and father. Louis had taken upon himself to meet with Keith Kennedy that morning and insist he not spoil Ivy's birthday, because Millie had let slip to him in a follow-up email that Ronan and his partner Ricky were flying all the way from Australia to attend. Fortunately, Keith had had the grace and maturity to accept he was wrong and came to the party with an apology in hand. Of course, there was more work to do on Keith's relationship with his son, but these things took time.

Louis had his own family relationships to continue

to work on. He could never thank Ivy enough for helping him to see how he'd been far too critical of his parents, viewing their relationship too negatively without seeing the positives. And there were so many positives now his focus had changed. His father had never had an affair…he had never walked out on his wife or son. His father had put all his own dreams and aspirations to one side so he could carry on his own father's business. That was a sacrifice that took enormous courage and commitment. His mother had suffered great sadness and Louis hadn't fully understood how it had impacted her mental health. But he was hoping the birth of grandchildren one day in the future would help his mother continue on her journey to a happier, more positive state of mind.

Ivy moved away from greeting one of the guests and came back to Louis. 'Darling, this is the best party I've ever had. I don't think I've ever been happier than at this very moment. I love you.'

He slipped his arms around her and planted a kiss on her lips. '*Je t'aime, mon ange.* I am happy too. More than I can say. More than I thought possible.'

And he would spend the rest of his life being thankful for his sweet, adorable Ivy.

* * * * *

COMING SOON!

We really hope you enjoyed reading this book. If you're looking for more romance, be sure to head to the shops when new books are available on

Thursday 17th September

To see which titles are coming soon, please visit
millsandboon.co.uk/nextmonth

MILLS & BOON

Coming next month

CHRISTMAS IN THE KING'S BED
Caitlin Crews

"Your Majesty. Really." Calista moistened her lip and he found himself drawn to that, too. What was the matter with him? "You can't possibly think that we would suit for anything more than a temporary arrangement to appease my father's worst impulses."

"I need to marry, Lady Calista. I need to produce heirs, and quickly, to prove to my people the kingdom is at last in safe hands. There will be no divorce." Orion smiled more than he should have, perhaps, when she looked stricken. "We are stuck. In each other's pockets, it seems."

She blanched at that, but he had no pity for her. Or nothing so simple as pity, anyway.

He moved toward her, taking stock of the way she lifted her head too quickly—very much as if she was beating back the urge to leap backward. To scramble away from him, as if he was some kind of predator.

The truth was, something in him roared its approval at that notion. He, who had always prided himself on how civilized he was, did not dislike the idea that here, with her, he was as much a man as any other.

Surely that had to be a good sign for their marriage.

Whether it was or wasn't, he stopped when he reached her. Then he stood before her and took her hand in his.

And the contact, skin on skin, floored him.

It was so *tactile*.

It made him remember the images that had been dancing in his head ever since he'd brought up sex in her presence. It made him imagine it all in intricate detail.

It made him hard and needy, but better yet, it made her tremble.

Very solemnly, he took the ring—the glorious ring that in many ways was Idylla's standard to wave proudly before the world—and slid it onto one of her slender fingers.

And because he was a gentleman and a king, did not point out that she was shaking while he did it.

"And now," he said, in a low voice that should have been smooth, or less harshly possessive, but wasn't, "you are truly my betrothed. The woman who will be my bride. My queen. Your name will be bound to mine for eternity."

Continue reading
CHRISTMAS IN THE KING'S BED
Caitlin Crews

Available next month
www.millsandboon.co.uk

MILLS & BOON

THE HEART OF ROMANCE

A ROMANCE FOR EVERY KIND OF READER

MODERN

Prepare to be swept off your feet by sophisticated, sexy and seductive heroes, in some of the world's most glamourous and romantic locations, where power and passion collide.
8 stories per month.

HISTORICAL

Escape with historical heroes from time gone by. Whether your passion is for wicked Regency Rakes, muscled Vikings or rugged Highlanders, awaken the romance of the past.
6 stories per month.

MEDICAL

Set your pulse racing with dedicated, delectable doctors in the high-pressure world of medicine, where emotions run high and passion, comfort and love are the best medicine.
6 stories per month.

Celebrate true love with tender stories of heartfelt romance, from the rush of falling in love to the joy a new baby can bring, and a focus on the emotional heart of a relationship.
8 stories per month.

Indulge in secrets and scandal, intense drama and plenty of sizzling hot action with powerful and passionate heroes who have it all: wealth, status, good looks...everything but the right woman.
6 stories per month.

HEROES

Experience all the excitement of a gripping thriller, with an intense romance at its heart. Resourceful, true-to-life women and strong, fearless men face danger and desire - a killer combination!
8 stories per month.

DARE

Sensual love stories featuring smart, sassy heroines you'd want as a best friend, and compelling intense heroes who are worthy of them.
4 stories per month.

To see which titles are coming soon, please visit

millsandboon.co.uk/nextmonth

JOIN US ON SOCIAL MEDIA!

Stay up to date with our latest releases, author news and gossip, special offers and discounts, and all the behind-the-scenes action from Mills & Boon...

 millsandboon

 millsandboonuk

millsandboon

It might just be true love...

Sensual love stories featuring smart, sassy heroines you'd want as a best friend, and compelling intense heroes who are worthy of them.

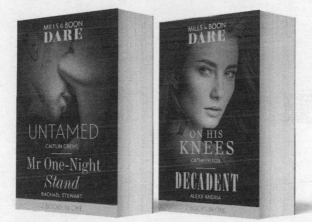